I0825301

LIAR'S DICE

THOUSAND VOICES
X

RANDOM HOUSE
NEW YORK

LIAR'S DICE

A NOVEL

JULIET FAITHFULL

Random House
An imprint and division of Penguin Random House LLC
1745 Broadway, New York, NY 10019
randomhousebooks.com
penguinrandomhouse.com

Library of Congress Cataloging-in-Publication Data
Names: Faithfull, Juliet author
Title: Liar's dice: a novel / Juliet Faithfull.
Description: New York: Random House, 2026. |
Identifiers: LCCN 2025037759 (print) | LCCN 2025037760 (ebook) |
ISBN 9798217153886 hardcover | ISBN 9798217153893 ebook
Subjects: LCGFT: Detective and mystery fiction | Novels
Classification: LCC PS3606.A385 L53 2026 (print) | LCC PS3606.A385 (ebook)
LC record available at https://lccn.loc.gov/2025037759
LC ebook record available at https://lccn.loc.gov/2025037760

Printed in the United States of America

1st Printing

First Edition

Book Team: Production editor: Cara DuBois • Managing editor: Rebecca Berlant • Production manager: Sam Wetzler • Proofreaders: Alicia Hyman, Catherine Mallette

Book design by Elizabeth A. D. Eno

Title page image: Pedro Costa Simeao/iStock

The authorized representative in the EU for product safety and compliance is Penguin Random House Ireland, Morrison Chambers, 32 Nassau Street, Dublin D02 YH68, Ireland. https://eu-contact.penguin.ie

For Margarita

Please see page 365 for a glossary
of terms used in the book.

Gemstones

JANUARY: Garnet

FEBRUARY: Amethyst

MARCH: Aquamarine

APRIL: Diamond

MAY: Emerald

JUNE: Alexandrite

JULY: Ruby

AUGUST: Peridot

SEPTEMBER: Sapphire

OCTOBER: Tourmaline

NOVEMBER: Topaz

DECEMBER: Turquoise

LIAR'S DICE

Chapter One

SEPTEMBER 1972

Outside the window, Christ on Corcovado stares at me with his peaceful soapstone eyes. My classroom is on the third floor, so I see him on the mountain, looking down. Everywhere in Rio is in front of or behind or beside Christ, so the statue is a way to remember. The favelas are under his armpits, so he can't see them. His sleeves hide the tiny shacks, the poverty, and the dirt. The statue of Christ is like a moon, guiding me in case I want to run away.

I am a watchful girl. I watched my parents for clues, and I always watched Mita for fits, but I didn't watch close enough, because one day they took her away when I wasn't looking, and suddenly she was gone, and it was too late. That's what I would say in my essay if I knew how to write: I'd say they didn't ask me, and if they had I would have said no. Everyone knows you shouldn't separate identical twins. They packed Mita away neat and tidy with her best helmet and her wheelchair and all her clothes, so there's nothing left of her in our new flat. They packed her up so well that sometimes I wonder if there's a locked drawer somewhere, where she still exists, only I can't find it.

Mr. P. checks his watch: "Ten more minutes." He rubs his hands down the front of his pants to get rid of the chalk. "No one should be nervous; this is not a test. Some of you come from different countries and school systems; I want to get a sense of where you are."

I am nowhere. It's already the second week of school, and I am still nowhere. I pick up my pen and pretend to write in my blue book. When Mr. P. comes near, I lean over so my hair covers the page and draw pictures: a flower, a swan. I'm good at swans and horses. I draw circles and waves and make them travel along the lines, little blocks of markings, so they might look like writing. I connect some of the shapes and not others, and I leave spaces in between. I draw writing.

Daddy said I'd pick it up in no time, but I'm not picking anything up. I must be slow, like Mita. Slow to read, slow to get my period, slow to make English friends. The normal things that happen to twelve-year-old girls aren't happening to me. Rows of zigzags form black worms on the page that curl around one another or stretch into lines. They are not pictures of anything I know. I look at the other heads bent over notebooks and wonder how it is that writing came to them and not to me. Did they wake up one day and it was there, fully formed, like a black bean sprouting? Or did it start slowly, line by line?

At least I'm good with numbers. I learned watching Daddy

play Liar's Dice at the club in Santanésia. I have his old cup, the faded one where the leather is almost white from the sun and the dice are turning yellow. The numbers are still there: tidy black spots that declare your luck. I love the rattle of dice, full of hope and energy like a samba. Every morning, I pray for a Bidu: a two and a one. If I get a Bidu, writing will come. If I get two Bidus in a row, Mita will live with us again.

Mr. P. claps the blackboard erasers against each other, the way he always does at the end of class. My stomach folds. *Write, stupid. Write.* I used to talk to Mita's hand, tell it to open. Sometimes it worked: Mita would uncurl her fingers and show me the white palm of her hand.

"Time is up." Mr. P. stands by the doorway as students file out. Each person hands him their blue book as they leave.

I sit at my desk, frozen. All I have are drawings and blank pages. I look out the window, at the asphalt below. Three floors. If I break my leg, I'll be stuck lying on the playground, with all the prissy English girls staring.

I decide to join the line and try to slip by, hoping Mr. P. won't notice.

His arm stretches in front of me like a gate. "Dolores, are you forgetting something?"

Priscilla, behind me, giggles. I give him my blue book and run to the playground. I run to a place I know behind the hydrangeas and sit on the ground, my heart slapping against my chest, and try to lose myself in the sweet smell and the pink of the flowers. I put my head down on my knees and cry a silent crying where my body shakes against itself like one of Mita's fits.

The first bell rings, then the second. We're supposed to be in line. I hug my knees, not wanting to move. I make myself stand up and straighten out my silly school uniform with the fake tie and join the queue, behind Marcos. He's always in detention, so he won't report me. There's a code among the last ones: We know we're in enough trouble as it is, so there's a kindness that doesn't exist for the middle kids, and certainly not for the clever ones.

Mr. P. stands outside French class. "Dolores, I need to speak to you."

"I have French now, sir."

"I'll talk to Monsieur Armand. Don't you worry. Come with me."

Instead of walking toward the detention office, Mr. P. heads to the front entrance and crosses the playground, to my hideaway. He pulls aside the hydrangea bush and sits in my secret place.

"Take a seat." He pats the ground.

I'm in huge trouble. I imagine Daddy getting a letter saying I've been expelled. He's so happy that I go to the British School of Rio, so happy because he wants to make me English, just like him. It's never going to happen.

"Lovely smell." Mr. P. picks up a handful of earth and lets it slide between his fingers. "You have good taste."

I can't tell if he's making fun of me.

"So why didn't you write the essay?" His voice is kind, and my throat locks up. I want to answer, but I feel ashamed.

"Can you tell me?"

I shake my head no.

"If you don't know how to write, I can help."

"I do know how to write." My body tightens. I stand up. "I do know."

Mr. P. takes hold of my arm. It's not a hard hold that hurts like Daddy's, but it's firm. He knows I'm broken, and I hate that he knows. Maybe other teachers know too, and Priscilla. Maybe the whole school knows.

"I can help you write," Mr. P. says. "Let's start tomorrow. I'll be here, in your spot, after school. How does that sound?"

My hand doesn't seem like a hand; it's more like an odd flower. He lets go of my arm. There are more words, but I hear them like echoes, like the whisper of leaves. The playground is enormous. I run across it into French class and sit at the back and watch Monsieur Armand pick his nose behind the flashcards.

DURING BREAK, I SEARCH FOR Andrea; I noticed her on the first day of school, but she disappears the minute the bell rings. She's Brazilian like me, and funny. As far as I can tell, there are only three of us Brazilians in my class. There's a whole sea of people with pale skin who wear socks with sandals and speak English. Back in Santanésia, it was just Daddy. I stand in the shade of a palm tree and watch the English girls play elastics. Two of the girls loop the elastic around their ankles and stand facing each other, as far apart as the elastic will allow, creating a double fence. The other girls jump in and out and over the band, twisting the elastic with their legs, then leaping their way out. If you trip or get tangled, you're out. I could play that game, but no one asks me.

Priscilla sees me watching and whispers something to Olivia.

I walk over to the iron gate. Soldiers march by in their uniforms and green berets. Rio is full of soldiers. One of them looks at me as he marches. Except for his short hair, he could be one of the boys in class six, he's not old. He half smiles as he gets closer. I wave at him, but he doesn't wave back. Maybe he isn't allowed. Mita loved to wave. She'd sit in the back of the car and wave at everyone who passed by. There was something frantic about her wave, as if she were trying to move every part of her body with her one good hand, as if all the words in her mouth that couldn't speak, all the jumps and twists and dances she couldn't do, were channeled into that wave.

The soldiers pass, then a businessman with shiny black shoes, and a woman in a tight yellow dress, carrying laundry on her head. A thin bearded man with two guitars. There is a hurriedness to Rio, a noisy rush of cars, radios, drills, bars, clubs, a rhythm that doesn't stop to take a breath. Every day: Catch the bus, school, the bell, French class, English class, break, every day there is a coming and going, as if all of life is a race you might lose.

Mita was slow. That's the word people used, but it didn't matter in Santanésia, because there was no hurry. Our life there was slow. We'd watch the hummingbirds hover above the hibiscus flowers. We'd swing in the hammock and listen to the *cigarras,* or help Mummy bake a coconut cake. The only timetable was the sun coming up and going down, and Daddy arriving home from the paper mill.

Olivia and Priscilla head toward me, with their ponytails and their leather sandals and white socks. I wish they'd leave me alone.

Rory swings across the playground like Tarzan. The rope is reserved for the older boys. It hangs from a huge tree, taller than any of the buildings.

Olivia stands next to me, close—and Priscilla next to her. I study Rory on the rope, how he makes his turn. There's some kind of trick to it I don't understand. He lifts his knee and swivels his body just before the rope begins to swing back.

Olivia fakes a cough. "Um, hello there."

"Hello," I say. My voice is too quiet. Rusty from so much silence.

"What are you up to?" Olivia asks.

I'm not up to much of anything, that's obvious. It's my turn to speak, like ping-pong, back and forth, but I have no words.

"Who are you for, Oxford or Cambridge?" Priscilla asks.

"I don't know."

"You have to choose," Priscilla says. "We're both Cambridge."

I have no idea what she's talking about.

Olivia plucks a light blue envelope from her pocket and hands it to me. "This is from my pen friend in South Africa. It's an aerogram."

The paper is thin and crinkly, not like any paper I've ever touched. It's more like the skin of an onion. When I open the envelope, it becomes a letter with writing inside. I fold it back into being an envelope again, like a magic trick.

"You can read it," Olivia says. "It's not private."

"Let me see you read it," Priscilla says.

I hand Olivia back her envelope.

Olivia points at some numbers printed over the stamp. "Ninth of September, 1972. One week. That's all it took to cross the Atlantic Ocean and arrive in Rio, all the way from South Africa."

Mummy doesn't let me call Mita on the telephone; she says international calls are too expensive. If I could write, I could talk to Mita. Send her aerograms every day. Tell her I haven't forgotten her: that I'll find a way to get her back.

"Do you have a pen friend?" Olivia asks.

"No, I don't." I don't even know what a pen friend is. The Union Jack folds and unfolds itself in the wind like a sail as I try to think of something to say. It's hard to get the motor of conversation going with English girls. Andrea wouldn't try. She does whatever she wants.

Moments pass.

"Let's go," Priscilla says. "I told you she's a dunce."

That's what the English girls and boys call me, and they're right: I am a dunce.

I look at the rope. There's no one in line; the bell is about to ring. I might not know how to write, but I know how to swing from a tree.

I run over and climb the steps that are carved into the thick bark of the trunk, afraid someone might stop me, grab me by the shoulder, and say girls are not allowed. I balance my way along the branch to the narrow platform and pick up the safety belt. It's heavier than I imagined, and even at the tightest setting, it hangs like a loose cuff around my waist. I try not to listen to the voices below. I pick up the rope and place my right foot carefully through the loop at the end.

I lean back and gather the force in my legs and behind my knees, I gather my energy plus Mita's energy—all that was stored up in her too-quiet legs—and leap off the tree. My loose leg swims the air, pedaling. I fly across the playground. Tufts of grass, slabs of stone, windows, orange tiles. I pick up speed as I glide through the air. I'm above the heads, above the teachers, above the school. Christ in the distance looks small from here, like a white bird perched on the top of a huge mountain. I expect a loud whistle, but I'm not going to stop. My legs tingle. My muscles slide inside my arms like eels. I'm above the wrought-iron gate. I can see traffic, the police station, a barefoot boy blowing a pink bubble. I prepare to turn—

"Psst! Psst! *Ei!*"

Andrea. Up in the tree, with Marcos. Smoking. I'm eye to eye with her. She waves at me with her cigarette. I lift three of my fingers from the rope in a small wave and miss the moment of the turn. I lose momentum. I pedal the air and manage to swing faster, but the arc is small, and the next time I turn, my feet graze the ground, and I land.

A couple of the older boys clap. Rory comes over and helps me unbuckle the leather belt just as the bell rings. My hands and legs feel shaky, the way they do when you get off a horse. "Not bad," Rory says, "for a girl."

I join the line heading back to class. Andrea pushes her way next to me. "That was incredible," she says. "You showed them."

"Girls should be allowed on the rope," I say, sailing up the stairs.

"D'you smoke?" Andrea asks.

"Of course," I say, as if I'm an expert.

"You can come with us next time, if you like."

Tuesday, Andrea helps me avoid English. She has this cream you rub in the soft spots beside your eyes, and it gives you a fever—so you go to the nurse. After school, I cross the playground to the Blue Bus and wait to climb aboard. I pretend not to see Mr. P. waiting for me behind the hydrangea bush. I slide low in my seat and stay down until the bus leaves the schoolyard.

The next day, Andrea is out sick. I find a spider and place

it on my arm and wait for it to bite, then I go to the nurse. The hurt is like a faraway toothache in my arm. She rubs cream on the bite and tells me to lie down on the metal bed by the window.

"Vat, you are having a bad-luck week?" Mrs. Von Tram says in her German accent. Andrea told me Mrs. Von Tram was in a concentration camp when she was little, that's why she has a permanent frown. Andrea thinks the school should have a friendly nurse, who gives you warm flannels on your forehead—but I'm glad to lie down and watch the sky, and be away from Mr. P.

Thursday, I search for another spider but find only a few ladybugs. Andrea is still out sick. The second bell rings. I head to English class and sit at the back.

"Dolores, you'll need to catch up. You're down two assignments. An essay about your parents, and a reflection on the moon. Observe the moon and write about what you see, think, and feel."

My cheeks burn. Mr. P. knows I can't write. He's doing it on purpose, in front of everyone.

"Yes, sir."

He hands me my notebook. "Well done. I liked the swan."

His voice is kind. I wait for the others to laugh, for the whole class to turn and stare, but they don't.

Mummy hides that she's illiterate, just like I do. She thinks I don't know, but I heard Daddy say it during a fight. He called her an illiterate fool. Mummy touched her nose, which she thinks is too long, just stroked the end of it. When he apologized, she said she was fine and walked away. Mummy is so careful; she cries in packets of tears, which she catches with a pink handkerchief, folded in a tidy triangle like a small sandwich.

Mr. P. asks for volunteers to read their essays out loud. Olivia waves her freckly arm in the air. "Daddy's an engineer and he's building the Rio–Niterói bridge," she says in her Scottish accent. "He's an expert on box girder bridges . . ." *Blah, blah, blah.*

Daddy likes to think of himself as an expert on Brazil. He loves telling foreigners that he lived in the jungle. That's how he talks about Santanésia. He calls it the middle of nowhere. I don't laugh at his jokes anymore. When he tells stories about the floods and winks at me, and says, "Remember how the snakes lined up outside our front door?" I say nothing. Inside the quiet essay I've started speaking to myself, I say in the middle of nowhere where we lived; in the middle of nowhere where I had a twin and we were happy sometimes, more than now. But I know it's not true for him.

Chapter Two

We sit on the terrace of the Copacabana Palace Hotel, supposedly celebrating my second week at the British school. Daddy sips his *tulipa* and beams at Mummy, who wears one of her two-tone dresses, light and dark blue with a horizontal line across the middle, so she looks like a flag. Her pink *morganitas* dangle from her ears like sweets.

"You look beautiful, Isabela." Daddy looks uncomfortable in a white Lacoste shirt. He didn't pull the crocodile off this time, for Mummy's sake. He doesn't like logos, but Mummy wants him to look posh. Daddy holds up his beer and touches his glass to hers. "Cheers. Cheers to the British school."

I hate their lies. They aren't celebrating me; they're celebrating Daddy's first paycheck from his important new job.

Now that he works for a cigarette company instead of making paper, he thinks he's Mr. Somebody. Well, I preferred it when he was Mr. Nobody. The bubbles of my Coca-Cola slide up my glass in tiny eruptions. Daddy waits for me to pick up my drink, but I don't. Mummy signals for him to leave me alone. She doesn't want a scene; she told me that. No difficult questions. Mita's been away seventy-one days. I cross each day off in my gem calendar, which hangs on the wall above my bed. We had one in Santanésia too. H. Stern sends them to Daddy every year. Daddy says it's bullshit, the whole idea of birthstones, but I like the photos of the different gems. They took Mita away in the month of Ruby, and now we are in Sapphire.

Daddy leans over and lights Mummy's cigarette. She's an ornamental smoker. She sips her cigarette without inhaling and leans back to look pretty. The flashing beam of the lighthouse sweeps its way across the beach every few minutes, back and forth, as if it's searching for something it has lost.

"This is a famous hotel, Dolores," Daddy says. "Take a look at these chandeliers."

I hate the beauty of Rio. I hate our new marble sinks and all our bathrooms and the long corridor with built-in cupboards where Mummy stores her new American appliances. I hate that we live on the twelfth floor, above the trees, above life. The chandeliers sparkle like dangling diamonds. Mita would have reached up with her good hand to touch them if she was here.

Daddy takes a gulp of beer. "So how was your week?"

I stay quiet.

"Tell us one thing."

"I hate that the school bus is yellow."

Daddy raises his eyebrows.

"Yellow," I say again, but they've forgotten. Already they've forgotten that yellow is Mita's favorite color; that her pajamas and the sheets on her bed have to be yellow—even her plate. That's why she loves Cremogema for breakfast. Because it's made of corn and yellow.

"I'll see what can be arranged," Daddy says, turning it into a joke. "I'll speak to the British consul. What color would you prefer? Pink?"

Mita's tongue turned yellow with the medicines. A whitish yellow like a dirty carpet, with spots at the back. I never told her, because it wasn't a yellow she would have liked.

Mummy smiles as she looks out at the flowered bamboo armchairs, and the pool that is lit from inside so it glints like an aquamarine gem. "It's elegant."

"Wait." Daddy leans past the waiter, who's arrived with some hors d'oeuvres on a silver platter. "Isn't that Freddie de Booze and Estelle?"

Mummy squints. She doesn't have her glasses on. "Leave them alone, Ian. Maybe they want to be alone."

Daddy walks over to chat with Freddie and Estelle, then the three of them come back to us. "Just a drink," Daddy says. "They have a dinner reservation."

Mummy forms a smile on top of her disappointment. It's all about the job. All this Rio life is about Daddy's job. "Of course," she says.

Freddie and Estelle order drinks.

"Excited about school?" Estelle asks.

"No," I say.

Estelle lights up a cigarette. "I'm sure you'll settle in. It's probably a little different from your old school, isn't it?"

"I never had an old school."

"The schools were dumps in the interior," Daddy says.

"The nearest one was in a bloody convent. You know how I feel about that."

Estelle turns to Mummy. "Did you homeschool her, then? That's brave of you, Isabela."

"Not really." Mummy leaves it vague. She doesn't want people to know that she's illiterate and grew up on a tenant farm outside São Paulo that didn't even have a toilet. I'm sure that's another secret they want to keep. They're such posers, the two of them.

Estelle looks at the gilded fan turning slowly above us. "We love this place. Bit run-down, but it still has glamour."

"It's the drinks that count. Forget glamour," Daddy says.

As if on cue, the waiter arrives with gin-tonics for everyone except me.

Freddie de Booze swirls his drink with his index finger, then points to the pool. "Orson Welles had to be fished out of there, frequently, they say. Took three chaps to lift the bugger." He gulps down half his drink. "Easy to see how a chap could get tozzled living here, night after night."

Estelle rolls her eyes and Daddy laughs. Freddie de Booze's name suits him.

A man squats in front of Mummy with a large camera and snaps photos of her, the flash going off over and over.

Mummy shields her eyes with her hand. A second photographer joins him.

Freddie de Booze stands up. "What's all this about?" he asks in his heavily accented Portuguese.

Daddy turns to the photographers. "It's not her. She's not Jackie Kennedy." Daddy's Portuguese is fluent, but you can tell he's a gringo.

The flashes continue. The photographers don't believe him.

"This is my wife, Isabela. Do you understand?"

Mummy fiddles with her rings, looking embarrassed.

Estelle stares at Mummy. "You know, there is a resemblance. She does look like Jackie, doesn't she, Freddie?"

"It's happened before, in São Paulo," Daddy says. "They gave us the bloody presidential suite!"

"I would exploit it," Freddie says. "Why the hell not?"

The photographers hover in the veranda, the way they do, waiting for famous people to arrive. There are always movie stars at the Copacabana Palace. Mummy slips her light blue slingbacks on and off with her toes. I miss the barefoot Mummy, who gutted fish, and cleared bamboo, and wasn't afraid of snakes.

I want to go back to our old life. Back to being the family who lived on top of the hill, with the gringo father and the twins. "The interior," Daddy calls it, but it was Santanésia to us. Home. Even after Mita was in her wheelchair and had fits, we were still that family. Four of us. You come in a pair, with two parents: You think you're a package that will stay that way always. The hummingbirds outside, the screech of the *cigarras.* The armies of ants that marched their way into the corners of our house, no matter how many times Mummy cleaned. I thought we'd always live in that house.

I take out my leather cup and dice.

"Dolores, please," Mummy says. "Why d'you have to bring it everywhere?"

"Is it a game?" Freddie de Booze asks.

"No. I'm checking my luck."

"She has my old cup," Daddy says. "Used to play dice, back in the interior."

"I play bridge," Estelle says. "Do you play, Isabela? Join us, Thursday nights. Just the girls."

"I'm afraid I don't know how to," Mummy says. "So nice of you to ask."

I swirl the dice, first in one direction, then the other. Please, God, bring Mita back. I lift the cup: one, five. Nothing.

"D'you know who was here last time we came, Ian? Biggs."

"Ronnie Biggs?"

"Sitting by the pool, in broad daylight."

Daddy turns to Mummy to explain. "The great train robber, Ronald Biggs. Escaped from prison seven years ago. Wandsworth, was it?"

"Right," Freddie de Booze says. "Then Australia. Now in our backyard."

"Bloody thug," Daddy says. "That poor chap he whacked on the head. Never recovered. How is that right?"

Daddy's always going on about how English people are honest, not like Brazilians, who lie to your face. "I guess the English aren't all honest after all," I say, looking straight at him.

Daddy ignores me.

Estelle uncrosses her long legs. "It's like the Wild West here. You can get away with murder."

One of the boys selling roses approaches. He's five or six years old and has only one arm. Once upon a time he may have had a rolled-up yo-yo of a hand, like Mita's hand, and they decided to cut the whole arm off.

The boy offers Mummy two roses, one red, one yellow. The petals of the red one are edged with black.

Mummy ignores him, so he walks over to Daddy. "*Compre uma rosa,* for your beautiful wife."

Daddy tries not to look at his missing arm. We hated it when strangers stared at Mita's hand, or her crooked foot.

Freddie de Booze shakes his head no.

"What the hell." Daddy reaches for his wallet and pulls out a five-cruzeiro note. He offers Mummy the red rose. "To my beautiful wife."

Mummy places the rose on the table, looking embarrassed. A few of the petals fall off.

"Runaways," Estelle said. "Handicapped ones. Their mothers abandon them. You have to harden your heart."

I look at Mummy and think, *Your heart is already hard.*

More children gather round, some with white roses, others with pink.

"I knew this would happen. *Vai embora.*" Freddie de Booze shoos them away with his hand.

"It's sad, but you can't encourage them, or they'll swarm like flies," Estelle says.

One of the boys hovers behind Mummy. Her handbag is wide open. Usually, she's so careful, suspicious of everyone, but she's too busy trying to impress Freddie and Estelle to pay attention. A small hand darts in and out quickly like a tongue and grabs Mummy's suede wallet, the one she loves so much. I swirl the dice and let it happen.

Freddie and Estelle stand up to say their goodbyes. After they leave, Mummy reaches for her handbag. She feels with her hand that the clasp is open.

"No," she says, a look of panic on her face. "It can't be."

"What's the matter?" Daddy's hands fist up.

Mummy rifles through her bag, fingers trembling. "My wallet. The one my sister gave me; it's gone."

"Think. Did you bring cash?"

"I'm not sure." Mummy sounds as if she might cry.

There must be a meanness in me that runs deep, because I don't say a word.

"It was him, the boy who sold us the rose." Daddy spots the one-armed boy a few tables down, offering the yellow rose to a tourist. "I'll kill the bastard."

"No. It wasn't him," I say. "It wasn't his fault."

"What d'you mean?" Mummy clutches her handbag on her lap.

"It was another boy. I saw it happen. He ran off. He's not here anymore."

"Why didn't you tell us?" Mummy asks. "Why didn't you say something?"

I point to the red rose sitting on the table. "You should have chosen yellow," I say. "You should have picked the yellow rose."

"What the hell is wrong with you?" Daddy throws two ten-cruzeiro notes on the table and stands up. "Let's go home, Isabela. I've had enough!"

They don't remember.

Chapter Three

SANTANÉSIA

For the longest time, I blamed the yellow sequins. I wished we'd danced in the traditional Ibeji costumes, the way we were supposed to—then nothing bad would have happened. I wanted to turn back the clock and start again.

Mita and I were seven years old, and we'd been chosen to lead the parade. It was Carnaval 1968, and the drought had gone on longer than anyone could remember. Banana trees wilted, and rivers ran dry. You could find dozens of tiny dried-up piranhas under the bridge, just their bones and teeth. Maria José, the most famous *mãe santa* in the valley, decided that only the Ibejis, the twin gods with their power of doing and undoing, could bring rain. She sent word she needed a pair of twins, and we were selected.

I hadn't wanted to lead the parade, not at all. I preferred to dance at the back, with the other children. But Mummy said it was time to get over my shyness. It would be good for Daddy's job, doing something important for the village—and of course Mita was thrilled. She was not one bit shy.

Mummy drove us to the *terreiro* to look at a drawing of the costumes. She didn't need a seamstress; she knew how to sew. I stared out the car window at the drooping leaves of the palm trees, wishing there was a way out. I could pretend to be sick, but Mita would be heartbroken and I'm not sure Mummy would believe me.

Mita reached over and stroked the inside of my elbow. She did this when I was upset. "*Ta malu?*" she said.

I shook my head no, even though I was mad.

Mita double-clicked her tongue. Two clicks meant *don't worry.*

"What are you girls up to?" Mummy looked at us in the car mirror. "Speak Portuguese or English." Mummy and Daddy didn't like us to speak our twin language; they thought we were too old.

The road was bumpy. Mummy swerved into the weeds to avoid the deep ridges of dried-up mud. "Maybe we should have asked Daddy to come," she said.

I was glad Daddy wasn't with us—he thought *macumba* was a load of codswallop; at least Mummy was tactful. She didn't go around saying that black magic and saints were all inventions.

"Yellow and gold," Mita said, as if we were in the middle of yesterday's conversation about the costumes. "Maybe with some stars?"

"Yellow's impossible." I'd told her that yesterday. I rolled the window all the way down. Yellow was Oxum's color; yellow was about beauty and riches, not rain. I hoped for glittery black top hats, because Ibejis were boy twins. Claudinha said we'd wear green tunics and carry a stethoscope; she'd seen figurines of Ibejis dressed up as Cosme and Damião, the doctor-saints. The truth was: We didn't know what to expect.

We drove past the *açude* and the dried-up sugarcane fields, down a dirt road until it almost disappeared. Maria José's hut was marked by a wispy white flag, but apart from that, it looked like anyone's bamboo hut.

We rang the old cowbell. Maria José came to the door, wearing a white turban. Her black skin glistened with sweat, the way it did after a possession.

"Ah, *as estrelas do show* have arrived," she said. "Come in, come in." Maria José opened the roll of drawings. Mita pushed her way up close to see. Her mouth puckered. The costumes were ugly. Lime-green pants under an okra-colored skirt that went below the knees—no sequins. How could we dance in something that didn't even sparkle?

"I won't do it," Mita declared. She didn't even say it under her breath.

I gave her a look. You don't speak like that to a *mãe santa,* to the person who calls spirits for the whole valley, you just don't. Even the governor consults Maria José for advice; how could Mita be so rude?

Mita pointed to the drawing: "It's ugly." Then tears came, one after another.

"I can add lace," Mummy said. "Would that be better?"

"No," Mita said, her hands in fists.

Maria José seemed more curious than mad. "What about you?" she asked me.

I knew Mummy wanted me to say something nice, or at

least in-between, like a side dish that wouldn't cause offense. I'd heard her tell Daddy that in Brazil you say yes when you mean no—it wasn't lying, it was just politeness.

"It's a little plain," I said.

Mummy frowned. "I apologize for the girls. They must be tired."

Mita sobbed harder, her body shook with sobs.

"Mita wanted sequins," I said, wanting Mita to stop.

Maria José knelt in front of Mita, and her seven or eight lace skirts knelt with her, forming a white flower on the ground. "What color sequins?" Maria José asked. "What color sequins were you thinking?"

A smile began to pull at Mita's lips. It took a second to make her happy.

"Yellow," she said. "Yellow sequins."

Maria José closed her eyes. Her face became still, like the *açude* on a hot day. Her wrinkles disappeared. She fingered the blue and silver beads around her neck and swayed. Maybe an *orixá* was entering her, I'd seen it happen. *Orixás* came and went from her body like guests. Once I saw a spirit turn her into an old man smoking a cigar. Even her voice and her laugh changed.

Maria José opened her eyes. "Yellow will work," she announced. "A short skirt with yellow sequins. We'll have the boys behind you, dressed like Ibejis, and you girls can sparkle in yellow: two suns leading the way. At the end of the dance, you will open your umbrellas, and the rain will come."

Mita let out a small yelp. Maria José laughed. "She's like a window, your daughter, wide open. The spirits can enter easily."

"I'm not sure about spirits," Mummy said. "But it isn't difficult to know what Margarita wants, is it, Mita?"

"Dolores wants it too," Mita said. She walked up to the tall statue of Iemanjá and ran her fingers along the blue filmy silk of her dress.

"Don't touch, Mita," Mummy said.

Maria José turned to me and raised her eyebrows. I liked the way she checked in with both of us.

"Yellow sequins are nice," I said. "Pretty."

"It'll be fun," Mita said, taking my hand and double-clicking her tongue. "Super-fun."

"Your other daughter's special too," Maria José said. "More of a protector."

"That sounds right," Mummy said, smiling. "Is it a skirt or a dress with yellow sequins?"

Maria José closed her eyes again. "A short skirt and a bustier, like a bikini top," she said. "We want to see them *rebolar.*"

Mita lifted her T-shirt and twirled the top half of her belly one way, and the bottom half the other way. She'd been perfecting that move all week. "Like this?"

Maria José laughed. "Marvelous!"

MITA AND I PRACTICED IN front of the mirror every day. Aparecida, our maid, helped us. We weren't the best dancers, but we weren't the worst. I had to work on separating my belly from my bottom: They seemed to want to move together as a unit.

"Pretend you're reaching for something with the top part of your body"—Aparecida shimmied her breasts, arms, and belly to the left—"and tell your feet to move the opposite way. Your *bumbum* will follow your feet. Then you put them together, like this," and all of her was *rebolando* at once.

I'd manage to connect the swirling energy from my upper body to my legs for a few seconds, then I'd lose it.

"Practice and you'll get it," Aparecida said. "Now it's your turn, Margarita."

Mita had confused feet—that's what we called them. We didn't realize then that it was a sign of trouble. During the turn, she tripped.

"*Pé no chão,* Mita. Remember your roots, keep close to the earth when you dance."

Mita tried again. Now her bottom wasn't moving, only her belly.

"*Bunda,* Margarita! Remember your bottom!"

Mita laughed and loosened up, and the music entered her. She went wild, undulating and turning, her body pulsing with samba.

Aparecida whistled. "When she gets it, she gets it! You'll be the best dancer out there!" Mita laughed, the samba inside her like a force.

"Now the two of you together," Aparecida said, "remember to dance in step." That part was easy. Whenever we ran, if one of us was ahead, the other would slow down. We didn't think about it; our bodies adjusted for us.

ON THE DAY OF THE parade, we had it down. We could shimmy our bodies this way and that, jump and turn, we could samba to every song. We'd opened and closed our umbrellas so many times that Mummy had to confiscate them so they wouldn't break.

"Will you come, Ian?" Mummy asked. "Take photos of the girls?"

Daddy hated the noise of Carnaval, because of the war. When the Germans bombed London, he lived in an underground shelter, and he could still hear bombs in his head. Fireworks, shouting, even playing could set him off. We were used to Daddy's ways.

"What the hell," he said. "You two are the main attraction, how can I miss it?"

Daddy wore a flowered green shirt for the occasion. He dropped us off at the Praça Tiradentes with the other children. Rows of boys dressed as Ibejis in tunics and pants, and girls in rose- and green-sequined skirts, maybe one hundred children—not just from Santanésia, but also from Barra Mansa, Volta Redonda, Querosene—from the whole valley. Mita and I were the only two in yellow.

We went to our place: out in front, facing each other. The drums pulsed their *batucada,* slow at first, then faster. The crowd behind us clapped, whistled, and threw streamers and confetti. I tried to pretend it was just the two of us, rehearsing in the kitchen. I could feel the prickle of nervousness collecting behind my knees, like tiny spiders. Mita widened her arms and curtsied. The crowd cheered. Mita's eyes sparkled. The drums picked up, followed by *cuícas,* then the *surdos, tamborins, chocalhos,* all the instruments playing. Mita and I locked eyes. Our sequins shivered as we waited. Then it came, our cue: the double beat.

I stepped forward and twisted my heel into the ground as if I were putting out a cigarette, the way Aparecida taught us. My hips dipped and my feet swiveled to the beat. Aparecida said invite the world into the dance. I opened my arms wide, looking at Mita as she shimmied toward me. Because we were identical and not pretend twins like the other children, people clapped extra-loud as we passed. I noticed Mita's left foot lagging behind. I locked eyes with her. Dance faster. Don't trip. I hypnotized her as I moved toward her; together, apart. I'd imagine I was Mita, and she was me, and we'd changed places, so my body danced in hers and she danced in mine. When she moved, it was me moving—I'd convince myself this was the case. It always worked, this trick. Our arms, legs, bellies, and feet, all melded together so it looked to the outside world like they were seeing double, not two separate children dancing.

Mita danced to the left, picking up speed. I moved to the right, and she stayed with me. Her feet flew, now it was me who had to keep up. The crowd clapped louder, the drums picked up, and we danced faster and faster, all the children following us, and behind them the teenagers and then the adults, but this year, us children were the stars. We danced for land, for rain, for the luck of the universe to shift, for the Ibejis to undo the curse that was drying up the valley. I felt it, the rhythm, the energy, the miracle happening, and it made me laugh.

We passed the *padaria,* the doorway where Mummy and Daddy would be standing. I didn't let myself look. I worried Mita might get distracted, so I stared deep into her eyes, hypnotizing her into myself, like a magnet coming home. Mita broke from my eyes and glanced up at Daddy. It was just a moment, but her feet tripped, one over the other, and she fell. I tried to pull her up, but her body was heavy. She wasn't helping, she was like a sack of potatoes. I was desperate. I yanked her arm. "Mita, get up!" But she was on the ground, shaking. Her eyes rolled backward so there were no middles anymore, they were like the white of an egg. Her body shook and her legs kicked, and Mummy held her head, and Daddy, too, crouched on the dusty road as the sea of children danced past us, looking back to see what had happened.

"Find Miguel," Daddy shouted in Portuguese, "get the doctor!" Voices above us. Someone said it was an emergency, another person shouted for Dr. Miguel, the music didn't stop, but there was a stir. Teenagers passed us, then adults. We waited. Dr. Miguel didn't arrive. He didn't arrive for the longest time. Daddy held Mita's legs, trying to still them, and Mummy and I each had one arm; they whipped about like loose belts. I tried not to look at her eyes. Her eyeballs, where did they go? How could they disappear like that?

Dr. Miguel finally arrived. I heard the snap of his black briefcase, even with the music. The band played "Mas que Nada," I sang the words inside my head: *Mas que nada, sai da minha frente que eu quero passar . . .* The words of the song matched everyone dancing past us while Mita's body jerked. The heat made the road wavy like a sea. Daddy wiped the sweat off his forehead with his scrunched-up handkerchief while Mummy's fingers stroked Mita's forehead. Dr. Miguel pulled out a syringe and a tiny glass bottle, the needle swallowed the liquid up, the liquid that looked like water. He flicked the syringe, *flick, flick, flick.* Daddy grabbed Mita's arm, which had escaped from his grip, and held it down while Dr. Miguel gave her the injection. Her arms flailed in the air when Daddy let go, the song went on, *obá, obá, obá . . .*

Once the backup band passed and the dancers thinned out, Daddy picked Mita up in his arms and we followed him through the crowd. Mummy took hold of my hand so I wouldn't get lost.

"We left the umbrellas," I shouted, "we have to go back!" My voice was swallowed up by the music, by the crowd, by the cars and lorries, which had started to leave. Mita's fit wouldn't stop. I didn't know it was a fit then; I thought she was possessed, and we needed Maria José—not Dr. Miguel. We needed Maria José's spiritual powers to bring Mita back. We pushed our way through the crowd, the stares, the murmurs, that was the first time I felt pity—I wasn't used to it then, that look in people's eyes.

Mummy and I slid into the back of our car and held Mita's legs, but they kept escaping and kicking in a wild way, as if there were an animal inside of her, mad to get out. Dr. Miguel followed us in his light blue Mercedes-Benz.

When we arrived home, Aparecida held the door open while Daddy walked in sideways with Mita, so her legs wouldn't bruise. He placed her in the center of their big double bed. We stood watching her for what seemed like hours. Sweat dripped off Daddy's arms, past his watch, and down his fingers.

Mita's shaking began to slow down, until it was only a slight tremor, like the gentlest of winds passing through her body.

Daddy offered Dr. Miguel a glass of his precious Glenfiddich, even though he couldn't stand the way Dr. Miguel watered it down with Guaraná. "Thank you," Daddy said. "I can't thank you enough."

Mita lay still on the bed, her cheek squashed upward, a trickle of dribble making its way from her mouth onto the pillow.

"Is she dead?" I asked. There was a gone-ness about her that scared me.

The space above Mummy's lips puckered like the stitches in a hem when you pull them too tight. "Of course not." Mummy hugged me close, even though I was sweaty.

Dr. Miguel took a small sip of whisky; he wasn't a big drinker. "She may sleep a long time—and be confused when she wakes up. Has she had other episodes?"

"Never," I said. I was the expert on my sister.

Dr. Miguel glanced at Mummy with that look adults get when they're hiding something. I'd watched the men play Liar's Dice at the club and I knew the look.

"Never," I said again. I was seven: I knew.

"She was two when she had the last one," Mummy said.

"It's not true. Mita was never like this." Mita had confused feet, but she'd never shaken before.

"You were too little to remember," Mummy said.

I didn't know then that adults could lie: that they were capable of hiding even the most important things from their own children.

"How long did that fit last, do you remember?" Dr. Miguel turned his crystal glass as he spoke, studying the color of the whisky.

Mummy glanced at Daddy.

"Less than a minute," Daddy said. "Not long."

"Any others?" Dr. Miguel asked.

"Well, there was the first one," Mummy said. "A few days after birth. They weren't sure if it was a virus or a fever that caused it."

"Did I have fits too, Mummy?" I asked.

"No," Mummy said. "Just Mita."

Dr. Miguel ruffled my hair. "You danced well today. Both of you did."

"Is she possessed?" I asked. "By the Ibejis?" The twin gods were angry because we didn't wear the right clothes. They were punishing us for our yellow-sequin skirts.

"Shut up with that nonsense," Daddy said.

I wanted Dr. Miguel to tell Daddy it wasn't nonsense. I knew he'd gone to consult Maria José a few times, Aparecida had told me. But Dr. Miguel didn't say anything. People were scared of Daddy's temper. Plus, he was a gringo—so they smiled and pretended to go along with his opinions.

Daddy offered Dr. Miguel one of his Cuban cigars. They were rare in Brazil, and precious.

"Thank you, I'll save it for New Year's Eve." He slid the cigar into the pocket of his shirt, so it looked like a sausage. "Does epilepsy run in the family?"

"I don't think so," Mummy said.

"Keep an eye out. If it's epilepsy, there may be other fits." Dr. Miguel closed his black medicine case. I remember the snapping sound the locks made, like two mousetraps, *snap, snap.* I wanted Mita to snap out of it, to come back and be Mita again.

Chapter Four

SEPTEMBER 1972

The Blue Bus is worse than school. A sardine tin full of English children. I walk past the rows of girls and boys in their school uniforms to the back, where no one sits. The bus stops and starts as it weaves its way through Rio. I'm used to traffic lights. Mita and I used to get so excited whenever we approached the one in Barra, betting on whether it would be red or green. Rio is dirty—not digging for worms, squelching your toes in the mud dirt, but city dirt. It's overflowing rubbish bins in the alleys; it's abandoned beer caps and cinema tickets; it's a deserted shoe with a broken heel. The swirls of oil in the canal look like slippery shadows.

The bus pulls through the school gate, and we file out. I go upstairs to Mr. P.'s English class. For once, I've done my homework.

"First things first: essays. I want them in a pile, right here." Mr. P. points to his desk. "In case some of you have short memories, the assignment was to write something risky, something hard to write. A secret you dare not say." The flecks of orange in his green eyes shine like tiny flames.

I'd drawn two girls: One has filled-out edges with long hair like mine, and she holds the hand of the other one, who is identical except she's made with small, broken-up lines, like the lines in the middle of the road—so she is there and not there. I place my blue book on the pile along with the others, and the bones near my heart start to close like wings. Mr. P. doesn't know it, but this essay is the only one that counts.

After class, I stay in my seat, hoping Mr. P. will smile or say hello, but he's busy sorting through the essays and doesn't look up. Maybe he's angry with me. He waited after school all those times, and I didn't bother to show up. I saw him sitting behind the hydrangeas reading, and I just walked by, pretending not to notice.

I head upstairs, to science, wishing I could take my blue book back. I should have kept Mita to myself. Mr. P. might be disgusted. Or sorry. He will never understand.

As I pass the staff room, I hear Mr. Wilson, the art teacher, with his snooty accent: "There's something wrong with her, that much is obvious."

"It's only the first month; give her time. At least she speaks English; that's a start. Michael Parker thinks he can help her." That's Mr. Walker's voice. The headmaster.

"Michael's a quack, you know that. Breaking all the rules. Can't teach anyone a bloody thing!"

They're talking about me. Michael Parker must be Mr. P. The headmaster and Mr. Wilson are talking about me.

I continue down the corridor, my cheeks on fire. They

know. They will tell Mummy and Daddy, and I'll get expelled. Or worse: I'll be sent to a Borstal. That's where they send dunces. I've heard the English girls talk about it. They don't just cane you there; they strip you naked and make you drink your own pee.

I slip into the lab room and try to settle my heart. Mr. Walker said give the girl a chance. I have time. I'll go after school today—and every day. I'll learn. I will. Mr. P. will teach me.

At least science is safe. On the first day, Mrs. Oliveira told us we'd all pass no matter what. She said the point of science is to be curious and ask questions; she doesn't care about A's, B's, or C's. We're doing a unit on animate and inanimate objects. There are two tables, one with a shell, a coconut, a rock, and an empty bottle of olive oil, and another table with living things: a black bean plant, exploding red tomatoes, a hibiscus flower, and a guinea pig. Mrs. Oliveira wants us to compare and contrast—but all I see are the samenesses. *Inanimate* means dead—at least that's what Marcos said. People are supposed to be living things, but I belong more to the other table, with the shell and the coconut.

Well, my essay, if I knew how to write, would say that sometimes things that look dead are not dead; you shouldn't give up on them. Like the rattlesnake in the middle of the road: Daddy drove over it two times, back and forth, but the head and the tail of the snake continued to move—instead of killing it, he doubled it. And Mita: What land does she belong to? When she was in a coma, she looked dead. Then she got better; at least, they said she was better. There isn't a table for in-betweens, and most things in life are in-between. Mrs. Oliveira wants us to say that the flower is alive because it grows toward the sun, and the caterpillar will become a butterfly. Along the sides of the road, people stand by bamboo huts and sell butterflies pressed between glass, turned into trays for tourists to buy. Bright blue butterflies with silver rivers along their wings, and yellow ones with orange spots, all of them pressed flat, so they are inanimate. It's only a matter of time before one table turns into the other.

I WAIT UNTIL IT IS quiet, and the buses have left, then I make my way downstairs. Please, God, let Mr. P. be there. This morning, I threw double threes. Daddy used to say you could fly on double threes; doublets are where luck is born. Mita and I loved it when he said that; it felt like he was talking about us.

I walk across the playground, afraid I've missed my one and only chance to learn.

Mr. P. is sitting on the ground behind the hydrangeas. "Peaceful here," he says. His dimples deepen when he smiles. I'm not sure how old he is, but he looks younger than the other teachers. I like the way his dark hair is messy. He picks up a long twig and pats the earth. "Sit down."

Mr. P. doesn't grit his teeth or show me his watch to point out my lateness; he's friendly and matter-of-fact. My stomach flips a little. Which possibly means I have a crush. I don't want to be like English girls, with their crushes. Andrea thinks it's pathetic to have a crush: You should love with passion, with your whole body and soul. Andrea held on to her heart when she said *body and soul,* or maybe it was her breast. Either way, I'm so not ready for that.

I sit a little distance from him. He doesn't seem to mind.

"I've been thinking about your drawing," Mr. P. says. "It's haunting."

I can't tell if haunting is good or bad. A sense of shame, like the shade of a tree, overtakes my body. This morning, I wanted to show him Mita, but now I don't.

"Can you tell me about the two girls?" Mr. P. says. "Who are they?"

I shake my head no.

"Does the drawing have a title?"

If I say no again, he might get mad or give up on me. Already I've missed so many lessons. "The girl who is there and not there," I say.

"What a title. Makes me want to know more."

I stay silent.

"Well, maybe one day you'll write her story, this girl who is there and not there? First step is to learn letters. We'll use this stick here as a pen." Mr. P. draws a clown hat, pointed, with a line through it, on the ground. "This is an *a,* the first letter of the alphabet, *aaahhh,* like when you go to the dentist."

I've never gone to a dentist. Mummy told Estelle it was one of those things she had to give up on, in the interior. Dentists and eye doctors.

"Aaahhh," Mr. P. says. The neurologist used to say that to Mita. He'd flatten her tongue with his ruler and tell her to say *aaahhh*—which never made any sense: How could you say anything with a ruler in your mouth? Even so, Mita tried. She'd try with all her might, that was something we loved about her. Her dribble would flow full force, like a flood from her mouth, "Aaahhh." Daddy always looked away. He couldn't bear her dribble.

"*Apple.*" Mr. P. draws another clown hat with a line through it plus two fences with fallen heads at the top, followed by a straight line and a curly worm. "This is how you write *apple.*"

There is no roundness or redness; absolutely nothing apple-like about his drawing. "Why like that?"

Mr. P. furrows his forehead. I worry he's angry, but maybe he's thinking.

"The alphabet is a set of pictures that make sounds." Mr. P. draws something that looks like a swan. "This isn't as good as yours, but can you see what it is?"

I nod. I wonder if he's making fun of me.

"Reading and writing are like that. It's looking at a picture and recognizing the words."

But the letters don't look like pictures. I've stared at them for hours, and they don't tell me anything.

"The letters aren't drawings of actual things. They are sounds. Each letter makes a sound, then you string them together to make a word."

I should already know this. He's treating me like a baby. My legs feel like running, but I don't run. I need to learn.

Mr. P. draws something curvy with the stick. "This letter here, is an *s. Sssssss,* it makes that sound, for *swan, sun, snake.* So: When I'm writing *swan,* I start with the sound *s.*"

My heart claps. I can feel it widen inside of me. He's showing me the secret code!

"I'm sure you can draw it," Mr. P. says. "Why don't you try making an *s;* it's curvy, like a swan." He offers me the stick.

I cross my arms and look at the school gate, the far one, where the buses come in. It's made of wrought iron, and the shapes curl around one another like *s*'s. It seems that there are *s*'s everywhere; but I don't want to try drawing one in front of him.

Mr. P. makes another *s,* and another. "You can practice on your own. The first step is to learn all the letters and the sounds they make, and after that you just join them."

He makes it sound so easy.

Mr. P. draws a fence with a fallen head on top: Maybe it's a skull. It reminds me of the skulls we used to find hanging from the fence at the fazenda. A dead horse, or a cow.

"This here is a *p,*" Mr. P. says, "like my name, Mr. P. Peter Piper picked a peck of pickled peppers." He draws three more skulls on fences, one after another, on the ground. Then he hands me the stick. "Your turn. Can you make a *p*?"

I take the stick, and a nervousness enters my body, a shaking that starts in my fingers and moves up to my elbow, then my shoulder. The whole right side of my body shakes, as if I'm spastic. I throw the stick to the ground. "I can't learn this. I can't."

Mr. P. grasps my arm. "You can. I promise you. I know you can."

I hate him. He's making everything worse. "Please leave me alone."

"Try. It's like drawing. You're so good at drawing. What does a *p* remind you of? I bet you had a picture in your mind as I drew the letter."

"A skull. Hanging from a fence."

"A skull. Hanging . . . yes. I see what you mean. You're more poetic than I ever would be. Can you draw a skull hanging from a fence?"

Draw. You know how to draw. I pick up the stick and draw a real fence, like the picket fences around the gardens of some houses, and then I draw a skull hanging from it; a skull with deep eyeholes and a jawbone that looks like a horseshoe.

"Great! That's better than a *p.* If you can draw this, you can make a *p.* You have to simplify." He draws a line straight down. "See? One line for the fence. The skull is on the side of the fence, like this." Mr. P. draws more *p*'s, one after another.

"Do you want to have a go?"

I take the stick and my hand starts to shake, all the way up to my elbow. I let it drop.

"You absolutely don't have to do it now. Maybe you can practice on your own? Just those three letters, a *p,* an *s,* and an *a.*" Mr. P. checks his watch: "My, time flies. Tomorrow? Same time, same place?"

I nod yes. Mr. P. stands up and pats the back of his trousers, which are brown from the earth. I wait until he's gone, then I find the stick and draw a *p*—exactly the same as Mr. P.'s *p*—and whisper to myself: "*P.*"

Chapter Five

Last night, after dinner, I drew ten *p*'s and ten *s*'s and ten *a*'s. It wasn't that difficult. I drew another five of each letter this morning. I can't wait to show them to Mr. P. He hasn't arrived yet. He's usually here before the buses. Marcos throws a paper plane across the room, then another one.

Mr. Wilson, the art teacher, walks in. "Quiet down, class. Mr. P. is out sick, so I will be teaching you English this week."

I swallow the sourness in my mouth. Mr. Wilson is a walking explosion. He hates pink. If you wear anything pink, he uses his ruler to thwack your bottom in front of everyone. His temper lives underground; you can feel it throbbing inside of him, a pulse beside his eye.

"Grammar is the foundation of all writing," Mr. Wilson says. "Let's begin with a game, shall we? A grammar game."

"Give me a noun," he says, standing in front of each person's desk. "Give me a verb." He walks from person to person, slapping his ruler against the palm of his hand, waiting for an answer. There's no avoiding. The first time you mess up, you stand next to your desk; the second time, you stand on top of your desk and hold the edges of your dress in, so no one sees up your legs. The third time, you are caned. You have to bend over and show your panties to the whole giggling class while he canes you with the rough side of his ruler. After the third time, you are eliminated from the game.

Always, I am eliminated. I can't figure out what makes one word a verb, and another a noun. I throw out a word—any word—and wait for the verdict, hoping to be eliminated as soon as possible.

We play this grammar game every day and school is unbearable. By the end of the week, when Mr. Wilson is about to cane me for the hundredth time, Andrea speaks up: "Stop it. *La ragazza non capisce.*" Her voice is loud, definite. I've noticed she speaks Italian when she's angry. She switches to English: "She no understand."

Mr. Wilson isn't used to being interrupted in the middle of his punishments. He focuses his blue eyes on Andrea. Andrea stares right back.

"I beg your pardon," Mr. Wilson says. "I can't understand your English. Please speak clearly."

The class titters, but Andrea isn't about to give up. "She no understand! Verb! Noun! No understand—never!" She sounds powerful.

I shake my head to emphasize Andrea's point.

Andrea senses she's gaining ground. "Never, never, never!"

The bell rings. Mr. Wilson tells us both to stay after class. Usually, there's a mad scramble to the door when the bell rings, but this time, students walk out slowly. Twenty-one necks swerve to watch.

Mr. Wilson bends down and puts his face close to mine, so close I can feel his breath. He smells of garlic. I want to step backward, but I'm afraid.

"What the hell is wrong with you?" he asks through clenched teeth. "Can't understand, my foot!"

He turns to Andrea. She adjusts the rings on every one of her fingers, including her thumb, and pretends not to notice him.

"Who do you think you are?" Mr. Wilson's thin body tightens—as if the anger is being squeezed up a toothpaste tube, all the way to his face. He's going to hit Andrea.

The sound of a plane cuts through the silence, making me jump. Children shout in the distance, the rusty metal swing twists back and forth.

Mr. Wilson cracks his knuckles, one by one. "You both make me sick." He breaks away from Andrea's gaze to look out the window. There's a struggle in his face, one part of it clenches up and the other tries to be calm. "Black Detention, both of you."

He walks over to the blackboard. "Go! Out of my sight!" I follow Andrea down the stairs and out to the playground. We stand in the detention line with Marcos.

"What are you here for?" Marcos asks. "Red or Blue?"

"Black." Andrea smiles at him, as if it is a feat she's accomplished.

"*Porra,* shit." He gives a long, slow whistle.

Red Detention means you stay after school to clean the

blackboards. Blue Detention means you get extra homework. I'm not sure what happens in Black Detention. It can't be good.

Andrea seems indifferent. She's part Italian, part Brazilian. She can read and write in English, but she has an accent and hates to speak it. She says it's an ugly language and her tongue doesn't want to go there. She wears her long, curly brown hair loose around her square face, and she doesn't try to disappear. When people stare, she swears at them in Italian and makes rude signs with her hands.

Andrea chats to me in Portuguese about *novelas* and *escolas de samba* and asks me interesting questions: Do I know where the *vira-latas,* the stray dogs, live in Rio? It's as if she's forgotten that we're standing in line waiting for a punishment.

Students stare as they pass by on their way to the buses. Andrea rolls her eyes and shows them in every way that she couldn't care less. Mr. Wilson watches her, which only makes her increase the drama. She kneels, searches in her satchel, and pulls out a pink lipstick and a small mirror. Pink, of all colors. She turns away from the sun and traces her lips with the creamy lipstick. Mr. Wilson's thumb presses lightly into the tip of each of his fingers, one by one.

He steps toward Andrea. "Hand me that."

Andrea ignores him.

"I said, give it to me."

Andrea outlines her upper lip carefully, then presses both lips together, to even out the color. She makes an O with her mouth. Then she slowly screws the cap back on and hands him the lipstick. "I don't think it's your color, sir."

Laughter bubbles inside of me, like Alka-Seltzer.

Mr. Wilson's face almost touches hers. "Don't test me. You understand?"

Andrea lifts her hair off her neck and lets it fall down her back. She arranges her curls around her ears.

The tip of Mr. Wilson's nose turns white. "I said, do you understand?"

Something in the hoarseness of his voice makes me step forward and stand between them.

"She understands, sir." My voice is reedy and dry. The glare from Andrea's mirror hurts my eyes. I stand there, determined to separate Andrea from Mr. Wilson.

Andrea sighs loudly, looking bored.

Mrs. Oliveira, the science teacher, approaches. "Mr. Wilson, a word, please."

A bead of sweat inches its way along Mr. Wilson's jaw.

"Andrew, I need to speak to you now." The *now* is sharp and loud. Mrs. Oliveira gestures with her chin to the other side of the playground.

Andrea catches my eye, and I look away. I don't want to make things worse.

Mr. Wilson follows Mrs. Oliveira to the shade of the *jabuticaba* tree. I hear Mrs. Oliveira say the word *control,* but can't make out much else.

"Thank you," Andrea whispers. "You saved me. He's such a pervert."

Douglas, a prefect in class six, dribbles a basketball, shoots, and misses. Mr. Wilson calls him over, and then they both walk toward us.

"Upstairs to the science lab, girls. Mrs. Oliveira has kindly offered us her room. I will stop in now and again to check up on you." Mr. Wilson sounds almost reasonable.

We follow Douglas upstairs.

"Mr. Wilson thinks he's so important, running that dumb eleven-plus exam," Andrea says.

"Shh. You're not allowed to talk." Douglas unlocks the door to the lab room.

Andrea sidles up to him, close. "We are allowed to whisper. I'll kiss you if you let us whisper."

Douglas's freckly face turns red. Andrea reaches and takes hold of his face in her hands as if it were a vase, leans in, and French-kisses him. A long tongue-kiss, the way you see in the *novelas.* My heart beats with surprise. Douglas's hands walk their way up like crabs, from her waist toward her breasts. Andrea breaks the kiss and steps away. "We didn't agree to that. Only a kiss."

She heads to the back of the lab and sits on one of the new stools, which turn from side to side.

I sit next to her.

"Where were we? Oh, yes, the eleven-plus." Andrea shrugs. "It's this important test they give you at the end of the year. I don't care if I fail."

"Me neither," I say, as if failing is a choice.

Douglas starts writing something on the blackboard. Andrea walks up front to see. She reads it out loud, in her strong Brazilian accent: "*Even though I find it extremely hard, I must try to behave more like a human being and less like a wild animal.*"

I can't tell if she's inventing, or if that's really what it says.

Douglas places the chalk on the narrow trough under the blackboard. "One hundred lines. Mr. Wilson said."

"One hundred? It's three whole lines, so he's actually giving us three hundred lines. That's not fair."

"Do you want me to call Mr. Wilson?"

Andrea glares at him and returns to her stool. She picks up her pencil and begins to write.

I open my notebook. I can't write one sentence; how am I going to write one hundred? Or three hundred. Usually, I draw something, but I can't do that for Black Detention. Mr. Wilson will have a fit. Even if I draw a hundred flowers or horses or trees. My stomach hurts.

After a few minutes, Andrea glances over and notices my empty page. "Oh, sorry, I forgot. I was so angry at Mr. Wilson for giving us lines, I forgot you can't write."

My head swims. I can't believe she said it out loud. I close my eyes, wanting to disappear. The words *can't write, can't write, can't write* echo in the empty lab room.

"It's okay. We'll probably be here until nighttime, but I'll do it for you." Her words hover above me like moths. Andrea takes hold of my hand. "Really, it's okay."

Can't write, can't write, can't write.

"It's not a big deal. Who cares about writing?"

I do. I care.

Andrea begins to write in my notebook. I hear the scratch of the pencil and her breathing, regular and strong, almost noisy.

After a while, I slip back into myself, like a gear. I feel my bottom on the stool, my elbows, my feet squashed up in coffin shoes.

Halfway down the second page, Andrea stops writing and begins to erase everything. "I have to start over in a different handwriting, or he'll be able to tell."

It never occurred to me that people have their own handwriting—like a face that is just theirs. "I'm sorry. Thank you for doing this."

"*De nada,*" Andrea says, with an impish grin. "You owe me, though. Big."

"I know. Big." I smile at her.

Andrea alternates between my notebook and hers. In

mine, she leans the markings forward, so each word tips into the next, as if it might fall over. In her notebook, the markings stand straight, like soldiers. I used to sing "Marcha Soldado" with Mita. We'd jump off the sofa, pretending to be soldiers with white paper hats. It's hard to remember that Mita, who could jump. It isn't exactly forgetting . . . it's more like colors fading in the midday sun; the aquamarine blue lightens into gray, and the gray turns white and suddenly there's only a whisper of a sister that is hard to conjure up.

"I'm a twin," I blurt out, before I can stop myself.

Andrea stops writing. Her brown eyes widen and take over her face. "Really? Fraternal or identical?"

"Identical. No one can tell us apart," I lie.

"Exactly the same? You're so lucky! I always wanted a twin. Do you like exactly the same things?"

"Yes," I say. "The same food, the same TV shows. *National Kid*. That was our favorite show."

"Me too. I loved his hand moves." Andrea makes the classic *National Kid* circular wave. "Why isn't your twin here, at school with us?"

I have to come up with an answer: "She has a hurt foot," I say, trying not to think of the word *spastic*—that's what the doctor called it. I'd hate it if Andrea found Mita ugly. Or laughed at her. Then I'd lose my only friend here in Rio.

"A hurt foot? Can she walk?"

"No." I decide to tell her that much. "She's in a wheelchair."

"That's so sad. She wouldn't be able to climb the stairs to get to class. Does she go to a special school, then?"

"Yes, a school with ramps." The lies slip out easily, like watermelon seeds, one after another. I tell myself I'm protecting Mita from being laughed at, but I'm really protecting myself. If Andrea doesn't have the right reaction, I won't be able to be her friend anymore, and I can't bear to find out.

"When you sneeze, does she sneeze too, at the exact same moment?"

No, that never happened. "We sneeze separately."

I tell her bits of truth and bits of lies, until I'm not sure anymore which is which.

"And peeing?"

"Separately."

"So what exactly is identical?"

"Freckles. We grow freckles in the same place." I show her the one above my pinkie finger. "Mita has one, the same size, in exactly the same place." That didn't change, even after her hand curled up and stopped moving.

"Do you have exactly the same feet?"

Mita's left foot veers to the right in a semicircle for no reason. I can't bear to see that look on Andrea's face, the look that Mummy, Daddy, Mita, and I all know—maybe everyone who loves someone who's deformed or different knows it.

"Our feet are exactly the same."

The door opens. Mr. Wilson strides across the lab toward us. He picks up my notebook and studies it. A frown develops between his eyes. He hands it back to me without saying a word. He picks up Andrea's notebook. The frown deepens into a lump with crevices, like a walnut. "Four lines," he says, pointing at his watch. "Four lines in half an hour. How is that possible?"

Before Andrea can answer, I speak up, doing my piece for both of us: "It's a very long sentence, sir."

"Too long," Andrea chimes in. "It's not fair."

"Not fair, is it?" The walnut between Mr. Wilson's eyes squeezes tighter, and new crevices form like lines on a map.

"Stand up." His voice is even.

We slide off our stools and stand next to each other. The heat from Andrea's body next to mine makes me less scared.

"Bend over."

Mr. Wilson walks behind us. I know the routine. I close my eyes and wait for the snap of his ruler, the sharp pain, like a burn. I wait, but it doesn't come. I open my eyes and look at Andrea, bent over. After a few moments, she stands up. I do the same.

A thwack, right next to my pinkie finger.

"Did I tell you to stand up? Did I tell you?"

"No, sir."

"Get back down, the two of you."

Before I'm all the way over, his ruler thwacks my bottom. The sting is so intense I yelp. Then he hits Andrea.

"*Porra,* that hurts." There's pain in Andrea's voice. The ruler snaps into me again, this time harder. I yell out. The plastic ruler hurts more than the wooden one. Mr. Wilson leans in, close to Andrea's bottom, bends the top of the ruler so it arches backward, and lets go. She scrunches up her face and manages not to scream. That's the advice she gave me: Don't give him the satisfaction of hurting you; pretend you feel nothing. I'm amazed she can do it. Her silence infuriates him, so instead of moving on to me, he snaps the ruler into her bottom again. Still: Andrea is silent. He snaps his ruler again. And again.

"Stop it," I say. "Stop it stop it stop it!"

He bends the ruler back and lets it unfurl onto Andrea's bottom at an angle, so the corner of the ruler cuts into her skin. Andrea bites down on a scream, then her face twists, and she begins to cry.

I walk over to Mr. Wilson, grab his wrist, and snatch the ruler from him. He's so surprised, he lets me do it. I don't care if I get expelled. He can't hurt Andrea like this. I go to the window and throw the ruler into the playground, all the way down. I watch it land. Then I turn, not knowing what will happen next.

Mr. Wilson looks stunned. His hands dangle next to him. His fingers open and close, open and close.

Andrea wipes her nose with her arm. She's half smiling, half crying. Blood dribbles down her leg. Andrea reaches back and wipes it, then holds her bloody fingers in front of her so Mr. Wilson can see. "Blood," Andrea says, in case he doesn't notice. "That is not allowed, to cane someone so they bleed."

Mr. Wilson grits his teeth. The rows of test tubes line up in their holders on the shelf above his head. The trickle of blood makes its way down Andrea's leg to her flip-flops. The fan creaks as it turns.

"Go. Get out, the two of you." Mr. Wilson's voice is tight with anger.

We leave without our notebooks. We run down the stairs, into the playground. Andrea stops and picks up his plastic ruler. "I'm going to keep this as a souvenir."

"A souvenir of what?"

"Our friendship."

If Daddy hears I had Black Detention, he'll be furious. I take the back lift, drop off my satchel in my bedroom, and walk down the corridor as if I've been home for hours. I hear Mummy's voice, low; it's the hushed tone she uses for secrets. I stand at the entrance to the living room, behind the bamboo palm, so she can't see me. She must be talking about Mita.

Mummy is with her new friend, Estelle.

"There was nothing in Rio?" Estelle asks.

"Those hospitals . . ."—Mummy shivers her shoulders—"filthy prisons."

"I don't know how you did it, Isabela. It's hard enough sending them off to boarding school."

"We couldn't risk another coma."

"Well, then, thank God for National Health."

"They have nurses round the clock. Margarita won't struggle so much to keep up . . ." Mummy sniffs a few times, and Estelle places her hand on Mummy's knee.

"And there's Ian's job," Mummy says. "You know how it is. If we get transferred . . ."

"We pay a price for the life we live," Estelle says.

"You do what you have to do."

"I suppose so," Estelle says. "Poor little soul."

Mummy stiffens her back. "This is better for Dolores. She can have a normal life. The doctor said think of the well child."

I step out from my hiding place and walk right up to Mummy: "The doctor was wrong!"

Estelle and Mummy exchange looks.

"It isn't better for me. How could you think that?"

"One day you'll understand," Mummy says.

"I won't. And Mita won't either. She'll never forgive you."

I glare at Mummy. Her fingers shake. I don't care. You don't do that. You don't just give your child away.

Chapter Six

SANTANÉSIA

The village was quiet, the way it always was the day after Carnaval. Sequins glittered among the cobblestones. The café was empty, tables and chairs folded up and stacked in the corner. I'd never walked down the narrow path to the village without Mita before, without her shoulder bumping against mine. It felt strange.

Church bells: the end of Mass. I took off my flip-flops and ran. I didn't want to see anyone.

I arrived at the shop out of breath, the beaded curtains in the entrance tinkled, announcing a customer. Geraldo worked Sundays, Easter, even Carnaval. People said he would burn in hell for putting money over Christ—but they were happy to go there when they needed something.

The cigarettes were on the wall above the porn magazines.

I stood on my tiptoes but couldn't reach. Geraldo wasn't anywhere. I rang the brass counter bell and waited. The sun shimmered through the colored beads, lighting the tiny corridor of a room.

Yesterday after the fit stopped, Mita slept for a long time, and then she was floppy. She couldn't sit up without pillows, and her head fell sideways like a broken daisy. But this morning, she ate two bowls of Cremogema and begged to come with me to Geraldo's. Daddy said no. He wanted Mita close to home, just in case.

I looked at the rows of shelves, noticing things Mita would notice: the wooden marionette man with a pipe glued to his bottom lip; a pair of green suede gloves with two gold buttons at the cuffs. A black lace bra with a tiny pink rose sewn between the two cups. Mita would love that bra. I could imagine the story she would invent; how Lampião bought it for Maria Bonita, and how she wore it the day she was ambushed by the police. It was the kind of bra a *bandida* would wear.

Daddy said Geraldo had women in Barra. He never used the word *prostitute,* but I was sure that was what he meant. After a few moments, I rang the bell again. Mita loved to ring it, even when Geraldo was right there in front of us. He always gave us a packet of free gum and said, "Share it with your sister." Sometimes he took off his glasses and said: "Am I seeing double?" It was a silly joke, but we liked it.

I heard the tinkle of the bead curtain and looked up to see Elói enter the shop, with his moon face and pale green eyes. Elói was our friend, but he had a mean streak. I don't think he meant anything by it: It was because of our fathers. Daddy and Tavares were enemies. They both worked in the paper mill and played Liar's Dice at the club, but they hated each other's guts. Whenever Daddy made a bet, Tavares called his bluff and upped him.

"How's Mita?" Elói said. The ash cross on his forehead looked like a stain.

"Fine. Everything's good."

"So why isn't she here?"

"She's making a cake."

I worried Mita might become floppy again, or worse. Another fit. Dr. Miguel said that could happen.

"What about the horse?" Elói said. Mita had wanted to see the dead horse under the bridge, but we'd been too busy practicing our dance. Elói and Mita loved to inspect dead things; they didn't get disgusted or frightened, like I did.

"There's always another horse," I said.

Elói's green eyes glittered. He looked like his father. "Mita's possessed. I saw it when she fell. She looked like a chicken after you cut off its head." Elói rolled his eyes upward and made a shaking crazy wriggle with his body.

I rang the bell three times in a row.

Geraldo appeared. When he saw me, he went straight for the Benson & Hedges. "Anything else?"

"Just the cigarettes, thanks." I placed the ten-cruzeiro note Daddy had given me on the counter. Daddy had said make sure the greedy bastard gives you change.

Geraldo handed me back the money. "This one's on the house," he said. "Give these to your sister." He added four packs of watermelon gum to the bag with the cigarettes. "I hope she gets better soon."

"Thanks." I walked out with the cigarettes and the gum. Everyone knew. Geraldo hadn't been at Carnaval—he'd been here at the store. But he knew. I imagined people gossiping.

The village was like that; it took minutes for a story to turn into a scandal.

Elói followed me into the street. I didn't want him with me. Since Mita's fit something about my edges felt torn and ragged. Like that cardboard girl we played with, where you carefully cut out her outfits along the dotted line, and then you balanced her clothes on top of her body with little flaps, but the clothes always fell off. All of me felt wobbly like that.

"Can I come over?" Elói asked.

I wasn't sure. Daddy said to keep things calm for a few days, and Elói wasn't calm. Mita would be glad to see him, though, I knew that. He made her laugh. "Maybe later," I said. "She needs to rest."

"Rest won't help," Elói said. "She needs a *cura* from Maria José, or she won't get better. That's what my mother thinks."

"Your mother's wrong. She's better already."

"I don't believe you," Elói said.

"Come and see." I wanted to show Elói he was wrong. Dead wrong.

We crossed the square and walked past the church. People were chatting on the steps. Dona Elena turned and waved. I waved back. My hand felt stiff, like a marionette hand. I could feel eyes following us. I wanted to run, but that would make things worse. I walked fast and pretended not to notice.

We walked along in silence, and I was glad. Our house was up the hill, by the reservoir. We could see it in the distance. The white house with our recently painted green shutters. All closed. Mummy had wanted to let Mita sleep in, so we'd spoken in whispers and kept the shutters closed. She must have forgotten to open them.

A banana tree lay across the path. It hadn't been there

when I walked to the village. Elói lifted the raggedy leaves, one by one, looking for loose bananas. The snapped trunk reminded me of Mita's knees, the way they buckled so suddenly during the parade. I began to have second thoughts. What if the excitement of a visitor started another fit? Elói could wind Mita up, and she didn't need winding up. What if she got floppy again and Elói made fun of her?

"This isn't a good idea," I said. "You shouldn't come. My dad is having a bad day." Daddy was moody, everyone knew. He got mad at the slightest things, like not saying please or thank you.

Elói's lips pressed together in a triumphant way. "I knew it," he said. "I knew there was something wrong."

"There's nothing wrong."

"I know how your father is. I'll be quiet."

"No," I said, the sureness growing inside me by the minute. "I said no."

Elói kicked the trunk of the fallen tree. I crossed my arms and waited. When Elói saw I meant business, he turned and headed back toward the village.

I stepped over the tree and walked along the path alone. The trunks of the banana trees were peeling. As I passed each one, I wondered if it would fall. The spiky grass of the fields seemed to tremble in the sun. Nothing felt permanent.

The front door was unlocked and I let myself in. Mita was on the sofa watching *National Kid.* "It's a repeat," she said.

I snuggled close to her, feeling my edges adjust. Mita's skin was warm. I was relieved. I realized I had expected her to feel wooden, like the marionette. I opened the paper bag and handed her the watermelon gum.

"Four? He never gives us four." Mita unraveled the cellophane cover and offered me a stick, tapping the pack the way Daddy did when he offered people cigarettes.

"When is Elói coming over?" Mita said.

"I don't know. Everyone was in church."

I'd never lied to Mita before. I assumed that we'd immediately know it, if one of us lied to the other. But Mita didn't seem to know it.

"I want to see the horse," Mita said. "We said we'd go after Carnaval."

I was about to remind Mita that Daddy wanted her close to home, but I decided not to. I didn't want her asking about Elói again.

We sat next to each other on the sofa, our knees up, chewing gum and watching National Kid fly above the buildings of Tokyo.

"The UFO," Mita said, knowing what was about to happen. The UFO appeared in the sky and shot down a Japanese plane.

Daddy came in from the veranda and grabbed the bag with the cigarettes. "Thanks, Dolores. I needed these! Why's the money still here?"

"It was a present," I said. "From Geraldo."

Daddy frowned. He stuffed the ten-cruzeiro note into his trouser pocket and lit a cigarette.

"I want to see the dead horse," Mita said. "Please."

"No, Mita." Daddy took a long drag of his cigarette. "We've had enough excitement for quite a while."

He dropped into his armchair and closed his eyes. His fingers held the cigarette loosely. I was afraid it would fall and burn the carpet. He'd been up with Mummy all night, watching Mita.

Mita studied Daddy's mouth. She thought she could tell by the press of his lips whether he would say yes or no. Loose lips meant there might still be a chance. Daddy's lips were partly open, but I knew he would never change his mind.

"*Na fa de,*" I said.

"*Ke-ke,*" Mita said.

"Don't, Mita," I said, switching from our language to English. Daddy was the only one who ever spoke English, and I wanted her to pay attention. "Don't ask him again."

"*Ke-ke,*" Mita said, but her voice was less forceful. She reached for my hand and put it on her belly, where she liked it. We leaned into each other and watched the old *National Kid* episode. I was glad it was a repeat. It felt familiar, like an old song you've heard a hundred times.

Chapter Seven

It was June, and the Ibejis still hadn't brought rain. Maria José had yellow fever, and people said she might die. Mita continued to be wobbly. Out of nowhere, her legs would buckle; her knees, elbows, and chin were always bright red with *mercúrio-cromo.* We had to keep an eye out. We spent most of each day in the pool, with the other children. In the water, Mita was a fish; her legs weren't a problem. She could stay underwater longer than any of us. But on that hot Saturday, instead of going to the club, we were headed to Volta Redonda, to buy boots.

Mita pressed her nose against the car window. "I don't want boots. It's too hot for boots."

Mummy stared at the road and pretended not to hear. No

one mentioned getting me boots. Maybe they were just for Mita, to stop her from tripping so much.

"Jaime wears boots," I said. "Maybe you can get cowboy boots, like his."

Mita gave me a smile. Everyone wanted to marry Jaime: me, Mita, Claudinha, Elena, every girl in the valley. "Maybe cowboy boots," Mita said. "The right kind of cowboy boots."

The mountain road was dusty. Dead trees and rocks everywhere. The motor coughed as the road got steeper. Daddy's hand tightened around the gearshift.

"I hope we don't break down," I said. Our car was always in trouble. Elói said Daddy was the poorest *estrangeiro* on the planet.

"The mountain road was a bad idea," Daddy said. "Police took over Contagem. There could be unrest."

"I'm sure it will be fine," Mummy said, adjusting the sunglasses on her nose. I could see her in the side mirror. I liked the idea of unrest; it sounded exciting.

"There used to be a mine here," Daddy said. The rubble on the side of the road glittered with pieces of amethyst, cracked beryl, and smoky topaz. We drove past a shack with a wooden table set out in front, covered with stones. Daddy stopped the car and reversed.

"Please, Ian," Mummy said. "Not today."

Usually Daddy stopped no matter what; he couldn't help himself. He was always on the corner of finding the most perfect gem in the world. A rare diamond, or a green brazilianite. But today Mummy's face was severe. Her chin jutted forward, and her hands were folded on top of each other like a parcel. Daddy put the car in gear and continued along the mountain road.

As we neared Volta Redonda, demonstrators blocked

the road, holding banners. A man with a beard slapped our car.

"What did I tell you?" Daddy said.

"Take the detour," Mummy said. "Don't react. Stay calm."

Daddy frowned. He didn't like it when Mummy told him to stay calm.

"What do the signs say?" Mita asked. "Is it a rude word?"

"*Abaixo a ditadura,*" Daddy said. "Since that student was shot, the protests are everywhere."

"What student?" Mita asked.

Mummy frowned. She didn't like Daddy talking about politics in front of us. Someone threw an egg. It broke on our windshield and slid down, yellow and slimy.

"Bloody lout." Daddy reversed all the way back to the main road. "We're going to be late."

"They'll wait for us," Mummy said. "We have an appointment."

"Why do we need an appointment to buy boots?" I asked. Mummy didn't answer.

People with signs took over the road at the next traffic light too. Daddy took another side road, then another. We arrived in front of a two-story house that didn't look like a shoe shop. "Here we are," Daddy said. "There's a tackle shop around the corner. I'll duck in while you're at the appointment." We all knew that Mummy preferred doing errands without him; he was impatient and got in the way.

The waiting room was boring. Mummy leafed through the pages of an old *Manchete.* A puzzle of a zoo sat on the coffee table. The body of the tiger was complete, but the cage was only half done, and there were no more pieces. Two small crutches leaned against the wall. I tried walking with them, but they were too short.

"They must be for babies," Mita said, taking the crutches from me. She knelt on the floor, placed one under each armpit, and walked a few steps on her knees.

Mummy said, "Mita, please. Put those back where you found them."

Mita stood up and swung one crutch in the air and knocked over a vase of flowers.

I rushed to pick them up before Mummy could get mad. The vase was plastic, and so were the flowers. "It's okay," I announced. "Everything is fake."

A bald man entered, carrying a clipboard. He spoke to me: "You must be Margarita?"

"I'm Margarita," Mita said. "That's Dolores."

The man looked from me to Mita. "You're identical," he said. We were used to that response.

"How old are they?" the man asked.

"They turned eight last month," Mummy said. We didn't like it when people talked about us as if we weren't there.

We followed him to a smaller room lined with shelves of ugly boots. Some were black, some were brown, but they were all short, square, and ugly.

Mita stepped backward. "No," she said. "I don't want boots."

"Mita, please." Mummy took hold of Mita's hand, but she shook it free. Mita's face was pale.

"They're for *aleijados,* these boots."

Mita was right. The girl who lived at the convent in Barra had those very same boots. One of her legs was thin and floppy, like an old string bean.

"It's only for a few years," Mummy said. "To straighten out your foot."

The bald man placed a metal tray with a sliding ruler on

the floor. He asked Mita to take off her *chinelos* and place the heel of her foot against the back edge of the metal plate.

"No," Mita said. "I won't."

"Mita, please," Mummy said. "We've come all this way."

Mita crossed her arms in front of her.

Mummy looked down at the pointed toes of her pale pink slingbacks, as if she might cry. She should have told us what to expect. But I knew if she had, Mita would have refused to come.

"I'll do it," I said. "My feet are the same size as Mita's." I slipped off my *chinelos* and slid my foot onto the metal ruler. "It's nice and cool," I said.

"Can you measure her instead?" Mummy asked. "They're identical."

The man looked doubtful. "I need the angle of the toes, where they turn. The exact pivot point of the twisted foot." He said *angle of the toes* and *twisted foot* so matter-of-factly, it made my heart hurt. We never mentioned Mita's crooked foot. There were good days and there were bad days, it didn't always show. We worked around it.

"I'll do it," Mita said, so quietly I wondered if I had imagined it. She kicked off her *chinelos* and placed her foot on the metal plate. The man adjusted the ruler until it touched the top of her toes and measured the length of her foot. Then he took out a ruler shaped like half a sun and placed it by Mita's toe. "How far do your toes turn," he said in his monotone voice, "on a bad day? Do they go here?" The man pointed his finger a little to the right. "Or do they twist all the way here?" The man pointed to Mita's pinkie toe.

"Here," Mita said, showing him an area midway between the first place and the second. She looked at me. "Right?"

I nodded yes. There was a hush in the room. I never knew

Mita had noticed the turn of her toes so exactly. I'd pretended to myself she didn't know.

After the man finished measuring, Mummy paid him. The man said it would be three weeks at least until the boots arrived. He said it was important that Mita wear them all day, every day. "Otherwise," he said, "there will be no improvement."

Daddy was waiting for us outside, with a brand-new silver fiberglass fishing rod. He placed it into the back of the car between me and Mita. On the way back Mummy opened her window wide, letting the wind mess up her hair. No one was talking. Usually, Mita would be the one to break the silence—but she was staring out the car window.

I placed my foot over hers, both of us barefoot. Then she put her foot over mine, and I put mine over hers, and we did this faster and faster, our feet changing places over and over, and we laughed as our movements became wilder until we were kicking each other and kicking the back of the seat and the fishing rod slid sideways and poked Mummy in the head.

"Stop it," Mummy said. "Cut it out, the two of you."

But we couldn't stop it. We kept swapping our feet in a frenzied way. They had a life of their own, our feet, and we couldn't stop laughing. Mita's laugh turned into a screech and for a second I thought she'd started to cry. But I was wrong, she was still laughing, only it was a crazy, sad kind of laugh.

Chapter Eight

OCTOBER 1972

I've been in school a whole month, and I still don't know how to read and write. I can draw the twenty-six letters of the alphabet, but that doesn't get me anywhere. When I look at a book, all I see is a series of letters with strange spacings. Mr. P.'s lessons aren't working.

Yesterday, Andrea invited me to spend the night. She is the only good thing in my life, apart from Aparecida. Daddy said he would think about it and let me know his decision in the morning. I want so much for him to say yes.

"They're kidnapping people," Daddy says over breakfast. "Especially foreigners. Andrea doesn't sound like an English name. What does her father do?"

"He's in business," I lie. If he finds out Andrea doesn't have a father, and her mother works as a prostitute, they'll never let me spend the night. Andrea's mother used to work as a cleaner at the British school, but there was some kind of scandal—and she left. Andrea doesn't know what kind of scandal. She said it probably involved sex or money, like most scandals, but her mother won't tell her.

"Well, at least you're making friends. Just one night."

I try to look happy, but not too happy, so he won't suspect. Daddy goes back to reading the paper.

"Look at this, Isabela," Daddy says, opening to the second page. "*Bombom de coco.*" He reads a list of ingredients out loud: condensed milk, eggs, grated coconut. "See?" He shows Mummy the page, even though she can't read. "The recipe is repeated in column after column."

Mummy frowns. "Why so many times?"

"Clever. It's a protest. Every time an article is censored, the journalists print a ridiculous recipe in the space where the story was supposed to run." Daddy chuckles. "Look at the ingredients! One kilo of sugar! Three hundred eggs!"

Mummy smiles. "Will they get in trouble?"

"Maybe. Who can tell? I admire them."

"I thought you were against the demonstrations?" I say. "You're always complaining about them."

"This is different. They're not blocking streets and closing down factories—they're taking a stand. It takes courage. This censorship business is absurd."

Mummy thinks Daddy should be more careful. I heard her say it the other day. Her friend Estelle agreed with her. Estelle said: "The company doesn't pay us to have opinions." But Daddy always has opinions.

I can't wait to sleep in the king-size bamboo bed with red silk sheets; to see the photograph of Andrea's Italian father in a soldier's uniform; to count the underwear shops that line her street. She told me there are least seven—in just two blocks.

At school, I hand in a note from Daddy allowing me to go home with Andrea Summer. (Andrea's real name is Santos, but I changed it, to make it sound more English.) I tell Mr. P. I won't be staying after school because I'm catching the Green Bus to Andrea's house. I worry he'll be mad and think I'm ungrateful, but he smiles and says, "Have fun. See you next week, then."

Today, there are only two other students on the Green Bus: Marcos and Rodrigo. Instead of turning left toward Leblon and Ipanema and the sea, the Green Bus heads to the mountains, to the part of Rio called Lapa—where most people don't want to live. "Under Christ's armpits," Andrea says. I look up. We are almost directly under his sleeves.

"No one can see their underarms, but you can smell them." Andrea lifts her arm and smells her armpit. She wrinkles her nose: "A little sour."

I smell mine. "Salty."

"That's good. Salty is what you want. Salty is sexy."

I'm not sure how to feel about *sexy.*

The road narrows to a long corridor of cement apartment buildings, connected by clotheslines and music blaring from radios: Roberto Carlos, samba and bossa nova. *Barzinhos* line the street, narrow bars where men drink standing up, calling out to women as they pass. They scratch themselves in front of us and stare. At a red traffic light, a man with a fat stomach reaches into our window, and Andrea slaps his hand. Things of this kind rarely happen on the Blue Bus, and when they do, Dona Silva shouts curses and reports the incident to the school. Dona Carla, the head of the Green Bus, doesn't seem to care. She sits, fat and wide across the front seat, rolling with the bumps, almost sleeping.

"She's a drunk," Andrea says. "Look under her seat: You'll see bottles and bottles of cachaça." We duck down to check, and sure enough, under the rows of metal poles separating the seats, we count six bottles, knocking into one another whenever the bus screeches to a halt.

"You can do whatever you like; she doesn't notice."

"I have a surprise for you." I pull out a carton of Pall Malls from my satchel and hand it to her.

"My absolute favorite!" Andrea counts the packs. "Ten: That's two hundred cigarettes! How did you get them?"

"My father," I say. "His company makes cigarettes."

"He gets them for free?"

"Yes, we have cupboards and cupboards full of them."

"*Que chique,*" Andrea says. "Thank you."

When we get off at Andrea's stop, she warns me: "Don't pay attention to the men, okay?"

"Okay," I say, not sure what to expect.

Andrea lifts her chin and walks down the street with a certain sway in her hips I haven't seen before. I follow, trying to move the same way. Men reach out from nowhere and she dodges them without a second look. I do the same. I'm used to men's hands, just from being a girl in the world, but not like this: They come from everywhere. I'm good at avoiding. Andrea notices and smiles. A huge gladness stretches inside my chest; a gladness that I found her, in the midst of all those English girls at the British school, I have a friend.

A skinny man with bony yellow fingers asks me if I need help carrying my books. Andrea grabs me by the arm and says: "Don't answer. Anything you say encourages them." We walk two more blocks, dodging and ignoring. Andrea stops in front of a large, cream-colored door, the paint peeling off in brown curls.

"Six floors up," she says. We climb the steep, narrow steps, feeling our way, because the bulb is out.

"Mamma, Mammina, we're here." Andrea throws her satchel into a corner and disappears behind the hanging beads. The beads sparkle in the afternoon sun and clink against one another like hundreds of tiny wineglasses. We had a bead curtain like that in Santanésia. Mita used to wheel her way through, leaning forward in her wheelchair, announcing herself. She loved the clinking sound. She'd go back and forth, back and forth, just to hear the shiver of music the beads made.

I stand in the doorway, feeling awkward. There are red velvet chairs and colorful orange and blue carpets in the living room—a combination Mummy would consider "flashy." A parrot sits on a perch by the window, cleaning himself. Andrea comes back, followed by her mother, a tall woman in a semitransparent flowing red dress, with long dark hair.

"Call me Glória, Tia Glória." She kisses me on both cheeks. "It's wonderful that you and Andrea have found each other." Her thin face dimples, just like Andrea's, only deeper.

"I've prepared *xinxim de galinha,*" Tia Glória says. "I hope you like spicy food?"

"I love *xinxim.*"

"Great, I'll leave it out for the two of you. I need to get ready."

"First homework," Andrea announces. "Then we can eat while we watch *Irmãos Coragem.*"

"First homework? Did I hear that right? It must be your influence, Dolores!" Tia Glória says.

"Andrea has a crush on our teacher," I say, wishing Andrea hadn't mentioned homework. Andrea says no one cares I can't write; it isn't a big deal. She doesn't understand.

"Who is this inspiring teacher?" Tia Glória asks.

"Mademoiselle Dubois," I say. "She's a substitute French teacher, and she wears very red lipstick."

Andrea sits on the sofa and opens her French book. The way we work is: She reads the poems out loud, and I help her understand their meaning, then she writes down the answers for both of us. I'm good at poems; they're like a story, with a surprise hidden inside—but I don't want to do it in front of everyone.

"Tell me what this means, *le souvenir,*" Andrea asks. "Is it a trinket like a charm of the Pão de Açúcar, that a tourist can take home?"

"*Meninas, meninas,*" a deep voice says from the corridor. I wonder how many people live here. A tall woman in pink velvet bell-bottoms saunters out in heels steeper than the cliffside of Corcovado.

"Wow! *Que linda!*" Andrea says. "I didn't know you were here."

"I've been hiding out trying to get some beauty sleep." The woman stares at me. "*Quem é a francesinha?*"

Andrea laughs. "She isn't French, she's Brazilian. Or mostly Brazilian. Her father's English."

The woman kisses me on the cheek. She smells of cloves and patchouli. "I'm Sofia."

"Dolores. Andrea's friend from school. *Um prazer.*"

"A friend from the British school coming to visit us! How lucky are we?" Sofia says, in a not altogether friendly way. She stares at me, then pouts. "Your queen ruined my life! Ruined it!"

"It wasn't her fault," Tia Glória says. "The queen wasn't her fault."

"She arrives and they move the whole lot of us, the whole *bairro,* for Queen Elizabete! Like we are broken furniture. Just so she can ride down Avenida Atlântica in her fancy car and wave at the cameras."

"Sofia, that was 1968—almost four years ago. Let it go," Tia Glória says. "What happened, happened."

"Can we go back to the poem?" Andrea chews on the end of her pencil. "I need to get it right."

"Ah, yes! The delicious Mademoiselle Dubois awaits!" Tia Glória winks at me. I wish Mummy was fun, like her.

"Let's try the other poem." Andrea finds the other sheet of paper. " 'Alicante.' I don't know what that means either! This is too hard."

" 'Alicante' by Jacques Prévert?" Sofia asks, her voice sulky. I want to tell her Queen Elizabeth isn't my queen, I've never even been to England—but I'm not sure it would help. She obviously doesn't like me.

"You know the poem?" Andrea says. "Really?"

"Just because I'm a *bicha* you think I don't know poetry? Us *bichas,* we read poetry with every cell of our bodies. Jacques Prévert: I love the man!"

I had no idea Sofia was once a man. I'm surprised she's so open about it. I try not to stare. She's truly beautiful.

"So what does 'Alicante' mean in French?" Andrea asks.

"It isn't French. It's a place in Spain." Sofia plucks the paper from Andrea's hand and begins to read in her smoky voice: "*Une orange sur la table / Ta robe sur le tapis / Et toi dans mon lit . . .*"

"I don't understand one *palavra,* but it sounds romantic," Tia Glória says. "Everything French sounds romantic."

Sofia shivers her shoulders. "It's beyond romantic!"

"*Une orange*—I know that!" Andrea says. "Orange. That's easy."

"Orange on the table," I say. We learned *on the table* with Monsieur Armand a few weeks ago. I like flashcards because Monsieur Armand reads them out loud, so I can memorize.

"Why is that romantic?" Andrea says. "An orange on a table?"

"*Ai!* It's the whole poem that's romantic. The picture it paints. *Ta robe sur le tapis / Et toi dans mon lit.*"

"Someone on fire?" Andrea says. "The orange is on fire?"

"*Lit* is not fire, it's a bed. Your dress on the carpet and you in my bed," Sofia translates.

"Now you're talking! They're making love." Andrea caresses the tops of her arms all the way to her neck. "Can you believe she gave us this poem?"

"I bet you Mr. Walker has no idea!" I say.

Tia Glória laughs. "I'm sure he doesn't. That man blushes if he sees a bare shoulder!"

Mummy would never say such a thing. She doesn't see things from our perspective.

A pretty black woman dressed in a tight green sundress appears. She says she's been mixing peroxide with lemon juice and Coca-Cola, to make her hair blond. Andrea introduces me to Luciana. Of course, I've heard about her already—how she dances for Mangueira, how her boyfriend drives buses back and forth to Bahia and writes samba songs. Luciana leans over. "How's my hair? Is it lighter?"

Andrea examines Luciana's thick dark hair. "No. No magic yet."

"Why do you want lighter?" Tia Glória says. "It doesn't go

with your skin." Luciana's skin is a warm, deep black, like jacaranda wood.

"*Contraste,*" Luciana says. "I want to stand out when I dance."

"I prefer you the way you are," Tia Glória says.

Andrea snatches the poem from Sofia's hand. "Let's get back to the poem. Tell me about the next line."

Sofia leans in to read. She's beautiful in an unexpected way, like a surprising flower arrangement where soft yellow roses are mixed in with prickly *quesnélias* and tall orange gladiolas.

Sofia looks up. She must have sensed me staring. "Never seen a *bicha* before?" she says. "Searching for the telltale signs?"

"Don't be mean," Tia Glória says. "You always have such an edge."

"It's easy," Andrea says. "Feet and hands. With Sofia, that's the only way you would know."

"Unless you pull down her panties," Luciana says. "You might find an unexpected present there if you do!" She makes a fist with her hand, then pops her index finger, so it sticks straight out.

Everyone laughs. I laugh carefully, not feeling exactly safe. I make a point of not looking at Sofia's hands, of not looking at her at all. Sofia reads the poem from the beginning to the last line: "*Fraîcheur de la nuit / Chaleur de ma vie.*" There's a beautiful sadness and a rhythm to the way she reads.

"Girl," Luciana says, "you're good at this. I had no idea!"

"There's a lot you don't know," Sofia says.

"Your mother was Polish, *né*? Not French?"

"*Uma polaca,*" Sofia says. "Came over during the war."

"The *polacas* are famous. Poems and love songs have been

written about them," Tia Glória says. "The most desired prostitutes in Brazil."

"White slavery," Sofia says. "Dirt-poor, but white."

"You mean you're not actually Brazilian?" Andrea asks.

"Officially I'm partly a Polish Jew. But don't tell anyone."

"So you're European after all," Luciana says. "No wonder you're such a snob. You're always talking about Europeans—but you are one!"

"I am and I'm not," Sofia says. "Like so many things!" We all laugh.

After we finish our homework, Tia Glória kisses us goodbye, and everyone leaves. We hear them clamber down the six flights of stairs. Andrea and I have the house to ourselves.

Tia Glória made her bed using red silk sheets, especially for us—not the polyester ones she uses for clients, but real silk. Andrea's skin is warm and smells of passion fruit because of the moisturizer she uses every night. Feeling her next to me makes my edges ache. I've never slept in the same bed as anyone, except for Mita.

"I lied when I told you about my twin," I say.

"You don't have a twin?"

"I do, but she's not like me. Not anymore."

"Not all twins are the same," Andrea says.

"She got sick, so they sent her away, to some hospital in England. I don't know if she's ever coming back." I say it quickly, before I change my mind.

Andrea pushes herself up on one elbow and stares at me. "That's terrible. What kind of sick? Does she have leprosy?"

"No, not leprosy. She has something called cerebral palsy. And epilepsy. That's what the doctors call it." Daddy tells visitors Mita has brain damage, but I don't say that to Andrea.

"Why can't she go to a hospital here in Rio?"

"I don't know. In case we get transferred. My dad's new job sends people to different places."

"That isn't a reason."

"No," I say. "It isn't a reason at all." I stare at the ceiling without blinking, trying to make my tears go away.

Andrea wipes the edges of my eyes with the bulb of her finger. "When are you going to see her?"

"I don't know. Daddy says we have to wait for home leave. That's when the company lets English people go to England. He says it might not happen for two years."

"Two years? My mother would die if she didn't see me for one week!"

"My mother doesn't care. She's cold. All she cares about is giving dinner parties and looking pretty. She doesn't miss Mita one bit."

"That's wrong." Andrea hugs me close and smooths my hair. "That's so wrong."

ANDREA AND I STAY UP so late, we sleep through the alarm. When we wake up, we scramble into our school uniforms, grab our satchels, and run down the stairs, without brushing our teeth. On the way down, we comb our hair with our fingers.

"I have a comb in here somewhere." Andrea searches her satchel and finds a comb with three teeth missing. "We have time," she says. "Let's go to the shop over there by the bus stop and do our hair."

We study our reflection in the window and comb out the knots. Mine is easier because I have straight hair. Andrea has a knot at the back like a bird's nest. As she struggles to unravel it, I see a photograph lying on the sidewalk, covered in footprints. It must have fallen out of someone's album. Daddy used to take photos of us when we were little, but he stopped after Mita got sick. I pick up the photo. I'm not sure what I expected, but definitely not this: two naked men and three women licking one another's private parts as if they were lollipops.

I show it to Andrea. "It's rude," I say, feeling a shiver between my legs.

"Disgusting," Andrea agrees. We study the photo even so.

"It's not sexy," I say.

"Not one bit." Andrea shudders. "Maybe a little?" she says. "A little bit disgusting and sexy?"

"I don't think so," I say. "No."

We can't stop looking. We notice other pictures inside the shop window. Maybe the photographer dropped this one as he was leaving.

"The Green Bus, the Green Bus," Andrea shouts.

The bus pulls away from the curb. We run after it, thumping on the back, until it stops and lets us in. Dona Carla snores in the front seat. She's supposed to make sure we arrive in school safe and sound, but she's always sleeping. We make our way to the back and examine the photograph.

"It's revolting that people do that," Andrea says.

"Are they forced?" I can't imagine why anyone would do such a thing without being forced. Aparecida told me that sometimes young girls are forced into prostitution, just to make ends meet. She said she doesn't judge it, but she'd rather be a maid, because at least you have a roof over your head.

Andrea inspects the faces of the women. "I don't think so," she says. "You can see if a woman likes sex by her eyes."

"This one has her eyes closed," I say. "What does that mean?"

"I'm not sure," Andrea says. "I don't have it all down yet."

The bus drives through the front gate into the playground. Andrea stuffs the photo into her satchel.

Our first class is art. I concentrate on my watercolor of a hummingbird, without looking at Andrea. If Mr. Wilson senses anything, he will make trouble. I blur the colors around the wings, trying to create a hovering, fluttering effect, but the paper is too wet. Andrea's satchel lies wide open on the floor next to her legs. I'm terrified the photo will slip out and Mr. Wilson will find it.

During break Andrea shows the photograph to one of the English girls, who is so disgusted and impressed she has to show it to her cousin. Before you know it, the whole class has seen it; it's all anyone talks about.

"Where did you find it, exactly?" Olivia asks, and Priscilla, who's so white and clever she never bothers to talk to us, wants us to tell her about the shop, every detail. I feel sort of proud and famous, though I'm not sure why: All we did was pick up a photo we found lying on the ground.

By the end of the day, Andrea has the photograph back in her satchel. I hug her goodbye and head to the Blue Bus, missing her already.

"How was your slumber party?" Daddy asks at dinner.

"Great," I say, forgetting to be silent.

Daddy looks at Mummy and smiles. "I told you it would be fine," he says, as if it had been his idea all along.

I'm tempted to tell them about my wonderful night, to say that people came after me at school, asking me questions, that I ate *xinxim de galinha* and slept so well I didn't hear the alarm clock . . .

"Oxford beat Cambridge in long jump," I say instead. "And we have a class trip to Paquetá next week. And the new Bunsen burners have arrived from England."

"You seem awfully chirpy today," Daddy remarks, looking pleased. He asks me what business Andrea's father works for.

Without thinking, I say, "Photographs."

"Photographs?"

"I mean film. He makes film for cameras."

"You mean he works for Kodak?" Daddy says.

"I think so."

Daddy pours himself a second glass of wine. "Cheers," he says, lifting his glass. "Cheers to settling in at the British school."

Chapter Nine

SANTANÉSIA

The boots announced themselves in all sorts of ways. They slapped the ground, one, two, like a hammer. Not the *flip-flip* of *chinelos* or the rustle of bare feet but a loud clomp so everyone knew Mita was coming. The boots slid down the bark of the trees; they couldn't grip like toes. Mita would try to pull herself up with her arms, and sometimes she managed, but other times she gave up.

When the boots first arrived, Mummy was strict. The man had been clear: Mita had to wear her boots all day long, even though she hated them. Each night when she took them off, I'd study her toes, looking for improvement. There were days when Mita's toes faced forward. Days when she moved easily and didn't bump into things, and we thought the boots were working.

Then there were bad days, when Mita's legs were tangly and slow. The boots made it worse, and our games didn't flow. We'd be chewing sugarcane in the fields, then someone would hear about an abandoned canoe under the bridge, we'd run over to see—only Mita couldn't run. We had to cross the smelly swamp behind the factory, and her boots weren't supposed to get wet. Mita stepped right into the mud anyway, we wanted to ruin those boots. They left strange tracks: two half circles, with a cross—like something God sent down to punish us.

And they were like tiny ovens, those boots. Mita developed white socks that never came off. I never knew she was white before. Every night, it was a production, to get the boots off. Mummy had to find the right angle—the leather was so stiff, it wouldn't bend. When the boots were finally off, Mita's feet lay stranded facing each other, little white curved feet that smelled of meat. Not steak or chicken, but liver. We hated liver.

The boots changed everything.

In August there were two more fits. Both times, Dr. Miguel came over with his injections. It seemed that Mita had something called epilepsy, so we had to make sure she didn't get too upset, because excitement triggered fits. The boots made Mita excited, so Mummy started to make certain exceptions. They were more worried about the fits than Mita's crooked feet.

We were happy that both of us could feel the tickle of the grass and squelch our toes in the mud again.

Chapter Ten

Mita kicked her legs under the stool. That night, Mita had on new *tênis* instead of boots, decorated with sticks of dynamite, bombs, and explosions, with POW! and a scatter of white stars along the sides. I could tell by the way she kicked her legs that she loved having her feet in stylish shoes, like a normal girl.

We were eight years old, and Queen Elizabeth II was coming to visit Brazil. We only had Carnaval queens, so I wasn't sure what to expect. There was a party spirit at the club. The thatched roof was decorated with colored streamers, and Celina, Mummy's best friend, arranged for a band to play as an introduction. Daddy wasn't too happy about the music: "Bloody racket," he complained, "why do we need music? Give me another caipirinha, please."

Mita and I sat at the bar with the adults. The barman said he'd made an exception for us, on account of Daddy being English. I knew the real reason was for the adults to be close to Mita, so they could catch her if she had a fit.

Dr. Miguel adjusted the TV and then we saw them: Queen Elizabeth and Prince Philip driving down Avenida Atlântica in an old-fashioned convertible. The queen's car was surrounded by police on motorbikes. Elói and Claudinha sat behind us, in the second row. I ducked so they could see better.

"I hope there isn't a demonstration," Dr. Miguel said. "That would ruin everything."

Tavares chewed on his toothpick and didn't say a word.

Elói had told us his father wasn't going to come; he wasn't interested in the queen. But he must have changed his mind. Daddy suspected Tavares was a communist, trying to organize something at the paper mill. Daddy thought Brazil was headed for trouble. Thousands marching in the streets of Rio. He didn't like the dictatorship, but he was against communists.

"Nice car," Mita said. "I want one like that."

"We were there a few weeks ago, Avenida Atlântica, remember?" I recognized the curve of Copacabana beach, and the wavy pattern of the sidewalk. Immediately, I wished I hadn't said that. Mita wouldn't remember. We'd driven down Avenida Atlântica on our way to the hospital in Rio, and Mita had been passed out in the back seat. Her fit wouldn't stop, and Dr. Miguel had said we needed a specialist.

"I remember," Mita said, though I knew she didn't. She'd started to forget things—and forgetting was a bad sign. The neurologist said every fit killed brain cells. It was important to catch them early and get them under control.

"Will everyone please shut up and watch?" Daddy said.

The queen waved at us from her car, and Claudinha said what we were all thinking: "She's not even beautiful." For some reason, we thought a queen had to be beautiful.

"The English aren't beautiful," Elói said. "Everybody knows that. They're ugly!" He said *ugly* extra-loud, looking at Daddy. All of the children laughed. It was funny, but I hid my laughter. People thought Daddy was *estranho,* with his white skin that burned and blistered instead of turning brown. Some said he was handsome, in a foreign way. I wished he was a normal Brazilian father, who didn't stand out so much.

"*Que chique,* they're so elegant, the two of them," Celina said.

"Her hat is strange," Mita announced. She liked being up front and commenting on the events. "It looks like a potty." People laughed.

"This isn't Miss Brazil," Daddy said. "Who cares what they look like?"

"People always care, Ian. What a woman looks like," Jurandi said. Jurandi was part of the group of men who played dice in the afternoons. I was glad Mummy was pretty. Not showy pretty, but an everyday, quiet pretty.

"That's silly," Mummy said. "Beauty doesn't put dinner on the table. It doesn't help you clean the house or gut a fish. You need to be able to do things."

Mita wasn't able to do certain things anymore. TV was risky. The flickering light could trigger a fit.

"So practical, Isabela," Celina said. "It's the farmer in you."

"Isabela can certainly gut a fish; I'll vouch for that!" the barman said. He and Daddy went fishing on weekends, but Mummy was the one who gutted.

"There was a luncheon at the Museum of Modern Art," Dr. Miguel announced. "I saw them arrive."

"Have you been glued to the TV all day long?" Daddy said, looking amused.

"It's not every day we get a visit from the queen, Ian. The government has been preparing for months. There's a whole protocol you need to follow, for royalty."

"We're not used to that here," Jurandi said. "We have generals, all we know is military rule."

"Wasn't there royalty, once upon a time?" Mummy asked. "With the Portuguese?"

Tavares had been quiet through most of the evening, staring at the TV. He signaled for a refill. "*The English,*" he said. "They think they are royalty. They have this attitude, like they're better than us, have you noticed?"

No one answered. I glanced over at Elói. He was pulling at his shoelaces. Neither of us liked it when our fathers argued.

"You think the generals are better?" Jurandi said. "They're a thousand times worse."

"This whole Rainha Elizabete trip is a distraction," Tavares said. "They're taking away our rights and they're hiding it with a show. A big international show while they legalize torture and censorship! All this pomp is *frescura.*"

Daddy frowned. *Frescura* was one of his words. He used it all the time—about having to wear a tie to go to a meeting in Rio, about having to shake hands with the governor, all the little politenesses of Brazil, which he considered excessive.

"We need shows and distractions," Celina said. "They make life bearable."

"For you, maybe," Tavares said. "D'you know how many people in Rio, in São Paulo, lost their homes for the queen to pass by? Whole *bairros* moved, *só pra inglês ver*!"

"It helps all of us when Brazil looks good to the *exterior.*

You're so negative." Celina glanced at Mummy and shook her head. She wasn't fond of Tavares either.

"Enough of politics!" Dr. Miguel pointed at the television. "The whole country is watching. This is a celebration! Please." Since he was the only doctor for miles and cured all of us at one time or another, Tavares gave him the thumbs-up and sipped his caipirinha.

The car continued down the avenue, making its way along Copacabana beach. It must have been windy, because the queen held on to the side of her hat as she waved with her long white gloves. Then the TV cut to an image of Corcovado, the Sugarloaf, and the bay. "What happened to the queen?" I asked.

"Advertisements," Daddy said. "They have to use every bloody occasion for propaganda."

"Maybe she's going to the bathroom," Mita said. "Queens have to go to the bathroom too." All of us children laughed, but Daddy ignored Mita's comment. He didn't like talk of bathrooms, or anything about the body. "Another one, please," he said, in a deliberately calm voice, and slid his empty glass across the bar.

The barman stirred the pitcher and poured Daddy another caipirinha. *Um Engov antes, um outro depois* . . . The hangover pill commercial came on the TV. Then a Coca-Cola advertisement. Dr. Miguel turned the volume all the way down.

"That's all there is?" I said. I thought the queen's visit would be like Carnaval, more of a show.

"There will be more soon," Dr. Miguel announced. "They're due at the British embassy at ten." He'd read every paper and magazine he could get his hands on and knew all the details. Daddy said he was obsessed.

The band played "Mamãe Eu Quero" and three or four

people started to dance. Mita watched from the bar, her foot tapping. I could feel the samba thrumming inside of her like an energy.

"Does absolutely everything have to turn into a party in this country?" Daddy said, smiling. He hated the noise, but he appreciated the spirit.

Then I saw him. Jaime. The boy we all wanted to marry. He had on his cowboy boots. He'd cleaned them up, so they weren't crusted with mud. The leather had a dull gleam that shifted as he walked. Mita kicked me under the bar. She'd seen him too. He'd gone to live with his aunt in Rio, so we hadn't seen him in ages. Amaro, his father, owned the biggest fazenda in the valley, they made coffee and sugar, and owned buffalo.

"*Ei,* Senhor Ian! I came for the occasion. Congratulations," Amaro said, as if the queen's visit were Daddy's doing. He called Jaime over. "Have you met my son?"

Daddy shook Jaime's hand and Jaime nodded hello to both of us. He was tall now, and his green eyes were darker than I remembered. Mita looked at him sideways, the way women did in *novelas* when they liked a man. She'd been practicing that look in the mirror. I couldn't believe she was doing it here, in front of everyone.

Jaime noticed. It was hard not to; she was being so obvious. He went over to her and asked for a sip of her Coca-Cola.

"Let's get this man a drink," Daddy said to the barman. "Haven't been to the lake lately." Jaime's father had a large lake on his property, where Daddy fished.

"Come anytime," Amaro said. "Caught three *tucunarés* yesterday."

"Nice shoes," Jaime said, examining Mita's *tênis*. Mita gave a huge smile.

The band started to play a slow samba, "Andança" by Beth Carvalho, and some of the older kids went to dance. Everyone knew slow dances were just an excuse to kiss. Daddy didn't like all the kissing that happened in Brazil. He said children are too young to kiss like that; in England children are children. In England, children are *boring.*

"Want to dance?" Jaime asked Mita.

Mita glanced at me, and I nodded yes. How could anyone say no to Jaime? Then I remembered her foot.

Mita slid off the stool, and Jaime took her hand.

"Where are you going, Margarita?" Mummy asked. "I'm not sure it's a good idea."

Jaime led Mita to the dance floor. She was making an effort not to drag her foot, I could tell. Last time Jaime played with us was a few years ago, before the fits and the boots.

Jaime put his arms around her neck, and they swayed, looking each other in the eyes. Mita's feet moved from side to side, I could see Daddy watching them.

"Relax, Ian. If you're like this now, imagine when the girls become teenagers," Amaro joked.

Daddy pretended to find it funny. "I'll need a bloody prison, to keep them safe," he said. The song picked up, and Mita stumbled—but Jaime reached out and held her up. Their foreheads touched.

"Ladies and gentlemen, the show is about to continue—" The barman turned up the volume on the TV and the band stopped playing. Daddy wiped his forehead and took a huge gulp of caipirinha.

Mita made her way back to the bar with Jaime. Mummy

cleared a space for her to sit, and the barman brought a stool for Jaime.

Mita nudged me with her foot. I nudged her back and pulled at my right earlobe. That was Daddy's signal in Liar's Dice. It meant *go for it.* Mita gave me a huge smile and slid the bowl of peanuts toward me. I took a handful.

"They're about to arrive at the embassy," Dr. Miguel said. "The British ambassador and Lady Russell."

"*Que frescura,*" Tavares said again. "The whole idea of a monarchy is disgusting. I can't take it."

Daddy's smile stopped midway. He twisted his cigarette and snapped it close to the filter. "Why are you here?" Daddy asked, extremely slowly, pausing between each word. "Why the hell are you here, then?" Mummy reached out and touched his elbow.

"Last I heard, having a drink at a bar is allowed," Tavares said. He sucked on his tongue, making a slurping sound. "Even here, in this *democracia brasileira,* drinking is still allowed." He stood up and finished his caipirinha. Then he slid his glass across the bar and walked out.

"Ignore him, Ian," Amaro said. "He's trouble. Don't pay attention."

Mita was holding hands with Jaime. He held her hand the wrong way, squashing her index finger on the inside. I wanted to adjust their fingers, to tell Jaime that Mita liked to be on the outside, but Mita didn't seem at all bothered. I was the one who was bothered. I rubbed my thumb and stretched my fingers out in front of me, one by one. I felt like the wife in a *novela* when she sees the husband kissing the maid in the kitchen, or one of the ugly sisters in "Cinderella." I didn't want to be that person. It was Mita's right, to have Jaime hold her hand. All this time, Mita had had to wear ugly boots; I should be happy for her.

I reached into the bowl for more peanuts and pretended not to notice. I focused on the samba show happening on the front lawn of the embassy. Women in sequin bikinis with parasols, men in top hats, and children—all dancing a special tiny Carnaval, just for the queen

Chapter Eleven

NOVEMBER 1972

Andrea has mono. I haven't seen her since our overnight. Mr. P. said she'll be out for another two weeks, maybe more; she has a bad case. The English girls get on my nerves.

"She would have mono, wouldn't she?" Priscilla says.

"She's such a slut." Olivia makes a loud kissing sound.

I tell them to shut up, but they don't shut up. Andrea wouldn't care; she'd shrug and swear at them in Italian.

Mr. P. starts class by saying he wants to tell us something important, something that will be remembered in history books. "Six months ago, May seventeenth, ten thousand children marched through the streets of London carrying banners that said 'No to the Cane.'"

He says *corporal punishment* is not a way to teach students.

There is a movement to end it. He looks at us with that thoughtful expression he often has, as if he's trying to puzzle something out. "A demonstration, led by children. You—" He points at us. "You children can make a difference in the world. I want you to know that."

I look at the door, afraid Mr. Wilson will walk in, or the headmaster, or the police. Mr. P. could be arrested. It's dangerous to talk about demonstrations.

"Were they successful, sir?" Priscilla asks, in her prissy voice.

"In a way," Mr. P says. "They drew attention to the problem, and that's an important first step."

"Were they arrested?" Marcos asks. He doesn't usually ask questions.

"A number of the organizers were arrested," Mr. P. says.

"And tortured?" Marcos asks. Marcos has an older brother who goes to university, and Andrea told me he's a communist.

"No, Marcos. In England, people are not tortured." He says this quietly, his voice serious. "But it's a good question. Nobody should be caned or tortured. Ever. Now let's get back to poetry, shall we?"

It's hard to change gears and shift to poetry. No one ever talks to us about things like this. You can feel a certain excitement in the classroom.

"Settle down, settle down, class." Mr. P. says that by the end of term, he wants us all to memorize by heart a poem we love and recite it to the rest of the class. "It doesn't have to be long."

I wonder if I'll ever be able to read a poem. I know all the letters. I've memorized their shapes, and I can draw them in cursive and in block letters, but that is not reading. Mr. P. says sound them out, but I don't know how to sound them out.

Whenever I try, I start to float. And then I'm above myself, above the letters, almost not there.

"Can you give us an example of a short poem, please, sir," says Priscilla, buttering him up.

"Certainly," Mr. P. says. "This is one of my favorites, by Philip Larkin: *They fuck you up, your mum and dad. / They may not mean to, but they do. / They fill you with the faults they had / And add some extra, just for you.*"

Priscilla blushes, and even Marcos pays attention. I like the way Mr. P. swears and says true things. He's almost not an adult.

"This is why I want you to memorize poems," Mr. P. says. "So you have them with you when you need them. Like a good friend. It's not about memory. I have a terrible memory. I forget my gym shorts; I leave my briefcase on the train. I've been accused of having my head in the clouds. But I remember poems. I want each of you to have a poem in your heart."

ON THE WAY HOME, I have the bus seat to myself. The traffic is slow; it would be quicker to walk. I hate the Blue Bus so much. I close my eyes, to block out the English girls. Car horns, laughter, bits and pieces of conversation, the sounds come at me in waves.

"*A Bear Called Paddington,* oh my God. I read that when I was two."

"*One, Two, Buckle My Shoe.*"

"She's a complete dunce!"

"Dolores is a dunce. Dolores is a dunce."

They're chanting my name. I feel with my feet for my satchel, but it's gone.

"Look at this one: *The Tiger Who Came to Tea*!"

They're talking about the books; the baby books Mr. P. gave me, to help me learn.

"She should go to a retard school, not the British school." More laughter. "Look at this, drawings!"

Priscilla has my notebook. I reach for it—but she holds it in the air, away from me.

Marcos walks up from the back, grabs my notebook, and hands it back to me. He collects the other books and stuffs them into my satchel, then sits next to me. "*Esquece elas,*" he says. "They're ignorant."

I keep my eyes closed. It's me who is ignorant: me.

Marcos nudges me when it's my stop. I stand up and make my way stiffly down the aisle. My body has locked itself up, like Daddy's fishing reel when he winds it in too fast.

At dinner, Mummy says I look pale and gives me a Cebion. I lie on Aparecida's straw mattress and stare at the shadows on the ceiling. Mita and I used to do that, we'd see capybaras, monkeys, and angels. Aparecida's room smells of cinnamon bread and grass, and after a while my breathing starts to settle. Thank God she came to Rio with us. She's the only one who doesn't act as if Mita never existed.

I reach under Aparecida's bed for the magazine. It's Thursday, the night we read *Noite Feliz*. I say *read,* but it's not really reading; it's looking. The stories in the magazine are told in photographs. It's stupid. Designed for stupid illiterate people, like me and Aparecida.

Aparecida comes in and sits on the edge of the mattress. She slips off her *chinelos* and massages the soles of her feet with almond oil. "*E daí?*" she says. Her sweat smells of lemons, it isn't rancid and meaty like English people's sweat. "What d'you think?"

"I'm only on page two. They're in bed."

"They're in bed and you haven't read on? I can't believe it!"

"It isn't reading." The photos look shiny and artificial. The month of Topaz is almost over, and all I can do is copy letters. Mr. P. is losing hope, I can tell. That's why he gave me the baby books.

Aparecida stretches her slim body next to mine. "*Ei,*" she says, "don't be a hog! Let me catch up!"

I turn back to page one, so she can see the story unfold.

"*Idiota,*" Aparecida says. "Why doesn't that girl learn?"

The last photo on the page is a close-up of a telephone on a side table. I notice a tidy rectangle of writing under each photograph. The writing must tell us the story. I'd never noticed it before.

Aparecida shakes her head. "The phone is bad news."

I take the magazine from her. "There are words underneath. We would know what happened in the phone call if we knew how to read."

"But we don't." Aparecida shrugs.

"I want to know."

"It will become obvious. We always figure it out."

"See the letters? Don't you want to know what they say?"

"Not really. I want you to turn the page."

I turn the page. Leila steps out of a taxi in front of a hospital.

"I bet you it's her father," Aparecida says.

In the next photo, we see the father in a wheelchair, wearing pajamas. It's different from Mita's wheelchair; there's only one long pedal for his feet, instead of two small ones that lift upward. The father's face looks normal, not twisted or paralyzed.

"Heart attack, probably. It's usually heart with men his age," Aparecida says.

"It could be something else. The letters probably tell us what's wrong with him."

"Who cares what he has," Aparecida says. "Take a look at the doctor. *Mãe do céu,* that man is a *pão*!"

I take the magazine from her and study the letters underneath the image. The first letter is a *p*. I try to sound out the letters inside my head, but it doesn't work. I throw the magazine on the floor. "I hate this!"

"What happened to you?" Aparecida says. "You're in such a mood."

"Nothing. Nothing happened. I'm stupid. A *dunce.*" I say *dunce* in English because I don't know how to say it in Portuguese. "I hate school. I'll never learn to read. Never. They'll send me away, just like they sent Mita."

Aparecida puts her arms around me. "You'll learn. Give it time. You need to be patient, like your sister. Remember how long it took Mita, after she got sick, to put on a sock? She'd pull at it with her good hand until she had it on. She never gave up."

I think of Mita with her sock: her jaw, the tip of her tongue, that focused look in her eyes. She was so stubborn and willful; we loved that about her. "I miss her. I miss her so much."

Aparecida hugs me tighter. "I miss her too. *Aquela safada.* She was always up to something. Remember the ant hospital?"

Before she was sick, Mita kept an ant hospital under her bed, with matchbox beds lined with sugar. Ants took over our bedroom. Mummy was so upset, she threw away all the little beds with the ants in them. Mita kept saying, "Stop it, stop it, they have a fever."

I slide off Aparecida's bed, go to my room, and take out one of the baby books from my satchel. It has a red cover with two black mice on the front. I hear Priscilla's mocking waterfall laugh, *Dolores is a dunce, Dolores is a dunce.*

I sit on my bed and make myself focus on the writing above the two black mice. The first letter is a *j*, shaped like the handle of an umbrella. J-A: jahhh.

J-A-N

J-A-N-E

J-A-N-E-T

I speak the letter-sounds out loud instead of whispering them. I'm tired of being so afraid, even when I'm alone in my own room. J-A-N-E-T. Jah-neet? Jay-net? *Janet.* That's an English name. One of Mummy's new friends at the club is called Janet.

I read the next word, three lowercase letters: A-N-D. *And.*

My mind is joining the sounds of the letters.

Janet and Joh- Johon? Joh-n. *John.*

Janet and John.

The letter-sounds join to become word-sounds, next to other word-sounds, all of them like soldiers in a row, telling a story. Can it be? Is this how it works?

We're in the month of November. I check my gem calendar, hanging on the wall next to me: a photo of a golden imperial topaz, and under it the letters: T-O-P-A-Z.

My palms sweat. I put the book down, afraid. Afraid of losing this ability I've only, just this minute, discovered. I can't bear for the letters to go back to being shapes, like Alice in Wonderland who became huge, then suddenly small again.

Chapter Twelve

SANTANÉSIA

Mita stretched her arms above her head. "I'm bored."

"Shh . . . don't wake them up. They're having a siesta." My crayon leaked onto the paper like a melting candle. It was one of those afternoons that stretched out, minute by minute, like droplets of water, *ping, ping, ping,* so hot and slow. I could feel a trickle of sweat slide along the crease of my elbow down my arm.

Mita unlaced her boots, her chin at an angle: daring me to tell.

"You're not supposed to." I hated the boots too; they were always in the way. Mita couldn't sit cross-legged under the coffee table anymore. I knew it was my job to help cure her foot, but it was too hot, and I was tired of it, all the carefulness. I wasn't sure the boots worked. It had been almost two years, and Mita's foot was still crooked; maybe even a little more crooked.

Mita managed to get the boot off and threw it clear across the living room toward the sideboard. It landed with a thud.

"If you break a glass, you're in trouble."

Now Mita was busy with her left foot, which was the tricky one. Mita pushed on the heel and pulled the tongue loose and tried again. It didn't budge. She used both her hands and rocked, as if she were doing a backward somersault.

"Don't say I helped." I twisted the heel of the boot sideways, back and forth, the way Mummy did each night, until it slid off. I placed it next to me before Mita could throw it. Mita unpeeled her yellow socks, which were scrunched up at the arch of her foot. There were wrinkle marks on her foot, and her baby toe was bright red from where it was forced to turn.

Mita stood up and walked barefoot on the cool terra-cotta tiles. She went to the cabinet and reached for Daddy's leather cup. Even on tiptoe, it was too high. Daddy had given up on tennis and joined Mummy for a siesta; it was too hot for anything. Mita was going to wake them up and set Daddy off again, I could tell. These days it was don't do this and don't do that—the more rules, the more Mita rebelled. The fights would lead to fits, and then Dr. Miguel would come over and give Mita an injection. I lowered my forehead onto the hard coldness of the marble coffee table.

Mita picked up a dining room chair and carried it across the room—she was on a mission. I turned my head, letting the marble cool my cheek while I watched her. I knew if she fell it would be my fault. There were days when her left leg buckled, but today it seemed fine. She climbed up on the chair and grabbed the leather cup.

"Got it!" Mita smiled a victorious smile. She brought the cup back to the coffee table and sat next to me.

"You have to cover when you shake, or the dice jump out."

"I do it my way," Mita said. The dice flew from the cup and spun on the terra-cotta tiles.

"I told you." I collected the dice and took the cup from her. "Let me have a go." I shook carefully, liking the delicate sound of the dice thudding against the sides, like a scatter of footsteps. I lifted the cup. Double threes.

"That's good," Mita said. "Lucky."

"I'm the lucky one," I said, and immediately wished I hadn't. We used to say that to each other, as if luck were an energy we could steal back and forth. But since the fits and Mita's spastic foot, grown-ups referred to me as the lucky one.

"A good throw means all your wishes will come true," Mita said. "You'll be the star of a famous *novela,* and Jaime will be your boyfriend."

"That's not my wish! That's your wish."

"Yes," Mita said. "I'll be the star." She started to sing the theme song from *A Grande Mentira,* her voice deep and sad, just like the *novela:* "*Foi mentira meu amor,*" then her voice got high and reedy, "*quiseram nosso mal . . .*" We burst out laughing. Mita couldn't sing high notes.

"My turn." She took the cup and sniffed it. "It smells like feet."

I smelled. "Sweat. Daddy's sweat." Elói said all Englishmen stink. I felt sorry for Daddy, he couldn't help being English.

Mita covered the cup and threw a one and a four. Instead

of handing me the cup, she turned her back to me and threw again.

"That's not fair."

"My hand keeps slipping. It's too hot."

"That's an excuse." Sweat collected in the webbing between each of my fingers. The feeble wind created by the fan disappeared in a second.

Mita dried her hands on her yellow dress and lifted her hair from the back of her neck. There were wet finger-marks where she held the cup. She kept getting low numbers. It was my turn, but I was too hot to care.

"What are you girls up to?" Daddy stood in the doorway, in shorts.

"Nothing." Mita quickly hid the cup under the table. The two dice were sitting there, right in front of us. White dice on white marble. Maybe Daddy wouldn't notice. Mita bit her lower lip. Her face was a dead giveaway.

"Margarita—"

Mita's lips quivered, then she started to laugh. She lifted the cup from her lap and held it in the air. "We were playing Bidu."

Daddy didn't seem cross. Mummy stood behind him in a pink dress, smiling. Then her face froze. Something was wrong. Maybe she could see that Mita had taken off her boots. She reached for Daddy's elbow. "Ian—"

"What?" Daddy's face went completely still. "Get up slowly, girls," he said, in the calmest of voices.

Mita frowned. She sensed something strange too.

I stood up. There was nothing to break: Mummy's crystal glasses were nowhere near.

"Mita, stand up," Daddy said. "Now!" The *now* came out loud and sharp.

Mita never liked it when Daddy was sharp with her. She stared at the leather cup in her hand and didn't move.

"Girls, stand up and walk toward me." Daddy pointed at his own chest, as if we didn't know who he was.

"Why?" Mita said. "Why can't we stay here?" Mita picked up the dice and dropped them in the cup. She didn't want Mummy and Daddy to see she was barefoot.

"Mita, do as I say."

"Come on, Mita," I said, sensing some kind of urgency without understanding.

"We were only playing." Mita pushed against the coffee table to stand up.

I turned to give her a hand, and then I saw it: a huge rattlesnake, unfolding itself slowly next to Mita's ankle. So close it could bite her if it wanted to.

Mita continued to shake the cup with the dice. The tension made her nervous.

"Gently, girls," Daddy said. "No sudden movements."

Mita didn't understand. She took a few steps toward me. The snake followed her like a river of silver water.

"Don't run," Daddy said. "Walk slowly."

Mita still hadn't seen it. She shook the dice harder, and they skittered onto the floor. "Oh dear," she said.

"Mita, keep moving," Daddy said. "For Chrissakes, keep moving."

Mita stood her ground. She never did things just because Daddy said so.

I had to hypnotize her. I stared at Mita, until I almost became her. "We'll get the dice later," I said, my voice calm and definite. "Follow me." I walked toward Mummy and Daddy without looking back. I could feel Mita following behind.

The minute we arrived Mummy slammed the bedroom door closed. "Thank God," she said. "Thank God."

Mita frowned, confused.

"There was a snake. The largest snake in the universe," I said. "Next to your foot."

I could tell she didn't believe me. We were used to rattlesnakes and anacondas, outside. A small grass snake might manage to slide under the door and get into our house, but nothing big.

"What the hell do we do now?" Daddy said. In England there aren't snakes, I don't think. Not snakes that come into your house.

"I want to see," Mita said. "I didn't get to see."

"I can handle it," Mummy said. "Now that Mita is safe." She inched the door open.

"Be careful," Daddy said. "I'm not sure about this, Isabela."

Mita pushed her way next to Mummy. "I want to see."

Mummy opened the door wider. "It's moving. Over by the television."

The snake slithered over and under itself, silver-purple with a yellow gleam to its underbelly, like a moving jewel.

"It's beautiful," Mita said. "I want to see close-up."

Mummy held her hand out. "No, Mita. Just me. Stay here with Daddy and Dolores."

"I'll get the gun," Daddy said, and for some reason that made us laugh.

"Don't be silly, Ian." Mummy fetched a broom from the cupboard. "Stay with the girls." Holding the brush part of the broom with the handle out in front, she walked slowly toward the snake.

"What the hell is she doing?" Daddy asked.

"She's catching the snake," I said. I'd seen Elói do it, with a bamboo stick.

"The broom will make it mad," Mita said. "I don't think snakes like brooms."

Daddy frowned. Mummy pushed the handle of the broom toward the snake. Its triangular face darted from side to side. Mita was right, the snake seemed nervous. Mummy allowed the snake to inspect the broomstick. The snake and Mummy watched each other. Slowly, Mummy began to pull the broom back in, toward her body. The snake noticed and slithered toward it. Mummy pulled back a little more, and the snake followed.

"Clever," Daddy said. "That's a clever move."

The fan fluttered Mummy's dress. The snake noticed and turned toward her. Mummy was barefoot. I didn't want the snake to bite her toes. They were painted pale pink to match her dress. Mummy inched the end of the broom back toward the snake. This time the snake hovered itself up in the air, as if it could fly. Then we heard it: a hollow shiver of a rattle, low at first then louder, picking up speed and rhythm, like rain through bamboo. *Click, click, click.* A tiny black tongue darted in and out, in and out, three times.

"Careful there," Daddy said under his breath. He squeezed my hand so tight, my fingers buckled one on top of the other.

The snake swam in the air and then collapsed onto the broom, curling itself over and under in small tires as it wound its way up toward Mummy's hands.

Mummy lifted the broomstick with the snake and walked quickly toward the front door.

Daddy ran over and held the door open. Mummy threw the broomstick with the coiled snake into the garden and pulled the door closed, then locked it.

"Thank God," Daddy said. "Where in the name of heaven did you learn that?"

Mummy smiled. Her face was flushed. "Sometimes, growing up on a farm is useful," she said.

Mummy went over to Mita and hugged her. Then, Mummy's eyes teared up. She didn't say anything, but the mood changed. Daddy said he needed a bloody drink after all that excitement and headed to the bar.

Later that night, I woke up thirsty. I untangled myself from Mita and made my way to the kitchen to get water. On the way back, I saw two cigarette ends glowing in the veranda. Usually, Daddy sat out there alone, with his whisky. I walked over to see who was with him. Mummy's voice was low and worried.

"I should have been there watching."

"Don't be silly. You can't watch her around the clock."

"If she gets worse, what will we do?"

"That won't happen."

"Celina said the paper mill might close."

"Rumors," Daddy said. "We'll be fine. It's a storm in a teacup."

"What storm in a teacup?" I asked, stepping onto the cool tiles of the veranda.

"Dolores, go back to bed. It's late," Mummy said.

"Why are you smoking? You only smoke for visitors. Is someone coming over?"

"Don't be silly. It's past midnight." Mummy stubbed out her cigarette and led me back to bed. She tucked me in next to Mita.

"You were great with the snake," I said, remembering the sound it made: a shivery dry rattle, like raspy wind.

Chapter Thirteen

NOVEMBER 1972

Mr. P. said it would be like this, like riding a bicycle: One moment it seems impossible, and then it all comes together and makes sense. I didn't believe him, but he was right. I've been reading for three whole days. Sometimes I get stuck. I run into a combination of letters that doesn't make sense. But if I keep myself calm, I figure it out. Soon, I'll be able to write to Mita and ask her the million things I've wanted to ask her all this time.

I don't dread school anymore. My stomach doesn't hurt, the way it used to. I even eat breakfast.

"Well, someone's been in a good mood! See? The British school isn't so bad after all!"

I almost tell him. I want to. I want to show off and say I

can write, but Daddy doesn't like show-offs. And it might make Mummy feel dumb. They don't deserve to know, anyway. They're so caught up with their dinner parties, that's all they think about. I decide the best approach is to act as if I'd been writing all along.

"I finished my homework," I say. "I had to write an essay."

"Good job," Daddy says.

Neither of them seems surprised. Mummy doesn't look upset.

Daddy lowers his newspaper and smiles at Mummy. "What's your essay about?"

"The French Revolution," I say, thinking about that phrase Mummy uses when she sees a woman wearing too much jewelry or a fancy outfit with the label on the outside: *Who does she think she is, Madame Pompadour?*

"Why don't you invite that friend of yours, Andrea, over? We've never met her, or her parents," Mummy says.

"Do they go to the club?" Daddy says. "We could try that *churrascaria* that just opened."

"Andrea doesn't like the club much. She prefers to stay home and read."

"A bookworm, is she?" Daddy says.

"I have to go, or I'll miss the Blue Bus!" I grab my satchel, run downstairs, and jump onto the waiting bus.

I walk to my seat, the one at the back with the window that doesn't open. I like the peacefulness of it. The water in the canal is so still—a mirror of upside-down trees stretching its way to the sea. Mita thought reflections were secret twins; she never accepted Daddy's explanation about light rays bouncing off the surface of the water . . . I wonder if Mita still searches for secret twins in the landscape, like she used to. I have so many questions. I want to know if the hospital is helping her. Do they make her do hand exercises with Play-Doh? I wonder if her bedroom is yellow. Are they teaching her to read?

I wonder about so many things. Now I have a way of finding out. I'll write my aerogram in English, in case she can't read. Then a nurse or a doctor can read it to her.

I love you Mita and I miss you, of course I'll say that . . . I'm not sure what to tell her about Mummy and Daddy. I could sugarcoat it: *They're busy in Rio, but they do miss you.* Or I could tell her the truth: *They've changed; you wouldn't recognize them. Mummy tries to be English. She cooks horrible food and pretends to be afraid of snakes. All she cares about are parties. They have parties every weekend, and sometimes in the middle of the week people come over for cocktails.*

The bus stops and starts its way to Botafogo.

School buses are yellow, I tell Mita in my head. *You would like them.* Maybe I'll tell her that words are everywhere. On buses, there's a message inside the rectangle above the driver's window telling people where the bus is heading—BOTAFOGO! IPANEMA! On the wall behind the Paissandu tennis club, someone spray-painted ABAIXO A DITADURA! *Down with the dictatorship!* And the cemetery wall says É PROIBIDO PROIBIR, *It is forbidden to forbid.* A whole world of secret messages appears when you can read.

All along, I've been thinking letters to Mita in my head; now I can write them into words and sentences, and I feel a huge gladness inside of me, like a balloon in my lungs that might explode with happiness.

Mr. P. told me that he's sure the story of my life is interesting; I should write it down; he'd love to read it. He said that. Yesterday. He gave me a book as a present. It has a green cover and looks like an official book, only it has blank pages, so I can use it to write or draw or doodle. I feel shy with how much I love Mr. P.

The Blue Bus pulls into the gates at Rua Real Grandeza. I jump off and walk across the playground to the class three queue. There's energy in my legs, a tingling, like an electric current all over my body. It's easy to ignore the whispers and the giggling.

I sit at the back of class, and my mind feels sharp, like a gem cutter polishing a diamond. Mr. P. is talking about punctuation, and how it is used in poetry. Punctuation shows you how to read a piece, when to take a breath and slow down, and when to stop. How do you know when to stop? It's not at the end of the line—which was how I thought it would work—it's when you reach a full stop. I love that full stop: a dot, like a freckle or a beauty mark, telling you things, giving instructions.

I think of a comma as a breath, take a full breath; it's a little curl in a sentence, like a hand saying slow down, Mita, slow down. Be careful, you might fall. Then there's the exclamation mark! Silly bloody cow! Daddy lives in the land of exclamation marks. There are no commas in Daddy's world, no breathing spaces or pauses.

At the end of class, Mr. P. reads us part of a poem called "Howl." He says, "You might consider it one huge run-on sentence, but this is poetry." He says punctuation is useful, but you don't always need it; sometimes it's good to break the rules. He tells us to write essays like that poem, everything and anything, to let go and let the writing pour out. I feel my fingers tighten around my pencil, knowing that if I did that, I would cry. Knowing I can't do that. I prefer using punctuation. It slows me down and keeps things measured, like Daddy's silver jigger controls how much gin goes into a glass.

Little full stops of alcohol, only with Daddy they behave more like commas.

"CAN I HAVE AN AEROGRAM?" I say before I can stop myself. We're having dinner and all I can think about is writing to Mita. Even if I can't write cursive yet, she won't care.

"I don't see why not," Daddy says. "Is it for school?"

"No, it isn't."

Mummy brings out a tray of Yorkshire puddings, some slightly burned at the edges. Last week, they came out flat. Daddy called them satellites.

"These look good, Isabela." Daddy holds his knife and fork in the air, as if he can barely wait.

"I need Mita's address. I want to write to her."

"I'm not sure it's a good idea." Mummy forks a Yorkshire pudding onto my plate, even though she knows I hate them. "It might make her sad to hear from us."

That makes no sense. Mummy must be jealous that I can write, and she can't. "How d'you think Mita feels, not hearing from us? Don't you think that's worse?"

Daddy puts his knife and fork down. He lights up a cigarette and leans back in his chair, his face impassive. I know that look. He doesn't want to give me an answer.

"How are the Yorkshire puddings?" Mummy says. "Overdone?"

"No. Perfect."

I look at Daddy, straight in the eyes: "Do you have her address?"

Daddy takes a long, slow inhale. "You'll see Mita when we go on home leave."

"And when is that?"

"As soon as we can. When things calm down."

"She's still getting used to it over there," Mummy says.

"She shouldn't get used to it. Her home is here, with us." I take a breath, trying to calm myself down and sound reasonable. Otherwise, I'll get nowhere. "Please. I've been writing to Mita in my head for so long, and now I know how to write, I want to send her a letter."

Mummy smooths a wrinkle on the tablecloth. She wants me to stop, but I'm not going to stop.

"All I'm asking is to write her a letter."

"It's not a good idea," Mummy says.

"I. Want. Her. Address." I say it slowly, as if I'm spelling it out.

"Selfish," Daddy says. "You risk upsetting Mita with a letter."

"Who told you that? Mita will be glad to get my aerogram. Glad to know at least one of us remembers her." My fingers ache from gripping my fork. "Please. You have to let me."

Daddy swallows and turns away. I realize he's trying not to cry. He should cry. I want them both to cry. He looks like a Yorkshire pudding: fat, puffy, and empty.

"I don't believe," I say, "that you are my real father."

"Don't be ridiculous!" Daddy says.

No real parent would send their daughter away to live in a hospital. "You don't care if she dies. You gave her away, like João e Maria." A shiver runs through me. "Maybe she's dead already," I say.

"How dare you. Of course Mita isn't dead." Daddy finishes his wine in one gulp.

"I'm not sure they have time to read letters in the hospital." Mummy's voice sounds wobbly.

"Maybe she'll read it herself," I say. "You don't know. You don't know anything. You're illiterate."

"Don't speak like that to your mother." Daddy glares at me.

"Why not? You say it. I've heard you."

Mummy carefully folds her serviette and places it next to her plate. Her fingers shake, and I feel sorry for my meanness.

"You can learn if you want to. People learn; it doesn't just happen. It's not like walking." Maybe Mummy doesn't realize.

"I've tried telling her," Daddy says. "Your mother doesn't believe she can learn."

Mummy rubs her nose. She wants this conversation to be over.

"Everybody can learn," I say, as if I'm an expert.

"Enough. I have a headache." Mummy pushes her chair back and leaves the room.

I wait at the dinner table, not ready to give up. Daddy smokes his cigarette all the way down to the end. "Don't lord writing over your mother," he says. "I'll give you the bloody address, but don't expect too much."

Chapter Fourteen

"*Querida Mita,*" Andrea says impatiently.

"We have to write in English, not Portuguese, remember?" I remind Andrea. I look around, making sure we're alone. Tia Glória isn't due back for at least another hour.

"Dear Mita, I miss you," Andrea says confidently.

"Yes," I whisper. "That sounds good." When I write *miss,* some ribbon of feeling loosens and travels along my body, like a snake. It moves from my chest to my arms, my legs, even my hands. There's so much new to explain: school, Rio, Andrea. The sea, Mita has never caught a wave. All the times we came to Rio, she was lying across the back seat, having a fit. She doesn't know how to let the small waves ripple by, how to wait for the one that is cresting, then paddle out in front, at exactly the right moment—so it swells under you and takes you forward. I feel Mita's presence, so close it hurts.

"Now what?" Andrea says.

"I want to ask her things, all kinds of questions: Are you okay over there? Is the hospital curing you? Are you happy?"

I write my questions out carefully, with question marks at the end. I love the shape of a question mark, how it stops suddenly and then there's a space and a dot underneath, it looks like doubt.

"Do you miss me?"

"Of course she misses you," Andrea says. "What a question."

"I haven't forgotten you, Mita," I whisper. I'm not sure anymore if I want to do this with Andrea. It feels private.

"Underline *haven't,*" Andrea says. "So she knows it's the truth." She reaches over and strokes my hand.

I underline *haven't,* twice. "I'm coming to visit, I promise."

"Tell her when," Andrea says.

"I don't know when. My parents refuse to give me a date."

"Soon," Andrea says. "You have to say soon, so she has hope." Andrea is big on hope.

I write *soon.* The two *o*'s aren't the same size, so I erase the corner of one of them and adjust it so they match. Then I add: *I can't wait for us to be a family again. Not having you here is terrible.* I write slowly, so I don't mess up.

English is hard. Mr. P. says Portuguese is easier for me because it's a phonetic language; the way you write it matches the way you say it.

"Now what?" Andrea says.

"I want to tell her about the sea."

"Tell her, then."

The waves come in, one after another, I write. *In per—* "How do you spell *perpetual*?"

Andrea looks it up in the *Concise Oxford English Dictionary* Mr. P. gave me. "P-E-R-P-E-T-U-A-L."

In perpetual motion, even though they say it doesn't exist.

"I like that," Andrea says.

I know I have the full stops in the right place, but I'm not sure about the commas. I study my sentence and add another one, just in case. The page fills up. "This is fun," I say. Telling Mita about my new life in Rio feels like having her back.

There are many English people in Rio, not just Daddy. I don't like most of them.

Andrea laughs. "She's going to love this!"

Except Mr. P. He taught me to write. I lift my pencil. "This next part is about you," I say.

Andrea leans in to read: *My best friend Andrea is like you. She's not afraid of anything.* Andrea's breath is hot against my cheek. "I didn't know I was like her," she says. "I'm your other twin."

The door opens and Sofia walks in. I slide the aerogram under my notebook.

"What are you *garotas* up to?" Sofia's dressed in a tight orange dress with matching heels. Today, her hair is jet-black and cascades off the top of her head like a fountain.

"She's writing to her sister," Andrea says.

My throat tightens. I told Andrea: Everything about Mita is private. Especially from Sofia. Sofia likes to tease, and sometimes it has a mean edge. I'm used to it now, but when it comes to Mita, I don't appreciate jokes.

"Sister? You have a sister?" Sofia sits next to me and adjusts the straps of her sandals. "They pinch. I had them specially made, but they pinch."

"Go lower. You're tall already," Andrea says.

"Attitude. I need heels for the look, not for the height." She rubs her feet. "How come I've never met her, this sister? What's her name?"

"Margarita."

"Margarita, hmm . . ."

It feels dangerous to hear Mita's name in Sofia's voice. Beauty is so important to her. If Sofia saw Mita on the street, she'd turn away with that look people get, as if there's a bad taste in their mouth. I know she would. "Can I see your signature?" I ask, changing the subject.

Sofia takes my pencil and scribbles a dramatic *s* like a whip across the page. "Easy. Fast and easy, that's the thing with signatures."

Andrea says: "I hate that my name begins with an *a*. You have to lift the pen; *s* just flows." She practices a few different *a*'s.

I can make *d*'s, but I'm afraid to do them in front of Sofia. I don't want her to know I only just learned how to write. I want her to think I'm clever.

"I smell a secret." Sofia narrows her eyes. "What are you girls really up to?"

I feel myself blush. This was a bad idea, writing the aerogram with Andrea. At least my lessons with Mr. P. are private.

Sofia sees the aerogram under my notebook. "Ah," she says. "I get it. You're writing a love letter to a boyfriend in Paris, right?"

I smile. The bones of my cheeks ache.

"Who is he, this boy?"

I feel my flush deepen. Sofia leans closer in and whispers: "You can tell me. I won't tell a soul. Love letters are my specialty."

My letter to Mita is a love letter. Or an apology. The word *sorry* floats in my brain like a song you can't stop thinking about.

"Look at her," Sofia says. "It must be true love."

"Can we talk about something else?" Andrea says.

"Where's your mother? I have news."

"Working," Andrea says. "She's going to be late today."

"She doesn't work Saturdays." Sofia checks her watch: "I hope it's not Antonio."

Andrea doesn't answer.

Sofia lights up a cigarette. "I told Glória, *não vale a pena.* Your mother promised she wouldn't—even if he pays double."

"I know," Andrea says. "She said she'd be back by two."

"I'll wait." Sofia traces her long legs with the nail of her index finger, then stops below the knee. "D'you have tweezers?"

"In the bathroom," Andrea says.

Sofia saunters past me. "You better get started with that love letter if you want my help."

Andrea rolls her eyes. "Ignore her. She's obsessed."

I slide my aerogram back into the safety of my satchel. "Does she have a boyfriend?"

"Too many," Andrea says. "But no good ones."

Sofia returns with tweezers and proceeds to examine her legs for any stray hairs that didn't come out with the wax. "*Aquela menina,* she didn't do a good job."

"My mother's obsessed with body hair too," I say. "She spends hours plucking at nothing. She's not even hairy."

"Your mother's lucky," Sofia says. "Mine are thick and ugly. It takes so much, just to stay on top of it."

"It's just hair," Andrea says. "We don't pluck it from our heads—but we hate it when it grows in other places."

"Some places are right, and some places are wrong," Sofia says.

Mita has a crooked hair that grows on her chin, where she had stitches. It pushes through dark and thick, announcing itself over and over, no matter how many times Mummy plucks. The skin underneath is shiny, like leather—on account of all her falls.

The door opens and Tia Glória walks in. Immediately, she ducks into the bathroom. "*Oi garotas,*" she says from inside. "I'll be out in a minute."

Andrea goes to the bathroom door and knocks. "Mamma, are you okay?"

"Just getting cleaned up. I'll be right out."

Andrea comes back and plonks herself next to Sofia on the sofa. "I hate him," she says.

"Who?" I ask.

Silence. Sofia pinches the tweezers open and closed.

"Why does she do it?" Andrea's voice is thick with tears.

Sofia shrugs. "Ask your mother. *Besteira,*" she says.

Tia Glória emerges from the bathroom, her face too powdered. A bruise shines through her makeup, and her left eye is half closed.

"Anyone hungry?" Tia Glória asks.

No one answers.

"Maybe a little," I say, feeling sorry for her.

"I'll prepare us a salad. I have artichoke hearts somewhere." Tia Glória smiles at Andrea, but Andrea ignores her. Usually, Andrea can't get enough of artichoke hearts; they're her favorite food.

"I'm not hungry." Andrea bites her cuticles. "Why? Why did you go back?"

Sofia stands up. "You need meat. And cachaça."

She returns from the kitchen with a bottle and a slab of meat. Sofia pours us shots. Tia Glória dabs the steak tentatively against her eye.

Sofia pushes the steak into Tia Glória's eye socket. She holds it in and presses.

"*Ai,*" Tia Glória says. "Be gentle." She takes a quick shot of cachaça while Sofia holds the steak to her eye. Andrea picks up her glass and downs it in one gulp. I do the same, trying not to choke. The cachaça burns my throat.

We drink until the edges of the furniture start to blur.

"Look at your friend," Sofia says. "She's tipsy."

"Topsy-turvy," I say, and Andrea laughs. We've had cachaça before, but not like this, quickly in tiny gulps, it feels electric.

"I better catch up." Andrea pours herself another shot.

"Can you believe my new sandals are tight?" Sofia wiggles each of her long toes separately.

"Maybe you can have them stretched," Tia Glória says.

"You need to have your brain stretched," Sofia says. "No money is worth it, Glória. I've told you a thousand times."

"I know," Tia Glória says quietly.

Sofia gulps cachaça right from the bottle. She wipes her mouth with the back of her hand. "Fuck the school bills, Glória. Don't go back to him for the money. She doesn't even like school."

"What school bills?" Andrea says. "My school bills?"

"Sofia's drunk. Don't pay attention." Tia Glória places the steak down on the coffee table. It's turned a bluish gray, as if it has absorbed her bruise. Her eye is swollen, but the color is back in her cheeks.

"You told me my father sends the money from Italy," Andrea says.

"He does. Sofia's drunk."

Andrea turns to Sofia. "It isn't true, is it? My father doesn't send us money."

Sofia inspects her legs with the tweezers.

"School's a passport. It opens doors. Especially a foreign school," Tia Glória says.

"I don't see any doors. Dolores, do you see any doors?" Andrea stands up. "All this time you've been lying to me, both of you. Do I even have an Italian father? I bet that's a lie too."

"Of course you do," Tia Glória says. "Don't be silly."

"I don't believe a word you say." Andrea walks past Tia Glória to her room. I follow her. She locks the door behind us and throws herself on her bed.

I sit next to her and smooth her hair out. "Grown-ups lie," I say. "That's what they do."

Chapter Fifteen

DECEMBER 1972

Dark green lab coats arrive at school from England, with our names embroidered on the pockets. They were supposed to arrive months ago, but they got stuck in customs. Maybe Mita's letter is stuck in customs. Every day, I check the table where Mummy puts the mail. I try not to have feelings, to merely take note. I am a scientist, searching for the absolute truth of things. I imagine myself a Brazilian Madame Curie, discovering the cure to all kinds of illnesses, never giving up.

We're studying hypotheses in science. Hypotheses are possible explanations for things that happen in the world, ideas that need to be tested. Mrs. Oliveira says the word *hypothesis* comes from the Greek language, meaning to "put under" or "suppose." Andrea also wants to be a scientist. Each week we devise two hypotheses, following the letters of the alphabet—then we design experiments to test them, using the scientific method.

We start with the letter *a*.

Hypothesis #1: aerograms. Dolores will receive an aerogram from Margarita in three weeks. We calculate that it probably takes one week for an aerogram to arrive in England, one week for the response to get back, and we add an extra week, just in case.

Each night I cross out another day on my gem calendar, making a fence of X's, like a prison. Mita went away in July (Ruby) and now it's December (Turquoise). It says on my calendar that turquoise is supposed to improve communication, but that doesn't seem to be happening . . .

"Maybe I wrote the wrong things," I say. "I should have written about gems. Or Lampião and Maria Bonita."

"It's not what you wrote," Andrea says. "I bet you it's censorship. We didn't account for that." The government opens people's letters; that slows things down. Also, it's possible Mita used normal stationery, not airmail paper: Heavier letters take longer. Andrea says we can't lose hope.

I tell her there's no room for hope in science; there's room only for truth. I try not to feel sadness, to report the facts as they are.

We decide to put our aerogram hypothesis on hold. Instead, we investigate arguments (they happen more between people with bad teeth; we find this to be true) and avocados (lemon juice works better than lime juice in stopping them from turning brown: also true).

Then we move on to *b*'s. First, we pick the words or subjects to be studied, then we make hypotheses.

Hypothesis #2: breasts.

"I suppose," Andrea says, "I suppose there's a perfect bra for each breast."

Andrea's breasts press against her school uniform in a way that made Tia Glória announce last week that it was time for a bra. She'd planned to come with us to Laura's Boutique, but this morning a rich client arrived unexpectedly, so we go by ourselves. On the way, we discuss our hypothesis.

"Some people have breasts two different sizes, like feet, what happens then? Some breasts are too floppy for bras," I say. Mummy's breasts spill out from her bra in all directions, even after she tucks them in.

"Laura will help us. She's an expert on breasts. She has a section for *travestis;* she set Sofia up to look gorgeous!"

Andrea's body is developing and mine isn't, and I'm glad. I prefer to stay close to my bones. Andrea loves the changes happening in her body. She grabs her bottom and pinches it, saying, "*Olha minha bunda, que grande!*" She doesn't think of it as fat; she thinks of it as extra, like a piece of chocolate cake with tons of icing.

Laura's Boutique has super-high stiletto heels, stockings, and black leather corsets in the window; apparently it isn't just bras.

"*Entrem, garotas,* come in," Laura says. "I was expecting you." She's thin and pointed, and her nose is crooked in the middle, like a fighter's nose. Her wide gray eyes are outlined with black kohl, and she wears red stiletto mules with furry pom-poms. When she talks, her elbows and hands move, so she's all angles.

I expected Laura to have large breasts. But hers are small and droop a little, like old pears. She isn't wearing a bra. Her light brown nipples show through her T-shirt. She grabs a tape measure and studies Andrea's breasts. "You can almost fit adult."

"I want something sexy," Andrea says.

"Of course you do," Laura says, smiling in a welcoming way. "I'll pull a couple out, and you tell me what you think."

While Andrea tries on bras, I walk to the section marked ESPECIALIDADES, the specialty area. Bras with the nipples cut out in a perfect circle, and bras where there is no bra at all, just the underwire outline of a bra, in black or red leather.

"Those are just to play." Laura winks at me. "They don't hold anything up."

"I don't have anything to hold up," I tell her. "So I might as well play!" We laugh. She has a cigarette-smoke kind of laugh that I imagine men find sexy.

Andrea appears from the dressing room in a black lace bra with a bow in the middle. It's pretty, but the wire underneath is too uncomfortable. Laura hands her some others, a purple one, and a black one that looks like it's made from a stocking. The minute Andrea comes out with the purple bra, we know it's right. The lace hugs the curve of her breasts like a pretty lampshade.

"You can tighten it here," Laura says, pulling at the tiny bow between the cups, "so it gives you more cleavage." Andrea's breasts press toward each other, creating a shadowy space between them, like a secret passage. She turns from side to side, studying the effect.

"I like it," she says. "And what's more, Gilberto will like it!"

Gilberto isn't her boyfriend yet, but he's her favorite of the many boys who want her.

Laura sifts through the racks. "I want to find something for your friend."

"*Eu não preciso.*" I don't want one of those horrible padded bras the English girls wear.

"*Aqui,*" Laura says. "Found it!" She hands me a beautiful red lace bra. "It's petite. It comes from France."

I step into the changing room with Andrea, who's trying on a black leather one for fun. I slip the bra over my breasts and Andrea hooks me up at the back. The lace covers my breasts like a soft curtain, making them look more distinctive and separate from me: my breasts.

"*Lindo!*" Andrea declares.

Laura opens the curtain to see. "That's it," she says. "I knew it. I've been searching for someone for that bra for ages. I knew one day the right person would come."

I realize we have to revise our hypothesis: I suppose there is a perfect breast for each bra, and not the other way around.

Laura doesn't let us pay one centavo for our bras. She says Tia Glória has a heart of gold, if she can pay her back in this small way, it's a pleasure.

As we walk along the street, the bra feels like a secret under my dress. It makes me move slowly and hold myself differently. It makes me want to wear lipstick and kiss a boy on the mouth.

On the way back from Laura's Boutique, we pass by a *padaria,* a nail salon, and a pawnshop.

"Is that Sofia?" Andrea says.

"It sounds like her," I say. "Who else says *for the love of God* like that?"

"Let's go in and tell her about our new bras," Andrea says.

"I don't want to. I'm not sure Sofia likes me."

"Don't pay attention. Sofia's edgy. She's like that with everyone—it isn't you. C'mon." Andrea pushes the door to the pawnshop open and walks in. I follow her.

Sofia's at the back, arguing with a man. "I'll go to H. Stern and have it analyzed! How dare you!" She pounds her fist on the rickety wooden table.

Andrea walks up to Sofia and kisses her on the cheek.

I linger at the entrance. Sofia feels unpredictable at the best of times, and now is clearly not the best of times. I've never been inside a pawnshop before. The shelves on the wall display silver coffee sets, trays, and ornamental vases. Two violins. There's a wooden cabinet with jewelry and watches.

"What are you buying?" Andrea asks Sofia.

"Selling. Not buying. But this *filho da puta* has the audacity to tell me that my emerald bracelet—the one that belonged to my great-grandmother—is fake."

"Why are you selling your bracelet? You love that bracelet."

"I need fast cash," Sofia says. "It's an emergency. I'll buy it back next week."

"It's always an emergency with you," Andrea says.

Sofia shows the bracelet to Andrea. "Does this look artificial to you?"

"Ask Dolores, she knows about gems."

Sofia looks at me and raises her eyebrows. "Come closer, *francesinha,* I'm not going to bite you! Tell me what you think."

I step closer in. Sofia wipes the bracelet on the leg of her orange bell-bottoms, then hands it to me.

The emeralds are set in gold, and each one has a quiet intensity. "Do you have a magnifying glass, please?" I ask the man.

"I know an emerald when I see one. I have three others in that case over there." The man points at the wooden cabinet. "This bracelet isn't worth much, whatever the child says!"

"Give her a magnifying glass," Sofia says.

The man frowns. He walks over to a gray file cabinet and returns with a magnifying glass.

I examine the emeralds from all angles, the way Daddy used to do when he had doubts. They have a few inclusions, but not many. I don't see any bubbles. "This is a true emerald bracelet. A beautiful one," I say.

Sofia looks triumphant. "What did I tell you?"

"I'm going to take it on the word of a child?" The man's voice is oily, that's what Mita called it when she didn't trust someone. She'd say his voice is oily.

"Let me see your other emeralds. I'll tell you if they're fake or if they're real," I say with more confidence than I feel. The only way to know for sure is to use a refractometer, but I'm not going to tell him that.

The man looks at me with suspicion.

"Show her," Sofia says. "Don't you want to know if you're being ripped off?"

The man opens the wood cabinet and brings out two rings and one brooch and places them on the wooden table.

Immediately, I see that one of the rings is fake. "Bubbles. See these bubbles?" I show the man. Sofia and Andrea lean in to look. "This is probably a goshenite beryl, painted over with varnish." Someone tried that trick with Daddy once, but he saw right through it. I turn the ring and look at the girdle. "And it's peeling here, see. It's a fake."

The man takes the ring from me, inspects it, and frowns. "What about the other ones?"

I pick up the other ring. "No. An emerald this size would be heavier. It's too light."

"What about this one?" the man says, his voice angry. "This one has to be real. Look at it!"

The color of the stone in the brooch is a deep blue green. Daddy bought an emerald this color once. He said it was probably from Colombia; the blue tint was rare in Brazil. "This one is real," I say. "It has a scratch along the side, here, but you could have it polished, then it would be worth more."

The man is listening. He nods his approval. Andrea is listening too, and Sofia. I feel like an expert.

I place the brooch back on the table. The brilliance of Sofia's bracelet makes the other gems look pale, even the blue-green emerald looks dull.

"I'll do it," the man says to Sofia. "I'll give you the five hundred cruzeiros you wanted."

Sofia picks up her emerald bracelet and slides it onto her arm. "You tried to tell me this is a fake?" She cups both of her breasts and lifts them. "*These* are fake. You don't deserve my emeralds. Come on, girls, let's get out of here."

The three of us march out of the pawnshop.

"What about your emergency?" Andrea says.

"I'll figure something out," Sofia says. "I know plenty of other places. But I'm not going to pawn this bracelet. It would break my heart to lose it. Especially now that I know it's real!"

"You didn't know?" Andrea says.

"I wasn't sure," Sofia says. "We didn't exactly come from money. But your friend here was convincing."

As we wait for the bus, Sofia puts on orange lipstick. She turns to me: "Want some? It's your color."

I take the lipstick and paint my lips orange.

"Look at her," Sofia says. "*Francesinha* has hidden talents."

I feel my bra, secretly cupping my breasts under my school uniform, and think that maybe Sofia's right. Maybe I do have some hidden talents.

Chapter Sixteen

FEBRUARY 1973

The water lilies float on the surface, barely moving. They're held in place by an underground root. I read about it on the wooden sign by the pond. Andrea lies next to me with her magazine. We're supposed to be studying biology, but instead she's examining nude photos of Jackie O.

"What if Mita's dead, would they tell you?" Andrea says.

I rip a blade of grass sideways. It rips in tidy lines like a green road. Daddy warned me sending an aerogram was a bad idea, so I'm not allowed to be sad.

"I don't want to be mean," Andrea says, "but have you considered that?"

I close my eyelids on my tears. Amethyst is supposed to

calm the spirit and balance emotions; that's what it says on my gem calendar. It's definitely not working.

"Maybe it's like the disappeared," Andrea said. "You never know if the police killed them, or if they're alive somewhere, hiding."

"Mita isn't hiding. She's in a hospital in England." I say it loud and sure, but inside, I'm full of doubt. I've sent her eight aerograms, and still no response. Mummy says the nurses are too busy to write back, but what kind of nurse wouldn't help Mita write to her family? I'm not sure about this English hospital. What if they're caning her there, or worse? I can't bear to think about it.

"You would know if she was dead," Andrea says. "You would feel it in your body like a knife. I saw a show about identical twins on *Chacrinha.* One of them was operated on in Pernambuco, and the other one was in Minas Gerais, and she couldn't stop screaming—it was as if she were the one being cut open."

It hurt my edges to think about that. "I'd know it. I would have to know."

I don't tell Andrea that sometimes I can't remember my own twin. When I write things down in my essays, they look so true: all those words marching one in front of the other. But maybe they're just stories.

I turn to the body section of my textbook and study the bones: *tarsals, metatarsals.* I say the names to myself as if I am a doctor in search of the causes of things. Where did Mita's twistedness begin? Was it the bone that was crooked inside her foot, or was it the meat and the nerves that swerved in the wrong direction?

They only teach us normal things at school, the way our

bodies are supposed to work. The lungs, the blood system, hundreds of capillaries like tiny rivers running inside us. I trace my finger down the vein of my arm into my hand, like Pedro Álvares Cabral discovering Brazil. I give it a name: *braço de prata,* silver arm. It's bluish silver, like a sardine of a vein. When I close my fist up tight, into a curled-up ball of a hand like Mita's hand, my vein swells, like a snake sliding down my arm.

"They would have to tell you, by law, if she dies," Andrea says. "When my daddy dies, they'll tell me—because he's in the Italian army. They always send telegrams to families when soldiers die."

"Well, Mita's not a soldier," I answer, prickly like the grass. "D'you remember your father?" I ask, changing the subject.

"Of course I do," Andrea says, with a sureness in her voice. Some days she remembers, and other days she doesn't, and she's always sure. Andrea turns over onto her belly. "Maybe what I remember is the photograph of him." She pulls out tufts of grass and sprinkles them on her arm. "When I think of him, it's always in his soldier's uniform, exactly like the photo by my lamp . . . and I remember his smell. The feel of his hands picking me up and lifting me over his head. And his smell."

"What kind of smell?"

"Cigarettes mixed up with . . ." Andrea wrinkles her nose, remembering. "Cigarettes, with that smell that stays after a fire? A dried-up, ash kind of smell. And trees. Not *bananeiras,* but trees that burn in fireplaces, like they have in São Paulo."

Andrea lived in São Paulo when she was little, before her father left.

"I can't remember Mita," I tell her. "I try, but no picture comes up."

"Nothing?"

"Not the way I remember the Cremogema I ate this morning, or Sofia's bracelet. Mita is fading." It sits between us, this truth, like an ugly slug you don't know what to do with. You don't want to pick it up with your fingers, but you don't want it sitting there, in the way.

"D'you remember the last time you saw her?"

"No," I say. "I don't." Daddy says I was there, in her room at Strangers' Hospital, but I can't remember it.

"D'you remember her smell?" Andrea asks.

I close my eyes and try to breathe Mita in. Very, very far away I smell her. Just the edge of a smell. "She smells a little sour, from the medicine," I say. "And sweet, like *canela.* A mix of cinnamon and chewed-up biscuits and . . . flannel pajamas, after they've been ironed."

"Well, then," Andrea says, her voice definite. "Well, then, you remember. A smell is remembering."

I'm almost remembering. I lie very still and breathe Mita in, breathe her smell and the tickle of her hair under my nose. The feel of our edges touching, my belly warm against her back as I curled around her at night. I feel the ache of her inside my body, but I don't see a photo in my mind, the way you do when you remember someone. Next to us, a blue hummingbird hovers above a red hibiscus flower—almost touching, but not quite. That's how my memory of Mita is. I can feel her behind the window of my eyes, pressing to come out: But whenever I open my eyes, she's gone. Almost there. Almost gone. I'm not sure which.

I turn over and look at the sun, trying not to blink. Maybe I'll go blind. If I can forget my sister, anything is possible. "I need to find out if she's alive."

"You have her address. Go. See for yourself."

Andrea makes it seem so easy. I imagine walking into the hospital, announcing I am Mita's twin, and I've come to get her.

"You'll need money. A lot of money," Andrea says. "I bet you it's expensive to fly to England."

"I don't have money." Sometimes Daddy gives me a ten-cruzeiro note to buy lunch at the club, or lemonade on the beach. "It's impossible."

"Nothing's impossible," Andrea says.

"Maybe I can sell my bike? I've never used it. I bet you it's worth something."

"A bicycle? You could get a hundred cruzeiros, max. You need a thousand, maybe two thousand."

"I don't have anything else to sell."

"Our bodies. We can sell our bodies." Andrea adjusts her bra under her dress. "Men pay a lot for girls our age."

"No," I say. "That's out."

"It's an idea. Your body is worth more than mine, I bet. Your skin is lighter, and they especially like *virgens.*"

"You're a *virgem* too."

"Technically. But in other ways, I'm not. I'm not sure how that affects pricing."

Andrea licked Gilberto's *piru* the other day. I don't like thinking about it. I close my eyes, still seeing the imprint of the sun like a floating jellyfish in the blackness of my eyelids.

Andrea's right. It is up to me. Mummy and Daddy don't care about Mita anymore. If she is dead, they wouldn't tell me. They'd want to avoid a scene.

"I need money," I say, "but I'm not going to sell my body. I'll get a job."

"It's not so easy. Jobs don't pay much. Do you want to be

a maid? Or shine shoes? Even if you work seven days a week, it will take years before you make enough to go to England."

"There has to be something we can do that pays."

"Sex," Andrea says. "That's the best solution."

"There must be something else. What about writing? Aparecida pays someone at the bus station to write João love letters when he's in Bahia. We can write letters for people who can't write. What about that? I'll ask Aparecida."

"Hmm. We'd make so much more money selling our bodies. It would only be a few times, then—" Andrea snaps her fingers. "England."

Chapter Seventeen

We hear the music even before we get off the bus. "Asa Branca." I sing along: "*Adeus, Rosinha, guarda contigo meu coração!*"

"Listen to you," Andrea says, "what a scene! I've never been here before."

There are three makeshift stages with live music and dancing, and thirty or forty *barracas* selling musical instruments, figurines, and specialty foods of all kinds. Everything from the Nordeste. Here, outside the pavilion, under the burning sun, migrant workers come with their families to *matar saudades* and remind themselves of home.

We find an open area and set up our folding card table. A man strides over and tells us the space is reserved. We find another location, but the same thing happens. Andrea sweet-talks the manager into letting us set up by the *trilho de forró.* It's a bit noisy, but maybe we'll work our way to a quieter place once we've established ourselves. We don't have a license, but Sofia said no one checks at the Feira de São Cristóvão. Anything goes.

We have stationery, stamps, and a large cardboard sign that says CARTAS DE AMOR: love letters to friends, family, and lovers. Andrea forgot that our customers can't read when she made the sign. I draw in a hand holding a pen, and a picture of an envelope with some hearts, hoping that makes it clear. The official letter writers are outside the bus station, which is at least a kilometer away, maybe more. We figured the fair would be a good place to set up shop. People come because they're homesick. They want to eat the familiar foods, hear the music, and see all the things they grew up with. It makes sense that in this atmosphere of *saudade,* they'd want to write someone a letter . . .

We sit and watch people stroll by while the accordion player warms up. I test my pen to make sure it works. Aparecida said bring pens, not pencils. When she sends letters to João, she always chooses writers who have pens. They are more professional. A banjo player joins in, then an older man, playing a *zabumba* drum. The music picks up, and people start to dance. No one stops at our table.

Andrea looks at her watch. "We're wasting time. My friend Flavia makes twenty cruzeiros doing a hand job. That's not selling your body, it's manual work."

"I'm not doing a hand job," I say. I don't exactly know what a hand job is, but I can guess.

When the band stops for a break, a middle-aged woman approaches. "You girls really know how to write?"

"Absolutely," Andrea says. "Who would you like to write to?"

"A man. A man I once loved. How much do you charge?" The woman looks uncertain.

"We'll give you a good price. What can you afford?" I say.

The woman feels inside her plastic shopping bag and pulls out a fifty-centavo coin. Andrea raises her eyebrows. We had agreed two cruzeiros was the lowest we would go. The tables by the bus station charge five cruzeiros per page.

"Do you have a little bit more?" Andrea says.

The woman shakes her head and starts to leave.

"Fifty centavos is fine for this first time," I say. "What is the man's name?"

"Valeriano. Valeriano Andrade."

"What d'you want to say?" I ask.

"Tell him I should have stayed in Sucatinga. He was right; it was a mistake to come here." She bites at the insides of her hollow cheeks.

"I miss you every moment of every day," Andrea says, taking over as if it were her letter. "How about that?"

"Yes," the woman says. "Say that."

"How long has it been since you saw him?" I ask.

"Forty years. I was thirteen. What do you know when you're thirteen?"

I won't be thirteen until May. Neither of us mention our age.

The woman closes her eyes. "Do you remember what you promised me that night at the bonfire? Ask him if he remembers. Ask him," the woman says, her face becoming animated, "if he steals fish from his uncle, like he used to."

I carefully write down her questions. When I look up, she's smiling. Even though one of her front teeth is missing, she looks beautiful.

When we've written a whole page of questions, I ask for his address.

"Sucatinga," the woman says. "The first house after the *praça.*"

"What number?" Andrea asks.

"Just write his name and Sucatinga. Don't worry, he'll get it." She walks away smiling.

Business picks up. We write a series of short letters about various grievances: a meddlesome mother-in-law, a distant son, an unhappy sister.

"This is starting to get old," Andrea says. She looks at the ring Gilberto gave her yesterday. "Imperial topaz. *Lindo, né?*"

She's already showed it to me one hundred times. It's a fake, but I don't say so. Andrea and Gilberto were friends when they were little, in São Paulo. Now he's here. He's our age, but he doesn't go to school, he works. Tia Glória thinks he deals drugs, but Andrea says that's not true.

I count out the money we've made so far. "Twenty-two cruzeiros and fifty centavos. Not bad," I say. "It will add up." I don't want Andrea to give up. I need to get to England.

A man in a flowered shirt approaches our table. I'd noticed him watching us from the *barraca* across the street. "I want to send a special letter to my lover."

"This one is mine," Andrea says, picking up her pen.

"*Querida* Filó, I miss your hands on my body."

I'm glad Andrea's the one writing. Something about this man makes me uncomfortable.

"Eu quero chupar tua buceta." I want to suck your pussy.

I look away. Andrea writes it all down. She doesn't seem to mind.

"You drive me crazy, *sua ninfeta gostosa,* you delicious

nymph." The man's voice is hoarse. He's fiddling with his zipper.

Andrea's so busy writing, she doesn't notice. "How do you spell *ninfeta*?" she asks.

"I think we should stop," I say.

Andrea looks up and sees the man pulling out his penis. "*Filho da puta!*" She crumples up the letter and throws it at him. "That's twenty cruzeiros now! You owe us twenty."

The man closes his zipper, smiling. He walks away without paying.

Andrea runs after him. "Twenty cruzeiros. You owe us."

The man keeps on walking. She grabs his arm, but he shoves her to the side and disappears into the crowd.

Andrea comes back. "*Porra, que filho da puta.* At least with a hand job you know what you're getting into."

"*Com licença,* do you girls have cards? Birthday cards?" A young woman with a thick braid of black hair and wide brown eyes stands in front of us.

"Only letters," Andrea says, her voice huffy. "And it will cost you two cruzeiros. We need the money first, before we write anything."

The woman reaches into her pocket and hands Andrea two cruzeiros. "My daughter, Catarina, turns fifteen tomorrow. I haven't seen her since she was a baby."

"*Ai,*" Andrea says, "*que triste.*"

I give her a look. I told her before we started: We're not supposed to have opinions; we're just scribes.

"What do you want to say?" I ask.

The woman stares straight ahead, silent.

"What did you write last year?" Andrea says, trying to get things started.

"This is my first letter. I couldn't bear to write, before."

The woman massages the side of her neck. "It's easier to forget than to remember."

The accordion player slows down his tune, as if he can sense her sadness.

"Ask her to please forgive me. I was going to send money. Find a way to bring her here. But nothing worked out." She takes out an embroidered handkerchief and dabs her eyes. "I left her in an orphanage. The nuns promised to take good care of her."

"You never went back to visit?" Andrea asks.

"I thought about it. Every year. I bought a bus ticket once. But then I didn't go." Tears stream down the woman's cheeks. "God forgive me. What would I do? Visit and then leave? I don't think I could bear that."

I wonder if that's how Mummy feels. Maybe that's why we don't visit Mita. Maybe it isn't Daddy's job and home leave. Maybe Mummy can't bear it.

"At least you haven't forgotten her," I say, breaking my own rule about staying out of things. "When she gets your letter, she'll know that. It's better than nothing."

"D'you think so?" the woman asks.

"Yes," Andrea says. "The worst is to just disappear."

BY LUNCHTIME, WE HAVE A line of people waiting for us. It seems we are a hit. Maybe because we're young, people don't feel embarrassed asking us to write. More bands arrive, and the fair spills out in all directions, hundreds of *barracas* with food and music and products from the Northeast.

My hand hurts from writing and my T-shirt is wet with sweat. We decide to take a break. We buy ourselves *acarajé* and *cocada.* Andrea sorts through a pile of checkered flannel dresses. "Oh my God, look at these! *Que cafona!*"

"I have a dress like that. Somewhere." Mummy always made us matching São João dresses, even when we didn't match anymore.

The accordion player begins to sing, and I sing along with him, liking the gentle sadness of the song: "*Por falta d'água perdi meu gado, morreu de sede meu alazão . . .*" *Lost my cattle for lack of water, my sorrel died from thirst . . .*

"How do you know all these *caipira* songs?" Andrea says.

"I told you: I am a *caipira.*"

So much in this fair reminds me of Santanésia. Not just the music, but the way people speak. The way they are with one another. I pick up a small clay figurine of Lampião from the stand next to us. "D'you know who this is?" I ask Andrea.

"I have no idea," Andrea says. "Some kind of cowboy?"

"Lampião, the one-eyed bandit. He'd torture his enemies and cut off their tongues. His girlfriend, Maria Bonita, was a *cangaceira* too."

"*Porra,* you know all this country stuff. Can you dance *forró*?" Andrea asks.

I show her the steps. I swirl my skirt the way Mita used to and swivel my hips, and the two of us join the crowd on the dance floor.

After our lunch break, we work nonstop, writing letter after letter.

I look up and notice it's dark. Nine thirty. We fold up our table and pack up our leftover stationery. Andrea counts our money as we wait for the bus. "Forty-five cruzeiros," she says. "In ten years, you'll be in England!"

"That's not funny. Next Sunday we'll make more. This was our first time."

"We have other avenues. Better ones. You're so *careta*. I don't know why you think a hand job is such a big deal."

"I like the fair," I say. All these people here who left the countryside and came to Rio to work. A part of them still lives wherever they came from: Pernambuco, Ceará, Piauí. A part of them never forgets. I'm not the only one who has a broken heart.

WHEN I LET MYSELF IN, Mummy is collecting ashtrays from the living room. "You're late," she says. "We were worried."

"I was at the Feira de São Cristóvão. It took a while."

"Isn't that in the Zona Norte? Is that safe?"

Nothing is safe enough for Mummy. The streets, the vendors, the beach, she's always worried something bad will happen. That's the reason they give for sending Mita away: to keep her safe.

"The *feira* reminds me of Santanésia. The music. The food. *Barracas* selling toys and clay pots, like ours. Why don't you cook with them anymore?"

"People don't eat like that here."

"I miss *xinxim de galinha* and plain old rice and beans." I hate shepherd's pie and Yorkshire pudding.

"Can you bring in the glasses?"

I pick up three empty gin-tonic glasses and follow Mummy into the kitchen. These days Daddy makes one after another, each time in a brand-new glass. It drives Mummy crazy.

"Remember the *cangaceiro* hat Mita loved? There were hundreds of them at the fair."

Mummy smiles. "I haven't thought about that hat in a long time."

Mita wore hers all day long, pretending to be Lampião or Maria Bonita.

"Where is it? Did you throw it away?"

"It's probably packed in a box somewhere."

Packed, just like Mita. They packed up all the things from our old life.

Mummy rinses the glasses, and I dry them. We are both quiet, remembering.

"I've never seen the farm where you grew up. São Paulo isn't far. Why don't we ever go there?"

"There's nothing to see. We didn't own anything. Everyone is dead."

I can feel Mummy closing up. "I have a job at the fair," I say. "Writing letters for people who can't write."

Mummy squeezes the sponge under the running water and doesn't say anything.

"Maybe we could write Mita a letter together?"

Mummy dries her hands and walks out of the kitchen.

Chapter Eighteen

Mr. Walker, the headmaster, picks up the microphone: "I'm afraid I have some sad news to give you . . ." I only half listen. Maybe the queen died, or something. Andrea hasn't arrived yet, and neither has Mr. P. He's supposed to be back from his trip, but he's not in the front row with the other teachers. I can't wait to tell him about my job at the fair.

Mr. P. enters the auditorium from the side door. He's wearing a suit and tie; he's never worn a suit before. He walks onstage and takes over the microphone. He has a tan and looks handsome; wherever he went, it was outdoors. I'm hoping Andrea will come today, though Mondays are iffy. Mr. P. stands silently, looking out at us. There's something somber about his face. He bites his lower lip and transfers the microphone from one hand to the other, then begins to talk. "There's no easy way to say this . . ." He says unfortunately the time has come, he's returning to England; he greatly enjoyed the exchange program, but he must return to his students in the UK. He says he's sad to leave, he's learned so much this year, *blah, blah, blah* . . .

I stop listening. My body shakes and my heart flaps like the wings of a hummingbird. It's so loud it's deafening, this hummingbird. If I had wings, I'd be in the trees, flitting from leaf to leaf, barely landing.

Mr. P. looks at me as he talks, but I'm not there. My body sits on the wooden bench, dressed in my prissy British School of Rio uniform, and maybe he thinks he's talking to me, but he isn't. Mr. Walker takes back the microphone. He says he will miss Mr. P. tremendously, we all will, and he wishes Mr. P. all the best in the future.

Everyone stands up and claps. I stand up and clap. *Clap, clap, clap.* We march to class. I try to slide by Mr. P., or my body does—which is all that is left of me—but he grabs my arm.

"Dolores, can we talk?"

I say no, I have to go. Maybe I say I don't have time, but he doesn't let go of my arm.

"I'm sorry . . . I should have said something before."

I'll keep myself to myself from now on. I twist away from him and run to my place behind the hydrangeas. My heart is wild, like a bird in a house trying to get out and smashing against a window. I don't have anywhere to hide. Mr. P. knows all my places; I showed them to him. I pray he will leave me alone, that he'll at least know that much.

I hear footsteps and the rustle of leaves and then he's standing there. My whole body tightens away from him. I want his eyes to go away.

"Dolores, I'm sorry. I should have explained my situation right away."

Grown-ups do that; they lie. I never want to talk to him again.

"I'm not good at goodbyes," Mr. P. says, his voice low. "The time went by so fast, I lost track. I can be scatterbrained like that. I'm truly sorry."

I cross my arms and say nothing.

"I'm going to miss Brazil, miss you."

Like hell you will, I say inside myself, sounding very English. "Like hell you will." My voice says it out loud before I can stop myself. Mr. P. looks surprised. I sound angry and grown-up. He pulls me to him. I let myself melt against his body and inhale his dried-up-sweat man-smell. He says "I'm sorry" in a whisper that sounds sorry and I can feel his heart beating against mine and before I can prevent it a crying sound comes out of me, a long moan, and then the crying pours out and he holds me and smooths my hair, the way Daddy used to when I couldn't sleep.

"Listen, Dolores, this doesn't have to be forever. I'll give you my address. I'd like to stay in touch." Mr. P. reaches for his briefcase and pulls out his green diary. He writes down his English address and phone number, tears the page from his book, and hands it to me. I put it in my pocket.

Mr. P.'s eyes are kind, and I believe him; a corner of me does.

"You mustn't stop writing," he says. "Promise?"

I can't promise that. I don't want to write anymore, not ever. First Mita doesn't respond, and now this. Writing doesn't change anything.

"The writing is in you. You'll have it long after you've forgotten me."

Mr. P. takes hold of my hand and looks at me sideways, wanting me to smile. He's asking me to be a nice girl, a good girl, all the things he helped me not to be. Now he wants me to follow the rules.

I didn't think he'd go away so soon—maybe not ever. I take back my hand and put it under my armpit. It feels cold. I pretend to listen, but I'm already in my own silence. It's like an atmosphere around me. Mr. P. turned into a grown-up, like all the other grown-ups.

"Are we okay?" Mr. P. asks, and I nod.

"I've been thinking. What if I visit your sister? I can let you know how she is. Would you want me to do that?"

My body twitches: my elbow, behind my knee, my neck.

"I have her address in my diary, I wrote it down." He leafs through the pages of his green leather datebook. "Queen Mary's Hospital for Children, Carshalton, is that it?"

Mr. P. helped me address that first aerogram. I should have done it alone. I should have kept Mita to myself.

My edges start to dissolve. Daddy in the hotel room, telling me Mita isn't coming back. Now I remember. They tricked me. They sent Mita away and didn't tell me until it was too late and she was gone.

"D'you want me to visit her?" Mr. P. says.

Mr. P. would get to see Mita, when I can't. What if he swallowed as if she were a bad taste, the way Daddy does?

"No," I say. "I don't want you to." My heart beats in my neck, in my cheeks, under my eye; it's an escaped hamster of a heart, I can't track it.

"You're upset," Mr. P. says. "Are you sure? I could tell you how she is."

"You would lie."

"Why on earth would I lie?"

"What if she isn't well?" What I mean is: *What if she's dead.* But I can't say that.

"I promise," he says. "To tell you how she is. Even if the news is bad."

I promise. People say that to each other. I used to believe promises were sacred, that God or the spirits were watching. *I promise from the bottom of my heart.* When we were little, we'd say that with a graveness that counted. I don't believe in promises anymore.

Chapter Nineteen

I stand by the school gate watching the traffic, the passersby, the police station across the street. The car horns, the shouts of children in the playground, everything sounds far away. The bee next to my ear hovers with no sound. The bottom window of the police station is black. It's been covered by a blanket. Andrea told me that means someone's being tortured. If they're screaming, I don't hear them.

"Psst! Psst!"

Something hits me on the head with a *ping.* A huge seed. Then another. I look up. Andrea, sitting on a branch of the almond tree, eating a *sapucaia.* The red straps of her bikini show under her dress. She signals for me to join her. It would take energy to resist. I climb up and balance myself on the branch next to her.

"What's wrong?" Andrea says. "You look upset."

"Mr. P. is leaving. Back to England. Today's his last day. They announced it in assembly."

"That's how you found out?"

"Yes."

"He should have told you," Andrea says. "He should have told you ahead of time."

Grown-ups never do. They never tell you the most important things. The window of the police station is no longer covered. A guard paces up and down in front of the building with his machine gun. A toy soldier in front of a toy police station. Everything feels plastic and fake.

Andrea puts her arms around me. "*Ei!*" she says. "You're in a trance. Come back." She smells of Johnson's baby oil and tangerines. Andrea is not plastic. She could never be plastic. She's too full of energy, too full of life. It's exhausting.

"Are you sad?" she asks.

The answer is obvious.

Andrea reaches over and strokes my hand, but I barely feel it. Mita's hand was like that when it got paralyzed; I would pick it up and let it fall, and she wouldn't even notice.

Andrea leans in close; I can feel her breath. "*Ei!* Your eyes look strange. It's like your soul flew away."

"Maybe that's what happened." I think of urubus, the way they fly in circles above a dead animal. Maybe my soul is up there, flying in circles.

Andrea pulls out a cigarette stub and lights it with a match. She takes a quick inhale, then offers it to me. I shake my head no. I don't have the energy to smoke. We sit quietly and watch the police station as if it's a film that's about to begin, but nothing happens.

"I know what to do," Andrea says after a while. "It will help, I promise."

She jumps from the tree to the top rung of the gate, then down into the street. I do the same. It's a relief to move my body through space, to follow her without thinking. Away from school, away from Mr. P.

We catch the bus to Ipanema. Andrea holds on to the rusty metal pole, but I don't bother. The bus is so crowded, the press of bodies holds me in place. I lose myself in the rhythm of stops and starts, the smell of sweat and perfume, the screech of brakes and car horns.

"Our stop. Arpoador." Andrea's voice breaks my trance. She pushes me forward and we make our way to the front of the bus and out, onto the sidewalk. The wind rushes at us, whipping my hair sideways and my stupid school tie, which I can't pull off because it's sewn onto the dress.

The waves are huge. The surfers paddle out in front and wait for the right moment, just before the tunnel of water crashes down. It used to be fun, to catch waves, but now it seems silly.

"We have to go to the very top," Andrea says, pointing to the rocky side of Arpoador. It isn't high, but it's windy, and has the roughest seas in Rio. That's why the surfers come here. The waves course in all the way from Greenland, with no land to slow them down.

I follow Andrea as she makes her way up the overgrown path, trying not to step on the cactus shrubs. I'm not sure why I'm going on this hopeless expedition. Mita isn't coming back. She could be dead. Mr. P. is gone.

A wall of wind pushes against us as we climb. I hear Mr. P.'s voice: *Unfortunately, the time has come.* I hear Daddy: *Mita isn't coming back. Better for all of us.* Andrea stops and waits for me to catch up. The path gets narrower and narrower and disappears into a series of ledges and mossy rocks. "It's slippery here." Andrea takes off her sandals and hides them in a crevice between two boulders. I push mine in next to hers.

The rocks are rough. Granite. Granite and quartz. All the mountains in Rio come from a huge volcanic explosion five hundred million years ago. I see blood on my toe, but I don't feel pain. I follow Andrea.

We pass a rusty sign that says DANGER. DO NOT PASS THIS POINT. RISK OF DEATH, with a skull and bones underneath the writing. Andrea keeps climbing. We make our way out to the farthest point, overlooking Praia do Diabo, where only a few crazy fishermen ever go. The waves slam into the rocks and explode into hundreds of tiny diamonds, then the sea sucks backward into a swirling foam.

Andrea pulls out a white handkerchief and holds it above her head. The wind whips it forward and she lets it go. The handkerchief sails in the air, swiveling and turning like an acrobatic bird.

"It's the right kind of day," she says. "The wind has to be steady and strong for this to work."

"For what to work?"

"It's called Leaning into the Wind," Andrea says, looking out at the open sea. Her hair blows behind her like a curtain. "You have to trust God. Or Iemanjá or the wind. Something. You have to trust life."

I don't trust life. Andrea, of all people, should know that.

Andrea walks to the farthest edge. She turns and looks at me, her back to the sea.

"Stand next to me. Open your arms, like Cristo Redentor." Her voice is a magnetic force, keeping me here, in this world.

I stand next to her on the lip of the rock and stretch my arms wide. I do it even though it's scary. Last week a tourist died here. He slipped on the rocks and was taken by a riptide.

"Now lean backward. If the wind stops, we fall and die. If it doesn't, we live."

"This is crazy," I say. Sofia always said Andrea has no common sense.

"Just wait. You'll see that it works."

Andrea leans backward, into the sheer drop below. She tips and I pull her back. I don't want her to die.

"You can't do that," she says. "That's the deal: You can't interfere with fate."

The roar of the waves is loud. The wind slaps against my shoulders. My hair blows forward and whips at the sides of my face. I lean backward.

"Let go," Andrea says. "You need to let go, completely."

My stomach churns. I press my eyes closed. The wind gives, and I'm suspended like a kite, half falling, half flying. Mita should have been the one to have this life, not me. I wait to hit the rocks, to feel the sharp, absolute blackness. But the wind holds strong, and Andrea and I sail, two flags at the edge of the cliff.

I'm afraid to open my eyes. After a few moments, I look at Andrea. She's at an impossible angle: If there's a shift in the wind, we'll tumble. But we don't. A band of yellow-billed terns fly above us, almost close enough to touch. The wind picks up and presses against our backs and tips us forward. And then, almost gently, we land on the rocks, on our knees.

Andrea has a peaceful, lazy smile on her face.

"You look high," I say. "I can't believe we did that."

"God chose for us to live," she says.

Andrea turns and sits facing the sea. She wipes the dirt

from her knees, picking out the slivers of rock that have dug themselves into her skin.

"Do your fingers tingle with life? And behind your knees?" She opens and closes her hands.

"Yes," I say, noticing a thread of energy there.

Andrea smiles. "Your soul came back."

Maybe one of those yellow-billed terns swooped in and delivered me my soul, opening its beak and placing it gently on the rock beside me. "Maybe it did," I say.

Andrea takes hold of my hand and we sit there, watching the surfers glide in. "Men are like that," she says. "They leave without warning."

So much of life happens without warning. It's a strange expression.

"My father left," Andrea says, throwing a stone into the sea below. "And Luciana's ex-boyfriend disappeared, on the day of their engagement party. And now Mr. P. We don't need them, you know? We really don't need them."

Andrea's right. I feel in my pocket for the piece of paper with Mr. P.'s address. *Michael Parker, Summerhill School, Suffolk, England,* written in Mr. P.'s messy scrawl. I hold it above me in the air and let the wind take it. I watch it fly around like a tiny kite, then nose-dive into the rocks below.

Chapter Twenty

SANTANÉSIA

Mita was shivering. I curled around her, but she didn't warm up. After a while, I turned so we were back to back. She kept on shivering. It was hard to sleep. I slid over to my own bed.

The next morning, when I reached for Mita, her skin was clammy. I thought she'd caught Elói's cold. There was a quiet motor in her body. "Mita?" I could hear the woodpecker like a machine gun, outside our window. No answer.

The minute Mummy came in, she wrapped a blanket around Mita, made her sit up, and yelled for Daddy to get Dr. Miguel. Something was wrong. I should have seen it. Mita continued to tremble. Then she held her arm stiffly out in front of her, fingers splayed like a starfish. Dr. Miguel came over and gave her an injection, but it didn't help. "How long has it been going on?" Dr. Miguel asked.

"Since this morning. She woke up like this," Mummy said.

I was afraid to tell them that Mita had been shivering all night. I should have known it wasn't a cold.

After a while, Dr. Miguel didn't have to say it: Daddy lifted Mita and took her to the car while Mummy packed a suitcase. I wanted to go with them, but they said I had to stay home with Aparecida.

Mita was in the hospital for a long time. I didn't count time then, but it was weeks, maybe a month. We turned ten, and Mita was still there. Aparecida baked me an orange cake with chocolate frosting and two candles. I blew them both out, but it wasn't a real birthday.

Mummy lived in a hotel in Rio. Daddy drove back and forth. Each time he came home, his mood was worse. He didn't know how he was supposed to do his job on top of all of this. He poured himself a whisky in the middle of the day, then sat on the veranda and smoked.

"When is Mita coming back?" Aparecida told me not to ask. She said Daddy would tell me when he knew. But I had to ask.

Daddy stared at the banana trees.

Aparecida was making *pasteizinhos.* I helped her fill each one and pinched the edges in. She slid the tray into the oven, then she gave me one of her Aparecida hugs where we hugged and swayed as if we were dancing.

The days were like that, waiting for Mita to come home. Slow and empty.

At night we called Mummy on the phone. I always said

hello, but I learned not to ask about Mita, because all I got was silence. Mainly Daddy talked. Sometimes he held the phone away from his ear. He'd hang up, and seconds later, Mummy would call back. There was a lot of that.

I watched *novelas,* even the ones on late at night. Daddy let me stay up as long as I wanted. One time, he arrived from Rio, poured himself a whisky, and went straight to the bedroom, without eating dinner. Claudinha came over to play, and Elói. But I felt lonely. I'd never realized before what a force Mita was; it was hard to play without her energy to push against. I preferred to be alone.

After a long while, Daddy called from Rio and said Mita was coming home. She'd be arriving in a company car, with Mummy and a driver. He had to stay in town for some meetings.

Aparecida and I weren't sure when they would arrive, so we took turns checking. We didn't know what a company car looked like. I imagined it would be two stories high and wide, like a company, but it was a gray Mercedes-Benz. We saw it round the hill.

The Mercedes-Benz slid quietly into our driveway, Mita and Mummy in the back seat. I ran over and opened the door. Mita looked sleepy.

"Don't just sit there," I said.

"Wait up, Dolores." Mummy unlocked her door, and the driver helped her lift a package from the trunk. The driver was an official chauffeur, with a dark blue hat.

"Do you have toys?" I asked Mita. Last time, Mita came

back from the hospital with a huge Topo Gigio. Mita didn't answer. Then I noticed how quiet her legs were. Both of them; not just the twisted one.

The folded metal package opened sideways into a wheelchair. Mummy pressed the seat down to make it flat. I never knew a wheelchair could fold up like an accordion. She wheeled the chair over to Mita's side of the car, then the chauffeur picked Mita up in his arms and placed her in the chair. The process was awkward; Mita didn't help.

Mummy said thank you very much and the gray Mercedes backed up and disappeared down the hill. Mummy pushed Mita and the wheelchair toward the front door.

We had to maneuver the steps. We didn't know yet that you had to tip the wheelchair backward at an angle and push, so we struggled. Aparecida lifted the front while Mummy and I lifted the back. Mita sat there, not moving.

Aparecida made us black beans and rice, and Mita ate from the tray balanced across her legs, using her good hand. The other one stayed curled up, like a knot. When she finished, I went over and squeezed Mita's good hand. Mita squeezed back.

She didn't smile. Maybe her face was paralyzed. I wasn't sure which parts of her worked and which parts were broken.

"Can you feel this?" I asked, pulling Mita's little toe, then the second, then the third. None of her toes worked.

"What about this?" I tickled her belly button.

Mita sucked her stomach inward. "Stop," she said. She hated anyone touching her belly button.

I was glad there was a part of Mita that was still Mita.

"Dolores, leave Mita alone," Mummy said. "We should put on her boots."

"She can't walk. Why does she have to wear boots?"

"Because she has to," Mummy said. "Or her feet will get worse."

"They already don't work; how can they get worse?"

Mummy didn't answer.

I wondered if Daddy knew about her legs not working; he was still away at those meetings. I imagined that he did.

We cleared space. We cleared space in the living room so the wheelchair could be next to the sofa, as if it were a normal chair. We cleared space around the dining room table so Mita could wheel herself close—though she usually wanted to sit separately, with a tray on her lap. We cleared space in the bathroom. I had to put all our toys away, every single marble, even the bathroom mat had to go, because the wheels could get caught and tip her over.

When Daddy arrived from Rio, he was in a company car with a chauffeur. Mita lost her legs, but we had a company car, which arrived then disappeared, like a gray shark into the horizon.

Daddy didn't seem surprised by the wheelchair. He didn't mention it. We acted as if it had always been there.

"Mita looks a bit subdued," he said.

"It's a lot to get used to," Mummy said. That was as close as we came to saying anything. I wanted to ask about brain damage. I'd heard Mummy tell Celina that Mita's fit had caused brain damage. But it didn't seem like the moment was right.

Mummy tucked a cotton blanket around Mita's legs; they were always cold. I didn't understand why Mita couldn't walk, but I didn't ask. It was not something you asked. I was learning that you do not talk about certain things: important things. I knew it in my bones, that it would be too sad.

Daddy said the company was helping with arrangements.

"Arrangements for what?" I said, worried Mita was going to die. Maybe they were talking about her funeral.

"We're getting a car," Daddy said. "A Vemaguet Rio. One of the new ones, with front-hinge doors and a hatchback."

"We can't afford that," Mummy said. "The car has to work, but it doesn't have to be new."

"Don't worry," Daddy said. "I'm working it out. Believe it or not, despite those bloody demonstrations, business is good. There's talk of a promotion. I don't want to count my chickens, but the political shake-up could be good news."

Mita didn't shake anymore, quite the opposite: She sat very still, in her wheelchair.

We parked her. We parked her mainly by the window, but also under trees in the shade. It was only a while later, after the wheelchair became a normal part of the furniture, that I realized Mita had stopped talking. And laughing. We were so busy adjusting to everything. We focused on details. Mummy lined the safety belt with flannel so it wouldn't cut into her when she leaned forward. I arranged Mita's feet on the pedals and tried to make sure they were comfortable. I brought her bits and pieces from the outside world: a snail, mating butterflies. She barely responded. When I asked her questions, she didn't answer, didn't even try. It became obvious, what I hadn't wanted to admit.

"Mita can't talk anymore," I announced, as if it were a fact. Her voice had gone, like her legs.

"I can," Mita said. It surprised us. We laughed.

"I'm glad to hear it," Daddy said.

Mita smiled. She didn't laugh, but she smiled.

She was still there, inside herself, inside the package of the wheelchair. She was still there. A huge sadness gripped my throat and pressed itself behind my eyes. There had been so many adjustments since the hospital, I hadn't left any space for it before.

That night, I crossed over to her bed. I snuggled around her, the way we always did, but hadn't done since the wheelchair. I'd been afraid of her too-quiet legs. I carefully placed my right leg on top of hers. She didn't respond in any way. Her feet didn't find mine, and she didn't push back against me so I could find myself; find the place where she stopped, and I began. There was just stillness. I wanted to pull away, but I didn't. Her legs and her feet were cold. I warmed them with my heat, and after a while they seemed more familiar. She reached over and found my hand and placed it on her belly, where she liked it. I pressed my nose into the space between her shoulder blades and for the first time in that whole month since she'd come back, I felt peaceful.

Chapter Twenty-one

MARCH 1973

When I arrive home from Andrea's, Mummy is waiting at the front door: "What have you and that friend of yours, Andrea, been up to?" she asks, her face all angles.

"Nothing."

"Don't lie. What did you do?"

"We watched *Irmãos Coragem*."

"That's not it," Mummy says, "you know it's not."

"We bought bras."

Mummy's heart-shaped amethyst earrings glint as she shakes her head. "Don't lie." She grabs my shoulder with her pointy nails. "Priscilla's mother called. She said you brought pornography to school."

"That was ages ago! We found a photo on the street, that's all," I whisper.

"Priscilla's mother said you were behind this. You and that Andrea."

"Priscilla wanted to see the photograph—we didn't force her." I can't believe Priscilla's causing trouble like this. "She was super interested, actually," I say.

Mummy pushes me hard against the wall, bumping my funny bone. She's never pushed me before. "How could you? How could you do this to us?"

"I'm sorry. It was an accident."

"Who is this Andrea? I've never seen her anywhere. I'm so embarrassed." Mummy's lips quiver; she's about to cry. Cry about this when she doesn't cry about Mita. All she cares about is Daddy's job and what people think.

The next morning at school, Douglas tells me to report to Mr. Walker's office. He makes a slicing action across his throat. The English girls whisper as I pass them in the corridor. I hold my head up high, as if I have requested this meeting myself. That's what Andrea will do when she arrives. She'll treat it like a joke.

I've never been to the headmaster's office. Queen Elizabeth stares at me from behind Mr. Walker's head.

"Sit down, Dolores." Mr. Walker looks at me with his floating blue eyes. "I have a delicate matter to discuss with you." He strokes the wooden desk with his long fingers. "This is quite unpleasant, I must say. But we might as well get to the bottom of it."

I think of the naked bottoms in the photograph, the funny look one of the women had in her eyes. Vague and cloudy, the way a fish scans you without seeming to see you. Queen Elizabeth looks like that.

Mr. Walker picks up my report card and studies it. His pale skin is dotted with thousands of freckles. Maybe they'll join up one day and make him black. He would look better black.

"What do you know about this Andrea Santos?" Mr. Walker asks, mispronouncing Andrea's name with his English accent. "Did she bring the pornography?"

Mr. Walker pronounces every syllable: *por-nog-ra-phy*.

"No, sir. I found it. On the street. While we were waiting for the bus. Someone must have dropped it."

"Where were you, to find a photo like that?" Mr. Walker studies Sir Winston Churchill, on the wall behind me. Churchill was honorable: It was thanks to him we won the war.

"We were at the bus stop, by Andrea's house. It isn't her fault, sir. She lives there."

Mr. Walker squints. "Look here, Dolores," he says. "I know your father. We play tennis together. You're a quiet girl—not a troublemaker. This is the first time you've been involved in anything like this." He shuffles the papers on his desk. I try to spot Andrea's report card. She's probably standing outside, waiting for her turn. The thought of her cheers me up.

"I've decided to put you on probation for the rest of the year," Mr. Walker says.

Thank you, God. Andrea and I can live with probation. Marcos is on probation; so is Rodrigo. You don't get thrown out of school; it's more like a warning. They give you extra chores, and you're not allowed to go on school trips. Daddy will be furious about it, of course—but maybe I can convince Mummy not to tell him. He's so tense about work and politics these days, she'll do anything not to set him off. Mr. Walker might be a problem. He plays tennis at the club with

Daddy. But I don't think he'd bring it up; he'd be too embarrassed.

"Thank you, sir. It won't happen again," I say. "You can be sure of that." I'm almost giddy with excitement. Andrea will laugh. Probation is no big deal.

"Andrea has been expelled," Mr. Walker says. "She will not be returning to this school."

My throat burns, my hands start to shake. "No—that's not fair," I say. I don't care that Mr. Walker is our headmaster. "You can't do that."

Mr. Walker's cheeks turn bright red between his freckles. He says it isn't "smart" of me to choose friends like Andrea, he hopes I will learn a lesson from this incident.

"Expel me too, then. I'm just as guilty as Andrea. Expel me!" I shout.

Mr. Walker adjusts his jaw the way boxers do after they've been knocked down. He stands up. If he tries to hit me, I'll hit him back. I'm not afraid. Not one bit.

Mr. Walker walks over to the door and closes it, then returns to his chair. "Don't be silly," he says. "You're a gullible child. That girl has led you astray."

"Please, sir, don't expel her. It was me. I'm the one who found it."

"Dolores, I am not going to expel you. You should be grateful. I'm giving you a second chance. You're dismissed."

There's a dark blue bottle of Parker ink sitting by the blotting paper; I consider pouring it all over his desk, over his face, over the walls. I don't want a second chance. I stare at the ink. My breath presses against my chest. If only Mr. P. were here. But he isn't. I stand up and leave.

I lock myself in the girls' bathroom. My stomach cramps

and my throat burns. That's what they do, grown-ups. They send people away, just like that. It isn't right.

I sit on the bathroom floor and hug my knees and wait until lunch break. Then I jump the school gate and head to the bus stop. The 39 bus goes to Andrea's house. A 36 bus passes, then a 72. Finally, a 39. I try to calm myself as the bus inches its way toward the mountains. They can't expel her and not me. It's the two of us or nothing.

I RING THE DOORBELL. I hear Andrea's laugh and some scuffling. The door stays closed. I ring again. My finger is slippery with sweat. I walk right up to the eye, which Tia Glória uses to check if it's one of her customers. I sense Andrea on the other side. I knock.

The door opens a crack. Andrea. With someone, I can't see who. A hand on her breast.

"I'm a little busy right now." Andrea giggles. "*Porra, menino,* stop! Is this an emergency?"

"Yes. It is an emergency."

Andrea opens the door. "What's up?" Gilberto stands behind her. Andrea jangles the bracelets on her arm as he kisses her neck. I try to ignore him.

"I'm sorry about what happened. It's not fair. I should have been expelled too."

Andrea shrugs. "I don't care. I hate school anyway. I'm glad it happened." Gilberto bites Andrea's neck, and she yelps. "Sorry," she laughs. "D'you want to come in?"

"That's okay," I say. I don't want to be here while she makes out with Gilberto. "I'll call you later."

When I get home, I go straight to Aparecida's room, even though it's her afternoon off and she's with João. I lie on her straw mattress, liking the spiky roughness of it and the smell of almond oil. I reach under the bed into her basket and feel for the figurine, the little Iemanjá figurine Aparecida holds when she is at the end of her rope. I hold it in my fist and stare at the ceiling and wait.

When Aparecida comes in, she sits on the bed next to me. She doesn't ask me what happened, she can tell I don't want to talk. She smooths my hair and hums, the way she used to when Mita and I were little.

Chapter Twenty-two

SANTANÉSIA

I'd uncurl Mita's fingers and flatten out her hand. *Stay. Stay like that.* Mita's fingers would curl themselves back in. *Come on, Mita. Try.* Mita would try. She'd grip with her mouth and grunt, but her fingers wouldn't listen.

Then I tried something else: I opened the palm of her hand and traced a circle, singing *Round and round the garden, like a teddy bear,* and maybe it was the song or maybe it was the touch of my fingers or maybe it was just a miracle! Mita's hand stayed open.

I did this day after day after day. Mita sang with me. *One step, two step, and tickly under there,* and Mita would laugh.

Mita could straighten her fingers and hold things. She began to push herself on the wheelchair. "Bloody hell," Daddy said. "It actually works."

Mita could wheel herself to the window or to the kitchen. If Aparecida was making *pasteizinhos,* Mita could surprise us and suddenly be there, in her wheelchair; she didn't have to wait for us to remember her.

And then, after one of Mita's long fits, the song stopped working. Her fingers locked in a tight fist that wouldn't come undone. Mummy told me to leave Mita alone, don't hurt her. But I couldn't leave Mita alone. I tried and tried and tried.

But the song never worked again.

Chapter Twenty-three

MARCH 1973

The accordion player waves at me as I set up my table. "Where's your friend?" he asks.

"It's only me today," I say, trying to sound matter-of-fact. All week, Andrea hasn't answered my calls. Now she isn't here. She said she wasn't angry, but obviously she is.

I organize the paper and the envelopes, and a queue starts to form. Word is out that we charge less than the official writers, so there's no shortage of customers. I write letter after letter. Some people I recognize from previous weeks: the woman with the missing tooth, and the two boys looking for their father. But there are others; it seems there's no end to longing.

I work all day and don't stop for lunch. The more money I make, the sooner I get to England. I looked up Carshalton in the atlas. It's outside London, in the countryside. Queen Mary's Hospital for Children, Carshalton. I try not to think about what I'll do if Mita isn't there.

Last week the fair felt like a party, but today it seems sad. Everyone coming to get a little taste of something or someone they miss. But the truth is, it's just a taste. Their old life is gone. I try not to think about Andrea. In a few days she'll forgive me. She doesn't stay mad long.

By late afternoon I only have two sheets of paper, and no more envelopes. I have to go home for supplies. Daddy still has tons of paper and envelopes from when he worked for the paper mill. He was friendly to me at breakfast; Mummy decided not to tell him. She said Daddy had a lot on his plate, she didn't want to add probation to the list. Her voice was cold, and she barely looked at me.

I count my money: seventy-eight cruzeiros. Almost double what we made last week. It could have been more if I'd planned better.

They're having their before-dinner drink when I get home. I walk up to Mummy.

"Is Margarita dead?"

Mummy puts down her sherry glass so hard the tiny stem snaps. It is her favorite, the violet one made of Czechoslovakian crystal, and she bursts into tears. Real tears. Not the quiet sniffles she hides in her pretty handkerchiefs.

Daddy glares at me. "Now look what you've done."

Shards of violet crystal glint on the floor.

"You say she's in the hospital, but I don't believe you. She must be dead."

"You're despicable," Daddy says. "Upsetting your mother this way. I knew the bloody aerograms were a mistake."

I look at the two of them, my mother and father, sitting

there on the sofa. I don't know who they are anymore. I don't know the truth of what happens in the world. Police kill people, throw their bodies under bridges, and call it suicide. The government lies. Parents lie.

"I have a right to know what happened to Mita."

Mummy wipes her eyes with a corner of a napkin. "Don't you think we miss her too?"

"Then bring her back."

Daddy chews on his bottom lip and stares at his whisky.

"If she's alive."

"Dammit, Dolores, leave it alone!" Daddy says. "She's in a place that's better for her."

"Then why doesn't anyone at the hospital answer my aerograms?"

"They must be busy," says Mummy.

"They? You don't even know who they are! How could you send Mita to live with complete strangers?"

Daddy's eyes tear up. This is my chance.

"Please, Daddy. I can't bear to live without Mita."

He pulls out his handkerchief and wipes his forehead.

Mummy leans over to pick up a shard of glass. "It's everywhere. I'll get the vacuum cleaner."

"For Chrissakes, stop being so selfish. Why don't you think of others for a change?" Daddy finishes his whisky in one gulp. "Don't you think it was hard for Mita, day after day, trying to keep up with you?"

I don't answer. The truth is, I've never thought about it that way. Maybe I am selfish. But I want her back. More than anything in the world.

I go to my room and lock the door. I open the *Concise Oxford English Dictionary* Mr. P. gave me. *Despicable:* "deserving of hatred and contempt." The example is in quotation marks: "A despicable crime." I sit at my nice white desk, which I'm ungrateful for, reading this dictionary that tells me I'm a criminal, and it feels true. There's something sharp and right about that word. *An eye for an eye, a tooth for a tooth.* People say that. I imagine my mouth with hundreds of tiny, pointed teeth, like piranha teeth—that's how ugly and despicable I am.

I reach for a notebook from my set of six, each one a different color. I choose black.

I uncap my fountain pen and lie on my bed—I don't care if the pen leaks and stains my bedcover.

> *She looks like an ordinary girl. If you looked at her you wouldn't know how despicable she is. You might just see a shy girl drawing in her notebook, or watching other girls play hopscotch, or staring at the sea . . .*

THE NEXT DAY AT SCHOOL, I'm still thinking about that word, *despicable.* The girls hover in groups, the way they always do, and the boys play by the wall. I walk across the playground, imagining I am guilty of murder: a despicable girl headed to the guillotine.

The bell rings. The beginning of another interminable day. That's another word I've learned from my dictionary: *interminable.* Endless.

Instead of class, there's a school-wide assembly. Mr. Walker announces that we are celebrating the vernal equinox. He says there are two moments in the year when the sun is exactly above the equator and day and night are of equal length. Today, in England, is one of those moments.

"Although the seasons are different here in the southern hemisphere, we follow the British calendar. Children in England plant tulip bulbs in spring." Mr. Walker runs his fingers through his thin blond hair. He says that we will be planting snapdragons and begonias, because tulips don't grow in the tropics.

We file out into the playground. I get in the begonia queue. Mr. Walker comes over and says: "Not you, Dolores. Come with me."

I follow him upstairs to his room.

"Probation students don't participate in celebrations," Mr. Walker says. "They clean up." He opens the bottom drawer of his desk and hands me a large black rubbish bag. "Hold it open," he says. He picks up the wicker bin and empties the *lixo* into the bag. "I want every classroom spick-and-span. Empty the bins, clear the drawers and the shelves, throw out old pencils, small pieces of chalk, leftover papers. Understand?"

"Yes, sir."

"I hope you are keeping your distance from that girl Andrea?"

I hold the rubbish bag in front of me and stay silent. He was wrong to expel Andrea. Wrong.

Mr. Walker looks at his watch. "I'll see you back here in an hour."

"Yes, sir." As long as I can be alone, I don't mind cleaning up.

I start in the lab room, straightening out the test tubes and lining up the Bunsen burners. I empty the bin and organize the papers on Mrs. Oliveira's desk into a neat pile. I open her drawer and push the rulers to one end, and the pens and erasers to the other. I throw away some elastic bands, a cracked marble, and a confiscated paper plane. I look around. It looks good.

Then I move to math. Mr. Williams is tidy. His drawer is empty. Just the rubbish and it's done.

Now English. Every morning Mr. P. began class by writing a poem on the blackboard. Sometimes they were funny limericks, and sometimes they broke my heart. He pressed down so hard as he wrote, the chalk often snapped.

I walk to the blackboard and find a row of the broken pieces on the ledge. I throw every one of them out.

The black of the blackboard isn't pure black. The ghosts of all the poems that were once there still hover, too faint to see. But you can feel them.

I move on to his desk. A narrow silver Biro sits forgotten by a pad of yellow lined paper. Mr. P.'s lucky pen. His initials, M. P., engraved along the barrel. I can't believe he left his favorite pen. I pick it up, liking the weight of it. I write my name diagonally across the page. Not following the rules, the way he taught me. The pen still has ink. I think of throwing it out, but then I slide it into my pocket.

I pull open the drawer. It's full. Two more Biros (neither of those works).

Times/Bartholomew Guide to Brazil, 1970. Some blue books. I open one of them and my heart swerves. Horses. Flowers. A wheelchair. My drawings.

It should have been me. I wonder if she's dead.

I can't believe Mr. P. left my essays at school, for anyone to read. "I will hold on to these, Dolores, I won't forget you. I'll find your sister. We can stay in touch." His voice sounded genuine. He didn't even bother to take them with him.

My hands shake as I sift through the other blue books;

they are all mine. The essay I wrote about my body and how I worried I would become crooked too, just like Mita. The essay about the ant hospital, and the essay about São João. He left them all.

I find a small datebook with a green leather cover. I open it and see various notes and addresses, in Mr. P.'s handwriting. Then I read:

> *She's a strange girl, twelve years old and illiterate. Brilliant in some ways, concrete in others. I'm not sure what's possible for her.*

Toward the middle of the book, I find a page with *Queen Mary's Hospital for Children,* underlined. A sharp pain throbs by my eyes, at the back of my neck. I throw the green datebook into the rubbish bag.

I throw my blue books inside too, and everything that's in the drawer. I dump it without sorting through. I don't care if there's something precious there, I just don't care. I run down the stairs, my legs so light I almost trip. I run to the huge metal dustbin behind the school, lift the lid, and throw my plastic rubbish bag inside. My heart pounds. Done. I am done with this cleaning.

I can't be here. I need to leave. But the gate is locked. And the students are everywhere, planting begonias. All of me trembles, like an overheated motor.

I run to the coatroom, grab my satchel from its peg, and lock myself in the girls' bathroom. I sit there on the toilet with my legs up, hugging my knees, and wait and wait, until the final bell rings.

Chapter Twenty-four

SANTANÉSIA

I was ten years old, and I didn't think of myself as a girl. I was a man-girl, playing dice. Daddy said I could come inside the clubhouse and have my beer only when I was dry, so I jumped up and down, waiting for the sun to dry my body and warm the goosebumps away. Then I slid onto the stool next to him, my pink T-shirt on top of my yellow bikini, hoping the wet stain didn't look too much like breasts. I wanted to be one of the men, and they treated me like one, offering me beer, and sometimes cigarettes. Mita didn't get to come anymore; it was only me who had this privilege. If Mummy walked in, everything would change. The men would stand up and offer her a seat, there'd be no rude jokes or accusations. I liked it that, with me, life continued as normal. I could watch the men play and sip my beer. The barman poured it into a small glass, just for me.

There were always peanuts in small wooden bowls on the counter. I rubbed them between my fingers and watched their grape-colored skins peel off like dried flowers. The stools and the bar were covered in fake red leather that smelled of smoke. I loved the sound of dice knocking into each other and sliding against the sides of the leather cups. I tried not to think of Mita, how much she would love to be here with me, watching the men play dice. She couldn't follow the game anymore. Soon it would be Christmas. Mita was still in the horrible wheelchair, and she was getting worse, not better. The medications had stopped working. The fits came two or three times per day, and they lasted longer and longer . . . The doctors in Rio couldn't figure out what was happening. Were the fits causing brain damage, or did Mita already have brain damage and that's what was causing the fits? I was glad to escape into the shade of the bar and listen to the dice.

Each man shook his cup with a different kind of violence. Daddy shook firm and quick, as if he were sure of his luck. He'd turn the cup and not check his throw for the longest time, it was unbearable. Then, casually, he'd sneak a look. It was hard to tell if he was faking or if he had a good hand.

Jurandi, the electrician, rattled his dice in the air, as if they were maracas, then clomped them down on the bar. He'd lift the corner of his cup before the dice whirled to a stop. Daddy watched his little finger like a hawk, because sometimes he'd use it to knock the dice over, to his advantage.

Dr. Miguel swirled the cup neatly and timidly in front of him, afraid the dice might escape. His dice slid into place quietly, making you expect a lower number somehow. It was always surprising when he won—even to him.

Tavares saw himself as the star player. Tavares and Daddy often faced off—especially now, with the demonstrations.

Daddy said Tavares was brewing trouble, he could feel it. Tavares's green eyes were unexpected against his black skin, and his bald head shone under the light of the bar. He liked to chew at the end of his cigar as he made his bet. He shook his cup long and hard, like a machine gun, then stopped suddenly. You never knew what to expect with him.

I wanted to ask Daddy about Xuxú. I was waiting for the right moment because he didn't like being interrupted in the middle of a game. Yesterday, he'd taken us to see a sloth, climbing up the telephone pole outside his office. We'd never seen a sloth before. We named him Xuxú because he was droopy, like the vegetable. Daddy said sloths were lazy, slow animals who slept eighteen hours per day. I'd heard Daddy tell visitors Mita was "slow" or "handicapped." Sometimes he said "mentally retarded." I hated that word. That's what the children in the village called her, *retardada*. Mita tried to say *sloth;* it was a hard word. She finally managed; her voice proud: "Ssslloaaaathhhh." Daddy told me to wipe up her dribble.

I wanted a report on Xuxú's progress, how close he was to reaching the top of the telephone pole. I hadn't had the chance to ask yet.

Tavares used a toothpick to poke at the gold tooth on the left side of his mouth. He didn't look happy.

"You first," he said to Daddy. "Gringos go first."

Daddy shrugged. "Sure, I'd be happy to." He piled all his red chips on the counter in front of him, looking mildly amused.

I could see Jurandi studying Daddy for clues. "*Aquele Ian é demais,*" he said. "You're having us on."

"Maybe," Daddy said. "Maybe not."

Jurandi signaled for another beer. "I'll pass," he said.

Daddy seemed pleased. He drummed the bar with his fingertips, quietly waiting. It was Dr. Miguel's turn.

Dr. Miguel rolled the peanuts between his fingers, edging their fluttery skins off then popping them in his mouth. He barely touched his beer. He picked up six chips and lined them up neatly in front of him.

"This time, Ian, I'm going to call your bluff."

It wouldn't be so bad if Dr. Miguel won. He helped us with Mita's fits; Daddy wouldn't mind losing to him.

Now it was Tavares's turn. Tavares's green eyes snapped from Dr. Miguel to Daddy, then down to his dice. He took all his chips, twelve of them, and placed them in front of him.

Daddy studied his mouth. Tavares's mouth twitched when he was lying, but his lips were quiet. His tongue reached out to lick his top lip. I wanted Daddy to pass. He still could, because Dr. Miguel was in the game.

"C'mon, Ian, what are you afraid of?" Tavares lit a cigar. "Too hot for you here in the tropics?"

Daddy scowled. I could hear the whirl of the fan. A fly landed on Daddy's hand, and he whipped it away. Sweat dribbled down the side of his face. The whole back of his shirt was transparent with sweat.

"Let's take a look, then," Daddy said, his voice flat, as if he wasn't interested. "Let's see who the bullshitters are."

Dr. Miguel lifted his cup: double sixes. He looked up expectantly, waiting to see what Daddy and Tavares would do.

"Go ahead, Ian," Tavares said. "What do you have up your sleeve?"

"You first," Daddy said. "This is your country."

"Bet first, show first," Tavares said. "Those are the rules. Even gringos have to follow the rules."

Daddy lifted his cup up slowly, no expression on his face.

"Bidu," he announced, and made a little salute with his hand. Thank goodness. Bidu beat everything, even double sixes.

Tavares lifted his cup. "Bidu to you," he said, his voice hoarse with excitement. He smiled and ordered a caipirinha. Although it was a tie, I had the impression Tavares had won.

There was a silence in the room. This was my chance to break in.

"Daddy," I said, "did you see Xuxú today?"

Daddy frowned. "Yes," he said. "I did."

"Where is he? Did he get to the top?" Yesterday afternoon, he was only a few meters away.

Daddy began to shake his dice, not looking at me.

"Tell her," Tavares said. "Answer the poor child, she wants to know."

"Yes," Daddy said. "He reached the top, all right."

"Oh good!" He made it. I couldn't wait to see him up there.

"D'you know what happened when he reached the top?" Daddy asked, in a mean voice that made me uncomfortable. He was so moody these days; he could be laughing one moment, furious the next. Mummy said he drank too much.

The men stared and I started to shiver, standing there in the shade in my damp T-shirt.

"Answer me," Daddy said, "answer me when I ask you a question."

"No," I said, "I don't know. I don't know what happened."

"He reached up to the wire and was electrocuted. He fell to the ground dead," Daddy said. "Your darling Xuxú is a dead sloth."

"Cheers to a dead sloth!" Tavares raised his glass, and the barman came over and filled everyone up. "Cheers! Cheers to a dead sloth!" They all laughed.

I stared straight ahead so my tears wouldn't drop and waited for the moment to pass. I wanted to go to the bathroom to cry, but that was the sort of thing girls did. I pretended I was deep underwater where no one could see, where my tears disappeared and all that existed was diamonds of light and ripples of blue green as I sank deeper—to where it was quiet and still. Being underwater is like being in the center of a gem where the blackness glows behind your eyes, even when you keep them closed. I tried not to think of Xuxú bleeding on the ground. I tried not to think of his little pointed face and his three fingers, wrapped around the telephone pole, holding on for dear life. I listened to the men speak from a faraway place, pretending not to care.

THAT NIGHT DADDY WAS QUIET at dinner and didn't finish his steak. Instead of having a brandy in the living room, he took his drink with him to the bedroom. I stood outside the closed door, wondering if he'd be mad if I came in. I pushed open the door; he was on the bed, smoking, and his shoulders were shaking. I thought he was laughing. When I stepped in closer, I saw his eyes were puffy. I'd never seen Daddy cry before.

"Daddy, are you all right?" I asked, feeling as if I might cry too. "What's the matter?"

Daddy stretched out his arm and pulled me next to him on the bed. "I can't bear it," he said. "I can't bear that the poor bloody sloth died." He shook his head from side to side, like he was saying no. "I should have stopped it, somehow. I should have done something."

Chapter Twenty-five

MARCH 1973

My essays were private, the most private things I've ever shown anyone. I find a stretch of beach without surfers, open my satchel, and take out my notebooks. I tear out each page: All the hypotheses, essays, and drawings I've ever made. The horses, the flowers, the theory about perpetual motion and the imaginary *Chacrinha* episode; Andrea's favorite. I read it, as if I'm reading something written by some other girl. An imaginary reunion between separated twins, with the Chacretes dancing in the background in their high-heeled boots and hot pants.

How dumb. I scrunch up that essay too and throw it in the pile with the other scrunched-up pages. Then I throw them all into the sea. The waves toss them back and forth, then swallow them up. I'm done with writing.

I look out at the horizon. Mita and I used to think we could reach it, like touching the end of a rainbow. But that was an illusion. Just like writing aerograms or trying to get to England by writing letters. None of those things are possible. Andrea was right. The only way out is to sell my body. It's the only thing I have of value, it seems. I don't care anymore. I'll do it; if it gets me to Mita, I'll do it.

It's dark when I get home. I almost don't see it, the cream-colored envelope on the side table: *Queen Mary's Hospital for Children* printed in the left-hand corner.

Mita. She wrote back. She's alive.

My body feels electric. A huge gladness swirls inside of me, thank you. Thank you, God. Even though I don't believe in God. Blood pulses in my fingertips. The envelope smells of dust.

I sit down on the sofa and read my name: *Dolores Hamilton,* in capital letters. Blue ink. The letters are symmetrical, like bricks; they don't have much personality. I touch the letters as if they could speak, afraid to open the envelope.

I pull out a flat card, the same color as the envelope, with only a few lines:

> *Dear Dolores,*
>
> *How are you? Thank you for writing. I am fine.*
>
> *Love,*
> *Maggie*

Maggie? Three lines. This can't be. This is a mistake. Maggie isn't Margarita. Daddy must have given me the wrong address. The card in front of me begins to dissolve, or maybe I'm the one who is dissolving.

I run to their room. Mummy stands in front of the mirror, holding her dangling amethyst earrings by her earlobes as Daddy ties the back of her halter-neck long-dress. Daddy looks up. "What's wrong?"

I hand him the card. So much is wrong.

"Well, that's nice," he says after reading it. "At least they responded."

"It's not her."

"What d'you mean, it's not her?"

"It's not from Mita. Look. Look at the signature. It says: *Maggie.*"

"Maggie's a nickname. Short for Margaret."

"Her name is not Maggie." My voice trembles with rage. "Her name is not Margaret. Her name is Margarita—*ta*," I say again, for emphasis. "*Margari-TA!*"

"Dolores, we're getting ready." Mummy points to my bare feet. "You're making a mess. Rinse your feet."

All she cares about is her fancy party.

Daddy gives me back the card. "At least she's fine. That's the main point."

"Do we have enough champagne?" Mummy says.

"More than enough."

My body veers from hot to cold. "How would you like it if someone called you by the wrong name?"

"Dolores, you're making a mountain out of a molehill. It's a nickname. The point is—she's well."

"A name is a person, it's who they are. Now even that is gone."

"It's never enough with you, is it? You're lucky they wrote back." Daddy walks over to the safe. "The imperial topaz?"

"It's too much, Ian," Mummy says.

"At least the diamond." Daddy rotates the dial of the combination lock.

"Not the diamond either. People will think we're swimming in money."

"What's the point of having beautiful gems if you never bloody well wear them?"

They're going to fight about the diamond again. They don't care about Mita. They don't care about the card.

The doorbell.

"I'll get it," Daddy says, in his excited visitor-voice, as if he's just finished telling a joke and the laughter is still there, dried up on his lips. "Hurry up, Isabela."

Mummy tightens the back of her earring until it makes her wince. She locks the jewel box and places the slim key under one of her shoes. "Go get ready, Dolores. Please wear something pretty." She walks past me to the party. I hear the sharp *clip-clip* of her heels down the corridor.

It's crystal clear what I have to do. Why didn't I think of this before? I go to the safe and turn the dials, the way I've seen Daddy do. If I went for Mummy's everyday jewel box, she would notice immediately. The diamond is perfect. Too valuable to wear. I turn to three, then counterclockwise to seven, then back to three. No. It must be one of his favorite numbers: threes and sevens. I know that from Liar's Dice. I'll sell the ring and rescue Mita. I need to go there myself; it's the only way. I scramble the dial and try again: seven, three, seven. Nothing. My fingers feel numb and jumpy. Please, God, for Mita, let me open it. I need to figure this out.

People arrive. Laughter.

I take a deep breath: seven, seven, three. *Click!* I pull the safe door open. A bottle of single malt whisky on top of some papers, and next to it, a flat beige rectangular jewel box. Inside, the imperial topaz bracelet and the earrings. They glitter against the black velvet. No ring. A door closes, someone in the bathroom. Voices waft down the corridor. I have to be quick. I move the bottle to the side and see a small black box. I snap it open. The blue sparkles like a quiet firework. I slide the ring into the front pocket of my shorts and return the empty ring box to the back of the safe. I hear the clip of heels approaching. I swing the safe door closed and scramble the lock as the bedroom door opens.

Chapter Twenty-six

SANTANÉSIA

We always made it a point to bring something back for Mita. I'd chosen a yellow beryl with underground tunnels I knew she'd love. Daddy didn't buy anything; he said the gems at the collector's house were average, nothing spectacular. On the way back, we stopped in Barra for a late lunch. Next to the *lanchonete* was a secondhand shop selling wigs, beaded handbags, and silver tea strainers. A ring in the window caught Daddy's eye. After eating our *misto quentes,* we went in for a quick look.

As Daddy studied the ring, his hands trembled with wanting. "How much for this old piece?" he asked.

The man smiled. "You're a smart man. You've found the most valuable thing here. It's a blue diamond. You don't see blue diamonds every day."

"It's a fake. See how dull it is." Daddy held the ring up to the dim lightbulb. The diamond startled us with its sharp midnight blue. It was cut flat, and the light trapped the blue, sending silver mirrors in all directions. Diamonds were usually cut in facets, in order to make the light bounce off the edges and sparkle, but this one didn't need a special cut.

"You can have it for one thousand cruzeiros," the man said.

"Don't be silly. It isn't worth five hundred." Daddy placed the ring back on the shelf.

"Don't buy it, then. I like having it around. I'd miss it if it were gone." The man scratched his greasy gray hair, then shuffled over to the chair behind the counter.

He was playing Daddy. I picked up a wig that seemed to be made of real hair and examined the rough cloth cap, wondering how each hair was attached. It was a long-hair wig, so some girl must have cut off all her hair to make it. I touched my bangs; I couldn't imagine someone else wearing them.

Daddy walked around the store, hands in his pockets, as if he'd forgotten about the ring. He showed me a wooden pepper mill, then placed it back down. I hated the silent battle it always was when he bargained. Daddy was greedy for the diamond, it was obvious. With gems, he wasn't good at bluffing. The man saw it, the way Daddy's fingers flicked against the palm of his hand, the way the muscle in his neck bulged.

Daddy picked up an old pipe and asked the price. "A bargain," the man said. "Twenty-five cruzeiros."

Whenever Daddy caught a large *dourado,* he'd tire it out first. He'd let it swim out to the middle of the reservoir, then he'd wind it back in, then let it out, back and forth. That's what the man was doing to Daddy. I wanted to go home, to leave that dusty shop and forget about the diamond.

It was late, Mummy would worry. I picked up the wig,

placed it over my hair, and went over to the tarnished silver mirror at the back of the shop. The wig made me look older than eleven, the black covered my honey-brown hair, so I was almost someone else. Mita was turning into someone else. The medicines made her mouth sour. Her tongue looked dirty, even after she brushed it over and over with her toothbrush. Sometimes it bled.

My new black hair made my eyes seem lighter. I looked like a different person. An evil girl, a girl who wanted to get away from her own twin sister. A girl who checked the mirror each morning, like the stepmother in "Snow White," afraid she would become crooked too, that whatever was happening to Mita would also happen to her.

"Take that bloody thing off," Daddy said. "You'll catch lice."

"Everything in this shop is clean," the man said. "That hair belonged to my wife."

Daddy frowned. I took the wig off. The black hair draped off the table like a curtain. I walked over to the trays with pressed butterflies. Each wing looked the same, unless you looked closely: Then you'd find all these subtle differences.

"Take the ring outside. See it in the natural light," the man said. "See what a beauty she is."

Daddy shrugged. "Very well," he said. "If you insist."

The man polished the ring with a red velvet cloth. "*É um milagre, esta pedra:* a miracle."

He dropped the ring into Daddy's open palm. Daddy's fingers shook, but not too much. Mummy wanted him to cut back on his drinking, she said it was starting to show.

We crossed the street to see better. Even though it was cloudy, oblongs of light shimmered downward and sideways all at once, the blue was dazzling.

"The cut is wrong," Daddy said, smiling. "But Mummy will love it."

He offered full price.

The man seemed disappointed Daddy had given up so quickly.

In the car, Daddy switched on the light by the mirror and held the diamond under its tiny beam. The blue flickered in our eyes and stayed there, leaving an imprint. "What a country this is," Daddy said. "What a bloody amazing place."

It was past dinnertime when we got home. Mummy was by the door, waiting. "I thought something had happened," she said, her voice on the edge of angry.

"Something did happen, didn't it, Dolores?" Daddy smiled.

This was the moment when most of the fights would start. Mummy would have the wrong reaction and Daddy would explode. "Where's Mita?" I asked. She hated their fights too.

Mummy looked around. "She was here a moment ago . . ."

Mita was sitting in her wheelchair, by the window. Mummy signaled with her eyes for me to go over.

"Hey, Mita. I have a surprise for you." I gave her the yellow beryl with its intricate inside tubes.

Mita examined it with her good hand, then she let it drop on her lap and looked away.

It was the kind of stone she loved.

"We had a bad time today," Mummy said. "Mita didn't want to take her new medicine."

"Mita," Daddy said, in a fake-strict voice. "Were you a naughty girl? Did you make things hard for your mother?"

The corner of Mita's lip started to smile.

"Margarita Hamilton," Daddy said. "You know you shouldn't do that." His good mood was contagious. Daddy pulled out the blue diamond ring and placed it casually on the dining room table.

"Something you might find interesting here, Isabela," he said, his voice plump with excitement.

Mummy picked up the ring. The lively blue surprised her, and she started to smile too. "Ian, you shouldn't have." She slid the ring onto her finger and held it out in front of her, as if she were looking at a beautiful gladiola. Daddy winked at me. For once, Mummy was completely pleased with her present.

Chapter Twenty-seven

MARCH 1973

Mummy heads to the mirror and adjusts the straps of her dress. She sees me in the reflection: "Dolores, why are you still here?" She turns sideways. "Is it too low-cut?"

"No. It looks fine."

"You're not dressed. I need you to serve the *salgadinhos.* Please, go get ready." She refreshes her lipstick, then returns to the party.

In my room, I pull out the ring, not sure if I dreamed what just happened. I place it under my pillow. I don't want to remember Daddy's face; how excited he'd been when we found the blue diamond. That father is not the same as this Rio father. And Mummy: She's more upset about my sandy feet than the card. They're not who they used to be.

I rinse my feet in the bidet and choose a white dress, one that Mummy will like. I notice the way my shoes line up in pairs, the way my Oxford dictionary leans against the amethyst geode on the shelf. Each moment has a sense of importance and finality, as if I'm already in some future life, looking back.

The laughter wafts down the corridor in waves. I listen to it the way you listen to music, feeling the rhythm, the way it bubbles low, then erupts. The English laugh quietly, a sneeze of a laugh, which dissolves in the air.

I step into the party. The breeze from the front window cools my face.

"Look who's here," Daddy's friend Harry says, lifting his glass. Harry plays doubles with Daddy and often comes over for lunch. "Tell me about school. Great place, eh?"

"I don't like it."

Daddy walks over. "Tell her," he says. "Tell her how silly she's being."

I look away. You won't think I'm so silly soon. When you discover me gone, and the diamond gone too. Then you'll pay attention; you'll have to.

"Jack loves the British school," Harry says. "It'll grow on you. You'll see."

"I'm not English like Jack," I say.

Harry raises his eyebrows and looks at Daddy with his light gray eyes. He's handsome; all the ladies think so. His skin is dark; people say his mother must have been Indian, but he denies this. Through-and-through Brit, he insists, though no one believes him.

Daddy stands close. "She doesn't realize how lucky she is," he says. I smell his sausage-meat sweat and feel the prickle of his edges against mine, even though we don't touch.

I don't say anything. In a few hours it won't matter. I'll sell the ring and be with Mita, and none of this British-school talk will matter.

"I agree with your father." Harry turns his crystal tumbler carefully, studying his whisky. He doesn't like fights. When he cheats on his wife, he's always extra-nice to her. I've heard the mothers talk at the club. His wife says that when she threatens to leave, he stays calm and tells her to think about it, because he loves her very much. She finds it infuriating, how calm he always is.

"Think about it," Harry says. "Give the British school a chance. You'll love it. I guarantee. Rugby, cricket. Great fun."

"They don't allow girls to play rugby."

"Well, you know, other sports. Rounders. Tennis. Time of your life," he says. "Next best thing to uni, isn't it, Ian?"

"Cheers," Daddy says, letting the subject drop. He never finished high school, let alone university. He was too poor, but he never lets on.

"Pass the peanuts," Daddy says to me. "See if anyone needs refills."

I offer people cashews and peanuts out of the aquamarine ashtrays Mummy uses as serving dishes. I wonder if it shows, this line I've crossed. Now I truly am a hooligan. A despicable hooligan. The dictionary defined *hooligan* as: "a violent young troublemaker, usually a young man." Well, this one is a young woman. I refill people's gin-tonics. I put an extra jigger of gin for Freddie de Booze because he likes his strong, then squeeze in some lime. He takes a huge sip. "Perfect," he says. "Cheers."

Amelia Clarke sways her way over. I met her at the club once, she was reading *Valley of the Dolls.* She doesn't mix in with the other wives or come to parties much. Maybe she's heard the rumors about her husband, Charlie, and wants to keep an eye on him.

"Have you seen the man?" she asks. Her pretty mouth is carefully painted dark red, lined with brown pencil. The men can't take their eyes off her, and neither can anyone else.

"No, but I can look."

"Thanks. Tell me if you find him in some corner or another." She holds on to the back of the settee to steady herself.

I walk around the party searching for Charlie. It distracts me from thinking about the diamond. Andrea will help me sell it. She'll forgive me; she doesn't stay mad long. I imagine the look of shock on her face when she finds out what I've done. I bet she never imagined I'd do something like this—I never thought I would either. It feels right, taking matters into my own hands.

I can't see Charlie, even though he's hard to miss. Taller than most of the men, and like his wife dressed to a tee, as Daddy would say. They wear clothes that you would look at. Tonight, Amelia has an off-the-shoulder red dress that wraps itself around her slim body in a swirl of pleats and unexpected turns that is both long and short: One side cuts up to her thigh and the other hangs above her pretty knees. Charlie's Italian suits are made from distinctive fabrics: black with a purple weave to it, or very light gray with a faint yellow stripe. He has belts that shine as if they are made of real gold, the leather embossed with swirls. Mummy says they are both a little much, but who is she to judge?

I make my way down the corridor: past my bedroom, the guest room, Mummy and Daddy's room, and their corresponding bathrooms. I check the study. No Charlie. Maybe he left the party.

I head to the *lavanderia,* at the back of the flat. Aparecida's door is open, but the second maid's room, the empty one, is shut. As I pass, I hear sounds—which is strange. No one ever goes there. We use it for storage: Daddy's old fishing rods, trunks, suitcases. The mattress is so badly ripped, pieces of straw poke through. I stand outside the closed door and listen. I hear the scrape of the bed moving, the sound of a muffled groan. I peer into the keyhole, but it's all black.

Aparecida waves her hand, signaling for me to leave. I ignore her. She walks over and takes hold of my arm. I twist away from her. She pulls me to the kitchen.

"*Quem é?* Who's in there?"

"*Não sei,*" Aparecida says, with a shrug.

"You're lying. Tell me. Tell me or I'll knock."

"Don't do that," Aparecida says. "You don't want drama. It will ruin the party."

"Who is it?"

Aparecida looks down at her toenails, which are pearly against her dark skin. She lifts all ten toes from her yellow Havaianas, then places them back down. There are indentations on her flip-flops where her toes land, and the outside edges are so thin they're disappearing.

"You need new flip-flops."

"I know it."

"Tell me."

"There are two men in there."

"Men? Are you sure?"

Aparecida nods.

"Is one of them tall, with curly dark hair? Handsome?"

"Mm-hmm. That's him."

"And the other one. Who is it?"

"I don't know his name."

"What does he look like?"

Mummy walks in. "Are the cheese balls ready?"

Aparecida checks. "Two more minutes, Dona Isabela, and they will be perfect."

"Thank you. Dolores, can you pass them around?" I nod yes. I have to see who's in there with Charlie.

Aparecida pulls out the tray of cheese balls using a dishcloth. She transfers each one onto the silver platter and hands it to me.

"*Vai lá,*" she says, gesturing with her chin toward the living room. "Pass these around and forget what I told you."

The door of the room opens; Charlie Clarke comes out and pushes it closed. He sees me and gives a wave, looking unruffled.

"Those smell great! Can I have one?" He picks up a *pão de queijo* and eats it in one bite, then heads back to the party. Aparecida gives me a look.

"*Vai.* Help your mother with the party," Aparecida says.

The door of the second maid's room stays closed. I take the tray of cheese balls to the living room. The party is in full swing: corks popping, an English-looking woman dancing a samba by herself, the rumble of conversation ebbing and flowing like a tide. I slide the tray of *pães de queijo* onto the buffet, knowing it will burn the wood but not caring.

I take the back route so Aparecida can't stop me. I arrive just in time to see the door open. Mr. Walker steps out. He closes the door carefully behind him and slides his long-fingered hand through his thin blond hair. I'm not sure who I expected, but not Mr. Walker. Not my headmaster.

"Sir," I say. "Mr. Walker."

He looks up, startled. He'd been watching the kitchen entrance; he didn't expect me to come in from the other side. "Goodness, Dolores, I didn't see you."

"Are you lost, sir?"

Mr. Walker blushes. The pink of his skin shows through here and there, in the small spaces where his face isn't yet a freckle. "Yes, yes. I was looking for the loo but found myself back here."

"The loo?" I say. "There's no loo here."

Last time I was this close to him, he expelled Andrea. I can still hear his plum-in-the-mouth Oxford accent, saying the word *por-nog-ra-phy,* syllable by syllable, as if I were a stupid child. I think back to that morning, Queen Elizabeth smiling down at me from her framed picture. How Mr. Walker drummed his fingers on the wooden desk and said he'd come to a difficult decision, how my stomach folded in and over itself as I waited. How he undid Andrea's future in a moment.

"I better head back, then." Mr. Walker steps toward the kitchen.

"Charlie Clarke went back to the party already," I say. "A few moments ago."

The pupils of Mr. Walker's pale eyes dart around like tiny fish. "I'm not sure what you're getting at, Dolores." His voice is reedy, as if something's stuck in his throat.

I'm not that girl anymore. I'm not sure if I say it out loud or just think it. That girl who was so afraid. Something hard inside pushes me forward: "Amelia sent me to find Charlie," I say.

Mr. Walker's graceful hand floats by his side gently, as if it is trying to find something to hold on to, but there is only the hot, humid air of tonight. Beads of sweat form a halo around his face. "What do you want?"

I hadn't thought about wanting anything. I wanted Mr. P. to stay at the British school, but that didn't happen. I wanted Mita to live with us, but she's in a hospital in England and no one seems to care.

"I want Andrea to come back," I say. "I want you to un-expel her."

"Don't be silly. I can't do that, Dolores. It's a done deed."

"Undo it, then." The idea grows inside of me like a bubble beginning to form. Andrea will come back to school; she won't be mad at me anymore. "Undo the done deed," I say.

Mr. Walker wipes the sweat from his face with his wrist. I look at him. *If you like men, that's your business. I don't care about you and Charlie Clarke, though I do feel bad for Amelia. What I care about is that you expelled Andrea for no good reason. You expelled Andrea because she lives under Christ's armpits, in the poor part of Rio, where you're not supposed to live if you attend the British school.* My thoughts are an energy passing between us like an electric current.

Mr. Walker's glasses slide down his narrow nose, and he pushes them back up. He has one of those long necks where you can see the swallow happen: It begins under the chin and moves its way down to the base of his chest like a snake. "Very well," he says. "I will send her a notice next week." He swallows and swallows and then he nods at me and heads through the kitchen, back to the party.

I return to the cheese balls. When I lift the tray, there's a perfect oval burn-mark on the shiny jacaranda wood of the buffet.

"Would you like a cheese ball?" I ask Daddy's boss, who is chatting up the women by the bar. He takes one delicately, with his paper napkin. I move on to the women. Mummy gives me a thank-you smile. I seem to have crossed over to a land where I do the most terrible things and smile.

I make my way to the study. Amelia is still sitting there. She stretches her beautiful stockinged feet and points them, then rolls her ankles. She's taken off her heels. "Eleanor Rigby" plays on the record player.

"D'you want a cheese ball? There are two left."

"Did you find him?" she asks.

"No," I say. "I looked. He's not anywhere."

She points her toes again. Her black tights have a delicate seam down the back. "Damn him," she says. "Damn the bastard."

Using her index finger, she pulls at the stocking, yanks it. She uses her nail to make a hole, then she pulls at the hole and watches the ladder climb all the way up her leg to her thigh.

"Ruined," she says. "This is how it happens. First it's one small thing, then it spreads." She yanks at the hole again. This time the ladder runs downward, like a tiny railway track all the way to her toes. "I don't care," she says. "I don't care if it's ruined."

Her eyes are dark blue, almost violet. They don't look hurt, the way Mummy's eyes do when Daddy shouts at her. They flash sharp, like the diamond.

Charlie walks in. His shirt is carefully tucked into his pants and his belt is studded with bronze buttons—but it isn't quite done up; the buckle is loose. I catch Amelia's eyes seeing the very same thing.

"You bastard," she says. "You can't even do your pants up." Charlie tightens his belt, making the prong slip all the way through the hole, and adjusts his cuff links.

"You've had too much to drink, darling," he says. "Maybe it's time to go."

Amelia sticks her finger in the hole of her tights, now the size of a small egg, and pulls. The ladder widens, spreading across her whole leg.

"Darling, don't be ridiculous." Charlie kneels, takes hold of her hands, and sinks his head onto her lap. "Come on, baby," he says. "You're imagining things. You don't have enough to do here."

Amelia stares straight ahead, as if she can see something far away.

I tiptoe out of the study. I'm never going to be like that. Even Amelia, who's the most independent of the wives, lets Charlie do whatever he wants. I'm supposed to go along too, and accept something unacceptable. I refuse.

Chapter Twenty-eight

When I wake up, the ring is under my pillow: small, pointed, and hard, like a promise.

The clink of dishes. Must be Mummy, cleaning up after the party. Daddy will be sleeping off his hangover. I pull on jeans and a blouse, zip up the ring in the pocket at the back of my purse, and head to the front door.

"You're up early. Coffee?" Mummy offers.

"No, thanks, I'm going for a walk."

"Thank you for yesterday. You were a great help."

I look down at my *chinelos.* I don't want her to be nice; not now. It's too late. "Be back later," I say.

I catch the bus to Lapa and walk up the six flights to Andrea's flat. I ring the doorbell four times, and she opens the door.

"*Porra,* it's early," she says. "What is it? Ten in the morning?"

"I'm sorry, but I really need to speak to you. I have news. First of all, you can come back to school," I say. "You're not expelled anymore."

"What? I don't know what you're saying."

I tell Andrea about the party and Mr. Walker and Charlie.

"You blackmailed him? That's impressive, I love that. But there's no way I'm going back."

"I was hoping you'd be glad," I say. At least a little glad.

"Thank you for standing up for me, but the British school causes problems."

I can't bear the British school without Andrea. "Please," I say. "Try. For me."

"No. My mum will go back to Antonio. To pay the bills. The only reason I ever went was because I thought it was from my father. Turns out that was a lie." She rubs her eyes. "I need more sleep. Can we talk later?"

"Wait. There's something else." I unzip the inner pocket of my handbag and show her the blue diamond. "It's worth a lot. It will get me to England, no problem."

Andrea holds the ring in the open palm of her hand. "I've never seen a jewel like this," she says. "Never. Where did you get it?"

"I stole it from my mother."

Andrea's eyes widen.

"Will you help me sell it? We need a pawnshop, but a fancy pawnshop. Regular jewelers might know Daddy. Maybe we can ask Sofia."

Andrea looks at her watch. "She'll be at the club. Let me put on clothes, and we'll go ask her."

The red lights of Clube Mônaco flash on and off across the street.

We walk inside as if we belong. Andrea taught me that: no hesitation. The club smells of stale beer and cachaça. Tables of men, playing cards and dice. I listen to the familiar *ping* of dice and scan the glitter of eyes and cigarettes through the smoke, looking for Sofia. Men glance up briefly, one or two reach out to touch us. Andrea slaps their hands. Even though I've never been here, the atmosphere feels familiar. Hope hangs in the air like a particle: a feeling you can nudge life in the right direction, change the course of things in a minute.

We search the tables until I see Sofia's coral nails, her long, elegant fingers, and her green beryl ring. I signal Andrea to come over.

Sofia's so absorbed by the game she doesn't see us. Daddy hated being interrupted in the middle of a game. "Maybe we should play first," I whisper to Andrea.

"No. Let's get down to business."

"Shh." The man playing with Sofia frowns at us.

I walk to the bar and hand the barman a ten-cruzeiro note before he can say anything about children *blah, blah, blah.* I come back with a cup and Andrea finds us chairs.

"*Puta,* what are these *crianças* doing here? This isn't a playground," the man says.

"If they can play, they can stay, that's how it works." The fat man on the left cracks his knuckles.

Sofia doesn't let on that she knows us. "They better know the rules, or they're out," she says.

"Fair enough." The fat man takes out a cigar, bites off the end, and spits it on the floor. His shoes are a shiny black leather that shows he doesn't walk anywhere, ever.

The man to the right of Sofia shrugs. His purple shirt is stained brown in places and missing a few buttons, so his thin, hairy belly is visible. "Pass." His voice tries to be neutral, but even in that short word the anger comes through.

Sofia picks up four chips and balances them carefully on top of her cup. Her coral nails glint.

The fat man doubles her bet, placing eight chips on his cup.

I shake my dice, warming up. The sound is shallow. The cup is made from cheap leather; it has the anonymous quality of a cup that has been passed around too much. Please, God, make this a Bidu. A Bidu would be a sign: I can reverse this downward spiral, sell the diamond, and find Mita. Please.

I turn my cup, and without looking at my throw, I up the fat man's bet to twelve: the highest possible bet. Daddy's old trick. I place my chips, two stacks of six, next to each other on my cup. It's a risky move. Andrea shrugs. She doesn't understand the game.

"I told you the girl can't play," the angry man says. "What is this?"

The fat man puffs at his cigar, sweat accumulating in the pleats of his neck. His pinkie finger fiddles with the edge of the cup.

Sofia's sharp eyes catch him. "Don't even try," she says. "I'm watching you."

Sofia lifts first: a low run.

The fat man smiles and shows double sixes.

"*Puta,*" the angry man says. "I thought you were bluffing."

"What do you care, you're not in this round," Sofia says.

Only a Bidu can beat double sixes . . . I lift my cup. I can't believe it! There it is: a two and a one!

"Bidu," I say, the magic from Santanésia entering my hands so they feel electric.

"*Gooool!*" Andrea claps. "We won!"

Sofia smiles. I smile too. This was a good idea, to play first.

The angry man stares at my Bidu as if it's some kind of insect. "Cheating," he says. "Someone planted her."

I hadn't noticed the barman come over. "Ah, yes," he says, "I had the child imported from the *jardim de infância,* just for tonight."

Sofia and the fat man laugh. I collect everyone's red chips and swirl my dice, letting them slide along the rim. Some ribbon of remembering takes me back to how life used to be. Daddy playing dice in the shade of the club, Mummy and Mita by the pool. Sitting across from Sofia feels like coming home.

I bet twelve chips again, without looking at my throw. I'm on a roll. If Mita were here, she'd screech with excitement. Soon, I'll be with her . . .

"That's crazy," the angry man says. "You can't do that twice. You didn't even look at your dice. That's a crazy move!" His voice floats around loose, going high, then low; he can't land it.

"What's it to you?" Andrea says. "She can do whatever she wants."

The fat man chews the end of his cigar as if he's starving. "Let her lose if she wants to, that's her right, isn't it?"

I lose the next round, and then I start to break even. Sofia helps me; she places her index finger on her cheek and bends her pinkie finger twice if she thinks I should up my bid. She taught me her signal when we were playing a few weeks ago. Daddy has his secret code and Sofia has hers. I need to gain the lead.

Andrea gets fidgety. I can tell she's bored.

Sofia places two chips on her cup. "I'll see you," she says to the fat man. He ups her by one. I match him.

"Sofia," Andrea says, interrupting. "We came here with a mission."

"Not now," Sofia says. She studies the fat man's face. "You're bullshitting me."

"You know these girls?" the angry man says, as if it is a crime. "What's going on here?"

"*Isso é um saco,*" Andrea says, standing up. "I'm going back to bed. Come get me when you have a plan, okay?" She kisses me on the cheek and leaves. Sofia barely notices. She's like Daddy when she plays; nothing else exists.

THE CLUB'S LIGHTS FLASH ON and off. "Break time," the barman announces through a microphone. "All games must take a break." I remember now: Sofia said there was always a midday break. Mornings are safest. After lunch, the police are more likely to raid.

The barman walks from table to table, collecting cups.

The angry man rattles his dice with increasing violence. "This is a setup. How can a child win? It's ridiculous. Against the law."

"You should have thought about that before you played," the fat man says. "It's too late to find your morals after you've lost. That's not how it works." He's defending me, but he's not happy either. He counts out his money in twenties and pushes the bills toward me. "Beginner's luck," he says. "Next time won't be so easy." He stands up and shuffles toward the door.

Sofia makes a big deal of handing me her money and then turns to the angry man. "Your turn, darling."

"Pay up," I say to the angry man. "If you play, you pay." I quote Daddy, wondering what he would think of this situation. He'd be furious that I'm in Lapa, by myself . . . but he'd like it that I won. That I held my own. I try not to think of them; Mummy thanking me, Daddy finding the diamond gone.

The barman stands watch. The angry man pulls out a hundred-cruzeiro note and throws it at me.

"Ten more," I say.

The barman laughs. "She doesn't need me, this one. She knows how to fend for herself."

The angry man walks off, flicking his fingers, as if he wants to get my energy away from him.

Sofia kisses me on the cheek. "You showed them," she says. "How much do you have?"

I sort through the bills, placing them in piles on the table. "Two hundred and eighty cruzeiros."

Sofia whistles. "You can afford to buy me a drink." She turns to the barman. "The usual, darling."

"I'll have a caipirinha, please." I'm not sure he'll give it to me, but I act confident. Maybe he won't guess that I'm twelve. I don't feel twelve, not one bit.

"Sofia, I need your help with something."

"What do you need help with? Is it about love?" Sofia bats her long eyelashes.

I used to feel so uncomfortable with her teasing, but it doesn't bother me now. "Yes," I say. "It is about love." I reach in my purse, unzip the pocket, and pull out the ring. The stone sparkles like a star in the smoky shade of the club.

"Put that away," Sofia says. "Now."

I notice a group of men watching us from the entrance. I should have been more careful. I slip the diamond back into the inner pocket of my purse. I slide half the wad of cruzeiros into the side pocket of my jeans, and half into my back pocket—just in case.

The barman arrives with a Cuba for Sofia and a caipirinha for me. As Sofia takes a sip, she whispers, "Watch your jewel, this place is full of thieves."

The club starts to empty out. The barman folds the tables and stacks them. Sofia stands up. "I'll be back in a second."

When Sofia returns from the bathroom, she gulps her drink standing up. "Loving Bidu is the one part of me that is anatomically correct," she says.

"I love Bidu too. What does that say about me?"

Sofia laughs. "It doesn't say anything. Or maybe you go the other way?"

I don't tell her, but I do feel like Sofia in a certain way. My body doesn't match who I am; it doesn't show I'm half of a pair. When people see me, they see a single person.

A thin man comes up behind Sofia and pinches her bottom. There's a meanness in the way he does it; it isn't appreciation. His pinstripe suit is too big, and his black flip-flops too small.

"I told you. Not in the morning," Sofia says.

"It's anytime I want." The man's voice swells as he says, "It's all day long, if I say so."

"Can't you see I'm here with a child?" Sofia pulls me toward her. Her fingers dig into my arm. I don't like it that she called me a child.

"Send her to take a nap," the man says. "It's past her nap time."

"Come, *francesinha,* let's get out of here." Sofia reaches for her purse, and I follow her past the tables and the men, out to the street.

She walks quickly for someone in heels. I slide the wad of money farther down my pocket and hug my purse, hoping no one saw me put the ring there. I check behind us and to the sides. No one's following. The sidewalk narrows and disappears in places. Sofia trips.

"Are you okay?"

"Sorry," Sofia says. "I took a *calmante* in the bathroom and it's making me dizzy."

Sofia leans against me as we walk.

"How far is your place?" I ask.

An orange Karmann Ghia slows down next to us and the window rolls open. "D'you want a *carona*?" a voice asks. "Get in and I'll give you a ride."

It's the man from the club, the one who pinched Sofia. Sofia looks up and down the street, her eyes panicked.

"Jump in," the man says.

Sofia turns and heads back toward the club. I follow her. The car stays pulled over, with its indicator lights flashing on and off.

"I thought you lived the other way."

"I don't live anywhere," Sofia says. "I live right here, you understand?" She's sweating. "This street, this corner, that car." She points to a car far ahead of us. "I live wherever I land." Her words slur.

"Maybe we should find a taxi," I say. I want to get out of here.

"A taxi, that's precious. They don't come this way, your taxis."

I hear the sound of a car in reverse. The Karmann Ghia

backs toward us fast, the engine making that high-pitched reverse sound cars make, only louder. He swerves onto the curb.

"Ride?" he says. "D'you want a ride," he shouts out like a command.

Sofia pulls out a cigarette. Her hand trembles so much, she has to flick the lighter three times before it takes. "You should go. I'll deal with this."

"Let's both of us go." I don't want to leave her with him. Something's wrong with her, maybe it's the drugs. "Please. Let's go to Tia Glória's house."

The man unlocks the passenger door. "Get in. Be a good girl and get in."

"Go," Sofia says. "Leave now." Sofia holds on to the side of the car.

I left Mita, sure I'd see her the next morning. And then she was gone. I can't leave.

"I want her with us," the man says. "She's in."

"She's not in," Sofia says, some of her edge coming back. "She's a child."

The man flicks his cigarette out the window and turns to me. "You better get in," he says, sounding reasonable, as if he's telling me the price of something on a menu. "It will be better that way."

Run, a voice inside of me says. The muscles behind my knees tighten. The street is empty except for a drunk curled up on the ground, hugging his bottle of cachaça.

"Go." Sofia slides into the passenger seat.

The man gets out of the car and holds his door open for me. "Hurry up," he says. "Be a good girl and get in the back."

If I run, Sofia could end up dead. If I get in, at least there will be two of us against him.

I've seen the headlines, bodies dumped into rivers, under bridges: I don't want to be one of those bodies.

Sofia's eyes close and her chin droops toward her chest. Tranquilizers never made Mita tranquil, just dopey; her body closed down. Maybe Sofia's body is closing down.

I get into the back seat. The car smells of perfume and sweat and sex. I'm not sure what sex smells like, but Andrea made me smell Tia Glória's sheets once, and they smelled like this: salty, fishy, and slightly bitter.

Sofia's eyes snap open. "Run like hell," she says. "Go!"

The man slaps her. I reach forward and pull his hair. He grabs my wrist and snaps it backward.

The pain shoots down my elbow to my ribs. I bite down on my lip, trying not to cry. Sofia's face is frozen. I see it in the car mirror.

"Your little friend needs to learn to behave," the man says. He yanks my wrist and twists.

I scream, not even trying to be brave.

The humid air presses against us. I hear my own breathing and Sofia's and his, all the breaths a different rhythm. A ribbon of pain travels from my arm into my jaw and my head. My teeth ache, and behind my eyes. "Give me the ring," the man says. "And the money."

I don't move, can't move. The pain is too much.

"Give them to me or I'll break the other one."

With my good hand, I take the money out of my back pocket and give it to him, hoping it will be enough.

"The ring." The man presses my hand backward, and the pain shoots up to my elbow. I want to throw up. I unzip the pocket in my purse and hand him the ring.

He lets go of my arm. The pain throbs like a pulse, spreading to every corner of my body. I've never broken a bone before.

The man puts the car in gear and takes off down the road. He eyes me from the rearview mirror. His face is narrow with shiny craters. His pores sweat. The car accelerates, hits the curb, and veers back onto the road. If we crash, there might be a chance to escape.

"Sofia." My voice is dry. I'm no longer the person I was a few minutes before: a person who had thrown a Bidu and won, against all odds; a person who was going to see her sister at last; a person with hope.

Sofia doesn't answer.

"We're going to have fun," the man says. "Aren't we?"

The man drives fast. We pass warehouses, shuttered buildings. I look for markers, like João e Maria in the forest, to find my way back. Mita and I hated that story: Why did they leave pieces of bread instead of stones; didn't they know the birds would eat them? We're in the Zona Norte, the industrial area.

My wrist sits on my lap. It looks like a knuckle, swollen and purple. My fingers are numb. Maybe I will die today.

Sofia's head rolls to the side as the car speeds around a corner. Her mouth hangs open. I remember car rides to Rio, with Mita passed out on my lap. Mummy and Daddy were with me then. I miss them. I miss them so much.

"Sofia. Sofia?"

Sofia's eyes stay closed. I see them in the mirror.

"Relax," the man says. "We're not there yet."

I don't ask where. He has a place in mind. He's kidnapping us.

We've been in the car half an hour, maybe more. I wish

Sofia was awake. Even if we manage to escape, how will we ever get back, we're so far away. Pain sharpens my focus. FÁBRICA KLABIN, I've seen that sign before. Daddy and I drove there once, for a job interview. Daddy said the car had better not break down, or we'd be screwed. I remember the abandoned park and the yellow seesaw.

The side of the mountain is dotted with small shacks, a favela. That's where he's taking us. I try to remember the favelas in the Zona Norte. Andrea and I looked them up once. This could be the Favela do Rato Molhado. We laughed that it was named after a wet rat. Now it doesn't seem so funny.

There's a traffic light up ahead. Sofia's eyes open. She sees me in the side mirror and places her index finger on her cheek. Her pinkie finger bends twice. The signal: Sofia has a plan.

The man glances at Sofia, and she quickly closes her eyes.

Sofia makes a show of waking up. She stretches her arms, yawns, slides toward the man, and reaches into his lap. She bends over him—I can't see her face anymore. She's throwing up on the man's lap. Gagging.

"Sofia, are you okay?"

She doesn't answer. The back of her head moves up and down, I hear small gasps. Maybe she's choking. I see the man's narrow face in the mirror, his mouth pinched in, his jaw clenched. His eyes squint with pain. Is she hurting him? The man makes a series of grunts and I realize—of course—they're having sex. She has his *piru* in her mouth. I'm afraid to look. He holds the steering wheel so loose I worry we'll crash. Then he lets out a prolonged moan. A film of sweat covers his pockmarked face, it shines a sickening yellow. The car comes to a halt. I feel embarrassed. I hear a scuffle, the sound of a zipper. Sofia sits up and catches my eye for a split second. She's telling me to be ready. She bends over and pulls on him, up and down with her hand. The man grits his teeth, it reminds me of Daddy when he's mad, then he groans a huge groan that is like a yawn and a scream and Sofia says: "Now!"

She opens the door and bolts. I scramble after her and we run along the side of the road. Sofia holds her coral dress out of the way, panting as she runs. We cross an empty parking lot, turn onto another street, then run along the uneven sidewalk and up a hill. Sofia stops in front of steel-gray double doors, each with a nailed-on Star of David. She pushes one of the doors open, pulls me inside, then closes it behind us. "Thank God," she says. "Thank God they always forget to lock it."

We're in some kind of garden. She runs down an overgrown path, and I follow, trying not to trip. I imagine the man close behind, the sound of the car in reverse loud in my ears.

Sofia points: "Over there." We bear right.

I hold my wrist as we weave our way among the tangle of weeds and slabs of stone—they look like tombs. Some of them lie to the side, broken. A cemetery, we're in a strange, abandoned cemetery. I listen for him: the *swish-swish* of Sofia's dress, the snap of branches, I listen for the man chasing us. Is he following? Every step is an arrow of pain.

Sofia stumbles. She stops running and holds on to her side, panting. Then she bends low and peers at a broken headstone: "*Porra,* this place is a mess!"

"Shh." I expect him to appear like a jack-in-the-box and surprise us.

"Where the fuck is she?"

"Who are you looking for?" I whisper. I let myself turn for the first time. I don't see him. I don't hear footsteps.

Sofia walks from headstone to headstone, her breath coming in gasps. The graves don't have names, only numbers: 372, 369.

"This is it." Sofia sinks to the ground and leans her head against one of the gravestones. I sit next to her. "He won't find us here. My mother will make sure of it."

"Your mother?" I'm afraid to speak out loud. The pain in my arm swells and throbs like a force.

"My mother." Sofia rummages in her purse and finds a pill bottle. She pours out a handful and swallows them without water. She shakes the pills in front of my face. "Want some?"

"No, thanks." Tia Glória's friend Flávia died from taking pills. I don't want Sofia to die. The graves make me think of Mita. She might already be dead. Buried somewhere in England, in an unmarked grave like this one. I wonder if there are special cemeteries for children.

"In a few hours, the factories close. It will be safer, with people around. We'll leave then," Sofia says.

A few hours. The swish of leaves. My stomach tightens, but it's just a grass snake. I cradle my wrist in front of me and let my forehead sink to my knees. Please, God, let the pain go away; let the man not find us. I want to be home. Sofia's eyes close. I close my eyes too and try to pretend, the way I always do, that I'm underwater, in the pool, sinking to the bottom . . .

"Mama, I'm here. I came." Sofia's voice startles me, breaking the silence. It's her voice, but different. Maybe it's the pills.

"Sofia?" She's right next to me, but she seems far away.

Sofia pats the ground with her hands, pulling out tufts of grass, until she finds a small stone. She places it on the palm of her hand and offers it: "Here you are, Mama."

I imagine Sofia's mother arriving, like a ghost. It wouldn't be strange here, in this secret cemetery.

"It wasn't supposed to go like this. My life wasn't supposed to go like this." Sofia sounds as if she is on the edge of tears.

I touch her arm.

"I'm a disaster." Sofia shouts into the darkness: "I'm sorry, Mama, for being such a disaster."

"Please, Sofia," I whisper. "He might hear."

"Not even a plaque with her name. I couldn't even afford that." Sofia hits the back of her head against the grave. "A number. That's all she is. A number in the weeds." She turns to me, her eyes glassy. "You've probably never lost anyone," she says. There's a change in her voice, a meanness. When Daddy's mood shifts like that, it's best not to respond. "You don't know sorrow. Girls like you, everything comes easy."

I look at the hundreds of shacks perched on the steep side of the mountain. No one chooses to be born in the Favela do Rato Molhado.

"I do. I do know sorrow." My voice surprises me, solemn and definite. I've never wanted Sofia to find out about Mita. Never. The way she hates ugliness. Maybe I'm ashamed. Maybe I am like Mummy and Daddy: ashamed of Mita. The ache in my arm throbs in my teeth, the back of my neck, it widens across my chest. "I have a sister. An identical twin." The words slip out, as if they can't be stopped. "They sent her away. I don't know if she's dead or not."

I press my wrist, wanting to cut it off, to make the pain go away.

"What's wrong with her?" Sofia asks. Her voice is calm, but I don't trust it. Mr. P. left my book of essays for anyone to find. What a mistake it was to trust him.

"Retarded," I say, using the word I hate, the word that cuts through my heart every time I hear it. "She's retarded and crippled." I say them: the two worst words in the universe.

"Was she born that way?" Sofia asks.

"I'm not sure; maybe a little. But then it got worse."

"Identical?" Sofia studies me with her critical eyes. "Your sister got the short end of the stick, poor girl. You're the lucky one."

Sofia's accusing me. It's what I've felt all these years. I look at the tangle of weeds and overgrown grass covering the headstones. I don't deserve to be the lucky one.

Sofia grips my shoulder and turns my chin, making me face her. "This *puta* life is a crapshoot," she says. "You got lucky. When you get a good throw, you play it, understand?"

I don't understand. The sharpness of feeling lucky aches in my lungs. "I want her to get a good throw."

"You can't control that," Sofia says. She looks up at Cristo Redentor, in the distance. "Even God can't." She pulls me close and puts her arms around me. I let myself lean into her, afraid she'll turn mean but too sad to care.

"What kind of cemetery is this?" I ask after a while.

"Our own private cemetery. Founded by *polacas,* Jewish prostitutes. The Jewish cemetery didn't want us, so we made our own. It was nice, once upon a time. It would kill Mama, to see it like this." Sofia picks up another stone and throws it into the weeds. "Number 237. Maybe it's just as well. If I'd made a plaque, the kids from the favela would have stolen it, anyway."

"What was your mother's name?" I reach in my side pocket. I only gave the man the money from my back pocket.

"Adele. Adele Friedman."

"Here." I tuck the money into Sofia's hand. It isn't enough to get me to England, but it will buy a plaque. "At least her name. No one can take that away."

Sofia begins to sob. Huge sobs that shake her whole body. I squeeze her hand, the way I used to squeeze Mita's hand when she was upset. I squeeze her hand and wait for the crying to slow down.

❧

When I open my eyes, it's dark and my legs drape across Sofia's lap.

"Awake?" Sofia says, her voice hoarse.

"Yes," I whisper. The more awake I am, the more my arm hurts. "D'you think he's outside the gate, waiting?"

"I don't think so," Sofia says. "But if he is, scream like hell, got it? People don't care what happens to a *bicha,* but you're a child. Make a fuss."

Daddy tells visitors life is cheap in Brazil, that's how he explains the poverty of the favelas, the dead bodies that show up under bridges. He accepts it, that some lives are cheaper than others, as if it's supposed to be that way.

We walk through the gray metal door into the street: no Karmann Ghia in sight. The ache in my arm pulses its way up to my shoulder and down my fingers. He's gone.

We walk to the bus stop by the Fábrica Klabin. The playground's still there, with the yellow seesaw. Sofia smooths her hair and adjusts her breasts as we stand in line. The woman in front of us gives Sofia a nasty look and moves a few steps away. She holds on to the cross of her necklace, as if she needs protection. Sofia doesn't notice. This must happen to her every day.

"We'll get off at Praça Onze. Plenty of taxis there, so you can get home. Plenty of police too, so we'll have to be quick," Sofia says.

On the bus, I sit doubled over, cradling my wrist. Sofia talks, to distract me. She tells me about the Society of Truth, about how in 1916 Jewish prostitutes built their own cemetery and synagogue, took care of one another. I only half listen. Every bump sends shooting pains up my arm. The hurt is so loud, it overtakes me. I hear a jumble of phrases: "white slavery," "not in life, not in death." My body begins to tremble. I wonder if I'm dying.

"Almost there," Sofia says. "I'll get you a taxi, but I can't go with you to Ipanema. The police are doing a sweep over there; I'd be dead meat."

At Praça Onze, Sofia flags down a taxi, and I climb in. The pain thrums through me so loud, I don't even say thank you.

Chapter Twenty-nine

A woman throws a bucket of bleach onto the sidewalk. I step out of the taxi and into the lobby of my building, holding my wrist close to my chest, hoping the porter won't notice. He walks me to the lift and presses 12.

The creaky lift inches its way up. My teeth hit one another, making a hollow sound.

Mummy opens the door. "You're hurt. Ian, quick!"

Daddy jogs over. "I'll call Dr. Fernandes and get the keys."

Mummy hugs me, not caring that I might wrinkle her dress. I'd forgotten this mother. The crying slides out of me in a stretched-out sob.

She drapes a shawl over my shoulders and sits with me in the back of the car while Daddy drives, like so many times before. But this time, Mita isn't lying across our laps having a fit. I didn't expect to be in this bubble of caring. It seems that illness connects us into being a family again.

At the hospital, Dr. Fernandes examines my wrist and orders X-rays. While we wait for results, he lets me sit on his swivel chair and gives me a pill and Coca-Cola.

"How did this happen?" he asks.

"I fell."

"How exactly did you fall?"

"Someone ran after me on the street, and I tripped."

"Someone you know?"

"A stranger."

Dr. Fernandes glances at Daddy. They suspect I'm not telling the truth.

"We usually see this type of injury in fights," he says. "Assaults. So close to the hand. And the bruising. Are you sure no one twisted your wrist?"

"Dolores, you can tell us," Daddy says. "We won't be angry." His voice is gentle. It's the Robin Hood Daddy who used to tell us bedtime stories. I have the urge to confess; to tell him about the diamond, about Sofia and the man, and how I'd won at Bidu. But if I tell, he'll blame Andrea. Or Sofia. I know he will.

"I fell," I say.

Daddy squeezes my shoulder. "Dr. Fernandes will take care of you, don't you worry."

I can't bear Daddy's kindness. I don't deserve it. I stole his most prized possession and lost it. Now I have nothing. I hurt them. And I won't even get to see Mita.

I'm a terrible person.

The X-rays come back: My wrist is broken in two places.

Dr. Fernandes traces the white ghost of my bone as it splinters at the base.

"You'll need a cast," he says. "It will be six weeks at least, probably eight."

The nurse brings in a wheelchair. Mummy slides the belt out of the way and Daddy guides me in, the same way he used to lower Mita. I wonder if they're thinking of her now. Mummy's lips pinch in at the corners with worry.

"She's in *choque,*" Dr. Fernandes says. "A break like hers is almost impossible from a fall. She may have been assaulted."

"How terrible," Mummy says. "We'll ask her about it again later, when we're home."

They're talking about me as if I'm not here, even though I'm sitting just below them. Once you are in a wheelchair, you don't exist anymore.

THE CAST MUFFLES THE PAIN and feels cold. Whenever we unfurled Mita's fingers, they were cold. Daddy pushes my wheelchair from the cast room down the corridor, back to the doctor's office.

Dr. Fernandes examines my cast and tells me to keep it dry; the beach is okay but no swimming. It might make sense to stay home for a few days, but my wrist should heal nicely.

Daddy shakes Dr. Fernandes's hand. "Thank you. I can't thank you enough."

Mummy stands next to me, her hand resting gently on my shoulder. I look up at her and smile. All of a sudden, my heart aches with love for her—and for Daddy—and for Dr. Fernandes. In fact, for the whole hospital.

"I love you," I say to Dr. Fernandes.

He smiles. "I see the medication is working."

Daddy laughs. "Thank God for that! Thank you."

"I love you, Dr. Fernandes," I say again. It seems those are the only words in my brain.

"AWAKE?" MUMMY HANDS ME A glass of fresh-squeezed orange juice. She sits on the edge of my bed.

I gulp my juice down. I am beyond thirsty.

"How d'you feel?"

"Fine. Great." I can't change my story. Daddy taught me. Once you make a bet, play it to the end.

"Did anything . . . bad happen?" Mummy looks embarrassed to be asking.

I want to tell her the truth, but it would be a mistake. "I broke my wrist. Isn't that bad enough?"

Mummy arranges the corner of my bedcover so it hangs straight. "Hungry?"

"Starving."

"The roast is ready." Mummy stands up. "D'you need help getting up?"

"No. I'm fine." The moon is huge, outside my window. "Is it nighttime?"

"The next night," Mummy says. "You slept two days. No wonder you're hungry!"

At dinner, Mummy serves me two helpings of chicken breast.

"More. Please."

Daddy beams. Eating is something he approves of. I place

a whole roast potato in my mouth, the hunger making me greedy. I cut a slice of chicken and try to fit it in too.

"Steady there," Daddy says, even though he always eats like this, with a sense of desperation. Maybe this is how hunger feels to him, like a race you can't afford to lose.

Mummy laughs. She doesn't tell me not to make a mess or ask me where my manners are. "There's another chicken in the kitchen. I roasted two."

"Delicious." My mouth is so full, it sounds like *deshishush.*

Daddy laughs. I focus on the green beans. Another potato.

Something adjusts inside of me, and I begin to slow my eating. I look around, as if I have just landed in a bright new world. The embroidered tablecloth and matching serviettes, the crystal wineglasses, the round vase in the center of the table, the spray of tiny coral roses. The same color as Sofia's dress. I think of her hooded eyes in the car, of the man twisting my wrist. Fábrica Klabin, the cemetery.

"There's a do at the embassy tomorrow," Daddy says. "Maybe we should give it a skip?"

"Let's give it a skip, and just be us for a while," Mummy says, smoothing the tablecloth and smiling at me.

I look at her graceful fingers and think of the blue diamond, how it's gone, and she won't ever wear it again. Thanks to me. When she finds it missing, she'll be so upset. She never had anything, growing up. She hates losing things. Even small things, like a handkerchief. Suddenly, I'm not so hungry anymore.

Chapter Thirty

SANTANÉSIA

Mita was having a bad day, so Daddy took me with him to Rio for the interview. The manager at Fábrica Klabin told Daddy the park was safe, he'd let his own children play there, but when we arrived, Daddy didn't like the look of it. The swings were rusty, there was *lixo* everywhere, and the park had an abandoned feeling to it. There was one tree.

"I don't like leaving her here alone," Daddy told the man. He unbuttoned his suit jacket, which was too tight. I told him I'd be fine, don't worry; I knew he needed a job. The paper mill was closing, and everyone was looking for jobs.

Daddy followed the man toward the building. Midway, he turned and said come and get me if you need me. I said I will, even though Fábrica Klabin was huge, and I wasn't at all sure I would ever find him.

I sat on the creaky swing looking at the dusty park and the empty warehouses with broken windows. I'd hate to live here, by the Fábrica Klabin. Mita would hate it too. In two days, we'd be twelve. Twelve had a one and a two in it, like a Bidu. It was a magic number; there were twelve months in the year; twelve apostles; I was hoping it would bring us luck. Maybe the paper mill wouldn't close and we'd continue to live in Santanésia. Maybe Mummy and Daddy would stop their fighting. The biggest maybe, the one that I almost couldn't bear to wish, was that maybe Mita would get better.

One of the rusty links suddenly snapped, and the swing tipped to the side.

I jumped off and went over to the seesaw. It was strange how it was bright yellow, when everything else in the park was rusty brown. I stood on the middle of the board and shifted my weight from side to side, trying to keep my balance. Sometimes I managed to go back and forth for a few rounds, and that felt like a victory.

After a while I went and sat by the entrance to the factory. I could hear clicks, and a *flip-flip* sound I imagined was paper coming out from the machines. Fábrica Klabin made paper and ceramics. The man had said the interview wouldn't take long. Daddy had gone on quite a few interviews. Mummy was worried. I'd heard her talking at the club. All the women were worried. Everyone in the village was connected to the paper mill.

It was humid, and the mosquitoes started to bite. I slapped them away, but there were too many of them.

Daddy finally came out with the man, smiling. "There you are," he said, as if he thought I might have gone somewhere. He shook hands with the man, I was afraid to ask how it went. Daddy always came back smiling, so it didn't mean much. I could read him at dice, but I didn't know how to read him at job interviews.

"Let's get the hell out of here. I'm starving." We headed for the car. I sat next to Daddy, in front. Daddy reached over and touched my knee. "Thank you for being such a good sport."

On the mountain road, we stopped at a *botequim* Daddy had heard about. It had decent food and great wine, and he said we deserved a treat. I had *pasteizinhos* and *batata frita,* but they weren't as good as Aparecida's *pasteizinhos.* Daddy ordered *espetinhos,* but he didn't eat them. He didn't mention the interview. Instead, he talked about Portuguese wine, how it was undervalued, didn't I think so? After a few glasses, he ordered a carafe.

"How about dessert, then?" Daddy said, and without waiting for me to answer, he asked the barman for the menu. It was late afternoon, and we were the only ones there. I wanted to go home. Mummy and Mita would be waiting. I'd wanted to come to Rio with him, but it hadn't been fun. I missed Mita. It was as if I had a little clock inside myself, and after a certain amount of time away, I had to go back.

Daddy read me the options: *flan* or *brigadeiros.* I thought of saying I wasn't hungry, but that made me feel like Mummy, spoiling the fun. So I ordered *brigadeiros.* The barman asked Daddy what he was doing in this part of the world, and Daddy said he was on a business trip, he'd just had a meeting at the Fábrica Klabin.

After the barman left, Daddy finished up his glass and put

it down on the marble counter too hard. "I wouldn't work there if they paid me," he said. I hoped the glass didn't crack. Then we would have to pay for the glass too.

Finally, we headed home. Daddy took the corners quickly. He was a good driver, but the mountain road always made me carsick. I rolled the window wide open, and let the air stream in.

"Look at that sunset, Dolores. Have you ever seen such a spectacle?" The wine had improved Daddy's mood. "What a great chap," he said. I knew he was referring to the barman. He'd given Daddy a bottle of the house wine to take home with him, and some extra *brigadeiros* for Mita. Daddy told the barman about Mita. The barman said having a sick child is everyone's worst nightmare. He didn't say it in an unkind way, but I didn't like it.

As we approached home, I started to have a bad feeling. Not about leaving Mita; I was always doing things without her these days, while she sat at home, like a potted plant. She was used to it. That's what we said: Mita is used to the boots, she is used to the wheelchair, as if it were a good thing. I worried Daddy had had too much to drink. Mummy would think so. The way his voice swelled and dipped, the way he talked about the wonder of huge butterflies. His mood was too good.

When we arrived, Mummy was concentrating on the gladiolas. Daddy stood watching her arrange them in the vase until she looked up.

"How was it?" Mummy said. "How was the interview?" She sounded tired.

"Stupendous!" Daddy said. "Well worth the trip, wasn't it, Dolores?"

I nodded yes. I could feel a fight brewing.

"We stopped for some food on the way back," Daddy said. "We found an amazing little place."

"And wine," Mummy said. "Obviously."

Here they go, I thought.

I looked for Mita. She didn't like their fights either; they set her off. She was parked by the kitchen window. I went over and kissed her cheek. "I brought you something." I carefully unwrapped the foil and placed the *brigadeiros* on her lap. Mita picked one up with her good hand, but then she put it back down, without taking a bite. Her eyes were focused on Mummy and Daddy; she knew they were going to fight.

"Did they seem interested?" Mummy asked.

"I wouldn't be surprised," Daddy said, "if they made an offer tomorrow."

He walked over to the fridge and pulled out the bottle of champagne Jaime's father had given him as a birthday present. Veuve Clicquot: the finest champagne in the world. Before Mummy could stop him, he'd untwisted the wire cage and was inching the cork out with his thumb.

"Ian, please. Don't—" Mummy said. "Why don't we wait until we know for certain?"

Pop! The cork flew across the room. Daddy grabbed three champagne glasses and filled them.

"It's a special occasion, Isabela. Come here, Dolores."

Daddy handed us each a glass. Mita wasn't allowed alcohol, on account of her medicines.

"To Brazil!" Daddy said. "*O país do futuro . . . e sempre vai ser!* The country of the future, and always will be!" He laughed at his own joke.

We'd heard that line about Brazil a hundred times. Daddy liked to use it on visitors from abroad.

Daddy held his glass in the air: "Cheers!" He polished off

his champagne in one gulp and refilled the glass too quickly, so it spilled onto the counter. Mummy went over to the sink and picked up a sponge to clean up. I could tell she was mad by the round-and-round way she wiped the counter, even after the spill was gone.

Daddy held his glass in the air again and waited for Mummy. "Try it, Isabela."

Mummy checked her watch. "It's too early, Ian."

I sipped my champagne.

Daddy downed his second glass.

I glanced at Mita. She was watching them.

"This is how you respond. To an occasion."

Mummy didn't say anything.

Daddy finished up the third glass. "Ungrateful," he said. "You're an ungrateful cow."

Mummy rinsed the sponge and placed it on the small plate where it belonged, as if she hadn't heard him.

Mita started to shake. Her legs kicked first, then her arms. She slumped over and her head moved from side to side.

We ran to her.

Mummy undid Mita's belt, and she fell sideways into Daddy's arms. He placed her on the floor and rolled her onto her side. I ran for the pillow. We held her as she shook. Her legs kicked the air in short, precise kicks, and her body curled and stretched out in spasms. Her shoulders shimmied as if she were dancing.

There was something wrong with this fit. Mummy and Daddy didn't notice, but I did. Mita opened and closed her good hand in a regular rhythm. Her movements weren't jerky enough.

"Mita, stop," I said. "You're bluffing."

Mita's legs kicked the air with even more energy.

"Don't be silly," Daddy said. "Keep her still, Isabela. Pull her tongue out."

Mita's eyes were pressed closed, the wrinkles pleated one on top of the other in a tight bundle. This wasn't the way her eyes looked during a fit. "She's bluffing," I said. "I can tell."

Mita slowed her shaking.

"She's pretending. I knew it! Mita, stop!"

Mita stopped shaking and opened first one eye, then the other—then laughed that hyena laugh of hers.

"I don't believe it," Daddy said. "Is it true?"

Mita screeched and laughed louder. Daddy shook his head and smiled. Mummy didn't seem happy: not about Mita, not about the champagne.

Mita looked pleased with herself. She'd stopped their fight. She reached out to stroke my arm.

She liked that I knew she was bluffing.

It made us close again.

Chapter Thirty-one

APRIL 1973

Andrea opens the door. "I'm so glad to see you. *A barra tá pesada.*" She looks at my cast. "What happened?"

So much happened. None of it good. "I broke my wrist."

"Come in," Andrea says. The *olheiras* under her eyes make her look older.

"You look tired," I say.

Tia Glória comes in with a pitcher of *batidas de maracujá.* "I just finished mixing. Your timing is perfect." At least she doesn't hate me. This is the first time I've seen her since Andrea was expelled. We sit on the sofa and Tia Glória pours each of us a small square glass.

Andrea wrinkles her nose. "It isn't sweet enough. I'm going to get more sugar." She goes to the kitchen.

I smile, feeling nervous. Tia Glória looks thin. She's all cheekbones and eyes. "I'm sorry about school," I say. "I'm really sorry." I don't tell her about bribing Mr. Walker. Andrea's right. She would go back to Antonio.

"It happens. We can't control what happens." She pulls a white hankie from inside her bra and dabs her eyes, smudging her makeup. "Please excuse me. It isn't you. Nothing to do with you girls."

Andrea returns, stirring her *maracujá* with her index finger. She plonks down next to me. "It's too quiet here. We need music."

"Not now," Tia Glória says. "You'll disturb Sofia."

"I don't care," Andrea says.

"Is Sofia here?" I want to thank her for saving me.

"She's resting," Tia Glória says. "She's not well."

"What's wrong? Can I see her?"

"She's not up to it."

"What d'you mean?"

Tia Glória folds and refolds her handkerchief, making a small, fat square. "She's hurt."

"Hurt?"

"They tortured her," Andrea says.

"Who tortured her?"

"The police, of course. Who else tortures people?" Andrea says.

"Shh, please. Don't wake her up," Tia Glória says.

"Is Sofia a communist?" I whisper. Poetry, speaking French, being Jewish. Sofia is full of mysteries.

Tia Glória smiles. "No, she certainly isn't a communist. Far from it!"

Sofia appears in the doorway, in her leopard-print robe.

Her right eye is swollen closed, and both her wrists are bandaged. "Can you shut up and let me sleep?" She slams the door closed.

"That's all she ever wants, is to sleep," Andrea says. "We can't be quiet the whole time. No one lives like that."

"She's recovering. It takes time." Tia Glória sips her drink. "Stupid. I told her not to go there. But she's *cismada* with foreigners, the ones from the hotels. Praça Onze has a reputation. That square is infested with police. Everybody knows."

Praça Onze is where we went to find me a taxi. "When did it happen?" I ask.

"More than a week ago," Andrea says. "That day we were going to sell your ring, but instead you played dice, remember?"

The day we were kidnapped. I put my glass down, thinking of that word: *despicable.* "It's my fault," I say.

"Don't be silly. How can it be your fault? She takes risks. Too many risks," Tia Glória says.

"She went there because of me." My voice chokes.

"She goes there all the time," Tia Glória says. "I tell her not to, but she wants to meet someone French. You know how she is."

"It was me. She took me to catch a taxi." My body starts to shake so violently, I feel it will come loose from my bones. I tell them. I tell them about the man who kidnapped us, about the cemetery. About Sofia walking me to the taxi stand at Praça Onze.

I wait for Andrea to withdraw, for Tia Glória to throw me out.

Andrea snuggles close and puts her arm around me. "We

don't know for sure it was that night," she says. "It could have happened the next day."

"It's one of her places," Tia Glória says.

"Even so." Andrea doesn't finish her sentence. She hands me my glass of *batida*.

I finish it up and Tia Glória pours me another. "In our line of work," she says. "There are dangers."

"Why did they torture her if she's not a communist?"

"Because they can," Tia Glória says. "They don't like *bichas.* They practice their tortures on them." She stands up. "I'm getting us some *brigadeiros.* We need something sweet. Keep your voices down."

Tia Glória never calls Sofia a *bicha.* We don't think of her that way.

"Let me see your broken arm," Andrea says.

I show her the white *gesso.*

"No one's signed yet. I want to be the first to sign." Andrea signs her name across my cast. "I'm sorry about the ring," she says. "That *filho da puta* ruined everything."

"I'm trying not to think about it," I say. "One day my mother will notice, and my life will be over."

Tia Glória brings out a tray of *brigadeiros.* Sobs from the bedroom. Gulps of sobs.

Andrea covers her ears. "Not again. I can't take this. It's too much."

Tia Glória shushes her. "We're lucky she's alive. Remember that."

"Nothing cheers her up," Andrea says. "Jokes, music, *fotonovelas.* She doesn't stop crying. All day long."

"Sometimes you need to cry," I say.

"Exactly right." Tia Glória offers me a *brigadeiro.* I have to put my drink down to pick it up. With only one hand, you have to plan things out. Mita had to do that all the time. I realize that some of the times Mita cried, it wasn't out of sadness: It was frustration. How difficult everything was.

"I've never broken a bone. Does it hurt?" Andrea says.

"Not really. Just a coldness."

The sobs pick up. Andrea sighs.

"Why don't you girls go out and buy her a *presentinho*? Something to cheer her up?" Tia Glória hands Andrea a ten-cruzeiro note.

Andrea stuffs the money in the pocket of her jeans. "Fine," she says. "But it won't work. Look what happened with the perfume."

"That was yesterday. We have to keep trying. You can't give up."

I follow Andrea down the stairs and outside. "What happened with the perfume?" I ask.

"L'Air du Temps! Mamma spent a fortune on Sofia's favorite perfume, and she turned away in disgust. She said she didn't like the smell anymore."

At the *banca de jornal,* we look at the magazines: *Picasso, Vida e Morte de um Genio,* that one is out. Nothing about death. Gal Costa on the cover of a *Manchete,* in a mini-top. Sofia loves Gal Costa. "What about this one?"

"I tried it already. She threw it on the floor and told me to leave her alone and let her die."

It's my fault she was tortured. It's my fault she wants to die. So many things are my fault. "When you lean into the wind, do you want it to happen? Do you want to die?" I ask.

Andrea walks over to the porn section. "I do and I don't. It's more of a flirtation, you know?"

I'm not sure how to flirt, so I don't say anything.

Andrea shows me a cartoon of a man putting his penis in

a pencil sharpener. “I don’t get this,” she says. She puts the *Playboy* back on the shelf. “I tried porn already. Nothing helps.”

“Poetry. French poetry. If anything can bring Sofia back, it’s poetry,” I say.

Chapter Thirty-two

"This has to be it," I say. There's no sign, but there are books in the window. A green awning flaps in the wind.

Andrea pushes the door open. A bell jingles. We step into a red room lined with shelves of books, one after another, in haphazard rows. Some books are maroon, like the ones in the library at school, some are dark green, and there is a shelf of colorful paperbacks.

Andrea pulls out one of the paperbacks: "*Où Est le Jardin?*" It's a grammar book. She slides it back into the empty sleeve of space on the shelf. "It's all in French."

"That's the point," I answer, looking at a green book about World War II. When Daddy discovers the diamond gone, it will be World War III. I walk over to the maroon section, hoping my Liar's Dice luck will guide me to the right book. Michel de Montaigne, *Essais.* There are too many hard words, and it's not poetry. I return Montaigne to his rightful place.

Andrea shows me a book of paintings by Raoul Dufy. "I like the colors, but boats? That won't work."

We're being watched. Looking is an energy; you can feel it. A tall man in a black turtleneck leans against the shelves, polishing his glasses with his sleeve. "May I help?" he says. His Portuguese has a slight accent; probably French.

"We'd like a poetry book," Andrea says. "French poetry. For a friend."

"Ah, *bien sûr.*"

"Do you have French poetry?" Andrea asks.

"*Mais oui,*" he says.

"Jacques Prévert," I suggest. "Our friend likes Jacques Prévert."

"Your friend is a romantic, then?" the man says.

"She used to be." Andrea shrugs. "Now I'm not so sure."

"Her heart has been broken, perhaps?"

Is he making fun of us? He seems genuine. Grown-ups don't usually take such careful interest.

"Definitely," Andrea says.

"Not her heart, but her spirit," I add.

The man nods as if he understands. He leads us to a section where the shelves are built into the wall and selects a narrow green book. "*Paroles.* This is his most famous collection."

I remember *paroles* from one of Monsieur Armand's flashcards. It means words, or lyrics. Andrea takes the book and opens it to a poem called "Cet Amour." One page is in French, and the opposite page is translated into Portuguese, so it's easy for us to understand.

"*This love / So violent / So fragile / So tender / So desperate* . . . sounds like Sofia, don't you think?" Andrea says.

"The desperate part does. I'm not sure about love poems."

"Listen to this: *Our love remains there / Stubborn as a mule / Lovely as desire / Cruel as memory* . . . isn't that wonderful?"

"You're thinking of you and Gilberto. It doesn't relate to Sofia." I turn to the man: "Sofia doesn't want to live anymore."

Andrea gives me a look.

"If we don't explain, we won't get the right book," I say. For some reason, I trust this man. Maybe it's the careful way he treats books. He hooks his index finger at the top of the spine and gently pulls each book free from the shelf. He is tender with books the way Daddy is tender with gems.

"She might need something darker, your friend?" the man says. "Rimbaud, Baudelaire?"

Andrea shrugs.

The man chooses a book called *Fleurs du Mal.* He reads it out loud in Portuguese, so we can understand. One of the poems is called "Spleen," and it talks about a mind tormented by disgust.

Sofia turning away from her favorite perfume. Her hollow eyes. The poem fits.

Sunlight streams in through the narrow window, making the dust dance in the air, as the man reads on: "*Dread / plants his black flag on my assenting skull.*"

The poem ends, and we are quiet. The awning flaps in the wind, like the wings of a bird.

"It's perfect," I say. "How did you know?"

"One can never be sure," the man says.

"It's a bit much. I prefer the love poems," Andrea says. "How much does it cost?"

The man turns to the back of the book, where the number 40 is written in pencil and circled.

"Twenty-five," he says.

"Are you sure?" I ask.

The man smiles. "I'm sure." He rings us up. It starts to rain, loud and hard, as if someone turned it on full force. The man slips the Jacques Prévert book of poems into the bag too. "Let me know how it goes, girls," he says.

As we head back, Andrea and I are bubbly with our inventiveness. We walk into the living room, wet through and hopeful.

"Shh, *meninas,* quiet," Tia Glória calls from the kitchen.

Sofia sits on the corner of the sofa, hugging her knees. Andrea walks over. "We bought you a present."

Sofia doesn't respond.

"Two presents, actually. D'you want to see?" She holds one book, then the other in front of Sofia's face.

Sofia doesn't move.

Andrea opens Jacques Prévert and finds the love poem she likes. She doubled over the corner, even though I told her not to. She reads it out loud, dramatically: "*This love / So violent / So fragile / So tender / So desperate*—"

"Stop!" Sofia says, her voice gravelly with anger.

Andrea is so caught up, she doesn't stop: "*Beautiful as the day / And as wretched as the weather . . .*"

Sofia's leg uncurls, and she kicks the coffee table. The vase with yellow daisies tips, and the flowers spill onto the floor.

"*Porra,*" Sofia says. "I said stop." She grits her teeth, the way Daddy does when he's mad.

Andrea closes the book, tears in her eyes.

Luciana appears out of nowhere with a sponge to absorb the water. She arranges the flowers back into the vase.

"Sorry," I say. "We hoped poems would help."

Sofia gathers her long legs into herself and lowers her head onto her knees.

Tia Glória brings out a clay tureen and some bowls. "Time for a little soup," she says. She holds a bowlful in front of Sofia. "It's your favorite, *sopa de couve.*"

Sofia keeps her head down.

Luciana sits next to Sofia on the sofa, and Tia Glória hands her the bowl of soup. Luciana takes a sip. "Mm, *que delícia,* Glória. Just what we need."

Andrea picks up the two books and heads to the kitchen. I follow her. "It makes me so mad," she says, throwing the books on the table. She turns on the water tap and splashes her forehead. "She doesn't even try!"

That's what Daddy says about me, that I don't try to make their Rio life work. "Maybe she can't try," I say. "Maybe she's not ready."

"It's rude. Plain rude." Andrea picks up the depressing book and sifts through the pages. "Perhaps it was the wrong poem. I think this one will work."

"I'm not sure today is right," I say.

Andrea marches back to the living room with the book.

Tia Glória signals no with her head, but Andrea ignores her.

"I don't care what you think. We bought this for you and I'm going to read it. Don't kick the table, because there's soup on it, okay? I'm going to read in Portuguese. French is too hard."

Andrea leafs through the pages. " 'Spleen,' part four," she announces; her voice is loud and determined.

It's a strange poem; it reminds me of an armadillo. Beautiful and horrible at the same time.

Sofia lifts her head and listens.

Andrea takes a breath, then continues. When she arrives at the final line about the black flag, Sofia reaches for the book. She reads the poem to herself. Her eyes follow the lines. Her lips twitch, as if she's sounding out the words. We sit with her, in the silence of reading.

When Sofia is done, she hugs the maroon packet of a book to her chest. She doesn't say a word, but there's a shift in the room.

Tia Glória opens the window. Raindrops hit the sidewalk and scatter, one after the other. None of us speak.

"*Ai,* it's too quiet," Andrea says. She walks to the record player.

"Nothing too drastic," Tia Glória says.

Andrea puts on a slow samba, one of the old ones.

Sofia places the book on her lap. She leans over and serves herself some soup with the ladle. "Good," she says, sipping from the edge of the spoon. "I like soup on a rainy day."

Chapter Thirty-three

"She was better for a few days. But now she's bad again," Andrea sighs into the phone. This morning Tia Glória found Sofia with a knife at her wrist and had to wrestle it from her. "It's too much."

"Let's go back to the bookstore," I suggest. Mita's medicines used to work at first, then she'd develop a tolerance; maybe it's the same with poems. "We need a different book."

Andrea says she doesn't have the energy for it. Plus, she's already made plans with Gilberto, to go to a dogfight. She didn't invite me because she knows I hate dogfights; but she needs a distraction.

I go to the bookstore alone. The man is there, and he remembers me.

"Why French poetry?" the man asks. "I need to know more about your friend."

I tell him Sofia studied at PUC, the Catholic university, but dropped out after her mother died. Then she had to move, because of Queen Elizabeth, and now she doesn't have a stable home. I tell him everything I know—without certain facts he might misunderstand. It might not be wise to mention Sofia's actual profession, or to explain that she's a *travesti,* and that she was arrested because of it.

"It isn't safe for students these days," the man says.

"Exactly," I answer. I don't mention the police, but for some reason I have the feeling he knows that Sofia was tortured.

The man, his name is Eduardo, takes me to another shelf, where the books are shielded by a transparent plastic curtain. He explains that the plastic protects photographs from too much light. He pulls down a medium-sized square book. "Take a look," he says. Each poem is paired with a photograph. A prison wall with barbed wire along the top, next to a poem about the stillness of a tongue that cannot tell a story. My tongue felt dead in my mouth, after Mita left. Like a slug. Visitors would ask me questions and I'd stay quiet, not able to answer. It made Daddy furious, my silence. He thought I was doing it on purpose. I close the book. "Poems and photographs at the same time is too much."

Eduardo nods as if he agrees and moves on to another shelf. I notice a doorway behind the atlas section. "What kind of books are in there?"

"That's my private collection," Eduardo says. "You're welcome to take a look."

I step into a small room lit by colorful Tiffany lamps. It's painted a purple-gray color that is warm and restful, like the shade of a tree. Two caramel leather armchairs face each other. Manuel Bandeira, Carlos Drummond de Andrade, Clarice Lispector.

"These are not French writers," I say.

"They're wonderful," Eduardo says, "my favorites."

I slide a thin slice of a book off the shelf: Vinicius de Moraes. "He's a singer. My father likes him."

"Your father has good taste."

I read the quote from the back cover: *Whisky is man's best friend, it's a dog in a bottle.* No wonder Daddy likes him. When Daddy finds the diamond gone, he'll probably need a lot of whisky. It makes me nervous to think about it. He's never hit me before, but I can imagine that happening.

Eduardo walks over to the record player and puts on "Apesar de Você": *Today you're in charge. That's it, it's been spoken. There is no discussion. My people talk sideways and look at the floor . . .*

"Wasn't this song banned?" Daddy thought it was clever, how the song pretended to be about love but was really about the dictatorship.

"It was."

I sift through his collection of records. Caetano Veloso, Vandré. "Roda Viva." Most of the songs banned. Caetano Veloso came back from exile last month. "Are you a communist?"

Eduardo smiles. "Not exactly, but I'm sympathetic."

"What if they find you, the police?"

"A few songs, a few books. This room reminds me that it won't always be this way. Brazil won't always be like this."

Chico Buarque sings in the background. *You who invented sin forgot to invent forgiveness . . .*

"Sit down and read. I'll make us some coffee."

I sink into the softness of the leather, with Vinicius de Moraes. "Soneto de Separação": *Suddenly, the laughter turns into a wail . . . the calm becomes the wind . . . Suddenly, no more than suddenly.* How true. Life can change in a moment and never be the same.

Eduardo brings out a tall silver coffeepot and pours us each a cup. "Milk?" he asks. "Sugar?"

"Black, please. With a spoonful of sugar." Eduardo sits opposite me and crosses his legs.

"I like this room. I've never been in a room painted this color before. You might think it would be sad, but it isn't."

Eduardo nods in agreement. "It's a warm darkness. Good for reading."

Eduardo introduces me to some of his favorite poems. Each one is like a small world, transporting me into a life, a place, a love lost or found.

The doorbell interrupts us. Eduardo places his cup down on the table. "I guess it's back to work," he says. "You're welcome to stay and read."

When I next look up, it's dark outside, only the lamp lighting the page. I stand up, my legs stiff.

Eduardo appears. "Ah," he said. "I didn't want to interrupt."

"I'm sorry. I didn't notice the time."

He smiles. "That's what books can do. I've been thinking about your friend Sofia." He hands me three books. "Let me know how she does with them."

THE POEMS BEGIN TO WORK again. Day by day, Sofia comes back to us. It reminds me of Mita, how she would emerge after a fit—sometimes it took minutes, sometimes days. Whenever it happened, it filled us with happiness. Mummy would bake an orange cake and we'd sit on the veranda and sing the songs Mita loved: "Cai, Cai, Balão," "Atirei o Pau no Gato," "Once I Caught a Fish Alive."

Tia Glória, Luciana, Andrea, and I take turns reading the poems out loud, in Portuguese and French. Sofia corrects our pronunciation. Tia Glória says she never liked school, but maybe she should have given it more of a chance; she had no idea poems could make you feel things, like songs.

Andrea and I go back to the bookstore for new recommendations. That's when I start to cook up my matchmaking plan. Sofia wants a Frenchman, and a Frenchman who loves poetry seems perfect. Andrea loves the idea. We can't decide if their first meeting should be at the bookshop or at a bar. Andrea says a bar is better: There would be music and drinks, and the right atmosphere for attraction to develop. We decide to wait until Sofia has fully recovered. I begin to imagine them together; a *novela* where Sofia falls in love, but for once, it's with someone nice.

Chapter Thirty-four

JULY 1973

Mita's been gone one year. This morning, when I looked at the Ruby on my calendar, all I could think of was blood. I don't want to speak to anyone. It feels even worse than our birthday, which I'd refused to celebrate. Visiting Andrea didn't help. She asked me what was wrong, but I couldn't tell her. My tongue was still in my mouth, like the poem said. I want the day to be over.

When I arrive home, I see Aparecida sitting in the living room, with Mummy and Daddy. Her back is too straight, and her hands rest on her knees in a stiff way. There's something wrong.

I drop my satchel and run over. "Is it your mother?" I ask. Aparecida's mother has malaria, but she'd been getting better with the pills.

"My mother's fine," Aparecida says.

Daddy buckles his cigarette into the ashtray. Mummy sips her sherry. Both their faces look grim.

"What happened?"

"I'll pack my bags and leave, then." Aparecida stands up and smooths the wrinkles on her flowered cotton dress.

"What do you mean *leave*?"

Aparecida walks toward the kitchen.

"Aparecida, what happened?"

"Ask your parents what happened."

She closes the door to her room and locks it. I knock, but Aparecida doesn't open. I hear the scrape of metal—she's moving her bed. I knock again. She's never locked me out before.

After a few minutes, I return to the living room. "Why is Aparecida leaving?"

Daddy swirls his gin-tonic with his finger. "Sit down, Dolores, we need to talk."

I half sit on the corner of the sofa, my legs jittery.

Daddy lights up a cigarette. "Your mother's blue diamond was stolen."

They know. It was bound to happen, but I managed to tuck it into some corner of my brain and not think about it.

"We've been taken for suckers," Daddy says, chewing his bottom lip.

"You can't trust anyone," Mummy says.

"I had to fire her. I had no choice," Daddy says.

"Fire? You fired Aparecida?" This is terrible. It never occurred to me they would blame Aparecida. "You can't do that. It wasn't her."

"Of course it was her," Mummy says. "I don't know how she thought we wouldn't find out."

"There was a robbery. On the seventh floor. Maybe that same robber stole the diamond. I'm sure it was the robber." My voice is too loud. I must be calm. Convince them.

"That was months ago," Mummy says. "On the other side of the building."

"Someone else, then. Someone else stole the diamond. I promise you: It wasn't Aparecida."

"We know you love her. We loved her too. I didn't see this one coming." Daddy drums his fingertips on the wooden arm of his chair.

I can't let Aparecida pay for my crime. It would be so wrong. "I did it. I stole the diamond."

"Don't be silly," Daddy says. "I don't believe that for one minute."

I stand up, my cheeks on fire. "I'm the one who should pay the price. Not Aparecida. I took it. How would Aparecida know the code?"

"She must have watched us," Mummy says. "Maybe we opened the safe while she was in the room."

"Seven-seven-three. That's the code," I say, looking straight at Daddy. "I knew it had to be some variation of seventy-three, like dice. That's your trick, right?"

Daddy turns pale.

"Do you believe me now?"

A knot of muscle slides from Daddy's ear down his jaw. He looks defeated in a way I've never seen before.

"Where's my ring?" Mummy asks.

"I lost it."

Daddy's hands fist up. "Bloody liar."

"It was stolen. When I broke my wrist."

Daddy sits there, not moving. I can't tell if he's angry or sad. I would prefer angry. I've hurt them. I thought I wouldn't care, but I do. I wanted to hurt them, but where did it get me? All I have is a sense of being despicable. Truly despicable.

"Why are you doing this to us?" Daddy says.

"To find Mita. I was going to sell the diamond and find Mita."

Mummy walks over and slaps me.

The surprise of it makes me tear up. I touch my cheek where it burns.

She grabs my shoulder. Her nails dig into me.

"Isabela." Daddy places his hand on Mummy's arm. "There's no point."

After a few moments, she lets go.

MUMMY KNOCKS ON APARECIDA'S DOOR. I listen from the *lavanderia*.

"It's me, Isabela. Please. Open the door."

Aparecida unlocks her door.

Mummy says she's sorry, they were mistaken, she knows that now. It was me who stole the diamond, they can't believe it, but it's true. "I hope you can forgive us."

Aparecida stays quiet.

"I'm sorry we jumped to conclusions."

Silence.

"We would like you to stay on. It was our mistake."

Aparecida doesn't answer.

I step out from behind the hanging clothes, into Aparecida's room. "I'm so sorry, Aparecida. I took the ring. It's my fault. I never meant for this to happen."

Aparecida looks at her toes. Her lips tighten at the edges, making slight dimples.

"Please, Aparecida. Please stay. Forgive me." Tears slide down my cheeks.

"I need to finish packing." Aparecida lifts a small suitcase and places it on her bed.

"I hope you're proud of yourself." There is hatred in Mummy's eyes. She turns and walks out of Aparecida's room.

Now it's just the two of us.

"I'm sorry. I truly am."

Aparecida opens her cupboard and starts laying her dresses, one on top of the other, into the suitcase. She scoops up her panties and bras from her top drawer and dumps them on top of the dresses.

I touch Aparecida's arm. "I can't bear it if you go. I already lost Mita, please."

Aparecida empties the second drawer, then the third.

When all her clothes are packed, Aparecida snaps the buckles of her suitcase closed. She reaches for the almond oil, sits on the bed, and begins to massage her feet.

"Please stay."

Aparecida pushes her thumbs into the arches of her feet. "I thought I was family, but I found out I'm just a servant."

"You are family, you are." Tears stream down my face. Every time Mita was in the hospital, Aparecida was there with me. She came with us to Rio. She never changed. She's always been my friend: "You are more my family than my parents."

Aparecida begins to cry. She reaches under her bed and pulls out the basket with *fotonovelas.* "You can have these," she says. "I won't need them." She caps the almond oil and drops the bottle in the basket with the magazines.

"Please, Aparecida, give me a chance."

Aparecida places her set of keys on the pillow. She picks

up her suitcase and walks through the *lavanderia,* to the back door.

I follow her and watch as she waits for the lift. Her flowered dress is so faded the yellow flowers almost disappear into white.

At the last moment, she turns. "And you: Stealing from your own family? *Isso não se faz.*" She shakes her head in disgust.

The doors of the lift slide closed.

I think of that game we used to play, Aparecida/Desaparecida, where Aparecida would hide and we'd go looking for her. Mita's excitement would mount as we'd search behind the bushes, inside the hammock, under the beds. When we'd finally find Aparecida, Mita's screech would be so loud, her joy so intense, it always made us laugh.

Now Mita is gone, and Aparecida is gone too. Going, going, gone.

Chapter Thirty-five

There are waves of laughter coming from the party. I know the sound so well: Too many gin-tonics, and the jokes spin out, and soon there will be squeals, and cigars with the brandy, before the dancing starts. You'd think they'd get sick of one another, having parties every weekend.

I pour myself a shot of straight cachaça and walk out to the *lavanderia,* trying not to look at Aparecida's closed door. I miss the sound of her *chinelos* in the background, the way she'd sing "Madalena," over and over, she loved that song. Yesterday, she was part of our family, and now she's gone. I stare at the wash, hanging above our marble sinks. Daddy's bleached white work shirts, with the buttons done all the way up so they dry straight, though he never wears them that way and hates anything tight around his neck. Mummy's pink-and-white Marks & Spencer underwear that cover her whole bottom, right up to her belly button. The cachaça disconnects the sadness from my brain, so I see things from a floaty, peaceful distance.

"Look who's turned into a young woman now." I see a faint swirl of cigarette smoke and turn to find John Carver watching me from the doorway. He came to visit us a few times, in Santanésia.

"Hello. Having a quick drink," I say, gulping the rest down. John lifts the bottle of cachaça he's holding and pours me another one.

"The backside of the party," he says. "More interesting, perhaps?"

"Backsides always are," I answer, sounding more flirty than I mean to. We both laugh.

John Carver is one of Daddy's youngest friends, and he comes over from England without his family. He tells me he's been stuck in "the interior" for six weeks, he's happy to be back in civilization at last. He's tanned dark, and when he lifts his arm to drink, I see the pale line of his English skin under his watch strap.

"How old are you now?" he asks. "Fifteen? Sixteen?"

"Yes," I say—leaving it open. Thirteen sounds much younger than I feel, so why correct him?

"Last time I saw you, I gave you a lesson about riptides."

"Came in useful," I say. "About a week later, I was caught in one. I didn't fight it, I let it take me all the way out and waited, like you said. Then I swam parallel and managed to get back." I tell it like a story, but really, I thought I would die.

The riptide pulled me under like a giant octopus, and I struggled in a panic, until my arms and legs ached. Then I remembered his advice.

"Good to be prepared," he says. "Learned that in the navy."

Daddy doesn't believe John was really in the navy; he says it doesn't add up. He also went to Oxford and spent time in Singapore and the Middle East. "Do the math, Isabela," Daddy said. "Could be MI6 or even the CIA."

More laughter from the living room, louder now, like a pulse. Daddy said he expects me to pass *salgadinhos* and refill drinks. It's the least I can do, after all the misery I've caused.

"Can I have a fag?" I ask, and John hands me a Pall Mall. He leans over to light it and I feel like Audrey Hepburn, in one of the old black-and-white films Mummy loves so much.

"Thanks," I say, taking a slow, long inhale. I never noticed how John's eyes shift from gray to green to dark gray. He really is handsome.

"God, it's good to be here in Rio," he says. "You have no idea."

Just then, the other English John comes out, John Davis. "What are you two doing out here?" he asks. His tall, skinny body leans this way and that, as if he might keel over, but his voice sounds sober.

I take another shot of cachaça, my third. I feel dangerous in an exciting way. If I were a boy I might pick a fight, but since I'm a girl, I'm not quite sure what I'll do.

"So how's the interior?" John Davis asks. "I rather liked it there, myself."

"Lonely," young John says, and blushes. "I miss my family."

"Course you do," skinny John says. "It's easier for us bachelors, to get sent down there."

I remember Daddy saying how disgusting it was that John

Davis liked young boys. "A right pervert, he is," Daddy said. "The whole village knows, and there's not a damn thing we can do about it."

"Yoo-hoo! Yoo-hoo!" A woman appears with a sunburned face, her upturned nose beginning to peel. I've never seen her before. "What is this, a secret conference?"

"Care to join?" Young John fills her up a glass of cachaça. "Dolores here is introducing us to the other side of life. Behind the flats."

"The maids' quarters," I say. "Here in Brazil, we still have maids." I take another gulp of cachaça, trying not to think of Aparecida.

"Still have them in England too," the woman says. "I'm Susie. You must be Ian and Isabela's daughter."

"One of them," I answer.

"You have a sister, then?"

"I do. My twin. They sent her away, but she does exist—or at least they say she does. They prefer not to talk about her."

Susie's smile collapses. I can see she doesn't know what to do with that information. The two Johns choose to ignore it.

"Quite boisterous, this party," Susie says, breaking the silence. "Are your dinner parties always like this?"

"If there's enough booze." I look up at the wash hanging above our heads and wonder how Mummy would like the visitors seeing this part of the house: Daddy's fishing rods sticking out from behind an old jacaranda cupboard, next to Aparecida's room. A dented pressure cooker next to some old suitcases. Pieces of Santanésia. Before Mita left. Before Rio and Daddy's important job. Then I see something metal above the cupboard, stacked on top of the suitcases. Could it be? I reach up. Wheels: Mita's wheelchair—folded up like a flat, narrow packet, on top of the cupboard. I turn the wheel and hear it whir. Mummy didn't throw it away after all.

"Can you do me a huge favor, please?" I ask handsome John. "Can you get this down for me?"

He easily reaches it. He lifts it up above my head and places it on the ground next to us.

"A wheelchair," Susie says. "Whose is it?"

"My sister's," I say, suddenly sad. Even though it's folded flat like a sandwich, it's as if Mita is in there, flat too, folded into an invisible postcard of a twin. I lean in with all my body weight and pry the chair open, separating the wheels to make space. It's rusty, so I have to push down hard.

There's a sound of champagne popping.

"We need to get back," John Davis says. "I think your mother's Baked Alaska is ready."

Susie follows him, and handsome John looks at me and raises an eyebrow. "Care to join us?"

"In a moment," I say. "Give me a moment."

He leaves. I sit in Mita's wheelchair. It's small, but I'm skinny, so I fit. There's a ragged edge that cuts into my underleg. I flip the pedals open and place my bare feet, one on each pedal. My toes are bright pink, and my feet look brown compared to Margarita's little white feet, how soft they were: like small fat fish with swollen bellies. I twist my left foot inward and imagine it curving, more than it can possibly go. I stretch into her deformity, trying to find myself in her, or her inside me.

I hear my own breathing, as if I'm a diver with an oxygen tank. It thunders inside me. I wonder how it feels to be paralyzed. When I turn the wheels, they make a squishy sound on the marble floor. My hands are black with dust and dirt. I propel myself forward.

I remember the tinkle of the orange glass beads as she wheeled herself through the kitchen doorway. Whenever there was cake batter Mita would appear—she'd smell it a mile away, and she'd arrive, pedals first, and the whir of her wheels, her face leaning forward, always leaning forward, wanting to lick one of the beaters, even before Mummy was done with the mixing.

"Wait a minute, Margarita," Mummy would laugh—this was before she forgot how to laugh—"you have to be patient."

"N-no!" Mita would wail, and Mummy would give her the beater, soaked in batter. She didn't mind the mess then.

I wonder if the bead curtain is still there, clinking in the wind, or has someone replaced it with a wooden door? Are the rooms pale green, or are they a different color now? There were stains along the walls like tiny rivers marking the different floods that came year after year. We were lucky, they never went above knee height. Mummy thought of painting over, but what was the point? The next flood would create another stain, and in some ways, they measured the years, like the marks in the doorway measured our heights. Little markings: Dolores here, Margarita there. A close race where we were millimeters from each other, but each mark counted. Some years Margarita was taller; others, I won the race. Until it was just me that got measured. Daddy found times to do it when Mita wasn't there, when she went to the *feira* with Mummy, or to the club. Then he would mark my height: How much I'd grown. I felt like a traitor, like occupied France during World War II. I enjoyed my own growing, but it was secret and hurtful. I knew it was a matter of time before Mita noticed the tiny new pen-mark Daddy made. Even though he made them smaller and smaller each time, I'd catch her looking and I'd see her eyes glaze with tears, but she never said anything and neither did I.

I wonder if our house still exists, up there on the mountain, with its flood-marks and its measurements. It belonged to the paper mill; when John goes to the village, does he stay there, with his boys?

I hear Mummy's footsteps and the creak of the oven door opening. I hear her slide the Baked Alaska out, probably onto one of the Royal Doulton serving plates, and carry it into the dining room. I imagine she's beginning to serve, to carefully cut into it, hoping it won't collapse, hoping the ice cream is melting just a little but not too much, so it holds. A perfect castle of a Baked Alaska.

I wheel myself across the kitchen. I have to use all my strength to get myself to move forward, toward the dining room. The tires are soft, and the metal rim makes a scraping sound against the marble.

"Perfect, Isabela!" I hear Susie say. "How do you time it so perfectly?"

"Stupendous," Daddy says in his visitor-voice. "Stupendous, Isabela."

The wheelchair is lower than our dining room chairs, so I have a great view of people's knees, with their napkins folded underneath the tablecloth and their hands resting on their legs or reaching for something above. It's as if I'm a little girl again, not tall enough to see what the adults are doing. It's hard to maneuver close in. I never realized how much being in a wheelchair separates you. Even when you are together with everyone, you're in your own world. I roll myself next to Susie and handsome John and pull on the brakes—just as Daddy is about to take a bite, his mouth open, beaming at everyone. He sees me and his mouth shuts. I watch him from below. He looks like a catfish. He opens and closes his mouth and then he frowns and looks over at Mummy, who is serving a tidy triangle of Baked Alaska—a little wobbly but standing pretty with the ribbon of strawberries on top of the sponge cake, and the fluffy egg whites perky and perfectly bronzed on top, like a golden hat.

"What the hell d'you think you're doing?" Daddy's voice is raspy with anger.

Everyone's eyes are on me, and I sit there, not having thought it all out. Just me, remembering Mita: wanting to announce her back into our family again.

"I found Mita's wheelchair."

Mummy puts her knife down, and her cheeks look flat and a little droopy, like a too-old pear. "That's dirty, Dolores. Not at all funny. Take it back into the kitchen."

"I'm keeping Mita's place for her until she comes back," I say.

Daddy twirls the stem of his wineglass between his fingers: "Get out," he says. "Get the hell out."

The other visitors eat quietly, pretending not to listen. Mummy picks up her napkin and wipes her eyes, and I realize she's crying. There must be a meanness in me that runs deep because I'm glad she's crying; it doesn't make me sorry. Not one bit.

"Can I have a piece of Baked Alaska, please?" I ask, my voice all politeness.

Susie leans over, cuts me a piece, and hands it down to me. I balance the plate on my knees, like Mita used to, and lean over to take a bite. The ice cream is cold and soft against the roof of my mouth, and the sweetness melts something in me.

"I wish Mita could be with us here, right now," I say.

Then I'm crying, tears sliding down my knees. I notice

how knobby they are and wonder whether I look like her. When Mummy and Daddy look at me sitting here, do they see Mita in me, or do they just see an angry daughter ruining their dinner party?

Daddy pushes his chair back and stands up, wineglass in hand, and walks into the living room. The two Johns and the other Englishman follow him. Susie starts collecting the plates, taking them to the kitchen. Mummy sits at the table, her slice of Baked Alaska untouched, melting into a swirly puddle of whites on the plate. She doesn't speak, and neither do I.

"Why do you have to be so selfish?" she says, her voice hurt and edgy at the same time. "I hope you're proud of yourself."

I don't feel proud; just a sequin of anger deep in my chest, and an ache of remembering that spreads itself all over my body.

"Isabela, come in here, I've poured you a sherry." Daddy's voice is light and airy, as if he's having the time of his life. "Come and show Susie your aquamarine."

Mummy stands up and folds her serviette carefully in four and lays it down on the table. She turns around and walks gracefully to the living room, in her blue silk dress and her silver strappy heels.

The dinner party resumes. I sit in Mita's wheelchair and listen to the laughter. The conversation floats across the bamboo curtain toward me. Ronald Biggs, the famous train robber again—*blah, blah, blah.*

I open and close my fingers, then curl them in and hold them tight, my nails biting into the palms of my hand. I imagine never being able to open my hand; that if someone were to carefully unroll my fingers one by one, the way I used to do with Mita's fingers, they would roll back in immediately, like a yo-yo. I imagine sitting in this chair for the rest of my life; my hips rusty with not moving, my legs becoming stringy and withered, like old green beans. I imagine my parents leaving me in a hospital in England and never coming back, how I would watch through the window every day, waiting for them, not believing that they could actually forget me.

Chapter Thirty-six

Sun slips through the shutters. It must be morning. My body is stiff from sitting in Mita's wheelchair all night. Mita has been sitting for four years. Her bones must ache.

I stand up and walk down the corridor, leaving the wheelchair behind. I feel walking: the absolute pleasure of each step, the freedom.

I pass the built-in cupboards Mummy loves so much, filled with bottles of whisky and cartons of every cigarette you can imagine: Benson & Hedges, Carltons, Marlboros, even mint-flavored ones from America called Kools. In the living room, I slide the front window open. The sea is dark violet. Waves slap against one another and explode into a ridge of spray.

Wind pours in and whips my hair this way and that. Mita's

hair had to be cut short so it would lie flat under her Styrofoam helmet. She couldn't reach up and touch it anymore.

Downstairs, the porter holds the door open for me. He doesn't ask questions, but he looks worried. I'm going to let the wind decide. Die or live. I am tired of this fight.

The surfboards are tied flat to the ground, one on top of the other like stacked cards. A red flag ripples in the wind. I abandon my *chinelos* and walk barefoot along the beach. Sand stings my face. A wall of wind pushes me backward.

I've messed everything up.

I've lost the diamond. I've lost Aparecida.

If I live, I have to accept it: Mita is gone. And I'm still here.

Mummy says it was a miracle that either of us survived. We were born too little.

But I don't want to live in a world without Mita.

I wonder what Mita wants. Now that she can't wheel herself into the kitchen, through our curtain of beads, to taste leftover cake batter from the beater. Now that she can't watch the hummingbirds from under the shade of the *jabuticaba* tree. Then, she was part of our life, even if she couldn't walk. She could collect snails and rocks, and when I placed a caterpillar on her leg, it tickled, and she laughed. I bet no one in that hospital in England puts caterpillars on her knees.

Sofia said I was born lucky. If I'm so lucky, why does it feel terrible?

I walk along Ipanema, all the way to Arpoador. I follow the path and climb the wet rocks, gripping with my toes. The waves surge in and explode over the rocks. I wait until each wave is spent, then I climb higher. I slip. My knee bleeds, and two of my fingers. I reach the top.

Ipanema, Leblon, and the Dois Irmãos are in the distance.

They're called the Two Brothers because they're next to each other, but quite different: One mountain is low and slopes to the right, while the other is tall and jagged.

Maybe it would have been different if Mita were my sister, and not my identical twin. Maybe life would have felt more possible.

The wind dies, and a strange quietness descends. A quietness that is louder than sound.

"I'm sorry, Mita!" I shout, louder than I have ever shouted in my life. "I'm sorry, I'm sorry, I'm sorry!"

The wind picks up again. I walk to the ledge that overlooks Praia do Diabo.

I open my arms wide, the way Andrea showed me. Eyes closed, I lean backward. The wind pushes into me.

I surrender to luck, to the wind, to the roll of the dice. *Sorry sorry sorry*. It's the only word I have. The wind holds me and holds and holds and then it gusts and dies. I fall backward. I fall—and try to reach with my fingers, to hold on to nothing—I try. I don't want to go down—no, I don't. Then the wind picks up, stronger than ever before, and throws me forward, flat on my face on the ground. The wind screams and my mouth bleeds and I am here.

The blood tastes of metal and I am still here.

Chapter Thirty-seven

SANTANÉSIA

I was in my pretty flannel dress with tiny apricot roses. Mita had the same exact dress, only her roses were yellow. We tried to put a yellow rose on her helmet, but when we looked in the mirror, it looked stupid, tucked in among the triangles of empty space and bands of Styrofoam. Mita plucked out the rose with her good hand and shredded it. I had a wide-brimmed sombrero with peach roses, and I took it off in solidarity, but later—minutes before the dance—I put it back on. Mita saw, but she didn't say anything. She looked down at her hands, tucked tidily on her lap.

São João, São João, acende a fogueira do meu coração . . . The bonfire spit sparks, and I noticed Jaime watching me as I tried to strap a straw hat on top of Mita's helmet so she wouldn't be the only girl without a hat. He walked toward me in his cowboy boots—not painted black socks, like the other boys, but real boots. He stood in front of us but spoke only to me, as if Mita weren't there. People ignored her because she was in a wheelchair. I felt a spark of anger glitter inside me, like the sparks that floated in the air above the bonfire, but Jaime's green eyes were kind and he seemed shy.

"Would you like to dance?" he asked. My heart accelerated. I looked at Mita and then tried to spot Mummy. She was across the way, talking to the other mothers by the accordion player. I couldn't catch her eye. Daddy was nowhere to be seen; probably getting as far as he could from the music.

Jaime shifted from one boot to the other, waiting for my answer. I leaned close to Mita's face and said, "Is it okay if I go, Mita, for this one dance?" Mita tried to focus her eyes, they were halfway closed. "Is it okay?" I asked, knowing I wasn't really giving her a choice. She gripped my hand tight. I had to untangle my fingers from hers, one by one.

I took hold of Jaime's outstretched hand, and we galloped toward the other children; children from Santanésia and São Lourenço, and Barra do Piraí, everyone celebrating. My flannel dress twirled wide when Jaime spun me around and he smelled of fresh-cut grass and ash and a smoky man-boy smell I thought was cologne, he smelled of trees. We hooked elbows and turned and turned until I was dizzy and laughing and he was laughing, white teeth, dark skin, dark from the sun and riding horses all day. We danced the next set and the next, until we decided to rest and catch our breath. I held my long hair off my neck, I remember the trickle of sweat down my neck, above my lips, under my earlobes. I forgot, almost completely forgot, about Margarita.

I remember the heat from the bonfire, how it made my cheeks burn, how his kiss landed like a breath, light and fruity then pressed in on itself with a question and all my worries about the tangle of tongues and teeth and where our noses would go, all those worries disappeared. We kissed back and forth, my hat slipping backward, hanging like a hammock behind me. I let myself kiss him knowing Vânia and Claudinha and all the other girls might be watching my very first kiss and not caring, because it was so delicious. It wasn't like truth-or-dare kissing, which was more like a feat to reckon with—like jumping from a high wall or a backward dive. No, this was a finding, losing, finding kind of kissing, more like a conversation where his tongue asked questions and mine answered back . . . Kissing wasn't at all like spitting, there was no saliva taste and saliva made me think of Mita and her *babas*—all of a sudden, I remembered to look.

Mita was slumped over.

I pushed him away.

She was completely slumped over in her wheelchair. I ran to her. The fit had already started and there was blood on her face when I pulled her up. I saw she'd bitten her tongue and her eye jerked upward, her lips, there was blood everywhere, on her lap down her chin and then it was on my hands and my dress. Mummy was there and Daddy. We wheeled her away from the celebration as the rain started, the black rain that didn't stop for so many days and nights like Mita's fit that didn't stop and it was all my fault because I was the one in charge of her.

Chapter Thirty-eight

Mita's fit was slowing down, the one that had started at São João and continued through the storm. Her shaking had settled into a quiet shiver, and then her body was calm, and she opened her eyes. The higher dose had worked. Dr. Miguel said he better get back before the flood arrived. Daddy didn't worry that the river might overflow or that Resende might become completely underwater. Mummy hummed as she made us hot chocolate.

Mita was back. That was all that mattered.

I promised God that I would never kiss again. Give me one more chance to be a good sister: just one. I vacuumed the living room and went with Mummy to the *farmácia* to pick up Mita's medications.

The pharmacist held her *figa* close to her heart: "It's going to be a bad one," she warned. "A flood like the one in the Bible."

Mummy nodded politely and said she was too tired to be alarmed. Daddy was taking care of the house. He'd blockaded the back door with sandbags and made sure he had extra batteries for the torch.

But by lunchtime, it was clear this was no normal rain. The world turned into a waterfall—a torrent of rain so loud we could barely hear one another speak. The drops were silver-black and hard, like hundreds of tiny bullets.

Usually, the electricity was the first thing to go, so we stayed inside with candles and flashlights. The clouds were so dark and the air so thick, it felt like night. We lit the candles early.

It was peaceful and cozy inside our house, the candles throwing shadows over the living room, Mummy laughing, opening cans for lunch. Cans of sausages and peaches, cans of green beans with no flavor. But nobody minded. Mummy didn't worry about getting it wrong, and Daddy hadn't expected too much, so he wasn't disappointed.

Mita was emerging. Her muscles were floppy but she could follow us with her eyes and laugh at jokes. It usually took a day for Mita to recover. I worried she would be mad at me for leaving her to dance with Jaime. Mita didn't seem mad; maybe she didn't remember.

We sat by the window and watched the storm outside. The wind uprooted whole trees. The branches of the old *jabuticaba* tree arched and quivered, like Daddy's fishing rod when he had a *dourado* on the line. We heard a cracking sound, and the trunk fell sideways. The branches disappeared into the swirling river of mud while the roots reached upward, like crooked fingers.

Mita was especially snuggly, the way she was after a bad fit. My job was to keep her awake. The longer she was awake after a fit, the better.

I pointed to a piece of corrugated metal and wondered out loud whose roof it was. It was sad to see pieces of people's lives float by. We recognized Maria's pink door, Alfredo's wooden duck collection.

A tree fell on the power line and snapped it. One end flew in the air and sparked, then we heard a *bang,* like a gunshot.

"Bloody hell, the transformer!" Daddy said. The wire flew around like some crazy out-of-control whip.

Mummy stopped opening cans and stood next to him, both of them holding hands. The flood had reached our front steps—so we knew Claudinha's house and Elói's and all the houses by the factory were long gone. We had the second-highest house in the village, on top of the hill.

"I've never seen it like this." Daddy's voice was almost glad, full of respect for the flood, as if he were admiring a rare tourmaline.

A carpet of snakes lined our front steps, we could see them from the side window. They slithered one on top of the other, making a fat necklace around the door.

The wire dove into the bamboo and there was this *whoosshhhh* like a waterfall, only it was fire. In seconds, the bamboo was alive with fire, spitting in all directions.

"I've never seen anything like this," Daddy said again.

The fire made me think of the bonfire and Jaime's kiss, the press of his lips, the deliciousness of it. I brushed my lips lightly with my fingertips, remembering. Mita leaned forward in her wheelchair, pointing with her good hand at the burning bamboo.

I didn't know flames could emerge from water like that. It seemed like a miracle.

The wind whistled through the trees, making an eerie kind of music. Wind was bad news, Daddy said, because it could carry the flames. All of us were busy watching, and then Mita fell over sideways onto the floor, her arms and legs flailing around like the power line. Her back arched and there was a flower of blood under her head, bright red on our terra-cotta tiles.

Mummy took hold of Mita's hands while Daddy grabbed her feet, but Mita shook them free, her body violent like never before.

The wind ripped through trees. The fire roared.

Daddy said be careful, dammit, she's strong. Her tongue: Don't let her bite. Mummy put her hand into Mita's mouth; Daddy grabbed her ankles. I had her arms. Her hand got loose and whipped into her own eye, making it bleed.

It reminded me of the catfish Daddy once caught, when the hook ripped from its mouth, all the way to its eye. Daddy said there was no point throwing it back; the catfish would never survive.

"Isabela, call Miguel," Daddy said. "For Chrissakes, call Dr. Miguel."

"We can't," Mummy said. "The power line is down." She began to cry, a swallowed-up crying that was more like a hiccup.

"The canoe. We need the canoe." Sweat dribbled down Daddy's face.

"She'll fall out," Mummy said. "She'll fall out of the canoe and drown."

Daddy let go of Mita's legs, and her body kicked itself

sideways against the table. Mummy held her head and pulled out her tongue.

"We have no choice," Daddy said. "Dolores, help me get the canoe."

The canoe was a crazy idea. Daddy couldn't swim. The only reason we had a canoe was because it was given to him as a present by Bruno, the barman. He didn't know Daddy couldn't swim. We weren't allowed to tell anyone.

I followed Daddy to the *lavanderia* at the back of the house, to the white sinks where Mummy broke chicken necks and let them dry. There were no chickens now, only the canoe, like a long thin slipper, shiny and green behind the sinks. We pulled it down and carried it to the back door.

"Boots," Daddy shouted, pointing to my bare feet. "To protect from the snakes."

Daddy moved the sacks of sand and plastic wrap to the side and pushed the door open. A mountain of snakes tumbled into the house, one after another—twenty or thirty of them—slithering over and under one another. Daddy went back into the house for Mita.

I held the canoe steady while Daddy placed Mita inside. Then Mummy and I climbed in.

"Here we go," Daddy said. He pushed the boat deeper into the water and heaved himself aboard. The canoe rocked madly from side to side.

"Careful, Ian," Mummy said.

"Keep it straight." Daddy handed me an oar while Mummy cushioned Mita's head so it wouldn't hit the sides of the canoe. The wind made small waves that rolled into us. The bamboo was still on fire. The flames whipped upward, into the sky.

Daddy worried the boat would get stuck as we crossed the

wire fence that divided the wild part of our garden from the "civilized part," as Daddy called it, where we had flowers and a lawn. I could see the tips of the fence ahead: small knots of wire twisted around themselves in a tight grip that reminded me of Mita's hand.

"Here goes," Daddy said. The wire scraped the bottom of the boat. Daddy rowed hard. Sweat poured from his arms as his muscles bundled and stretched, but the boat wouldn't move. "Dammit, we're caught."

Mummy picked up the spare oar to help.

I put my oar in deep and pulled against the water. The rain made the wood slippery and hard to grip. *Save Mita, save Mita; this is your fault.* My arms trembled with effort.

"Just a bit more," Daddy said. He pushed down on the wire fence with his oar, and the canoe lurched forward.

"We made it!" Daddy said. "Thank God for the canoe."

As we approached Dr. Miguel's house, Mummy stopped paddling. She pulled out her lipstick and her mirror that snapped open and shut like a secret box. The boat veered to the left.

"Bloody hell, Isabela, what are you doing?"

I paddled on the other side of the canoe, trying to keep us on course, while Mummy concentrated on her lips. She clicked the mirror closed. She was always calmer after putting on lipstick.

"Look out!" Daddy said.

The boat hit a rock and lurched sideways. Daddy counter-balanced just in time. He jumped into the shallow water and pulled the boat onto the shore. Dr. Miguel's house was on top of the tallest hill; the floods never reached it.

Daddy picked Mita up in his arms. The fit was still happening. Her legs kicked and her body twitched, like a motor that wouldn't turn off. "Go ahead, you two, I'll bring her."

We ran to Dr. Miguel's house, the wind sweeping us uphill. We were out of breath when we rang the doorbell. It was one of those doorbells that imitate a piano, playing higher and higher notes. Dr. Miguel and Tia Cecília always had the latest gadgets. Mummy said they wasted their money on silliness—they weren't careful, the way she was, with money.

"*Miguel, tem alguem na porta!*" Tia Cecília's deep man's voice, shouting out orders.

Bombinha, Dr. Miguel's daughter, opened the door. "What d'you want?" she asked in a rude voice.

"We're here to see your father," Mummy said. "Please tell him it's an emergency."

Bombinha chewed her gum without responding. She blew a bubble, a huge pink bubble that became lighter and lighter, then burst. She drew the gum back into her mouth and started chewing again. I hoped it would explode in her face.

Dr. Miguel arrived at the door. "Isabela," he said. He saw Daddy behind us, with Mita jerking in his arms. "*Meu Deus do céu,* bring her in."

Daddy walked in sideways so Mita's legs wouldn't hit the doorway and bruise.

"Put her in Brigite's room," Dr. Miguel said. He was the only one who called her Brigite. Everyone else called her Bombinha because she was such a bully.

"*Ei,* that's my bed!" Bombinha said. "I don't want her on my bed, she's wet."

"*Por favor, filhinha,*" Dr. Miguel said. "Please be kind."

Daddy placed Mita carefully onto Bombinha's bed. The candle on the dressing table stretched our shadows tall and thin against the wall. They flickered and shifted, like ghosts.

Daddy held Mita's arm while Dr. Miguel pushed in the needle, as he'd done so many times before. We stood and waited for the injection to work.

Dr. Miguel rubbed his hands down the sides of his pants. "Whisky?" he offered.

"Please," Daddy said.

"What about you, Isabela?"

Mummy shook her head. "No, thank you."

I hoped he'd offer me a Coca-Cola, but he seemed to have forgotten about me.

"The flood has reached Barra," Dr. Miguel said as he handed Daddy his whisky. "It's a bad one."

Daddy downed his glass, then pulled a face. He couldn't stand Brazilian whisky. Dr. Miguel sipped his in a careful manner.

Mita continued to shake.

A toilet flushed, then Tia Cecília came into the room. "The girl is sick," she said. Mummy nodded.

Her name is Mita, I wanted to say. Outside the window, trees swayed with the wind. I hated Tia Cecília's prodding fingers and her oily short hair. We had to put up with her because Dr. Miguel was our doctor. "She means well," Mummy said whenever we complained.

"*Ela não vai parar,*" Tia Cecília said, shaking her head from side to side.

Dr. Miguel looked at his shiny black shoes. "She's right. The medicine isn't helping."

"What do you recommend?" Daddy asked, his voice calm as could be.

"She needs the hospital in Rio," Dr. Miguel said. "She needs a neurologist."

We were quiet. Rio was hours away.

"We'll go to Rio, then," Daddy said, in his cheerful Liar's Dice voice. The one he used when he was losing.

"How?" Mummy asked. "It's too far for the canoe."

"Tavares has his boat in the water," Dr. Miguel said. "He's come by twice already. He's bringing me some antibiotics this afternoon. I'll ask him. I bet he'd take you to Piraí, for a price. He can drop you off near Macedo's Garage. He'll lend you a car."

"I hate the bugger, but we have no choice," Daddy said. His voice wasn't fake-cheerful anymore.

Tia Cecília shook her head, as if she knew the plan wouldn't work.

Mummy reached over for Mita's curled-up hand and stroked her fingers. "We'll do what we need to do," she said. She pressed her lips together as if she were blotting lipstick. Her face looked pale.

TAVARES'S BOAT WAS PAINTED A white that was slightly yellow, like his teeth (except for the gold one). As the boat approached the hill, I could see him at the wheel, his gold tooth flashing like a coin. Before reaching us, Tavares turned his boat around and backed his way in. We waited at the waterline. Daddy had Mita in his arms. She was shaking, but the kicks had lessened. She was like the boat, idling.

"That *safado* is going to charge you an arm and a leg for this ride," Tia Cecília said.

She was right. Tavares would do anything to beat Daddy

at Liar's Dice, and now he could charge whatever price he wanted.

Daddy shrugged.

"Put her here on the floor," Tavares said. "It's safest."

Mummy glanced at the dirty wooden boards at the bottom of Tavares's boat, which smelled of bait and fish. She had the same look on her face that she had when she took Daddy's ashtrays to the kitchen, holding them away from her body. Tavares saw the look.

"It isn't a yacht, but it's the best I can do." Tavares's voice was prickly.

"We're very grateful," Mummy said.

Tavares started the motor. "We have to get going," he said. "Before the girl dies."

Daddy glared at him.

Tavares maneuvered the boat out toward the mountains. He liked being the one with power. He couldn't make decisions about the factory; those were up to Daddy and the other managers. But on the boat, he was *chefe.*

I prayed for Mita not to die. Twelve is too young to die. If she died it would be my fault. Only I knew that; nobody else. The secret of my badness felt sharp in my chest. Mita's face was crusted in blood, especially around her eye. Just give me this chance, I'll be better.

I reached my fingers in front of her nostrils. Breath. If Mita was having a fit, she couldn't be dead. Dead people don't have fits.

Mummy made her way over with a blanket she had found and placed it under Mita's head. She sat on the floor next to us, looking seasick.

Tavares turned the key up a notch, and the motor roared louder. He gave a long blast with his horn, and we sped away from the village. After we passed the reservoir, the undertow began to pull at the boat. Tavares increased the power, making it hard to talk. I was glad. Daddy and Tavares were a bad mix any time of the day.

I made my way to the boat's cabin. Tavares rested his hand on the wheel as he took sips of cachaça from a square bottle. There was a photograph of a naked woman taped next to the compass. It wasn't his wife, and it wasn't his mistress either. She was black, with peroxide-blond hair. She faced away from us, looking back, over her shoulder. There was a tattoo on her bottom, a picture of a mouth and teeth. One of the teeth was painted black. It was the front tooth: exactly the same one as Tavares's gold tooth.

Tavares saw me notice and smiled. "*Bonita, né?*" He leaned over and touched the tip of my nose with his greasy index finger.

She wasn't pretty, but I said, "Yes, *ela é linda.*"

"My own little *puta,*" Tavares said.

I worried Daddy could hear, but luckily, the motor was loud. I slid past Tavares and went back to Mita, warming her hand with mine. "Please, Mita," I whispered: "Please come back."

People stood on the roofs of their homes and waved as we passed by. I waved back. Mita would have loved that. She loved the way everyone became especially friendly during the floods. The wind slapped at our faces and made the water choppy. Mita rolled a little to the side with each wave and Mummy reached out to steady her.

"*Cuidado!*" Tavares yelled.

A tin roof from a house blew directly toward us.

Daddy shielded Mummy with his body. I lay over Mita,

trying not to squish her. The roof hit the side of the boat, making it list sideways. Water gushed in at the front.

"*Puta merda,* that was close." Tavares put the motor in reverse and slid the boat away from the roof. He made his way to the side that had been hit and leaned over, feeling for damage. For such a big man, he was nimble. When he pushed against the side of the boat, the wood gave in, making a hole.

"That's what I was afraid of," Tavares said. He pulled a plastic bag from his pocket and stuffed it into the hole. "This will have to do for now."

"Need help?" Daddy asked.

"No," Tavares said. "I'll let you know."

They were talking to each other like normal people. That was a relief. We set back on course, all of us keeping an eye out. After about an hour, we saw Piraí.

"I'm going to drop you off at Macedo's Garage," Tavares said. "Ask for a Vemaguet."

"Thank you," Daddy said. He squeezed Mummy's shoulder. Mummy tried to smile, but she was seasick. Mita's body was quiet. Her eyelids fluttered, like a caught butterfly.

The water was shallow as we approached. Tavares kept slowing, to make sure we didn't hit bottom. When we heard a scrape, he put the boat in reverse. "This is the end of the line," he said.

"I can't thank you enough." Daddy sounded truthful.

Tavares idled the motor, not looking at Daddy.

"How much do I owe you?" Daddy reached into his trouser pocket for his wallet.

Tavares shrugged. "You don't have to pay me," he said. "I did it for the girl."

Daddy was silent. None of us expected this. "Please," he said, "let me give you something. Your boat was damaged."

"Just a nick," Tavares said. "I can fix that in an hour."

"Thank you," Daddy said. "Thank you." He went to shake hands, but Tavares ignored him and jumped off the boat. He held it steady so we could climb out.

Daddy picked Mita up in his arms and stepped into the water. Mummy went next, lifting her dress and holding her shoes in the air. She waded over to Tavares: "*Muito obrigada,* we'll never forget your kindness."

Tavares smiled. "My cousin has a kid like her," he said, nodding toward Margarita. "*Boa sorte!*"

Chapter Thirty-nine

Mummy was still in Rio, with Mita. She'd been there all month, ever since the flood. Daddy and I would drive back and forth on weekends. This time, we broke the record: three and a half hours from Santanésia to Strangers' Hospital, nonstop. Mummy wouldn't have liked it, the way he took the corners, like Emerson Fittipaldi. But she didn't have to know.

When we walked into the room, the whooshing was so loud, it hurt my ears.

"Bloody hell," Daddy said. "I can't hear myself think."

The room was full of noise: beeping, sucking, humming, the drone of something like a vacuum cleaner, the *thud-thud* of Mita's heartbeat on the monitor. Mita lay on the bed, surrounded by a tangle of tubes.

"She's settled," Mummy said. "No more fits."

Mita's hand was sweaty and warm, like a normal hand. A good sign: "Mita, it's me. I'm here."

Mita's eyes were closed. There was no movement under the eyelids, no tiny explosions at the corners of her eyes. She wasn't having a fit. Plastic tubes came out from inside each of her nostrils, looped behind her ears, and met under her chin, where they connected to a machine. The narrow bridge of her nose was crusted with blood.

"They were going to take her off the ventilator," Daddy said. "Wasn't that the plan?"

"Later," Mummy said. "They haven't come by yet."

The machine sounded like the ocean, perpetual motion. I was obsessed with the idea of perpetual motion. I'd seen a program about it on TV: It seemed to be the opposite of death.

"Why is she on a ventilator?" Last time I came, there were no machines. She'd been having fits on and off, quiet ones, which shivered her body in an underground way, but she hadn't been on a ventilator.

"They're taking her off today," Daddy said.

The whooshing sound overtook the room, with its strange echo. It seemed to come from the machine and from Mita, at the same time. Every time her chest lifted with an inhale, it was followed by the sound of waves crashing, which I realized was Mita's exhale. Mita's breathing was controlling the machine, or maybe it was the other way around, the machine was controlling her breathing.

Daddy lit up a cigarette.

"I'm not sure you can," Mummy said. "In here."

Daddy took a long, slow inhale. "She looks better."

My heart felt glad. "Mita is better." I kissed her cheek,

which was soft, not papery like last week. "Is she in a coma?" I wasn't sure what a coma was, but I'd heard the doctors talk about it, how Mita's nonstop fit had induced a coma. That was the word they used: *induced.*

"No," Mummy said. "She came out of it."

I didn't understand why Mummy sounded sad: Mita was out of the coma. The machine made her better. I climbed onto the narrow space on the bed next to Mita, half of me dangling off the mattress.

"Careful there," Daddy said. "I'm not sure that's a good idea."

Mummy lifted the tubes and threaded them under the pillow, clearing the way for me to get closer.

I slid my head next to Mita's head. The pillow was flat, worse than nothing. Mita liked fluffy pillows. "We should bring her a pillow from home," I said. "Next time."

Daddy looked over at Mummy. A roll of ash fell from his cigarette to the floor. Neither of them noticed.

Mita's body had goosebumps, so I snuggled her to warm her up. The loneliness of sleeping only next to myself began to dissolve. I inhaled, expecting that Mita smell, which was part cinnamon, part sour medicine, part talcum powder—but she didn't have a smell. Not clean or dirty, sweet or sour, nothing. The whooshing sound made me sleepy. "Maybe I'll take a little nap," I said. "Right here."

There was a knock on the door. A doctor I'd never met walked in, carrying a clipboard. He shook Daddy's hand, then walked over to us. "So this is the twin sister." He looked from me to Mita, back and forth, the way people did. "I see it," he said. "The similarity."

I was grateful. I was trying to hold on to the Mita that was like me, worried she might slip away completely. When people saw us, they said "poor little thing," or "*vai com Deus,* go with God." I hated it. I was the ripe mango, and she was the bruised one.

"Is she stable?" Daddy asked.

The doctor said yes, her numbers look good. He pointed at the wavering red zigzags on the machine. "The oxygen level has gone up, and there's some brain activity."

"Thank God for that." Daddy looked around for an ashtray, noticing ash was falling.

Mummy walked to a metal dustbin and stepped on a pedal to make the lid open. "Here," she said.

Daddy flicked his cigarette inside.

I stroked Mita's arm. Each week her skin was lighter, like watercolor paint when you add too much water. The color swims around, then starts to lighten and disappear. I realized all of her could be white, not just the inside of her curled-up hand and her feet and ankles, which were covered by the boots. Maybe all of Mita would turn this pale, ugly color.

"She's quite loving, isn't she?" the new doctor said. "A caretaker. She'll make a good nurse."

I felt prickly with gladness that he'd noticed.

"Maybe too much," Mummy said. "But she enjoys it."

Mita's eyes opened wide for a second, then closed. We all saw it.

"She's coming back," Daddy said. "She's coming back to us."

Mummy reached over and kissed her cheek.

"It's having her sister here," the doctor said. "Makes a difference. She'll be sleepy when she wakes up, and she may have difficulty talking. Don't expect too much."

We were used to that. We were used to having Mita be sleepy for days, after the hospital. She'd emerge gradually, each day a little bit more, until she was all there. Maybe a slightly different all there, but still: Mita.

"Is Mita coming with us to the hotel?" I asked. Sometimes we did that. We stayed an extra night in Rio so Mita could sleep at the hotel.

"No." Mummy's voice choked up. "She's staying at the hospital."

She sounded so sad. "Tomorrow," I said, trying to cheer her up. "After they take the ventilator off, she can come home with us."

Mita shifted her body and made that little moan she made in her sleep, a happy sound. We laughed.

"She can hear us," I said. "She hears every word we say."

"Could be," the doctor said. "Patients respond to the human voice, there have been studies."

The doctor asked Daddy if he was ready to sign the papers. They moved away from the bed and whispered something I couldn't hear. Daddy went over to the table by the corner. The doctor said Mummy had to sign too. He smiled and asked me to take care of my sister while they did paperwork.

I said you can trust me, don't worry. I must have fallen asleep to the whooshing sound of the machines.

When I woke up, Daddy and Mummy were standing by the hospital bed, as if they'd been waiting for me. Mummy looked tired.

"She's back from the dead," Daddy said, checking his watch. "We have to get going." It was his Liar's Dice voice.

"I want to wait for Mita to wake up." I snuggled close to

her, not ready to go. "I want to talk to her, now that her fit has stopped."

"Not today," Mummy said. "I don't think that's going to happen."

"What about that bicycle we talked about," Daddy said. "We could go buy it in a few minutes."

"Now? You said it was for Christmas. Christmas is ages away."

"It has to be now," Daddy said. "Unless you don't want it anymore?"

I placed my hand on Mita's chest, feeling it swell up, then deflate, the whooshing sound coming from the machine and Mita at the same time, like an echo.

"Can't we buy the bicycle tomorrow? I'm tired." Daddy was in such a hurry these days, back and forth from Santané-sia to Rio, with his meetings.

"It's up to you. It's now or never. You choose."

I heard the ultimatum in Daddy's voice. I knew it from dice.

I imagined myself sailing down a steep hill on the bike, jumping it onto the sidewalk, leaning backward so the bike's front wheels left the ground, I'd seen a boy in a Coke commercial do that.

I kissed Mita's cheek and rolled off the bed. "The bicycle, of course. I choose the bicycle."

Daddy smiled. "Right you are."

We went to Sears and stood on stairs that moved by themselves, all the way to the fourth floor. There was a whole area for bicycles: pink ones, gleaming silver ones, there was even a yellow one, which I showed Daddy.

"This one could be for Mita," I said, though I knew a bicycle would be too hard.

"No, that isn't possible, Dolores. The bicycle is just for you."

I chose a red bicycle with silver stars and sparkles along the frame.

I WOKE UP IN THE hotel room. A blade of sun escaped through the thick velvet curtains where they met in the middle, slicing my room in two. My own room: with a connecting door to Mummy and Daddy's room. I slid out from under the tidy sandwich of tucked-in sheets and went to their room. Daddy sat in the armchair, smoking, a drink in his hand. It was too early; Mummy wouldn't be happy. I looked around, but she wasn't here. Maybe she was taking a shower, although I couldn't hear water running.

"I'm hungry."

"What about room service?" Daddy offered.

Mummy hated room service. She thought it was ridiculous to pay extra to eat from a bed, but I loved everything about room service: the trolley, the food covered by a domed silver lid like a surprise, my own private restaurant.

"Is Mummy here?" I said, afraid she'd be angry.

"She's gone to be with Mita."

I should have noticed the slide in Daddy's voice. I did notice. But I was focusing on room service, what to order.

Daddy picked up the phone by the bed. A square phone with square numbers you pressed instead of dialed, like something from *The Jetsons.*

"Anything I want?" I asked, sensing the possibility in the room.

"Anything."

I ordered spaghetti carbonara, toast and jam, and chocolate profiteroles: the kind of breakfast no one has. Daddy repeated my order into the telephone. "Shower and pack up," Daddy said. "Before the food arrives."

When the waiter rolled in the trolley, my meal was covered by the silver dome, just the way I'd hoped. And my favorite, the Parmesan cheese: in a silver pitcher, where you pressed your thumb on the top of the handle and the whole lid opened up at once, with a special semicircle carved out for a mini silver spoon. The smoothest, freshest Parmesan cheese, I sprinkled it over my spaghetti and started to eat.

"Aren't you having anything?" I asked, noticing that all Daddy had was a drink.

"Not this time."

I twirled the spaghetti around and around my fork like a true Italian and leaned into my mouthful, sucking in the last little tail that almost escaped.

Daddy didn't notice my technique. Usually, he hated for me to eat like that. He liked me to cut it up with a knife and fork, but no one does that.

"Are we going to meet Mummy there, at the hospital?" I wasn't sure how we were going to fit the bike and Mita and the wheelchair, all of us in the car.

"We're heading home," Daddy said.

"So we're picking them up on the way," I said. It wasn't a question.

"No. It's just the two of us."

"Why? I don't want to. I want to wait for Mita."

"Mita isn't coming back," Daddy said, his voice quiet.

"Why not? She's better, the doctor said so. They're taking her off the ventilator."

"She is better. Mita is going to a hospital in England. One

that is especially for children like her." Daddy stared out the window at the sky. Our room was on the tenth floor, so we were close to the sky. "Mummy took her early this morning." He checked his watch. "They're probably halfway there by now."

I lowered my forkful of spaghetti and placed it down on the plate. "For how long?"

"To live. She's going to live there."

"She lives with us. Here."

"Not anymore. You have to understand. This is better for her."

I didn't understand. My mouth was sour. My hands were cold. I started to shiver.

"No. You can't do that."

"It's already happened," Daddy said. "We made the decision. It's better for her this way. She doesn't have to compete with you anymore, to keep up. Everyone there is handicapped. She'll be happier." He said other things I don't remember.

No. I said no. The no screamed in my eyelid, the inside of my wrists, my fingers; my ears rang, tiny explosions inside myself, one after another—was it a fit coming, it felt like a fit: blood vessels popping in my thumb, behind my eyes, the echo of my no so loud in the hotel room. Someone knocked on the door, asked Daddy if everything was all right. I screamed *no* again, *no* and Daddy said my child is having a tantrum—that's what they said when Mita fell to the floor refusing to wear the boots, refusing to take the medicine, refusing what was offered to her in this life, and now it was in me, this throbbing, this sense of being tricked.

Daddy opened the mini fridge and broke the top off the tiny gin bottle and downed it in one *glug*. For God's sake. His fists squeezed tight. His teeth—I could hear them, his voice pulsing, his hands gripping. I kicked him. My fingers were black with grease—I must have pulled the chain off the bicycle. I had beating hearts in every fingertip in each toe beside my eyes.

I kicked his shins he held my wrists in a grip that hurt and said dammit, Dolores, stoppit, he shook me silly he shook me and shook me and it worked. I stopped.

I stopped crying. I stopped saying no. Daddy held me down on the green carpet of the hotel room there was spaghetti everywhere and Parmesan cheese and the bicycle on its side, chain spilling onto the carpet, my cheek pressed against the floor and a screaming high-pitched whistle in my ears. At some point there was only silence.

Chapter Forty

JULY 1973

Out there on the rocks, luck kept me alive. I leaned all the way back and surrendered myself to the choppy wind and it held me. It held and held and then, in a gust, it pushed me forward, and here I am. Alive.

I walk back along the sidewalk, trying to adjust to this truth. The black-and-white tiles form an interlocked pattern, one rectangle inside the other. I can't imagine separating them. But that is what has happened to me. My life is here, in Rio. Without Mita.

Sand blows along the empty street, looking for a place to land. The porter holds the door open. He seems relieved to see me.

I find Mummy cross-legged on the kitchen floor, polishing Mita's wheelchair. Still in her blue silk dress. The melted Baked Alaska from the dinner party sits by the sink in a puddle. She cleans each spoke of the wheel with a chamois leather cloth and doesn't look up. Her eyes are swollen. I kneel beside her.

"Mummy—"

She pushes me away with her hand. "Leave me alone." She folds the cloth in half and moves to the rim.

"I'm sorry. I'm sorry, Mummy." I watch her polish the wheelchair, thinking of all the little ways she took care of Mita: lining her helmet with soft felt, so it would be more comfortable; embroidering yellow daisies on her pillowcase; poaching us slightly runny eggs, just the way Mita liked them.

I find an old dish towel under the sink, slather on some of the purple polish, and tackle the other wheel. The rust comes off easily. There is a relief in making the metal shine.

After we finish the wheels, Mummy examines the torn seat, feeling along the jagged tear with her pale pink nails.

"Maybe we can sew it?" I suggest.

"The needle won't go through. It's plastic."

We polish the side guards and the handles, centimeter by centimeter. Mummy sits back on her heels to take a look.

The chair gleams in the fluorescent light.

"What happened to your face?" Without waiting for an answer, Mummy leaves the kitchen and returns with gauze and *mercúrio-cromo.* I lift my face so she can clean the cut, which has begun to throb like a tiny heart. Mummy unscrews the top of the bottle, swirls the swab, and applies *mercúrio-cromo* to my chin. I try not to flinch.

"It's going to bruise," she says. Mummy's used to cuts and bruises because of Mita's falls.

"Thank you." I reach over and touch the jagged edge of plastic where the seat is torn. "Maybe we can tape it."

I find some duct tape and slide a sticky loop under the tear. I press and hold. When I let go, the seat looks better: only a thin scar along the side. Mummy nods her approval. Something adjusts inside of me, some rectangle of feeling smooths itself out around the edges, like a cutting machine polishing the angles of a gem. My breath fits inside of me again.

Mummy pushes the pedals down from their upright position, so they face each other like tiny ironing boards.

The rust has settled deep into the pedals' grooves. I tackle one while Mummy does the other. We take turns using an old toothbrush. The grooves are there to prevent feet from slipping, but Mita's feet never slipped. They never pushed. They sat quietly, curled up and soft, as if they were waiting for a blessing.

The business of polishing absorbs us. Mummy sits across from me on the floor, her lips set, removing every stain.

Finally, Mummy puts her cloth down. "Looks good," she says.

"Almost like new," I answer. It feels as if Mita is with us, as if we're preparing to receive her back.

"You aren't the only one who misses her, you know." Mummy swivels the ring on her finger.

"You don't show it," I say.

"It doesn't help, to walk around parading your feelings."

The jangle of keys. Daddy, back from the club. I imagine him throwing his racket on the sofa, the way he always does. I hear him open the window, then slide it closed. The wind must be too strong; it could knock over the vase of gladiolas.

"What the hell—?" Daddy stands in the doorway.

"It isn't perfect, but it's better than it was," Mummy says.

Daddy comes over and feels along the rip with his index finger. He's the same way with gems—he always sees the flaws first. "Not bad," he says. "Not bad at all."

I expect some comment about me ruining their dinner party, but he squats next to Mummy and kisses the top of her head. She doesn't pull away, even though he's sweaty.

"Bloody weather. It's crazy out there." Daddy notices the cut on my chin, now painted neon red with *mercúrio-cromo.* "What the hell happened to you?"

"I fell."

I see in his face that he doesn't believe me. Mummy stays quiet. It's as if their worrying has been all used up and there's none left. There are tiny lines under Mummy's eyes, like rivers on a map.

"I'm starving," Daddy says.

Usually, Mummy drops everything to fix him food, but not today. She picks up the chamois leather cloth and goes back to polishing the inside rim of the wheel, making it sparkle.

Daddy waits. When he realizes Mummy isn't going to rescue him, he walks to the fridge and forks a slab of leftover roast beef straight from the serving dish.

After he's finished eating, Daddy kneels down beside us. He pushes the wheelchair back and forth, back and forth on the kitchen floor. The wheels make a squelching sound. "Remember how Mita loved to race down the hill so fast? It scared the hell out of me. What a daredevil." His voice clogs up.

"Please, bring her back. I'll never leave her again. I promise. Give me a chance."

"What?" Mummy looks confused.

"That night," I say. "The night of the São João Festival. I didn't watch her. It was my fault you sent her away." I start to cry.

Daddy hands me his dirty handkerchief. "Dolores, it has nothing to do with you."

I let my forehead rest on the cool metal handle of the wheelchair. I like the hardness of it. I knock my head against the metal, gently at first, then harder—the way Mita used to—each hit lessening the pressure inside. Mita used to knock her head against the wall, against the bed frame, against the tiles of the kitchen floor. Selfish. Selfish. Selfish. All the things I've done, running off, dancing, not paying attention. The rhythm picks up inside me.

"Dolores, stop." Daddy places his arm along the metal bar, blocking me. "For Chrissakes, stop it!"

"I didn't watch Mita, and now she's gone. It's my fault. Sofia, my fault. Aparecida fired, my fault. I deserve to die."

Daddy takes both my hands and holds them. "Dolores, listen. It wasn't your job to protect Mita. It was ours." He looks at me intently. "You need to understand that."

Mummy smooths the hair back from my eyes. "I was arranging flowers on the hats and didn't look. If anything, it's my fault."

"I had to get away from the bloody music," Daddy says. "We couldn't watch Mita every minute of the day."

"Yes, we can. We can watch her. Give me another chance."

"Dolores, it wasn't you. It wasn't that day," Daddy says. "Mita was on a waiting list for years. It was going to happen sooner or later."

"*Waiting list?* What do you mean?"

"We put her name on, just in case," Daddy says, his voice quiet.

"You planned this all along?" I don't know how to fit that piece of information inside myself.

"We knew the fits might get worse," Mummy says. "The doctors told us that."

"We hoped the time would never come," Daddy says. "But it did."

"When? When did the time come?"

"After the medications stopped working," Daddy says. "When the fits got worse."

"You tricked me. You didn't tell me until it was too late. I never got to say goodbye."

"Maybe we should have told you ahead of time," Mummy says. "But we wanted to get you settled. It all happened so quickly." There are tears in her eyes.

Daddy reaches over and squeezes her shoulder. He looks so sad.

They do miss Mita. But they made this decision to put Mita on some list, and it was like a game of dominoes, where one starts to fall and the next one collapses, and before you know it, they're all lying flat on the table, and this is where we are now.

I look at our white marble kitchen counters, the glistening white tiles, the shiny new fridge. So different from our bungalow in Santanésia with its flood-stained walls and terracotta tiles. It's hard to imagine Mita here.

"It's not fair." A gargled sound comes out of me. "It's been too long. I can't remember how it feels to be a twin anymore. Sometimes I think I invented Mita. She doesn't seem real."

Mummy takes my hand. "Of course Mita's real."

Daddy pushes the wheelchair back and forth, leaving thin trails of tire prints. The three of us sit on the kitchen floor, not talking. Spent.

"Let's go, then." Daddy's matter-of-fact voice breaks the quiet: "Let's go tomorrow."

"Ian—" Mummy places her hand on his shoulder.

"A few days. They can't fire me for a few days."

Mummy says: "Are you sure?"

"Dolores has a point, dammit. It's been too long. For all of us."

"One year and thirteen days." I try to make my voice factual.

"What d'you think? Ready for a trip?" Daddy says.

"More than ready." I suddenly sound like I'm some other girl. A girl who believes her luck can change.

"Better start packing," Daddy says. He sounds pleased, as if he wanted this all along.

I'm afraid to speak in case he changes his mind. I reach out with my bare feet and touch my toes to the arch of Mummy's foot. She looks at me and smiles. The hum of the new fridge takes over the kitchen.

Chapter Forty-one

LONDON

"These chairs are surprisingly comfortable." Daddy leans back in the orange plastic bucket chair. Mine is cracked on the side.

"They keep it quite clean," Mummy says.

The air smells of rubbing alcohol and bleach. The aluminum bucket with the mop in the corner looks exactly like Daddy's fishing bucket, in Brazil. Maybe aluminum buckets are the same, all over the world. I imagine a silvery-pink tilapia inside, stretching its gills to breathe.

Daddy checks his watch. People in England are on time, that's what he's always said: But here we are, waiting.

My heart slaps against my chest like a trapped bird. I'm about to see Mita. It's been more than a year; Ruby to Ruby.

I don't need to count off the days on the calendar anymore. I'm here. I'm with Mita again.

Daddy prepared me at the airport. He said he's gone out on a limb for me, I'd better keep my part of the bargain. No scenes, no running away, no begging to have Mita come live with us. Did I understand? I said yes, I understood. Your mother thinks this is a mistake, that it will upset you too much, make things worse—not better. But he decided to take the gamble. It will be hard, such a short visit, one week. Not what he wanted, but all that is possible, did I understand? I understood. He said the last series of fits caused severe brain damage. Irreversible brain damage. The best we can hope for is that the medication controls the fits, stabilizes them. No cure. Am I prepared? I said yes, I am prepared.

Daddy doesn't believe in miracles. He doesn't know that impossible things happen every day: Uri Geller bends spoons; Zé Arigó cuts out cancer with a kitchen knife. You can't let go of hope; Andrea taught me that. Even in your lowest moment, there's always some corner of magic to hold on to. I don't say any of this: If there's a miracle, let it announce itself.

Any moment now, I will see Mita. My stomach cramps. I've imagined our reunion so many times, in so many ways. Mita sees us from across the room and runs over, showing us her cured legs; she laughs at the shock on our faces, the surprise of it. That's my favorite version. Sometimes I picture finding a Mita who is handicapped, but only a little handicapped—the way she was at first. She has to wear the ugly boots, and maybe she has a fit once in a while, but she's well enough to come home.

The door opens. A nurse approaches, her white hat

perched on her brown curly hair like a bird about to fly off. Daddy stands up and we follow suit.

"You must be Maggie's family? I'm Sister Elizabeth." The nurse stares at me. "Are you her twin sister? They're quite different, aren't they?"

"Not really," Mummy says. "Maybe."

"Thank you for accommodating us at such short notice." Daddy's fingers hover in the air, searching for something to do. There's a No Smoking poster on the wall, with an image of a cigarette and a large red X through it.

"Maggie's in the dayroom," Sister says. "We told her you would be coming."

Her name is Margarita, I say to myself. *She also goes by Mita.*

Daddy gives me his Liar's Dice let-this-one-go look.

We follow Sister through orange double doors to a corridor, to another set of double doors. Sister turns to us. "They can be hard, these reunions. It may be wise to keep it short."

Who the hell do you think you are? I wait for Daddy to say it—I'm sure that's what he's thinking.

"Very well," Daddy says. "If that's what you advise."

The doors open, and we're assaulted by the smell: stale vomit, antiseptic, talcum powder, and a vinegary, sour-body smell I can taste in my mouth. Mummy rubs her neck and Daddy puckers his lips. "God," he says.

"Sorry?" Sister's face is severe. She looks more like a nun than a nurse.

I scan the room. Handicapped children everywhere; some parked in wheelchairs, some in green plastic armchairs, some on the floor. "A Horse with No Name" blares from two large speakers that hang from the ceiling. I can't see Mita.

"Maggie was here only moments ago," Sister says.

A small girl with frizzy ginger hair whirls toward us, faster and faster, her hair following her like a spinning halo. She smashes into Daddy full force, then falls to the floor.

"Christ!" Daddy says. "What the hell—"

"Jocelyn, please," Sister says. "Slow down."

The girl picks herself up and smooths out her dress with its red flowers. Her forehead is wrinkled, the skin baggy under her eyes. She has an old-lady face in a girl's body. Stiff black boots. Her legs are covered with bruises.

I check the wheelchairs one by one. No sign of Mita.

Maybe she isn't in a wheelchair. Of course, why didn't I look? I examine the upright girls: a tall blonde with dungarees and a balloon; a delicate black girl clapping to herself. No Mita.

Then I see her. By the window, in a padded wheelchair. Her knees knock against each other like folded deck chairs, they're so thin and white: But they're her knees. I know them. Her cheekbones jut out in angles.

I run over.

Mita stares out the window at the rain.

I touch her arm. "Mita?"

I squat so I'm at her level. She doesn't notice me. Her eyes follow each raindrop as she turns the page of a catalog with her good hand. "Mita. It's me. Dolores. Your twin."

Mita doesn't respond. Maybe she's deaf now. I swivel the wheelchair to face me. "Hello, Margarita."

Her eyes narrow. They're light brown, like mine. "The color of honey," Mummy always said. Mita doesn't recognize me. How can she not know me? "Mita, it's me. Dolores." I double-click my tongue, hoping she'll remember our language.

Mita turns back to the rain. She still wears an ugly helmet, only this one isn't covered by leather. The Styrofoam is dirty white and crumbles onto her hair like popcorn.

"Hello there, Margarita," Daddy says in a hopeful voice. "Are you my cheeky girl?"

Mita gives him a brief glance, like a fish does as it swims by.

Mummy tries to hold Mita's hand, but Mita shrugs her off. None of us expected this. Mummy's face looks old. I didn't know age could happen like this, in a moment.

Mita isn't better.

Daddy said she wouldn't be, but I didn't believe him.

"Hello there, *chanka.*" Daddy drums his fingers on the rim of the wheel. "Look who's here."

Mummy bends over, so she's close to Mita's face. "Margarita, it's Mummy." She strokes Mita's curled-up hand.

Mita stares past Mummy, toward Sister.

"H-h-hhellooo," she says. A ghost of a smile forms, as if her face, somewhere, still remembers how to smile. Mita reaches toward Sister. It's that same reach, where her fingers splay wide open with wanting.

Sister gives Mita's hand a pat. "Aren't you a lucky girl," she says. "To have your family come and visit?"

Mita turns back to the rain.

"She likes the outside, Maggie does," Sister says. "God knows what she sees out there, but she spends hours looking."

Mita always loved the outdoors, I want to tell her. *The hummingbirds in glittering colors, the huge yellow and blue butterflies with their cellophane wings, even the spiders. I know my sister.*

Mummy tucks the wool blanket around Mita's cold legs. Her skin flakes, like old paint. *Ashes to ashes, dust to dust.* I rest my arm next to hers, side by side. Mine's so dark, compared to her white, translucent skin. Our wrists are identical.

Sister Elizabeth snaps her clipboard. "Maggie's been having lots of fits these past months. She's on some new drugs. We're hoping they will help."

"Is that why she doesn't remember us?" I ask.

Sister studies Mita's feet, perched on the pedals of the wheelchair in stained pink socks. "Some of the kids remember and some don't. Maggie hasn't had many visitors. Not remembering is a way of coping."

I swallow the sourness that spits up from my belly. Daddy scowls. Mummy rubs the tip of her nose. No one speaks. We stand around Mita, not sure what to do.

"Well, I have work to do. If you need anything, you can find me in the kitchen." Sister walks out of the dayroom, her spongy shoes making a squeaky sound, like air seeping out of a balloon.

"Hi, Margarita," I try again. "I'm Dolores."

"It might take her a little time," Mummy says.

Daddy looks out the window. "I can't stand the smell."

THAT NIGHT, I LIE AWAKE in my converted sofa bed while Mummy and Daddy sleep, feeling more alone than ever before. I've lost Mita. Lost the Mita that I knew. She might as well be dead. It's selfish to think this. I am full of selfish thoughts.

I stare at the plastered ceiling of our hotel room, which is decorated like a wedding cake. It's strange to be sleeping in the same room as Mummy and Daddy, but the hotel was too expensive for me to have my own room. I hear someone turn, probably Mummy, because Daddy is always out like a light.

"What's the matter, Isabela?" Daddy whispers. They don't know I'm awake.

Mummy sits up in bed. Daddy sits up too.

"I didn't think Mita would be like this," Mummy says. "Maybe we made a mistake."

I hear her sniff. She's crying.

"It's better than the dumps we saw in Rio," Daddy says. "We need to remember that. We can't do an about-turn now. It wouldn't be fair to Mita."

"Deal with it, that's all you ever said. Whenever Mita had a bad day, you left. Gems. Fishing. Any excuse to leave the house." Mummy's voice is angry in a way I've never heard before. "We were too focused on the job," Mummy says.

"Dammit, Isabela. You made the bloody decision. I didn't force you. I said all along, it's your call."

"I made the decision you wanted me to make. I was exhausted."

"You made the right call. It was hard, but it was the right call." Daddy puts his arm around Mummy's shoulders. I can't tell if he's crying too, but maybe he is.

After a while they lie back down, and I hear Daddy snore. Mummy is quiet.

Chapter Forty-two

The sour hospital air makes it hard to breathe. I want to leave, to run away as fast as I can with my legs that work. I want to smell the grass and the sea, the musky sweat of bodies on a crowded bus, orange trees and bread in the *padaria.* The smells of life. Instead, I pretend to be happy. Happy to be with my twin, at last. Trying to play the part that is expected. That I expected. I want to feel love, but instead I feel a sharpness that is cruel. *How can you forget me?* I study Mita's sunken cheeks and her dead catfish eyes: *You are not my sister. I don't know you.* I don't want to think this. *Maggie is an ugly name. This is a death.* I take hold of Mita's hand, trying to stop my thoughts. It isn't Mita's fault. None of this is Mita's fault.

"Maggie?" I say Mita's new name.

Mita smiles at me, in a polite way.

"I brought you Sonhos de Valsa." I offer Mita one of her favorite *bombons,* hoping she will recognize the purple-and-gold foil cover. Mita throws it across the room.

Daddy gives a short laugh. "She thinks it's a bloody ball."

I unwrap another one and hand it to her. Maybe she'll remember the taste. "See, Mita? It's chocolate."

Mita tries to put it in her mouth all at once, but it's too big. She no longer has upper teeth, so she gums it for a while—then it drops to the floor. Mummy wipes the chocolate from her face with a folded paper towel. Mita used to hate it when Mummy did that. She'd turn her face violently from side to side and tuck her chin into her neck, avoiding the wipe. Now she sits quietly while Mummy cleans her up.

After fifteen minutes (we keep checking the clock), a man arrives with a tea trolley and places a yellow mug in front of Mita.

"T-t-tea!" Mita shouts out in an excited voice.

"You don't like sugar with it, though, do you, Maggie?" the man says as he pours tea into Mita's mug. He has a warm, Indian accent.

"Yes," Mita says. "S-s-sugar!"

"I know, Maggie. I'm just taking the mickey." He drops three white sugar cubes into her mug.

"I'm Dolores, Mita's twin sister."

"Prakash," the man says, shaking my hand.

Mummy shakes Prakash's hand too. "Thank you for taking care of our daughter."

"It's my pleasure. Maggie's very affectionate, aren't you, Maggie?" Prakash reaches over and smooths Mita's hair. "How long has it been since you've seen her?"

"One year," I say.

"I have family in Delhi. One year is a long time."

"It is," I say. "Too long."

Prakash moves on with his trolley, and Mita finishes her tea. I notice an Argos catalog resting on her lap.

"What are you looking at, Maggie?" I'm not used to calling her by that name. It sounds so wrong.

Mita shows me a tractor, a sewing machine, a Jeep. Is she pointing at random pictures, or is she really interested? I have no idea. No idea what she likes and doesn't like anymore.

I pull out a small box from my bag and open it. The bracelet sparkles in the fluorescent light: blue with glints of silver, deep purple, glittery orange. All the gems from Brazil. Mita leans toward it. I wonder if she will try to eat it. She hovers her hand above the bracelet, like a helicopter.

"Pick it up, Mita. Can you pick it up?" We used to do exercises, to keep her good hand going. I'd roll up balls of Play-Doh and have her pick them up and squeeze them.

Mita lowers her splayed hand toward the bracelet. Her eyes focus on the gems and her tongue slips out from between her lips with concentration. The tip of her middle finger crooks a tiny amount. The palm of her hand grazes the colored gems, but she can't do it, she can't make her fingers bend. I take the bracelet and slide it onto her good arm.

She swivels her wrist back and forth, watching the colors glitter: She knows it's a bracelet. Her smile is so wide, *babas* pour from her mouth. Mummy holds a Kleenex under her chin.

Mita sees Sister across the room and yells: "L-l-l-look!"

Sister is busy folding a tablecloth and doesn't hear.

"L-l-l-look!" Mita yells louder.

"Do you want me to get her?" I walk over and ask Sister if she has a moment, please. Mita wants to show her something.

Sister follows me. Even from across the room, the bracelet gleams like a quiet firework.

Mita stretches the arm with the bracelet toward Sister, smiling. "L-l-l-looook!"

Sister wipes her hands on her apron. She has the wrong face.

"I'm sorry, Maggie, but we can't have sharp objects in the ward. It's dangerous. We wouldn't want anyone to get hurt, would we?" Sister tries to take the bracelet, but Mita snatches her arm back.

"N-n-ooo," she says.

"Maggie, give it to me. You know it's not allowed."

"N-nooo." There's determination in Mita's mouth. This is the Mita we know. Daddy crosses his arms in front of him. There's an underground smile on his face he can't hide.

"Maggie Hamilton," Sister says. "Give me your arm. Now!"

Mita tucks her arm with the bracelet under her armpit. All her energy pulls inward; I can feel it: the energy of saying no, the energy of living.

Sister grabs Mita's wrist. Mita pulls back. We watch, hoping Mita will win. Mita twists her body away from Sister and doubles over, hiding the bracelet.

Mummy fiddles with the clasp of her handbag, as if she doesn't notice the struggle. None of us offer to help. *You don't know who you are up against. Go, Mita.*

Mita whips her body from side to side. Sister manages to grab hold of Mita's wrist and forces her arm straight. She rolls the bracelet off and pockets it into her apron.

Mita's *no* turns into a wail. Her mouth curves downward, her cheeks, even her eyes droop.

Daddy looks out at the rain. I want him to say something.

His jaw shifts. "Excuse me. That bracelet belongs to my daughter."

"I'll keep it in the office. You can pick it up on the way out. Please check with me before you give Maggie anything else. It puts everyone at risk." Sister walks across the room with the bracelet.

Mita yells louder. She leans her body forward and tries to turn the wheel of her wheelchair with her good hand, but the brake is on. Sister doesn't look back.

"You gave her a run for her money," Daddy says. "Good girl."

"We'll get you something else. Something that's allowed." I stroke Mita's arm. Her wail courses through our bodies.

Mummy smooths Mita's hair through the triangles of her helmet. "She's a bit strict. I suppose they have to be."

"Bloody Nazi," Daddy says.

THAT NIGHT AFTER DINNER, DADDY paces the hotel room, restless. "I'm going to have a pint at a pub. Dolores, you've never been in an English pub, have you? We're on holiday, let's have a drink."

Outside, it's raining. We walk the streets with our black umbrellas. Mummy stayed in the hotel to rest. Daddy wants a real pub, not some tourist trap. We find a corner place that isn't crowded, just a few men drinking pints. Daddy orders a Guinness, and we sit at the bar. I take a sip: bitter. I had hoped it would taste like chocolate.

"Can I have a caipirinha?"

"You can have lime juice," Daddy says. "Children aren't allowed to drink in England, you know that."

Lime juice here comes from a bottle. It's oily and doesn't look or taste like limes. We've only been away two days, and I already feel homesick. Smoke hovers above the bar, trapped by all the closed windows. I'm glad to be away from the sour smell of the hospital, but the gladness feels wrong.

"You okay?" Daddy says.

"Yup," I say. "Fine."

I don't want the sadness to land, this sadness that collects in the back of my throat. I study the bottles behind the bar: Hendrick's gin, Smirnoff vodka, Johnnie Walker. I've never heard of Pimm's No. 1, or Tarquin's Pastis. No cachaça.

After his second Guinness, Daddy orders a whisky and looks around as if he suddenly remembers me, sitting on the stool, next to him.

"Darts? Want to play darts?"

The barman gives Daddy some darts and we head to the dartboard. No one else is around.

"Use at least three fingers to hold the barrel." He focuses on the dartboard and throws. Almost a bull's-eye. Then he hands me a dart. I aim it and shoot. It goes wide.

"You'll learn," Daddy says. He takes a huge gulp of whisky. "In three days, we leave. Just the three of us. Understand?"

I'm not sure how to understand that. "Is Mita ever going to get better?" I've asked before, but this time is different.

He doesn't take his eye off the dartboard. "No," he says. "She's never going to get better."

Daddy hands me another dart. "Limit the movement of your arm," he says. "Snap your wrist, when you release, and follow through. It's important to follow through."

I throw and miss the dartboard entirely.

"Steady there," Daddy says. "You could hurt someone."

"Some families keep handicapped children at home."

"Each family has their own circumstances."

"Is it because she's ugly?" I'm tired of not saying what I think. "You stopped taking photos of us when Mita got crooked."

"Don't be ridiculous!"

"You used to take hundreds of photos and develop them in the bathtub. Then you stopped." The pain of it swells inside of me. I throw my dart quick and strong, the anger of remembering entering my wrist.

"That's my girl," Daddy says. "Good throw." He rolls the darts against one another in his hand.

"You were ashamed. Ashamed of us."

Daddy places his darts down on the dusty table, picks up his whisky, and takes a last leftover gulp. "You're wrong," Daddy says. "Dead wrong."

He stares at the dartboard, holding his empty glass. The suspended dust swirls in the darkness of the pub. Elton John sings "Rocket Man": *And I think it's going to be a long, long time . . .*

"Dolores, I miss Mita too," Daddy says. "We all do."

I need to remind him that Mita is still Mita. She belongs with us, no matter how sick she gets.

"She still has her spirit," I say. "You saw that, with the bracelet."

Daddy smiles. "She certainly does."

I'm gaining ground.

"And if she saw us every day, she might recognize us."

"She might," Daddy says. "And she might not. That's not the point."

"What is the point, then?"

"The point is to keep her safe," Daddy says.

"But the medications work. Even when Sister took the bracelet away, she didn't have a fit."

"That was today," Daddy says. "We don't know about tomorrow."

"We can't lock Mita up *just in case.*"

"It's too big a gamble."

"I thought you were a gambler."

Daddy's eyes glitter above his drink. He catches the barman's eye and the barman nods. There's a secret language of drinking and bars, and Daddy is fluent in it.

"One false move and she could be dead," he says. "It's not a risk I'm willing to take anymore. Ever. This way is better for all of us."

"It isn't better for me."

"Dolores, you might not understand this, but we did this for you. So you can have a normal life."

"For me? That's crazy! This hurts me. There's nothing you could do that would hurt me more. And it isn't better for Mummy. I heard her, the other night in the hotel room. She thinks it's a mistake." I don't care if I set him off. I'm not going to be like Mummy, tiptoeing around his temper. "This is only better for you. You and your job."

Daddy faces me. I see anger in his face, and a coldness. "You don't understand a thing. You're a child. What if I get transferred? I can't move to Africa or the Middle East with a handicapped child."

"So it is the job. I knew it! It's not for Mita, it's for your career."

"A day will come when Mummy and I won't be around anymore, and who will look after Mita? Here in England there's National Health. This way we know she'll be taken care of."

"Taken care of? She's locked up, like the blue diamond. You said it yourself, what's the point of having something precious if it's locked up and hidden?"

Daddy grits his teeth. Bringing up the diamond wasn't a good idea. He holds up a dart and aims. "Dolores, Mita is staying here. That's been decided. It isn't up for discussion."

He throws a bull's-eye. Some of the men at the bar clap.

"Oy," the barman says. "Give the young lady a chance!"

Daddy laughs a fake laugh. "Your turn," he says.

He's not going to change his mind.

Chapter Forty-three

We arrive each day, with Kit Kats and other treats. Mita starts to recognize us—not like a twin or a mother or father, but as nice people who bring her sweets. She takes my hand, as if I'm a new friend. Now I know how it feels: tiny shards of crystal, exploding inside. A heart doesn't break, it shatters; like Mummy's Czechoslovakian sherry glass did when it fell.

Every day it rains, and every day Mita watches the rain. She leans forward and studies it through the closed window.

"Mita. D'you remember Brazil? Santanésia?"

Nothing. It's as if she doesn't hear me. I lean in close, trying to smell something of the old cinnamon-biscuit Mita smell, but it isn't there. Maybe the stench of the dayroom overpowers her smell. Or maybe she doesn't smell like herself anymore. I uncurl her fingers and let them furl around my index finger the way they do, to clasp me without knowing. Her fingers are strong; a surprising strength for a hand that in every other way doesn't work. It does know how to hold on.

I look out at the rain that fascinates Mita, trying to see what Mita sees. The raindrops glimmer like Daddy's lures, which swiveled to fool the fish. The rain catches Mita's attention the way a lure catches a fish, hooking her away from me, away from the dayroom, away from the smell, and suddenly: I understand. Who wouldn't want to lose themselves in the freshness of the shiny rain, if they were stuck here day in and day out? Through her eyes I see colors hidden in each raindrop. I used to think of rain as transparent, or gray, but now I see it twist with colors like a sequin. In the rain, I see Carnaval, I see dances, I see a thousand mirrors of the world. The more I look, the more I discover. I lean against Mita's shoulder. She fidgets, but she lets me. Her helmet rests next to my head. I smell her breath, vinegary; it's her new breath. My heart stretches so wide I think it might rip with sadness, but it doesn't. It widens to make more space. I breathe in deeper and realize I'm used to the smell of the dayroom. Perhaps you can get used to anything.

Time moves slowly. I snatch quick glances at the clock on the wall. Twenty minutes before I check again, I promise myself. *Focus for twenty minutes. Surrender yourself to Mita. Be a good sister.* Daddy goes out for a cigarette, then comes back. We've said all our phrases, and Mita has said hers. She has eaten too much chocolate.

To pass time, I start to sing a Brazilian children's song: "*Boi, boi, boi, boi da cara preta.*" Mita sways to the music. She grips the arm of her wheelchair with her good hand and leans forward. Her face comes alive. She remembers. My heart pulses in my neck, and on the inside of my wrist. I sing more: "*Pega esta criança que tem medo de careta.*" Mita's head moves up and down with the tune.

Daddy squeezes my shoulder and kneels next to us. "D'you remember this one, Margarita?"

"Call her Maggie," Mummy says.

Daddy sings: "*One, two, three, four—*" and Margarita shouts out: "*Five!*"

"*Once I caught a fish a—*" Daddy stops.

"*Live!*" Mita's smile takes over her face.

Daddy, Mummy, and I look at one another, thrilled. Mummy crouches next to us, and we sing songs from our childhood. Mita remembers them all. "*São João, São João, acende a fogueira do meu—*"

"*Coração!*" Mita sings at the top of her voice.

"Well done, darling," Daddy says.

Mita waves her hand in the air toward him, and he takes hold of it. "Hello, Margarita," he says softly.

Mita turns to me: "D-D-Doloraaahh."

"Yes, it's me, Dolores. It's me." I put my arms around her, and she hugs me back with her good side. Our bodies press against each other like two hands praying.

I reach through the triangle space of Mita's helmet and stroke her wiry hair. Everything is different, even Mita's hair. A huge sadness overtakes me. "I'm sorry. I'm sorry, Mita."

Mita looks at me uncertainly. "*S-São João,*" she sings in Portuguese.

She wants us to sing again. And we do, we all sing. "*São João, São João, acende a fogueira do meu coração . . .*" I remember the bonfire, Jaime walking over and choosing me. Not Mita. How unfair life is. The melting velvety feel of kissing him, how I got lost in it and forgot to look, forgot Mita.

Sister Elizabeth says it's time to leave. "There's been a lot of excitement today, we don't want her overexcited."

Daddy nods his head. "Time to go," he says brightly. "Be back soon."

Mummy rummages in her handbag and pulls out a yellow Jelly Baby; you can tell it's hard for her to go. She offers it to Mita.

Mita begins to realize that we are about to leave. She ignores the Jelly Baby and tightens her hold around my wrist in a grip that won't let go.

"Now, you be a good girl, Maggie." Sister Elizabeth unpeels Mita's fingers from me. "You be a good girl and behave yourself, or there won't be any more visitors."

"Nooo." Tears slide from Mita's cheeks, onto her white knees. Now that Mita remembers, it feels different to leave. "Nooo," Mita wails.

Mummy looks uncertain.

"C'mon, Isabela." Daddy walks toward the door.

I take hold of Mita's hand. "I'm staying with Mita."

"Go," Sister Elizabeth says, nodding toward the door. "I'll take care of Maggie, don't you worry."

"Dolores, Isabela, come," Daddy says, sharply.

Mummy kisses Mita on the forehead. "We'll be back tomorrow, my love," she says, and leaves.

Now there's only me.

Mita presses my fingers so tight, my rings cut into me. Her skin is clammy. Beads of sweat form tiny pearls along her hairline. The left side of her mouth begins to quiver. Her eyes roll. Her legs kick the air, small kicks. I know this. She's having a fit. Mita's fingers loosen their grip.

Sister pulls out a syringe. "Go," Sister says. "It's time for you to go."

I could refuse to leave. Sit down on the floor and wait until they call the police to remove me. But I don't.

Every step I take across the dayroom is deafening.

We look through the window, from the outside. Mita sits in her wheelchair, shaking. We stand in the rain and watch, like so many times before; Mita's fit bringing us back to some circle of remembering where we are a family again. This family: with a child who has fits. This family: that waits for it to pass.

And then we drive away. We cry all the way back to the hotel. Even Daddy cries. The song plays over and over in my head: *São João, São João, acende a fogueira do meu coração . . .*

TODAY IS OUR LAST DAY. Daddy takes out the plane tickets from the inside pocket of his jacket and checks them. We're heading straight to the airport from here.

"Time to leave," Daddy says.

Mita's face starts to crumple.

"Wait a second, I forgot." Daddy reaches into his jacket and pulls out a small black camera. "Dolores, stand next to your sister. Let's take some photos."

"Ian, where did you get that?"

"Next to the hotel. When I went out for cigarettes."

Mummy frowns. The shops near the hotel are expensive, she doesn't like Daddy spending money.

"Lean in," Daddy says. "Closer."

I rest my head next to Mita's helmet.

"Say cheese!"

"Ch-ch-cheese!" Mita shouts. She remembers.

"Hold on." Daddy lifts his hand in the air. "How do I focus? Oh, it's automatic. Okay, one, two, three—"

"Ch-ch-cheese," Mita and I sing out together. The dribble slides from the side of Mita's face down her neck. Mummy reaches to wipe as Daddy clicks.

"Dammit, Isabela, I just took a photo of your arm."

Mita laughs. We all laugh. Daddy clicks and clicks, some with Mummy, some just the two of us. And then the film is done.

"Okay, then, *chanka,*" Daddy says.

"Mo-m-more!" Mita's face is animated.

"Maybe tomorrow," Daddy says.

Mita smiles. She believes him.

MUMMY AND DADDY ARE IN the car, waiting. I hear Daddy rev the engine. I take a last look at Mita through the rectangular window that's cut into the double door.

Rosa, a Filipina nurse who works the night shift, taps me on the shoulder. "You're the one who sends Maggie aerograms, right?"

I nod.

"Sister reads them to her, you know."

"She never mentioned it."

"Sister is tough on families. It upsets her, that people leave their children here. Come, let me show you something."

Rosa walks over to the staff room and unlocks a cupboard. She pulls out a flowered box and hands it to me. Inside, I find all my aerograms, carefully folded. Some of them have been taped together where they are torn. "Maggie asks for them, and we read them to her. It's part of her nighttime routine. Sometimes she won't let go, though, and they tear. You know how she is, with that hand of hers."

I smile, knowing Mita's grip. "Thank you. Thank you for showing me this." A knot of gladness twists in my chest. It was worth it. The lessons after school. The English girls laughing. Feeling like a dunce. It was all worth it.

I hear a car horn: three short honks and a longer one. Daddy.

I hand Rosa back the flowered box with the aerograms. "Thank you. It means so much to me, that you read them to Mita. I'll keep writing."

"And we'll keep reading them to her," Rosa says. "Don't you worry. And don't forget to sign the visitors' book before you leave. It's on the table outside Sister's office."

I walk out of the staff room and see it there, in dark blue leather: the visitors' book. A pen next to it.

I open the book. Visitor. I am a visitor to my own twin sister. There's a narrow column for the date, then NAME OF PATIENT, NAME OF VISITOR, and ADDRESS. I quickly sift through the pages, looking for Margarita, even though I know no one's come to visit her. Some people wrote messages in the address section, like *See you soon, darling!* or *Keep smiling.* I wonder who these visitors are, and why they have left their children here, and was there a sad brother or sister standing by? There is no way of telling. I almost miss it, but some corner of seeing catches the *M* of Mita's name: Margarita Hamilton. Under NAME OF VISITOR: Michael Parker. I recognize Mr. P.'s messy handwriting. He didn't forget. He came.

My fingers shake as I feel in my handbag for the paper coaster I stole from the pub at lunch. I copy Mr. P.'s address:

Summerhill School, Leiston, Suffolk, England. Mr. P. visited Mita. He said he would, and he did. He does care.

I turn to today's page and write: *27 July 1973. Margarita Hamilton. Dolores Hamilton (her identical twin sister). Rio de Janeiro, Brazil.*

I don't write a message in the address section. I'll send Mita an aerogram the minute I arrive in Brazil. She might not understand the words, but she'll know it's from me, and I haven't forgotten her. She'll clutch it, the way Rosa said she does, and not let go.

I walk out the front door and get into our rented car, and we drive away. Our week is over. We drive away and leave her.

The windshield wipers *click-click* back and forth and the rain slides sideways across the window. I watch fields fly by, bare trees with branches like bony fingers. We're heading home: and Mita is not part of that home. Back to palm trees and elephant leaves and wild grass that pushes through the sidewalk cracks, back to the sea and the mountains. We're leaving this prison of a place with all its stale air, and Mita will stay here.

I write an *M* on the foggy car window. There's a layer of mist above the street, as if we're driving through the center of a cloud. The tidy green fields pass by, one after the other. I still feel Mita's grip, the way Sister had to unpeel her fingers from my wrist each time I said goodbye, Mita's *nooooo* disappearing into the air, dissolving into silence.

The rain outside the car is quiet too, each *drip-drip* like the second hand of Daddy's watch, moving around the circle of a day, this day, which is now over. We're going back home. There is a ripped-up feeling inside my lungs.

I want to go back. I miss Rio. I miss the sea and the mountains, I miss Andrea. The bookshop. But I'm not sure anymore, what *home* means. The Rio we're going back to is a Rio without Mita. Now I see our story like a book that has already been written, and all this time I've been trying to change the ending.

Chapter Forty-four

RIO DE JANEIRO

The minute we arrive from the airport, Andrea calls. Sofia is better. The fashion show is tonight, and Sofia is one of the models. Andrea says she's been trying to get hold of me all week. I say I'll be there. I don't mention England. Yesterday, I was in the hospital, feeding Mita Jelly Babies, and now I'm going to a fashion show.

I walk along the beach, trying to get used to being back. The sand is firm and packed, the way it is after a storm. It flooded the whole week we were away. The city is cleaning up. It will take a few more days for the life, the dirt, the traffic, the sweat, the radios with samba, the bars, the flies on the sandwiches, for all of life to begin. "*Bom dia, bom dia.*" People smile, happy to be alive, to pick up where they left off.

The rocks of Arpoador glisten in the distance. Ipanema,

Copacabana, Leme: one beach leading to the next, like a bracelet sparkling. I pass Posto 9, where Vinicius wrote "Garota de Ipanema." The bar on the corner is always packed with tourists because of that song—though it's just a bar, like any other. A few blocks down, the *farofeiros* arrive by bus from the suburbs, with their coolers and their sandwiches. Sofia wouldn't be caught dead here, though she isn't always welcome in Posto 9 either. Even on the beach, there are divisions, places where you belong or don't belong.

Tourists are out in front of the Copacabana Palace Hotel, with their too-large bathing suits. A kite lies stranded on the sand. I walk from Copacabana to Leme, the everybody beach: where Sofia, Tia Glória, Andrea, and I usually go. The smell of sewage is more than usual, because of the rain. Every time there's a storm, a canal of brown water stretches like a dark tongue into the sea. After a while, you don't smell the sewage; you get used to it. Maybe you can get used to anything in this life; maybe you have to.

I walk along with no destination. I feel loose, like a tooth that isn't ready to fall. It dangles on the gum at an angle, not in or out. The tongue plays with it, wanting to push it back in, to feel it solid there, in line with the other teeth. Once it's gone, the emptiness feels strange, a space in your mouth with too much air.

I look up at Corcovado, Christ's arms a horizon over Rio. They made him out of soapstone, which is only a 2 on Mohs' hardness scale. Maybe marble would have been too hard, there would be a coldness there that wouldn't fit. I imagine the statue made from pink-and-white marble, like Mummy's bathroom; how it would change everything. It would be too shiny in the sun, like a piece of jewelry. Soapstone blends in with the earth and the trees, it is durable but quiet. Lighter than marble: Maybe that's why they chose it. They had to take the pieces up the mountain by train and then assemble them. I read about it, how it took years, and hundreds of men, how it was done as an act of hope. That was how it was described in the book: an act of hope.

THERE ARE AT LEAST TWENTY people already in line when I arrive at the Chapeuzinho Vermelho school. Andrea catches me up on the details. Azevedo is the lookout. If he sees the police, he'll whistle. He has a referee's whistle; if we hear it, we leave. If the police ask, we came to see our niece or nephew in a play.

"We shouldn't be standing around like this," Tia Glória says. "We don't want to attract attention."

The fashion show takes place in an elementary school to trick the police. In the three years since it moved here, they've never stormed a show. But Tia Glória says this year is worse. The government is obsessed with security, and they're practicing their tortures on *travestis.* Not just Sofia: Last week, it was Caetana and Denise.

"You're spoiling the mood," Andrea says. "Relax."

The doors open and we file in. Our seats are in the second row. You can hear the band warming up behind the curtains. Tia Glória keeps glancing back at the entrance.

"I have a surprise," Andrea says. "I hope you're not mad, but I invited him and he's coming!"

"Eduardo?"

"I tried calling you, but you didn't pick up. It's the perfect occasion!"

"What if it doesn't work out? It could ruin Sofia's big day."

"It will work out," Andrea says. "Trust me."

"Does Sofia know?" I ask.

"No. Too much pressure. It's better if it just happens." Andrea adjusts herself on her seat and looks around. "He's not here yet. I hope he comes."

"He doesn't seem the type not to come," I say, as if I know men.

"Listen to her," Luciana says, "next thing you know, Dolores will arrive with a boyfriend!"

"Never," I say.

"I don't believe in never. Pass me the nuts, will you?" Tia Glória grabs the bag of cashews. "What d'you think she'll wear?"

"I hope she chose the Zuzu Angel dress," Luciana says. "The crochet on the silk was something else."

"No way!" Andrea says. "I love Zuzu, but not for this occasion! I voted for the green velvet bell-bottoms."

"Zuzu never found out what happened, did she?" Tia Glória asks.

"She dresses Liza Minnelli, and still, she gets the runaround. I don't know how she does it," Luciana says. "If the police took my son, I wouldn't be able to get out of bed."

"They haven't found his body yet," Andrea says. "So there's still hope."

The drums play a *batucada*, and Ivete, Sofia's friend, saunters out in a long black strapless dress and a top hat: "*Laidees and gentlemene,*" she says into the microphone, with her Portuguese accent. "I present to you the Fourth Annual Chapeuzinho Vermelho Fashion Show!"

People clap and whistle. A few family members in the first row stand up and throw streamers.

"What number is she, in the *passarela*?" Luciana asks. "Is she number eight?"

"Seven," Andrea says. "She swapped to seven because it's Dolores's lucky number."

"Seven is better," Tia Glória says.

Andrea elbows me. "Look who's arrived!"

Eduardo. In a long-sleeved white shirt and a gray waistcoat, with his black-rimmed glasses. He stands at the entrance, holding a red rose. He has a wrapped package under his arm.

"He's tall," Tia Glória says. "A nice face. *Inteligente.*"

"He's not her usual type," I say, "but he's nice."

"He's sexy in his own way," Andrea says. "A professor kind of way, you know? And he's French! Actually French!"

"D'you think we should have told him ahead of time?" I ask. The stares, the looks of disgust that came our way when people looked at Mita. I can't bear for that to happen to Sofia, not on her comeback day.

Tia Glória shakes her head. "The *detalhes* come later. After a few *drinques;* after he sees how beautiful she is. You know the French, they're very open over there."

The usher leads Eduardo to an empty seat across from us. As he walks by, he waves. Andrea and I wave back. I'm nervous it won't work, but also hopeful. Sofia must feel that every day; that she has a secret to hide. She can't be herself. I remember when I couldn't read, how I tried to hide it. Sofia's secret is harder. It's a secret that gets you tortured. That can make a man beat you up. Every man she meets, she has to worry.

Andrea is sure Eduardo will fall for Sofia; she's a true believer. I don't know much about love, but I hope it's like writing, a code that opens a door and lets you in. Luciana says that after all the poems he's sent her, and all the buildup—a little thing like a penis isn't going to mean much. "What's a *piruzinho* that sits there like a hangnail? Nothing, really," she says. "The man would be a fool to turn down Sofia's beauty, her high cheekbones, and her intelligence—for a hangnail." We laugh.

The band sets up below the stage. The tambourines, guitars, a saxophone, a *cuíca,* a *cavaquinho,* all the instruments warming up.

"What song did she choose in the end?" Tia Glória asks.

"She was torn between 'Sabiá' and 'Sangue Latino.' I voted for 'Sangue Latino,'" Andrea says.

" 'Sangue Latino' is too much for her shoulders," Luciana says. "I told her."

Since the *pau de arara* and the *eletrochoques,* Sofia's right shoulder locks, and her arm goes numb.

"She needs a dance that's more in the hips and legs, that keeps the arms low. There are sambas like that, I showed her," Luciana says.

"You know she won't listen," Tia Glória says. "She always does her own thing."

The band opens with "A Banda," one of my favorite songs. I sing along, with the others. Next, the band plays "Walk on the Wild Side." Valeria slinks out in a purple micro-dress with wide bell sleeves and psychedelic tights. Her eyes are huge.

"Mary Quant, from Londres. Don't her eyes look great?" Luciana is the makeup and costume consultant for all the shows.

Valeria smokes from a long black cigarette holder. She blows smoke rings at us as she gyrates. Halfway through the song, she throws the cigarette on the floor and steps on it with her shiny white leather boots. She pulls out a joint and lights up. *Hey babe, take a walk on the wild side . . .* She hands the joint to someone in the audience, and it passes from person to person along the first row.

"*Puta,*" Andrea says. "It will be done before it gets to us."

"They're pushing the edge," Tia Glória says, but she's smiling. There's a spirit of secret fun in the room that's contagious.

"Don't be so *careta,*" Andrea says. "It's not like you don't break the law every day. A little *maconha* is nothing!"

By the end of the song, Valeria's big eyes are almost shut, she's so stoned. Her Mary Quant eye shadow glimmers in the lights.

Next, a tall black woman in silver-green sequins undulates across the stage, like a snake. The only instrument that plays is a flute. Every so often the music pauses, and the woman hisses, *sssssssss,* into the microphone, then the flute begins its melody. All of us are mesmerized.

When the dance is over, the crowd gives the snake woman a standing ovation.

"Who is she?" Andrea asks.

"Lourdes, from São Paulo," Luciana says. "Sofia told me she was good, but: wow!"

When it's Sofia's turn, my stomach hurts. I don't want her shoulder to lock. I hope the police won't come. I hope Eduardo will fall in love with her. I hope so many things. Tia Glória watches the front entrance. I listen for the warning whistle.

"You walked into the party like you were walking onto a yacht." Sofia's voice, accompanied only by a guitar. She struts out in a red leather catsuit. A few people whistle.

"It looks like real leather," Tia Glória says.

Sofia's catsuit hugs her hips and her long slim legs. She bends toward us, close to the audience, her deep voice low, full of feeling. "*I had some dreams, they were clouds in my coffee . . .*" Her breasts show, perfect and realistic, above the low V-cut neckline and the zipper.

"She's good! I didn't know she could sing!" I say, surprised by Sofia's easy way on the stage.

"She thinks her voice is too masculine," Tia Glória says. "That's why she stopped."

"Her shoulders look good," Luciana says. "Loose."

Sofia controls the stage with her gravelly, sexy voice.

"She should go professional," Andrea says.

Sofia gets a standing ovation too.

The show ends, everyone claps, then the thirteen models take a bow and leave the stage. The crowd throws streamers and the band play a *batucada.* We stand up and clap louder, whistle, shout: "*Mais um! Mais um!*" demanding another song.

Sofia appears from behind the curtain and moves center stage. A single spotlight follows her. She unzips the tight leather sleeves of her catsuit and lifts her arms in the air—her shoulder doesn't lock. There are white bandages on both of her wrists, stained with blood.

"What's she doing?" Tia Glória says.

"The blood is realistic," Andrea says. "That's exactly how her wrists looked."

Sofia slit her wrists in the police station. She said dying was better than torture, any day.

The other twelve models walk out and stand next to her.

They lift their arms, and they too have white bandages stained with blood on their wrists.

Sofia starts to sing in a low voice. We lean forward to hear: "*Caminhando e cantando e seguindo a canção.*"

The song from the 1968 International Song Festival. Mita loved that song. It came in second: Everyone thought it should have won. Everyone. Including Daddy. The government banned the song the very next day. It didn't pretend to be a love song with a double meaning about the dictatorship; it was direct.

"She's asking for trouble," Tia Glória says.

People cough and turn to check the entrance.

Andrea starts to hum the tune. I catch her eye and begin to hum too. Tia Glória frowns at us, but we continue. Luciana joins in. I let my hum blend in and disappear into the other hums, like a bee of a sound. Every day, the government sends people away and tortures them. Artists, students, *travestis.* For nothing. Everyone knows, but no one talks—just like home.

A single guitar accompanies Sofia's voice: "*Come, let us go, to wait is not to know . . .*"

People begin to sing out loud, softly at first, then louder: "*In the barracks they learn an old lesson, to die for your country and live without reason.*" I sing with them. We all know the words.

Tia Glória gives up her worry and joins in, all of us singing the protest song.

When the song ends, Sofia is in tears. Tia Glória cries too, everyone laughing, crying, hugging, all around us. I have goosebumps. Hope is an energy; you can feel it in the room. We make our way to Sofia, who is surrounded by fans.

Andrea pushes through and hugs her. "You were amazing."

Sofia dabs her temples with a handkerchief. The leather must be boiling hot. Her eyes are lively.

Eduardo hangs back, behind the circle of people.

I take his hand and pull him in. "Sofia, this is Eduardo, the poetry man from the bookshop."

Sofia stretches her arm out and Eduardo kisses her hand, the old-fashioned way.

"Inspired," he says. "Unforgettable." He gives her the rose and the package.

"Do you think he knows?" Andrea says in her too-loud whisper.

"Maybe," I say. "Maybe it doesn't matter." Sofia is so beautiful and talented, I'm hoping it doesn't.

Chapter Forty-five

I decide to stop by the bookshop. Andrea never gets to the beach before noon, and I want to know how Eduardo feels about Sofia. He seemed interested, but I couldn't be sure. The awning is torn, and the lights are off. It's closed. I try to read the title of the book in the window, but the glare from the sun makes it hard. I remember the way letters looked, before I could read; how I saw them as shapes, pieces of some snake that had been chopped up. Now they are words, poems, books.

I press my nose against the glass: *Oublier:* to forget, in French. I can't make out the other word. There's a map of Europe underneath, I recognize Spain, Portugal, and the boot of Italy.

Not so long ago, I assumed life would unfold day by day, in a certain fashion. There would be twists and turns: Bridges might collapse; you might find a dried-up river with the bones of a horse at the basin. There would be unexpected things. But our life would happen within a certain space, a rectangle on a folded map. Whenever we traveled, we'd unfold the page to see where we were going. But always, our home was Santanésia; it was a given. Mr. Williams says that about math problems: What are the givens? And the givens were: That I was a twin. That Daddy was British and moody but kind inside. That Mummy was Brazilian and pretty, and that we were the family that lived on the hill. Some givens could change. The shutters would be painted green one year, blue another. Daddy might get a promotion . . . but part of the givens of a family was that we were a unit. One person doesn't get taken out, like the joker in a pack of cards. But that's what happened. The givens were all shuffled and whole people disappeared, and this is the hand I've been dealt. This is where I've landed.

Rio wasn't on our rectangle. We had to unfold the map to get there: when we drove Mita to the hospital after a bad fit; when we made trips to Sears to buy roller skates and ride on the escalator; when we ate hot dogs standing up, at Bob's. But those were adventures, deviations, and then we'd go back home.

But home shifted and Mita shifted, and even my body has shifted, everything rearranged. Do I have to accept that I have a brain that isn't damaged? That I'm able to read and write and jump, even if Mita isn't? Do I go back to school, like some single girl who has never been a twin? I've promised Daddy I will; not the British school—I've convinced them not to send me there. I hate Mr. Wilson. There's a French school they're considering, and a Brazilian Jesuit school.

The lights in the bookstore turn on. The front door opens,

and Eduardo stands there, barefoot. I've never seen him barefoot before. He has tidy toes, all lined up, the same size. Everything about him is even.

"Are you wanting some poetry, Mademoiselle?" he says, smiling. He holds the door open, and I walk in.

"I thought you were closed." It's a relief to be in the peaceful shade of books. "Why are you barefoot?"

"Flooding at the back entrance," Eduardo says. "Lost forty books. Some of them can be salvaged, however."

"Can I help?"

"I have two more shelves to go, I will show you."

I follow him to a back room, which is painted a minty green. The books here are wide, in various shapes: atlases, encyclopedias, dictionaries, maps.

"This is the reference section," Eduardo says. "Not poetry, thank goodness. I didn't lose any poems."

We carry the wet books to a wooden table by the window. The ones that aren't too damaged we leave open, in front of two fans that Eduardo has set up to dry the pages. "*Un peu primitif,*" he says. "But the best I can do."

I want to know how Eduardo feels about Sofia, but I'm shy to ask. Andrea would grill him immediately. It isn't just shyness, it's fear. I can't bear to lose too many dreams all at once.

We work quietly.

I pretend to be interested in a book about Mesopotamia. I study the map as if I'm looking for something. After a while, I put it down. I don't like pretending with Eduardo.

"Did you like the fashion show?" I ask.

"Very much," he says. "Though it was a bit of a surprise."

He knows. He knows about Sofia. The map of Mesopotamia looks like a potato.

"You could have told me. You could have told me about Sofia. You know that, don't you?"

"I wasn't sure. I wanted you to give her a chance." He's disappointed. I let him down. Let our friendship down.

"I see." I can't tell if he's mad or not. His voice is careful.

"I'm sorry. I should have explained some things . . ."

"It might have been helpful," he says. Then he smiles. He isn't too mad.

Eduardo adjusts the fans so they blow the pages in the opposite direction. One of the pages from a book called *Apostrophe* floats to the floor.

"Loose." Eduardo picks it up and slides it back into place and closes the book. "The dampness loosens the glue binding. How about some coffee?" he says, gesturing toward the gray room.

As he pours me a cup, I notice a photograph leaning against the books. A younger Eduardo, with his arm around a pretty *mulata* smiling at him.

"Is that your girlfriend? Or wife?" My heart beats a little faster. Maybe he's married. I've only ever imagined him alone, with books. Maybe he has this whole other life.

"Yes," he says. "She was both."

"Was?" He's probably divorced. Daddy says the French all sleep with one another and get divorced. Not as bad as the Americans, but almost.

"She died. Cancer."

"I'm sorry." I imagine a whole family. Andrea and I hadn't considered this. Our plan was a silly soap opera. I sip my coffee, feeling sad. Helping Sofia be happy was something I thought I could do. But it turns out I was wrong about that too. Wrong about so many things.

"She was a jazz singer," Eduardo says. "I met her in Paris and followed her here."

"Brazilian?"

"From Bahia."

"How long ago did she die?" I probably shouldn't ask, but this room makes me want to say things.

"Five years ago," Eduardo says. "It's been a while."

I sip my coffee, feeling awkward. I should never have fancied myself a matchmaker; I've barely kissed a boy, except for Jaime.

"You were right about my loneliness," Eduardo says. "Perhaps I needed a jolt."

"But not that much of a jolt?"

"Sofia could be the right kind of jolt. I'm not sure, of course, but maybe."

"Really?" Eduardo's smiling. If he didn't like her, this would be his chance to say so; but he isn't saying that. Maybe some things are possible. Not Mita, at least not right now. But maybe Eduardo and Sofia.

The doorbell rings. A customer. Eduardo places his coffee cup down and goes to take care of them. I scan the poems on the shelf for something to read. Cecília Meireles, I've never heard of her. *I did not have this face I have today, / so calm, so sad, so thin . . . In which mirror has my face been lost?* Now, when I look in the mirror, I just see me. It used to be Mita there, looking back at me. So much has changed.

I feel a presence and look up.

Sofia stands in the doorway, wearing jeans, cowboy boots, and a blue cotton shirt. She looks like a student.

"Did you come here to check up on me, *francesinha*?"

"I didn't expect to find you here," I say, kissing her on both cheeks. I'm about to whisper *Go for it,* when Eduardo appears, right behind her.

"Did you find anything interesting to read?" Eduardo asks. He seems a little formal and awkward.

"I'm not sure," I say. "I need ten different poems at least."

"He'll find you something," Sofia says. "He has a book for every occasion."

"I will bring in another cup."

Sofia lowers herself into the other armchair and crosses her long legs dramatically. "*Ai,*" she says. "I'm still recovering from last night!"

Eduardo returns and pours Sofia a coffee.

As Sofia takes a sip, she looks across at me and I give her the signal. Two bends of my pinkie finger: *Go for broke, no matter what your hand.*

She sees it and signals back, two times: *I will.*

Eduardo senses something, but he doesn't know the language of Liar's Dice. He looks from me to Sofia.

Sofia stretches her long arms. "What a sleepy day," she says.

I stand up. "I need to go; I'm meeting Andrea at the beach. Thanks for the visit."

"Take the poems with you," Eduardo says. "For company."

I hug the parcel of the book to my chest, liking the hardness of the cover, keeping the sadness at bay. I hear Sofia's laughter as I step into the brightness of the day.

By the time I get to the beach, a thin veil of cloud has covered the sun. *Mormaço.* The kind of weather where tourists get burned. I stretch my towel out on the sand, lie on my belly, and reach into my bag for the green book Mr. P. gave me. I've never written in it; not one word.

I find my set of felt-tip pens and choose yellow. I write in large capital letters: THE GIRL WHO WAS THERE AND NOT THERE. I like it that the yellow doesn't show up much on the white page; it's almost invisible. You have to look carefully to read it.

Once upon a time there was a girl who was there and not there. Ever since she was born, she was good at disappearing. She weighed less than two pounds, so she was almost not there from the beginning. When she hid, it took hours for anyone to find her. She hid in the tall grass by the river with black bubbles behind the paper factory, where no one would think to look, it smelled so bad. She hid on the very bottom of the pool, holding her breath and lying low, like a catfish. Then she'd come up for air, laughing. Her father said she was always up to some mischief.

That girl had a twin sister who looked exactly like her, just as little, when they were born. She wasn't as good at disappearing, but she was good at finding her twin. The clues she looked for were birds and stones and gems.

I stop writing. This isn't right. I want to cross the whole paragraph out, but that would look ugly. I should have used a pencil. Mr. P. used to say don't worry about mistakes. It's good to keep going, write whatever comes to your head. Stream of consciousness, he called it. I brush off some sand that has found its way onto the page, pick up my pen, and try to think of my story as a stream, winding its way through a forest . . .

One day, her sister disappeared for good. She shook and fell, and her eyes rolled white, and no matter where she looked, the girl couldn't find her. Her twin wasn't in her body, she wasn't in her bed, she wasn't anywhere.

For good means forever. Why is forever good? I hate that expression. I close the book. This is enough writing for today; at least I've started.

I think of Eduardo's gray room, with all the banned books and records he loves so much, how he's made a room to hold them and keep them safe, until the day Brazil is free again. I want my green book to be like that: a place to hold on to Mita and our old life together. A place where she still exists.

I'm not writing for others anymore. I'm writing for myself.

I have Mr. P.'s address in my bag, and an aerogram, but I'm not ready to write to him yet. Maybe tomorrow. I looked up Suffolk in the atlas, and it is more than one hundred miles away from Mita's hospital in Carshalton. I asked Daddy, and he said it would take more than two hours to make the drive. Mr. P. went out of his way. That has to count for something.

I watch the volleyball game, knowing exactly which boy Andrea will choose. The muscles climb up his arm like an eel when he serves. He looks my way and smiles. I look down, embarrassed. He thinks I'm watching him for myself. He doesn't realize I'm choosing for Andrea. Where is she? I pull down on the hem of my shorts, which Mummy said were too short, they don't hide a thing: Why wear them? I told her that was the point: Sexy is something posing as nothing. As if I knew what I was talking about. Mummy rolled her eyes. There's something softer about her now. She framed one of the photos we took at the hospital and set it on the jacaranda sideboard, next to the gladiolas. I saw it this morning. This new Mita, who is even more crooked than before, but still Mita.

A shade blocks my sun. It's him, the boy from the volleyball game.

"*Ei,*" he says. "Can I sit?" He drops himself onto the sand next to my towel.

The waves fold in on themselves. Their end is contained in their beginning; they're dying even as they're born.

"I haven't seen you here before," he says.

"Funny, because I come every day."

The boy laughs. "Well, I'm seeing you now." He reaches over for a handful of sand and almost touches my hand.

Andrea would enjoy him approaching like this, but I don't. There's something too electric about him. I feel the heat of his touch though he isn't touching me. A trickle of sweat stains his cheek, his skin is jacaranda-brown and his eyes are gray. A glittery, warm gray, like the room in the bookshop.

"What are you writing?" the boy says, looking at my green book. "Is it homework?"

"Yes," I lie, wanting to keep my story private.

He sits next to me and watches the game, as if we're old friends. A boy on his team smacks the ball into the net.

"*Porra,*" the boy shouts out to his friends as he looks at me. "Don't get distracted just because I'm distracted!"

They laugh and look at me, the boys playing volleyball. I pretend I'm comfortable with this sort of attention. This is my new self that I'm trying on.

Andrea arrives. She bends over and kisses me on both cheeks. "Who's your friend?" she says.

"Rafa. My name is Rafa."

"Andrea," Andrea says, kissing him on both cheeks too.

I don't say anything. I want the boy to go away, but he doesn't.

"What about you?" Rafa says. "D'you have a name?"

I look at Andrea, trying to let her know I don't want him around, this boy. She pulls her rolled-up towel from her straw bag and shakes it loose. "Her name is Dolores," Andrea says, setting her towel next to mine.

"Nice to meet you, Dolores," the boy says.

I give him a small nod.

He stands up. "I'll see you soon," the boy says to me, "since you come here every day." He smiles and jogs back to the volleyball court.

"He's interested," Andrea says. "Definitely."

"Don't," I say. "I barely talked to him."

"You should have talked more! He's a *pão.* Now that we've found someone for Sofia, it's your turn."

I don't want a turn. I'm afraid of having a turn. Last time I kissed a boy, it was Jaime, and look what happened. Any boy I love would have to love Mita too, and I don't know if that's possible.

"Is that a new bikini?" I say, changing the subject. It's made of black macramé with shells that dangle from where it's tied at the sides. "I like it."

"Isn't it adorable?" Andrea pulls it higher, toward her belly button. She takes out the Johnson's baby oil mixed with Coca-Cola and rubs it on her shoulders, arms, and legs. "Want some?" She offers me the bottle.

I pour oil into the palm of my hand and rub it into my legs.

Andrea lies on her belly and undoes her bikini strap to avoid tan lines. She stares at me from her towel. Her eyes remind me of black tourmalines, the way they glint. Black tourmalines are a 7 on Mohs' hardness scale, the same hardness as other tourmalines, but they are cheaper. Just because they're black.

"Something's different about you," she says.

Does it show when your heart breaks? Maybe it changes you. Maybe that's why the boy came over, maybe he sensed it, this change inside me.

"I feel different," I say.

We watch the volleyball game. The boy with the gray eyes serves an ace and everyone claps. He looks over at us.

Andrea waves. "Where were you all this time? You almost missed Sofia's show."

There's a kind of dishonor, sunbathing on the beach with Andrea, feeling salt crystals tighten into stars on my belly, while Mita is in the vomit-shade of the hospital.

"We went to England," I say.

Andrea pushes herself all the way up, forgetting about her bikini top—so it dangles loose, in front of her muffin-shaped breasts. The boys on the volleyball court whistle.

"Take it off," one of them shouts. "Take it all off!"

"*Porra,*" Andrea says, catching the ends and tying them behind her back. She ignores the commotion, not one bit embarrassed. "How could you not tell me something like that?"

"It was a short trip." I sit up and make swirly circles in the sand with my fingers. *Round and round the garden, like a teddy bear . . .* Mita loved that rhyme. I'd make circles with my fingertips on the palm of her hand to trick her into letting me open her curled-up fingers. The white palm of her hand, the smoothness of it, scared me. It was hard to see her life line. I wasn't sure what that meant. The map of crisscrosses on my palm looks like an equation, one of those complicated ones with no answer.

"*E daí?*" Andrea says. "You saw Mita. That's amazing! I want to know every detail."

What do I say? I went to see Mita and left her there? I'm glad to be back. It feels wrong, but it's the truth.

"She didn't know me."

Andrea shifts from her towel to mine, so she's lying right next to me. I feel her heat like an energy. "Who did she think you were?" she asks.

"No one."

"No one?"

"Not at first. Then she remembered."

Andrea is quiet. Silence is unusual for her. I expected a row of questions, one after another. A sense of shame descends, so pointed it's hard to breathe. She's disappointed. This is the wrong story, not the story she wanted, I wanted. But it's the only one I have. My throat is tight.

"Did you cry?" Andrea says. "When your twin remembered you, did you cry?"

She's looking for a *novela,* the drama of reunion.

"No," I say. "I didn't." Maybe I'm more like Mummy than I know. It doesn't mean I have no feelings. I see that now. "I was happy to have her again."

Andrea reaches to hold my hand. Our fingers are slippery with oil and sweat. The waves lap against the sand gently, reminding me of Mummy's slippers at night, the *flip-flip* as she walks down the corridor when she can't sleep. I like the sound.

"Did Mita come back with you? Can I meet her?"

"No," I say. "We left her there." Tears slip down my cheeks and Andrea strokes them away.

"*Coitadinha,*" Andrea says in a hushed tone I've never heard before. "Is it better for her over there?"

"No," I say. "It isn't better. But my parents say it is." It's the story they have to tell themselves, so Daddy can keep his job, and Mummy can be less worried, and we can continue to have this Rio life they want so much. It makes them sad, but they're not going to change their minds.

"Will you go back to visit?"

"Daddy said soon, maybe after the holidays."

"At least you know she's alive," Andrea says. "It's not like with the disappeared, where you keep waiting and you never find out."

"Yes, she's alive. And she remembers me. At least I have that much."

I lift handfuls of sand and watch the grains sift through my open fingers, like falling rain. Hope fists up in my belly, a knot of hope I don't want to have, that feels too large and too small at the same time. I hate the way hope is a wish that is too wide for this world. My wish that Mita comes back, and we can be a family again—that is a wish that won't happen, can't happen, won't happen . . . But it's still there. A grain of sand. Tiny. Almost invisible. But it is a particle and has its own truthfulness and weight. And it still sparkles in some corner like a leftover sequin from Carnaval.

Epilogue

THREE MONTHS LATER

I take a sip of water and stretch my fingers. The sky is ribboned with orange and the mosquitoes are beginning to bite, but there are still people waiting in line to see me. The accordion player catches my eye and waves, and I wave back. We are a little family in this corner of the fair. I bring coffee, he brings me *acarajé* to eat during my break. Andrea said she might stop by, but it's dinnertime. She probably won't come. She's training to be a manicurist, and working two jobs, so she comes home exhausted. She needs the weekends to recover.

"You're the letter writer, right?" A man stands in front of my table, looking uncertain.

"Yes," I say.

"Everaldo told me about you. I was expecting someone older."

"I'm an old soul," I say, picking up my pen. "Who do you want to write to?"

The man reaches into his pocket and hands me an address scribbled on a beer coaster. "Mãe Tatá de Oxum, at the Terreiro Casa Branca." He sits on the edge of the metal chair. "Ask her to please send me that *pião-roxo* from her yard."

"D'you want a few leaves, or the whole plant?" I ask. Maria José used *pião-roxo* to clear negative energy. Sometimes she made a tea with the leaves; other times she'd prescribe a bath.

"One branch is sufficient," the man says. "My wife is expecting. She's due next month. November twelfth."

"*Pião-roxo* is powerful," I say. "Good luck."

The man smiles. "Thank you. We've lost two babies already, so I need it."

"I hope the *pião-roxo* helps," I say, wondering if the babies were twins. "I'll think of you in November."

Maybe Mummy should have tried *pião-roxo.* Maybe our birth would have been different and Mita wouldn't have had brain damage. But that is water under the bridge, as Daddy would say. There is a lot of water under the bridge.

I tidy the pile of envelopes on my left, ready to be taken to the post office. A Sunday's worth of wishes and missings and laments. Maybe these letters make life more bearable; like a prayer or a song or finding the perfect poem. It's an energy sent from one person to another, and it has its own kind of magic.

I write a few more love letters, a request for emergency money, and a letter of complaint to Presidente Médici telling him that Brazil's economic miracle isn't a miracle at all. I'm almost out of paper. Two more people, and I'll call it a day.

I look up to see Daddy in front of me, holding a fishing

rod. Mummy beside him, in her Jackie O sunglasses. They look like tourists.

"So this is your setup, is it?" Daddy says, smiling. "Quite popular. We've been standing in line for a while."

Mummy sits on the metal chair. "How much do you charge?" she asks.

"Two cruzeiros a page, but for you it's free," I say. I can't believe she's here. They're both here.

"I'll pay," Mummy says. She takes out her wallet and hands me two cruzeiros.

"Really? You want to write a letter?"

"Why not?" Mummy takes off her sunglasses and holds them on her lap.

I pick up my pen. "Who do you want to write to?" I say, even though I already know.

ACKNOWLEDGMENTS

This novel took decades to write, and I've been so incredibly lucky to have the support of many people along the way.

Most important, I want to thank my sons, Luca and Rafael Higonnet-Faithfull, for bringing me such joy and (as they got older) for encouraging me to finish. I finally did it!

I want to thank my agents, Gráinne Fox and Veronica Goldstein, for being such wonderful, warm, and talented editorial agents! Veronica, you read my novel almost overnight and immediately saw what it needed. I still don't know how you did that! Gráinne, without you, I would not have written the epilogue; you pushed me to dig deeper, and I think the novel is better for it!

I also want to thank Lucy Luck in London; I'm glad you are part of the team, championing my book in the UK.

Jenna Bush Hager, I'm so grateful that my book found its way to you! After the unforgettable meeting in your office (where we all cried!), I knew my book had found its home. Our twin connection was part of the magic that has sometimes appeared in my life, and your faith in this book means the world to me!

Special thanks to my editors at Random House, Sara Birmingham, Azraf Khan, and Melanie Tutino. Sara, you have such an eye for the whole, helping me see where to cut and where to add new scenes when needed. Melanie, your line edits were so perfect, and your questions helped me clarify my intentions in so many places. Azraf, you've been so steady and quick to answer my concerns—and patient with my technical difficulties. I'm so lucky to have such a team.

I also want to thank Cara DuBois, Hasan Altaf, Erin Richards, Rebecca Berlant, and everyone at Random House who helped bring this book to the world. I am so grateful for your care and attention.

This novel would not exist without Kendall Dudley and his Thursday-night writing group. So many key scenes were written there, with the inspiration and energy of this special group of writers. Thank you, Kendall, Bee, Ellen, Suzanne, Henry, Carolyn, Beverly, Lisa, Connie, Heidi, Suz, and so many others.

Kendall, thank you for the decades of friendship and support, and for setting up the GoFundMe that got me to Ireland and started the ball rolling. Your creative and joyful influence has changed my life.

Louise Piantedosi, I cannot imagine this past year without you by my side. You have been a dear friend, editor, coach, confidante, and finder of last lines. When I think of us, I am reminded of Anne Sexton and Maxine Kumin, calling each other on the phone and leaving the line open while they wrote . . . you are one of the best writers I know, and I am so grateful for our friendship.

For decades I had been writing bits and pieces, not sure

how to sew them all together. Thank you to all my teachers at GrubStreet (and the Novel Generator and the Novel Incubator), who helped me transform them into this book.

Michelle Hoover, you are one of the finest teachers I have ever had: generous, smart, and tough. Without your guidance, my scattered, intuitive draft would never have found its form. I've learned so much from you, thank you.

Thank you too to my Year 9 Novel Incubator classmates—John McClure, Aube Rey Lescure, Kasey LeBlanc, Nicole Vecchiotti, Joan Nichols, Sara Shukla, Cameron Dryden, Michael Giddings, and Susan Larkin—for your feedback and friendship.

Aube, you led the way, and our connection goes deep, both of us writing about rebellious adolescents and badly behaved expats and navigating the world from multiple countries and perspectives. I can't imagine the journey without you.

John, you've been such a good friend and editor: I always know I'll get the full, complex analysis when I send you a piece, and it is something I treasure. I'll never forget how you outlined my whole novel according to *Save the Cat!* and helped me realize that I did have structure after all!

Kasey, you've been so openhearted and generous—even setting me up overnight with a website when it seemed I suddenly needed one. Thank you.

Nicole, I've so appreciated your advice about writing and publishing. You've been there at so many crucial moments with your humor and wisdom.

Thank you, Bob Fernandes, for being such an amazing beta reader. I will treasure your feedback letter forever! Your encouragement gave me hope when I was plagued with doubt.

Annie Hartnett (and my Novel Generator class), thank you for helping me trust the process and believe that I could find my way, even without knowing where I was going.

Thank you, Amy Greene, Jeannette de Beauvoir, and Anna Solomon, for your thoughtful feedback.

Bill Madden-Fuoco and Janet Damaske—what would I have done without our little group? I hope our group continues in some form forever.

Phillip Freeman, your belief in my book meant so much to me. Lily Shi Naseer and Eve LaPlante, you've helped me go the distance.

Ruth Drasin, you've been there through thick and thin with me; I cannot imagine life without you. Thank you for reading my novel (some sections many times!) and being so insightful about the characters, for being such a good friend, and for making me the most delicious salads ever!

Natasha Lifton, thank you for your friendship and the many glasses of wine we had on my porch while discussing your fine-tuned feedback. You could have been an editor!

Ann Epstein, it's been lovely to share the ups and down of my writing life with you this past year. Thank you too, Bernard Edelstein, for the technical support you gave me in Brazil so that I could stay there a few more days.

Antonia Fried, thank you for encouraging me and inspiring me to write. I think of you as one of my early influences!

I am especially grateful to the Irish Writers Centre's Novel Fair and the panel of judges for believing in me and helping me to believe in myself.

Betty Stenson—your warmth and humor are part of why I fell in love with Dublin.

Adele Pressman, this novel would not exist if you hadn't helped me collect and bear all the disparate pieces and hold them in a non-simplistic way. You were there at a crucial turning point in my life and made all the difference.

George Vaillant, thank you for our many late-night discussions about writing and psychoanalysis, for understanding survivor's guilt, and for introducing me to Viktor Frankl.

Nancy Bridges, your example of taking every August to write and publish a paper, and the way you balanced work, children, and writing, helped me to believe it could be done.

There have been so many important teachers and mentors in my life, some of whom are no longer with us. Cynthia Rich, you introduced me to writing freshman year, and it changed me. Arturo Vivante, you believed in me; thank you for all those Wednesday afternoons; I'm sorry it took me so long! Mary Robison, you were patient with my writing blocks and believed in me. Grace Paley, Michael Cunningham, Elizabeth Strout, Pam Houston, Julia Glass, and all the teachers I was lucky enough to have at the Fine Arts Work Center in Provincetown (some of whom may not remember me), thank you.

Fred Leebron, I studied with you twice, and you know more about writing than anyone I have met! Thank you for meeting with me in New York (long ago), and for your guidance at Tinker Mountain Writers Workshop. Your encouragement over the years helped me to not give up!

Fredinho Woods de Lacerda, you have been an amazing research assistant and friend, helping me on so many fronts, from questions about the geography of Rio (is Lapa under Cristo's armpits? Could the statue be seen from the British school in Botafogo?) to the setting of certain scenes (Feira de São Cristóvão). You've helped me with Brazilian slang, descriptions, and remembering our old haunts in Rio. I could not have written this without you!

Ricardo Woods de Lacerda, thank you for coming with me to Feira de São Cristóvão and to the rocks of Arpoador. I am so grateful for your help with my research.

Célia, thank you for the morning on the beach at Arpoador, and for all the photos. Thank you too, Simone and the whole family, for being a resource on Rio, Feira de São Cristóvão, and even for discussing the age girls in Brazil start thinking about boys!

Thank you to Nick Wollak and Josefina Durini for hosting me in Brazil (two times!) and for being part of my research team on the ground. Nick, meeting you by sheer coincidence, and then sharing the magical trip to Santanésia, where I discovered that imagination can be a form of memory, and things that I thought I had made up were in fact true—I will never forget it.

Marina Vanderput, thank you for arranging our small EA reunion, for connecting me to people at the British school, and for helping me with research.

Sandra Norén, thank you for arranging the interview with Sérgio. I am so grateful for your help and friendship.

Beatriz Kushnir, PhD, professor of history at the Federal University of the State of Rio de Janeiro, thank you for taking the time to meet me for coffee in Rio. Your research on the *polacas,* the Jewish prostitutes in Rio, and your work on censorship and freedom of the press influenced my novel.

James Green, professor of Latin American history at Brown University, thank you for taking time to clarify the (pejorative) words used to describe trans people in 1970s Brazil and how they were reclaimed by some in the gay and trans community in an effort to lessen their sting.

Thank you, Allen Shawn, for taking time to talk to me

about your memories of your twin sister. It was incredibly helpful.

The Pauline Scheer Fellowship at GrubStreet and Kitty Pechet made the Novel Incubator possible and not just a dream.

Special thanks to Andrea Sorgato and Alexandra Goresh for their care.

Finally, I am grateful to Margarita, for inspiring my novel, and for Marielena (my triplet who only lived one week), who deserves a novel of her own!

GLOSSARY

a barra tá pesada: Brazilian slang for "things are heavy," or challenging.

acarajé: A Brazilian fritter made from black-eyed peas deep-fried in *dendê* oil. This dish comes from Bahia and originated with enslaved Yoruba people from Nigeria.

açude: Dam.

A Grande Mentira: A popular Brazilian telenovela in the late 1960s, about a cleaning lady who is accidentally hit by a young millionaire's car, leading to a romance.

aleijados: Cripples.

Zé Arigó: Brazilian medium and faith healer, also known as the Surgeon of the Rusty Knife. He performed surgeries without anesthesia and claimed to have cured millions, including Brazilian president Juscelino Kubitschek, singer Roberto Carlos, and British consul in Brazil H. V. Walter.

bairros: Neighborhoods.

banca de jornal: Newsstand.

batida de maracujá: Passion-fruit drink with cachaça.

batucada: Brazilian high-energy rhythmic drumming style, often found at Carnaval and other celebrations.

bicha: Widely used and often derogatory slang term for a gay man; sometimes informally used to refer to a trans person (Sofia refers to herself this way in the novel). More recently, this term has been reclaimed by some in the LGBTQ+ community.

Bidu: A popular bluffing dice game played in Brazil.

Ronald Biggs: English criminal known for his role in the Great Train Robbery of 1963. He lived for thirty-six years as a fugitive, first in Australia, then in Brazil, where he became a celebrity, recording two songs with the Sex Pistols.

Borstal: A British reform school for young offenders. The Borstal system was abolished in the UK in 1982.

botequim: A tavern for drinks and cheap snacks.

brigadeiros: Brazilian chocolate truffles.

calmante: A sedative or tranquilizer.

cangaceira: Female bandit, part of a band of nomadic outlaws that roamed the Northeast of Brazil.

careta: "Square" or "lame," as in "don't be so *careta.*"

carona: A ride, especially if hitchhiking.

cavaquinho: A small, four-stringed Brazilian musical instrument, similar to a ukulele.

Chacretes: Professional dancers who assisted Chacrinha on his TV show.

Chacrinha: Brazilian comedian and radio and TV personality. Also used to refer to his eponymous television shows.

Chapeuzinho Vermelho School: Little Red Riding Hood School.

chinelos: Flip-flops, also known by the popular brand name Havaianas.

cigarras: Cicadas.

Cremogema: Popular brand of instant porridge in Brazil, enriched with vitamins and minerals.

cuíca: A Brazilian friction drum with a high-pitched, squeaky sound.

dourado: Freshwater fish known for its golden color and aggressive fighting style.

Engov: Popular over-the-counter medication in Brazil, used to treat hangovers.

espetinhos: Skewers or kebabs.

estranho: Strange.

Fábrica Klabin: Brazilian paper producer and exporter.

farofeiros: A pejorative term used for people who come from the outskirts of Rio to the beach and bring picnic lunches, including *farofa,* a toasted flour made from yucca.

Favela do Rato Molhado: Slum of the Wet Rat, located in the Inhaúma neighborhood of Rio de Janeiro.

figa: Brazilian amulet, a symbol of good luck and protection against the evil eye.

filho da puta: "Son of a bitch."

fotonovela: A story told in sequential images, similar to a comic book, but using photographs instead of drawings. It originated in Italy and Spain in the 1940s and is very popular in Latin America.

francesinha: "French girl."

frescura: Slang, meaning fussiness, excessive or affected behavior.

Uri Geller: Israeli British illusionist and psychic, known for his international television performances (including on *The Tonight Show Starring Johnny Carson*) and his ability to bend spoons with his mind.

Guaraná: Brazilian soft drink made from the guarana plant.

Ibejis: Twin gods in the Candomblé religion, originating from the Yoruba traditions of West Africa. They are believed to bring good fortune, blessings, and prosperity to a community.

Irmãos Coragem: Brazilian telenovela from the 1970s about a simple man who finds a valuable diamond, which is then stolen by the most powerful man in the region, whose daughter suffers from triple personality disorder.

isso é um saco: Slang for "this is a drag," or annoying.

jardim de infância: Kindergarten/preschool.

João e Maria: The children in the Brazilian adaptation of "Hansel and Gretel."

Lampião and Maria Bonita: Lampião was a notorious bandit of the 1920s in the Northeast of Brazil, and Maria Bonita was his girlfriend. They lived as outlaws for nearly two decades, wiping out entire police stations and taking over towns, until they were finally captured and killed in 1938.

lanchonete: Snack bar or casual eatery in Brazil.

lavanderia: Laundry area.

maconha: Marijuana.

mãe santa: Also known as a *mãe-de-santo;* a priestess of the Candomblé religion, responsible for the well-being of the entire community.

"Marcha Soldado": Brazilian children's folk song about discipline and the consequences of disobeying orders.

matar saudades: To kill one's sense of longing for or missing a person or place.

misto quente: Popular grilled ham and cheese sandwich.

mormaço: Hazy, overcast, sultry weather.

National Kid: Japanese TV series about a superhero who adopts a band of children. It was not popular in Japan, but gained cult status in Brazil in the late 1960s.

***novela* (telenovela):** A prime-time TV soap opera with a recurring cast of characters and a melodramatic storyline.

olheiras: Dark circles under the eyes.

orixás: Deities or spirits in the Candomblé religion.

pães de queijo: Brazilian cheese bread made with tapioca flour.

pão: Literally, "bread"; Brazilian slang for "hot" or "good-looking man."

para o inglês ver: Literally, "for the English to see"; idiom meaning doing something only for outward appearances, without genuine intent. Informally, *só pra inglês ver.*

pasteizinhos: Small fried savory pastries filled with cheese, meat, or seafood.

pião-roxo: A medicinal plant also known as bellyache bush, used for treating abdominal ailments.

polaca: Literally, "Polish woman"; the term became synonymous with "prostitute."

porra: "Fuck."

puta: Literally, "whore" or "prostitute"; used as an insult or swear word in Brazil.

quesnélia: Flowering plant common in eastern Brazil.

safada: Mischievous.

salgadinhos: Small savory snacks served at parties.

São João Festival: Festa Junina, a major Brazilian celebration held in June, honoring Saint John the Baptist. It embodies a mixture of Catholic, indigenous, and Afro-Brazilian influences, with traditional foods, dancing, and clothes.

Society of Truth: A mutual aid organization founded in the early 1900s by Jewish prostitutes in Rio de Janeiro. Excluded by the Jewish community, they established their own synagogue and cemetery, the Cemitério Israelita de Inhaúma.

sopa de couve: Kale soup.

tênis: Tennis shoes or sneakers.

terreiro: Sacred space for Candomblé rituals and ceremonies.

Topo Gigio: Fictional mouse created as a character on an Italian puppet show in the 1960s.

travesti: The definition of *travesti* is controversial, but the term usually refers to a person who doesn't identify with the gender they were assigned at birth, originally pejorative but recently reclaimed as an identity term in Brazil. *Travesti* identities are heterogeneous and multiple; they have been described as a "third gender."

tucunaré: Peacock bass, a large freshwater fish common in South America.

tulipa: Draft beer glass shaped like a tulip.

Vemaguet: A Brazilian station wagon that was produced in the 1950s and 1960s by Vemag under license from the German manufacturer DKW.

xinxim de galinha: Popular Afro-Brazilian chicken and shrimp dish from Bahia.

xuxú: Chayote squash, a popular and mild vegetable used in various Brazilian dishes; also spelled *chuchu*.

ABOUT THE AUTHOR

Juliet Faithfull is a Spanish-British-American writer who grew up in Brazil. *Liar's Dice,* her first novel, was a winner of the Novel Fair at the Irish Writers Centre and a semifinalist for the James Jones First Novel Fellowship. She was awarded a Pauline Scheer Fellowship by GrubStreet's Novel Incubator program in Boston, and her short stories have been published in *Bellevue Literary Review* and *Urbanus Magazine.* A graduate of Harvard University and Smith College School for Social Work, Faithfull works as a trilingual psychotherapist and lives in Cambridge, Massachusetts, with her two sons.

juliatfaithfull.com
Facebook.com/authorjulietfaithfull
Instagram: @julietfaithfull

ABOUT THE TYPE

This book was set in Bembo, a typeface based on an old style Roman face that was used for Cardinal Pietro Bembo's tract *De Aetna* in 1495. Bembo was cut by Francesco Griffo (1450–1518) in the early sixteenth century for Italian Renaissance printer and publisher Aldus Manutius (1449–1515). The Lanston Monotype Company of Philadelphia brought the well-proportioned letterforms of Bembo to the United States in the 1930s.